"Just a kiss..."

Drake could hear Edwinna's heart pounding in the darkness. He drew her near. She remained stiff but didn't refuse him. He took one of her arms, pressed a soft kiss to the wrist, to the throbbing pulse point there, and draped it behind his neck. Then the other. Even the skin of her wrists burned him.

He brought her nearer and molded her body to his, thigh to thigh, waist to waist, chest to breast.

"Just a kiss."

She began to tremble. "Drake—"

"Don't be afraid of my body, Edwinna. It means you no harm. May I kiss you? Just a kiss?"

Her heart pounded against him. "Yes."

"Oh, Edwinna." He dipped his head and began to kiss her mouth, then pulled back for a startled moment. Her mouth was so hot. Unaccustomed to kissing, she knew only his way of doing it—with mouth bold and open—and it utterly thrilled him.

A whimper came from her throat. He kissed her ear and whispered hoarsely, "Let's be together as we should. Come to bed . . ."

Also by Jo Ann Wendt

THE GOLDEN DOVE

Published by
POPULAR LIBRARY

Beyond the Savage Sea

JoAnn Wendt

POPULAR LIBRARY

An Imprint of Warner Books, Inc.

A Warner Communications Company

POPULAR LIBRARY EDITION

Popular Library® and the fanciful P design are registered trademarks
of Warner Books, Inc.

Cover illustration by Gregg Gulbronson
Cover lettering by Vladimir Studio

Popular Library books are published by
Warner Books, Inc.
666 Fifth Avenue
New York, N.Y. 10103

 A Warner Communications Company

Printed in the United States of America

First Printing: July, 1990

10 9 8 7 6 5 4 3 2 1

CHAPTER

* **1** *

Barbados, the Caribbean
December 1659

Edwinna Crawford left the boiling house at a run, her long, thick braid swinging as she loped. She was dressed in a shirt, men's breeches, stockings, and shoes. She and her plantation overseer, Matthew Plum, had been at work there since dawn, seeing to the installation of a new sugar boiling kettle. Now, as she ran breathless up a cane path in the morning sun to Crawford Hall, her smooth brow creased with worry.

Harvest would begin in two weeks and she desperately needed a good harvest. Last year, rats had infested the island, invading the fields, feeding on the sugary roots, causing the cane to rot where it stood. To destroy the rats, she'd had to burn field after field. She'd nearly lost her entire sugar crop—a financial calamity she could ill afford. Crawford Plantation was already deep in debt.

Now she had a new worry. Her uncle, George Crawford,

had ridden in. He hadn't come for a social visit. He hated her as much as she hated him. What did he want? He was a planter, and *no* planter went on casual visits two weeks before harvest. There was too much to do. Had he come about that clause in her father's will? Matthew Plum had warned her. Simon Tarcher, who served as Speightstown's magistrate and her trusted lawyer, had warned her, too. She tried to cast off a sense of foreboding, but couldn't. Her uncle was greedy and clever.

The path sloped steadily upward, past a sea of tall green cane that rustled in the trade winds, billowing, wave after green wave. There were endless fields of cane rolling richly over the plateau that formed the broad spine of the island. Cane covered the island, broken only by patches of mahogany forest and by deep dark ravines, descending in terraced fields to the jewel blue Caribbean Sea three miles away.

Ordinarily, Edwinna's heart leapt at the sight. She loved planting, harvest, and the hard, exacting work of making sugar. But today she took no joy in it. Why had George Crawford come? Why?

The trade winds blew gently into her face as she ran, bringing the familiar smells of sea, fertile soil, and ripening cane fields. Out of habit she stopped at the top of the hill, the highest point on Crawford Plantation, and looked down over the miles of billowing cane toward Speightstown. Nestled beside the bright blue sea, the tiny sugar port shimmered in its white sand cove. It was a beautiful cove, but a cruel one. Today was execution day there. She hated for any human being to die condemned to death by slow drowning, shackled to boulders in the cove to await the incoming tide. She hated suffering in any form.

Yet, she firmly believed that pirates had to be executed. They were the scourge of the Caribbean—their ships were more numerous than sharks. She knew, firsthand, the disaster they could bring down upon planters. You could toil two years to bring forth a sugar crop—planting the cane, growing it fourteen to sixteen months, harvesting it, grinding it, boiling it, curing it three months in the curing house, sorting it, packing it into kegs, loading it on the backs of burros, taking it down to the sugar ports on hazardous trails that wound through mosquito-filled ravines. Two years! And when you sent it off to sea, a pirate ship could swoop down out of nowhere and take it all in ten minutes.

Kill them. Let the punishment fit the crime. Live by the sea, die by it. *Still*, she thought, shuddering, *it is terrible to die that way*.

Crawford Hall dominated the hilltop, visible from all directions, its gabled red tiled roof and white stucco walls awash in the brilliant Caribbean sun. Built by her father with his first sugar money, it was constructed of quarried limestone coral and ballast stones that had come from England in the holds of cargoless ships. Fearful of slave uprisings, Peter Crawford had built it like a fortress. The walls stood two feet thick. There was no window glass in Barbados, but each window was fitted out with two sets of stout wooden shutters that could shut out storm or siege. A ten-foot-tall limestone coral wall covered with lush tropical flowers encircled the house, meeting in the front at wrought-iron gates, which her father had kept tightly locked day and night.

Edwinna left the gates open. Unlike her father, she'd been born in Barbados. She had no Englishman's fear of black skin. She'd lived among blacks all her life. If she locked her gates at night, she did so not as a precaution against her blacks but against her whites. Most of the white bond slaves were convicts straight out of Newgate Prison in London. Slyer, less trustworthy men she'd never met—except for her uncle, George Crawford.

She gazed out again at the beautiful panorama of sky, cane fields, sea, and Speightstown nestling in its cove, and her throat tightened. She thought of the letter Simon Tarcher had sent up to her, with the bizarre solution to the problem of the clause in her father's will. She'd read the letter so many times she knew it by heart. It was a desperate, frightening solution, but Simon Tarcher could be trusted. He and Matthew Plum were the *only* men on Barbados she was willing to trust.

But perhaps she would not be forced to the wall. She hoped her uncle had come on a different matter. If not, she would have only until noon to get to Speightstown. By midafternoon, the tide would be in, the executions over. She took a deep breath, straightened her shoulders, and strode through the open gate into her house to face George Crawford.

He waited for her inside, in her dining chamber, seated at the table, hovering over a bowl of kill-devil punch someone had been foolish enough to make for him. The bowl stood half emptied. She could smell the rank, raw scent of rum, could see its effect in her uncle's flushed face. He'd brought his disgusting son with him—Clive, with his handsome looks and evil ways.

Clive looked her over with bold eyes and smiled. Edwinna didn't return the smile. She'd had little use for him when they were children and had none now. He was a bully who took what he wanted. She kept her distance.

"You should keep your gates locked," George Crawford said crossly, starting in on her without greeting.

"Yes, Uncle." She refused to argue over trivia. She didn't like him enough to bother arguing with him about anything. Her uncle was a tall, handsome man of fifty who dressed with fussy vanity. He had been her father's twin—identical in every respect. Edwinna had learned early in life to be wary of both of them.

Not one to short himself on comfort, he kept his Negro body slave, Caesar, standing behind his chair to attend to his every whim. Caesar was required to wear full livery, buttoned high on his neck. His black face glistened with sweat.

"And you should whip your house slaves, Edwinna. They are never around to serve me when I come. Never."

"I sent them off on chores this morning."

Untrue. She'd sent them nowhere. They were terrified of George Crawford. Like children, they'd run off to hide. Her uncle had a vicious reputation. In a fit of temper, he'd flogged one of his slaves to death. He'd been reprimanded by the governor, of course, but that amounted to a slap on the wrist—a slap in exchange for a human life.

"Where is Kena?" Clive asked smoothly.

He knew exactly how to goad her. She clenched her fists.

"Leave her alone, Clive, or so help me . . ."

Chuckling, Clive sat back in his chair and threw up his hands in mock alarm. "Say, now. This is a friendly family talk, isn't it?"

Out of the corner of her eye, Edwinna saw Kena standing in the corridor that led to the kitchen, clutching her two-year-old son, Tutu, in her arms. Loyal Kena had stayed near, but her lovely eyes were large with fright and her light-skinned, mulatto features were fraught with worry.

"That is no way to talk to your cousin," George Crawford scolded her. "And you should dress like a woman, not like a man." His eyes raked her with scorn.

"I dress for my work, Uncle."

"Exactly!" He pounced on the point as if waiting for it. Leaning forward, his long, carefully combed hair sweeping over his silk clad shoulders, he gave the table a sharp rap. "Planting and making sugar is man's work, not woman's. Women haven't the knack. Clive and I have been in Bridgetown, discussing this very issue with the governor."

Her chest tightened. It *was* the matter of her father's will. The governor was its executor. By the terms of the will, her twin brothers, Thomas and Harry, would inherit the plantation when they reached the age of twenty-one. Meanwhile, Edwinna had the right to manage it for them, with one stipulation—she had to marry by age twenty-six, or she forfeited management of the plantation to George Crawford.

It was an unfair stipulation. Marry? Be ruled by yet another man? A husband? She would rather put her head in a noose. But she would turn twenty-six tomorrow. That's why her uncle had come, of course. She drew a tense breath.

"Uncle, you know I have been planting and making sugar since I was sixteen. You know that in the last ten years of my father's life he took no interest in running the plantation. He left it to me and Matthew Plum to do, and we make some of the best muscovado sugar on the island. The governor knows that. My sugar factor in London writes that the refineries always bid highest per hogshead for mine."

She'd erred. His drink-flushed face darkened. The sugar shipped from George Crawford's plantation bore a poor reputation and fetched a mediocre price in London. It tended to be either overboiled and scorched or underboiled and so full of molasses no one wanted it. She and Matthew Plum well knew why. His boiling house slaves hated him. He boasted all over Bridgetown that he made his boilers test the consistency of the cooking sugar with their bare fingers. His slaves took their revenge where it counted—in the boiling kettle.

Swiftly she changed her tack. "Uncle, women plant," she said quickly. "Lady Maud Locksley plants. Dinny Fraser plants."

"You are *not* Maud Locksley. Nor are you Dinny Fraser. They are widows. Their plantations belong to them. This is not your plantation, Edwinna."

"Nor is it yours!"

He leaned forward, livid, the vein in the center of his forehead throbbing. "For twopence I would flog you. You owe me filial obedience. You are my niece."

She owed him *nothing*, but when George Crawford became angry, he tended to vent his temper on his slaves. For Caesar's sake, she choked down her resentment, but she was frightened. If he got his hands on Crawford Plantation he would ruin it. When Thomas and Harry came home from sea, they would have nothing.

"Yes, Uncle." With a trembling hand, she smoothed the hair that had come loose from her braid.

Clive put in suavely, "We are only thinking of Thomas and Harry's best interests, Edwinna, as we told the governor when we asked him to reexamine the will."

She gave him a dark look. He wasn't thinking of Thomas and Harry; he was thinking of what he could steal from Crawford Plantation.

"I'm doing my best, Clive," she said sharply. "I am running this plantation as best I can. You know it. The governor knows it. Everyone on this island knows it."

"And in the meantime," her uncle charged on, "your credit in London and in the American colonies is stretched thin."

She felt as if she were being backed to the wall. It was true. Her credit *was* stretched to the breaking point. She needed a sugar profit of two thousand pounds sterling each year, just to break even, to keep the plantation maintained and repaired, to replenish equipment and supplies and cattle, to feed and clothe her slaves, to buy provisions from Virginia and Massachusetts—salted fish, dried corn, barreled pork. Last year she'd made no profit.

"Everyone's credit is stretched thin, Uncle. Last year every planter on the island lost his crop to rats. Even you."

He wouldn't hear it. He was drunk and uglier than ever.

"Enough of this. You know the terms of your father's will and you have not followed them. You have not married. You have defied your father's wishes."

She raked a hand through loose strands of hair. She'd never felt so helpless in her life. "Uncle, I have no wish to marry. The will was unfair. Even the governor said so."

"He does not say so *now*. Not in the light of your failed crop and your mounting debts." He quaffed the rest of the rum punch, wiped his mouth with the back of his hand, and rose unsteadily. Caesar leapt to help. "Enough of this, Edwinna. As Clive pointed out, tomorrow you will be twenty-six. I mean to go to Bridgetown then and obtain the governor's signed order. I will be back here in two days, and I will run this plantation as it should be run." Over his shoulder he said to Caesar, "Get my horse, you black ape." Caesar bolted.

She gave Clive a furious look. Clive was behind this. She might have known.

"Then I will marry, Uncle. I will marry today."

Clive smiled. "Who? Some bond slave? Some riffraff out of Bridgetown? Trickery, Edwinna. The governor will not buy trickery. He is no fool; nor are we."

Her thoughts on Simon Tarcher's letter, she raised her chin resolutely. "I am doing no trickery. I am betrothed, and have been for six months. I have proof of it. My betrothed is in Speightstown. He's come from London and will gladly wed me today."

Clive laughed and went out to see to his horse. George Crawford lingered to give her a look of contempt. Striding through the dining chamber with unsteady steps, he saw Kena in the corridor, Tutu in her arms. He jabbed a finger at them.

"Them small black apes will be the first to go. They don't earn their keep. They can't work proper until they are ten years old. Why waste money feeding 'em? I mean to sell the whole lot of 'em to the first slaver that puts in to Carlisle Bay—every jack one of 'em under the age of ten."

"Uncle, you cannot do that. I won't allow it. Nor would Thomas or Harry!"

"I can and I will. As for them old ones that don't earn their keep? A bit of castor bean ground into their food will hurry them on their way. They are always yammering about the afterlife they want to go to, aren't they? I'll help 'em on their way. This is not an almshouse, Edwinna. This is a plantation. I mean to run it as such."

He strode out of the house and into the yard. She watched him go, chest pounding. He tripped over his own drunken feet and went down, and when Caesar came running to help, he gave him a crack on the head. Patient Caesar helped him across the yard, out the gate, to his horse, and up into the saddle. For thanks he got another blow. George and Clive Crawford rode off, Caesar on foot, trotting in their dust.

Edwinna watched until they were gone. Kena stole up behind her, clutching Tutu, her eyes huge with fright. Edwinna put her arms around her.

"Don't worry. It's all nonsense. I would never let Tutu be sold, never. Nor would Thomas or Harry."

Kena gave her a trusting nod. A delicate young woman of nineteen, Kena had eyes as lovely as a doe's and long, soft black hair that fanned out upon her shoulders like a shawl. Edwinna loved her very much and Kena loved her. Oblivious to the tension, Tutu gurgled happily and lunged for Edwinna. She took him in her arms.

"Kena, run to my bedchamber. There is a letter from Simon Tarcher on my nightstand. Fetch it." Kena flew, eager to help.

Chortling, Tutu poked a finger into Edwinna's mouth. She kissed it. He was a sweet baby. His skin was ebony black, like his father's, a boiling house slave who'd died. For a moment, she closed her eyes and pretended Tutu was hers. She could never have a child of her own. She wasn't a real woman; she hadn't had her woman's flow in many years. Besides, even if she married, she had no intention of letting any man commit the marriage act upon her.

"Do you love me as much as I love you?" Edwinna asked. Tutu nodded, fuzzy head bobbing, dark eyes shining. She laughed. He didn't even understand the question. Kena came hurrying back with the letter. Edwinna gave Tutu back to her, unfolded the letter, and anxiously reread it, although she already knew it by heart. Kena watched, tense, scared. George Crawford terrified everyone. When she'd read the letter a final time, she crushed it into a ball.

"Run to the stable, Kena. Tell Jeremy to saddle my mare."

"Where do you go, Mama?" Kena said, her pretty face worried and loving. All of Edwinna's slaves called her Mama, though in truth, Kena had every right to call her Edwinna. Edwinna scarcely heard or saw Kena. Her mind's eye was rereading every line and word of Simon Tarcher's letter.

An extreme solution, but it would work. It would keep her uncle and cousin at bay until Thomas and Harry returned from sea and reached the age of inheritance. And she trusted Simon Tarcher as completely as she trusted Matthew Plum. Both were honorable men. They loved her and they loved Thomas and Harry. Her chest throbbed in indecision. But she must do the deed, or lose the plantation.

"Mama?"

She pressed her lips together, unwilling to show the anxiety she felt.

"To Speightstown, Kena. To save my plantation."

Drake Steel stood waist deep in crystal blue Caribbean waters and watched death come for him again. It came, this time, in the guise of a rumbling roller that crested over him and dashed the back of his head into the boulder he was shackled to. With the roller came large pieces of coral, lumbering over the ocean floor, careening into his ankles like runaway cart wheels, grating away his skin.

After the wave had engulfed him, its bubbles prickling in his hair, up his nostrils, in his ears, like the nipping bites of tiny feeding fish, it surged back to the sea. He slung wet, dripping black hair out of his eyes and wrenched ferociously at his wrist irons. Embedded in the boulder with spikes, they refused to budge. For the hundredth time he shouted, voice hoarse with seawater, edged with panic.

"I am not a pirate!"

His shout was lost in the thundering din of the surf. Overhead, sea gulls screeched. All around him, shackled men screamed and shrieked and cursed.

Anyhow, who would heed him? Not the motley assortment

of humanity watching above the beach: hard-faced planters, ragged bond slaves, naked black African slaves, a few painted whores. One of the whores ate her lunch as she watched, placidly gnawing on a greasy rib as if executions were daily fare in Speightstown.

His heart thundered louder than the incoming surf. He swung his head in panic and scanned the horizon. Out beyond the reef the Caribbean was rising, mounding like glittering silver cloth. This was the equator. The tide would not come in fast, but it would come in! Watermarks above his head on the boulder testified to it.

He wrenched wildly at his irons. The skin on the inside of his wrists tore away. Blood and flakes of iron rust trickled down his wet, outstretched arms into his armpits. This couldn't be happening—not to him. He wasn't a pirate. He was a London wine merchant.

When a thundering roller had engulfed him and retreated, when he could breathe, he screamed again, his voice raw, hoarse.

''I am not a pirate!''

Tears filled his eyes. Jagged panic stabbed at him. Was this how it would end for him—with no more dignity than a cat stuffed in a sack and thrown to the sea?

Each seventh wave was a higher one. A glittering mound of water came rumbling in over the reef now, its color a clear translucent blue-green, full of sunlight and death. All around him the din increased, the panic rose. Sensing the turn of the tide, men clamored and shrieked.

I'm going to die, he thought with astonishment. He wrenched at his irons like a maniac, skin tearing, blood running, flesh fiery and burning. *Anne, beloved*, he thought as the rumbling wave crashed over him. *William . . . Katherine. Dear God, what will become of my children?*

CHAPTER
* 2 *

The noon sun blazed overhead, a white hot ball of light burning with Caribbean brilliance by the time Edwinna rode into Speightstown. She was warm, sweaty, and tense. Although the distance was short—only three miles from Crawford Plantation—she hadn't come alone. It wasn't safe. Runaway slaves lurked on the outskirts of every plantation, hoping to steal food—frightened, starving creatures who so feared recapture that they would kill to prevent it.

Dismounting at her sugar storehouse, she gave her reins to her bond servant and hurried through Speightstown, a hamlet so small it consisted of a single dirt street. A sutler's shop stood at one end, dilapidated and listing slightly from the pounding it had taken in the last hurricane. A sailor's drinking house and brothel stood at the street's opposite end, silent now, since everyone had gone to the cove to watch the executions. She began to run.

She found all of Speightstown gathered at the cove, some watching silently and some with hard-hearted amusement.

She pushed her way through the crowd and went directly to Magistrate Tarcher, who stood at the edge of the cove above the rocks and boulders, his sparse white hair feathering in the trade winds, his elderly face grim. He didn't relish executions, either, but it was his duty to oversee them.

"You're late," he scolded, turning abruptly as she approached. His sharp eyes appraised her. More gently, he said, "So, you've decided. It's a wise decision, Edwinna."

"Yes. My uncle visited this morning." She had to raise her voice to make herself heard over the surf's rumble. "You were right. He means to take Crawford Plantation out of my hands. He means to loot Thomas and Harry's inheritance. He and Clive."

He scowled, bushy white brows meeting in a V above outraged eyes. He'd been godfather to Thomas and Harry at the twins' christening eighteen years earlier. The surf rushed in with a watery rumble. Drawn by the sound, Edwinna glanced into the cove and blanched. A dozen men struggled in the water, shackled to a dozen boulders. She swiftly looked away, feeling pale, light-headed.

Simon Tarcher pointed into the cove. "I recommend that one, Edwinna. He claims not to be a pirate."

"They all claim that."

"Ay. But his claim had the ring of truth. He says he is a London wine merchant—a Mr. Drake Steel. He claims he was a prisoner aboard that pirate ship, not a pirate. I believed him. I was sorry to condemn him, but the other blackguards swore he was one of them. My hands were tied in the matter. Look."

Edwinna didn't want to look, but she forced herself. She followed Simon Tarcher's outstretched arm into the cove. She saw a lean, darkly tanned man whose glistening black hair clung wetly to broad shoulders. It was pitiful to see such a strong-bodied man struggle for his life, but there was something gallant in the way he did it. While the others spent themselves screaming for mercy or shouting vile curses at

God, he did not waste his strength on such useless pursuits. He saved his strength to gulp lungfuls of air between waves and to wrench ferociously at his wrist irons. For a moment she found herself praying desperately that he would break free, swim out to sea, and somehow save himself.

Out on the reef, a wave hovered like a low, watery mountain, then broke and came rumbling in. It crashed over him. His head disappeared. She pressed a fist against her mouth and held her breath until the wave washed away and his head popped out of the water, and he, too, could breathe again. Then she found herself breathing as raggedly as he.

"This is obscene."

"He is a widower. Two children, so he says . . ."

Children. It struck a chord in her.

"I liked him, Edwinna. I believe you could trust him to do no harm to Crawford Plantation."

"Trust a pirate? You jest."

"Edwinna, yes or no?"

Her chest pounded with the magnitude of the decision she was making. But she must do it or lose the plantation. Thomas, Harry. Children. He was a man who had children. She tore her eyes away from the barbaric sight.

"Him, then, yes. Him or anyone. I don't care. I only want to save my plantation. Mr. Tarcher, I cannot watch this another instant. I'll wait in your house." Desperate to leave, she swung around to push her way through the crowd, then turned back.

"Hurry," she said urgently. "Before he drowns!"

Exhausted, at the end of his strength, Drake had counted himself a dead man when suddenly he heard a faint shout amid the rumbling surf and the unholy screams. Blinking salt water out of his eyes, he twisted in his irons and craned his neck to scan the low cliff above the cove. It was the magistrate who had condemned him! He'd clambered halfway down the rocky escarpment, flanked by two barefoot bond slaves.

His heart thundered. "I am not a pirate," he shouted hoarsely with the last of his strength.

Securing his balance on the wet rocks, a bond slave supporting each elbow, the magistrate flourished an arm and shouted. The shout rose and fell, waxing and waning in the din of screams and surf and screeching gulls. Drake frantically tossed his head to clear his ears of seawater and strained to hear.

"Mr. Steel . . . a woman . . . intercede with the governor . . . pay your fine . . . if you will agree . . . wed her . . . marry her . . ."

Deafened by the clamor, he missed most of the words but grasped the gist of it. He had a chance to live. To live! Grabbing a great huge lungful of watery air, he roared, "Yes—anything. Yes—"

A wave crashed over him. Unprepared, he caught a faceful of water. Coughing, choking, he thrust his head out of the wave and twisted to see the magistrate. Panic surged. Was this some perverse form of Caribbean sport? Dangle a man's life before his eyes like carrot, then snatch the carrot away?

To his terrified relief, the magistrate signaled, and the two barefoot bond slaves clambered down the wet, slippery rocks, plunged into the foamy swirling water, and dog-paddled out on the wave's ebb. But fear still hammered.

"Hurry," he demanded hoarsely when they reached him. The youths found their footing in the deepening water and attacked his wrist irons. The rusty clamps wouldn't give. "Hurry!" Men shackled nearby saw what was happening and sent up a torrent of begging screams. Drake ignored them.

A wave came rumbling in. The youths ducked under. Drake took it full in the face. The force slammed him into the rough boulder. "Hurry," he urged when he could breathe again. He slung wet, blinding hair out of his eyes with a toss of his head. The two combined their efforts and attacked one clamp. At last it creaked open. Drake tore his wrist free and attacked the remaining clamp himself. Fear gave him strength. It sprang open.

A long, low breaker came rumbling in. Drake and the two youths plunged into it, and the wave, full of pieces of coral and gritty sand, swept them onto the rocky escarpment. Strong and surefooted, the youths grabbed hold of boulders, found their balance, and scampered up the rocky slope. Weak from his ordeal, Drake was tumbled over the rough boulders like a stick of driftwood. It took all of his strength just to claw a firm hold on a boulder and hang on as the receding wave tried to tug him back into the sea.

When the wave washed away, he lay panting, breathing in the musty smell of seaweed. Overhead the sun burned like a torch. Then, he slowly pulled himself up the rocky slope. The screams of doomed men followed him. When he reached the top of the cliff he wanted to collapse on the hot, sun-warmed earth and weep with relief, but somehow he managed to stay upright. He staggered drunkenly to the magistrate, who watched him come with eagle-bright eyes. He was a stern little man with bushy white eyebrows and sparse white hair that ruffled in the trade winds like spiky feathers.

"I am not a pirate," he said, shaking with a sudden chill as the hot sun began to toast his cold body. "I am a wine merchant—Drake Steel. If you will kindly write the Steel Wine Shop, Thames Street, London—" He breathed hoarsely, exhausted. "My brother-in-law will vouch for me—"

The magistrate totally ignored him.

"Do you see that cottage at the end of the street?"

Even in his exhausted and shaken state, he felt a flash of anger. In London, the Steel name, *his* name, got at least a small measure of respect. Even the damnable Cromwell government, which had stripped his father of house, money, and business, and had hounded the gentle old man to death, had paid the name token respect.

Light-headed, panting, he dragged his gaze in the direction

indicated. Speightstown was a miserable hole—a jumble of sugar storehouses and drinking houses. His eyes hurt. Under the merciless assault of the Caribbean sun, everything shimmered in white-hot light. Through a haze he focused on the distant cottage and nodded.

"Go there. I will deal with you there, Mr. Steel. You will be wed to Mistress Crawford within the hour."

"I am not a pirate."

"Go!"

With what was left of his strength, Drake shot him a savage look. Then, too shaky and light-headed to protest, he obeyed. He had no choice. But before he went, he lunged into the midst of the gawking spectators, who backed off and made way for him. He grabbed his silver timepiece from the derelict who'd won it in the lottery. The timepiece had been Anne's bridegroom gift to him. He would kill to keep it. He grabbed his boots from another. Seeing the fury in his eyes, no one demurred.

Slinging his boots over one shoulder, he staggered across the rough beach grass and into the sun-baked lane. He stopped only once to look back, to listen to the surf and the faint screams of the doomed men, then strode on. Lying, thieving, murdering bastards. Let them die.

The street, less a lane than a pig path, lay hot underfoot and sent aching trails of warmth up the strained, chilled muscles of his calves and into his thighs. He shivered in the hot sun. He couldn't think. His mind felt dazed, pickled in seawater. It occurred to him, vaguely, that he had gone to pieces. He couldn't pull himself together. A big, strong man like himself, and he could only pant and shake.

Baking in the sun, the lane smelled of pigs and discarded fish heads. Pale yellow land crabs skittered silently in the shadows of the windowless sugar storehouses that were built flush to the lane.

Midway to the magistrate's cottage, the day's ordeal overwhelmed him. He stopped in the lane and shot out a hand to steady himself against a storehouse wall. William, Katherine. Dear God, he'd almost made them orphans. He staggered on, panting, the roar in his lungs louder than the surf. His mind flew dazedly to thoughts of escape. But escape to where? How?

Shaded by tall, leafy mahogany trees in which squawking pelicans roosted thick as crows, the magistrate's yard was blessedly cool. The shade eased his sunburned eyes. Aware suddenly of a raging thirst, he went first to the coral water drip, a tall stone contraption. The water that dripped through the coral, purifying, gathering in the catch basin below, looked to be as pure and clean and cold as anything he could want. Taking the dipper, he squatted and slaked his thirst, drinking until his belly ached. Then he hove to his feet and found the backyard privy. When he came out he felt better, but so weary he wanted to sleep for a week.

The back door of the limestone coral cottage stood open to the trade winds. Drake stepped inside. After the excruciating brightness of sun and sea, the cottage was dim as a tomb, soothing to his eyes. Stumbling against a footstool, he made his way to a bench along the wall, sank down, dropped his boots, let his head loll back, and wearily closed his eyes.

Dear God, death had come so near. Until he'd been dragged down into the sea and clamped into wrist irons, he hadn't realized how fleeting life could be, how precious. Now he knew. Oh, God, he knew. Trembling, eyes closed, he sat there savoring life's everyday wonders: air pumping in and out of his lungs, his heart alive and beating, the island breezes feathering his wet clothing, the scent of a jasmine bush in the yard. Even the persistent buzzing of a fly somewhere in the cottage seemed suddenly so sweet a sound it brought tears to his eyes. How precious life was!

When his chest stopped heaving, when the powerful emotions abated, he suddenly became aware that he was not alone in the room. He opened his eyes. A woman stood on the opposite side of the room beside a tall livery cabinet, her arms crossed and tightly clenched at her waist.

He stood with a jolt and paid for it with a spasm of light-headedness. He shot a hand to the wall and steadied himself. His skinned wrists chose that exact moment to begin burning like the fires of hell. He couldn't help himself—he winced. Her wary eyes watched, flashing for an instant with sympathy, then retaining their original wariness.

"I am Drake Steel of the Steel Wine Shop, Thames Street, London. You would be my . . . benefactress?"

Edwinna felt near to panic. *I chose the wrong one!* She thought. *This one is too handsome!* He hadn't seemed so big and handsome when she'd stood at the cove and watched him struggling in the sea. He's seemed pathetic and, somehow, valiant. A man with children, fighting to live. Her heart had gone out to him. But now?

Now he frightened her. His shoulders were immense. He had midnight-black hair and olive skin that was tanned by sun and sea to the deep rich color of mahogany. His eyes were a fiery blue and so expressive she could almost see his thoughts reflected in them: his outrage, his indignation at the ordeal he'd been put through. He was a proud, handsome man. She tore her eyes away. Oh, she knew all about handsome men! Her father had been the handsomest man in Barbados—and a brutal drunkard.

She gripped her elbows so hard her bones ached. What should she do? She couldn't throw him back into the sea. It would be inhumane. She nodded brusquely.

"I am Mistress Crawford, of Crawford Plantation."

Drake suffered a moment of acute anxiety. Had she changed her mind? He did not want to marry this woman or any woman. He was still in mourning for Anne. But God! He didn't want to die.

"I am not a pirate," he said quickly. "I was a prisoner aboard that pirate ship, not a pirate."

"They all say that."

He stiffened. He felt his hackles rise, but he was in no position to indulge in the luxury of temper. He wanted to live, damm it. He had children to live for! If that meant he had to grovel, he would grovel.

"Nevertheless, I am *not* one. I will explain if I may."

"Do."

He flushed. She had a bold, strong-willed manner—he disliked that in a female. His eyes flickered over her. She was tall and slender with fine, wide shoulders and even features, but he would scarcely call her pretty. He blinked as his eyes came to her breeches. He'd never seen a woman wear breeches before. The curve of her hip and thigh were plainly outlined.

"As I said, I am a London wine merchant. Seven months ago I set sail for Portugal. It was to be a wine-buying trip. A storm blew the ship off course. North African pirate ships swarmed out and captured us. They murdered the crew and divided the passengers among them to take as slaves to sell in the slave markets in Tangier. Three of us were impressed into seamen's service on the *Black Queen*, the pirate ship that was captured last week."

He waited, anxious, his life in her hands.

"What happened to the other two?" she asked bluntly.

"Dead. One of fever off the coast of the Floridas, one of despair. He . . . hanged himself." He did not add what was unfit for a woman's ears to hear: that the despairing young man had been too slight of build, too timid to defend himself from homosexual advances. The bastards had taken him to their bunks and used him as a woman.

"So you see, I am not a pirate."

She shrugged. She did not believe him. Though her mistrust angered him, he realized she had every right to believe him a pirate. He looked like one, he'd been condemned as one; when captured, he'd been found crewing a pirate ship. He tried diplomacy.

"Nevertheless, I intend to prove I am who I say I am. In the meantime, I am deeply grateful to you for saving my life, but if there is any other way than marriage to save my skin . . ."

"There isn't. They will drown you or hang you."

"A petition to the governor . . ."

"He will give you your choice—hanging or drowning."

"A petition to London."

"London cares little for what goes on in the Caribbean. It pays scant attention to planters' petitions, so why would it pay *any* attention to a pirate's petition?"

"I am *not* a pirate."

"So you say. No one in Barbados will believe it."

Drake drew a heated breath. This was impossible. "You do not understand. I am a poor candidate for marriage. I am a widower, still in mourning."

"*You* do not understand. You are lucky to be alive. And if you think I want to marry you or anyone else, you are sorely mistaken, for I do not. I am marrying to save my plantation. By the terms of my father's will, if I am not married by the age of twenty-six—which is tomorrow—I forfeit my plantation to my uncle." She wore her hair in a braid, but raked at it as if it were loose—a nervous habit, he suspected. "I think it a fair trade. You save your life and I save my plantation."

"It's fair," he admitted, but he felt overwhelmed with frustration, fatigue. There was nothing more to say. He swallowed angrily. Then, lest he end up back in the sea—she looked bold enough to do it—he shut his mouth, retreated to the bench, and sat. She sat on the bench opposite.

He looked at her. Plainly she believed him a pirate. So why marry him? Why not marry someone of the island? He could only think of one outlandish reason. She was a female with a bizarre sexual appetite for "pirates."

"Do your wrists hurt?"

He looked down at them. They were as bloody and raw

as anything hanging in the shop windows on Poultry Lane in London.

"An understatement," he said dryly.

"I thought they might, so I brought balm from my store-house. I'll dress them, if you like."

He looked at her in surprise as she fetched a bowl of god-awful smelly balm from the livery cabinet, plus linen bandage strips. She knelt in front of him.

"Hold out your wrists."

Orders from headquarters. He held them out. She was gentler than he'd expected. The rancid smell of the sticky yellow balm curled into the air, making his nostrils flare.

"What's in it?"

"I don't know."

"Wonderful."

She frowned. "My slaves swear by it. We buy it by the barrel. It comes from the Gambia River area in Africa. Whenever my slaves hurt themselves or become ill, they smear it on their bodies. They even eat a bit of it. The next day they are well."

"I do *not* intend to eat any."

"Well, I did not say you had to."

She was a stiff, humorless woman. He watched her in curiosity. When, in the course of rotating his wrists for her, their hands touched, she jerked back. He could have sworn he saw a flicker of terror in her eyes. What was wrong with her? Was she insane? Even if he *were* a pirate, he was hardly in a circumstance to do her harm.

A bell began to toll somewhere in the rotten miserable hamlet, its echo waxing and waning in the trade winds, signaling that the executions were over. A chill shot up his spine. Dear God, how close he'd come to dying. He panted a little. She heard the tolling and flinched.

"They deserved to die," he said. "I saw them murder helpless men, rape women, cast innocent little children into the sea."

"Perhaps you did those things, too."

"I am *not* a pirate."

"As you say."

This was an impossible woman. When she'd finished bandaging his wrists and put her things away, he sat back and kept silent. The slow, measured tolling went on. By and by it stopped. Footsteps sounded in the yard. Smoothing his windblown, feathery hair, Magistrate Tarcher entered the cottage, acknowledged Drake with a glance, and said to the woman, "Did you explain the situation to him?"

"I . . . not everything."

The magistrate scowled. "Edwinna, he deserves an explanation."

"I deserve more than an explanation," Drake said. "I am *not* a pirate." Both glanced his way, but ignored what he'd said. Edwinna. So that was her name. It suited her. It was a bold name. Drake glanced at her. Chided by the magistrate, she'd at least had the grace to flush. He got his first real glimpse of her eyes. They were lovely—long-lashed, a clear brown.

Tersely, without wasting a word, Magistrate Tarcher put the matter before him. Drake was a merchant, a man of business; he grasped the situation. Basically, the woman was in a box. Unless she married, and at once, she would lose control of the family plantation, which her brothers were due to inherit at twenty-one. He could understand that. He was grateful to her for saving his life. He would gladly work his tail off for her for a couple of years. But marriage?

"If there is any other way to save my skin . . ."

"None," the magistrate said crisply.

"I am *not* a pirate."

Tarcher eyed him sternly from beneath bushy white brows.

"Mr. Steel? I detest executions. I have no wish to witness another tomorrow. Now, come to the table and sign the papers. I need to send word to the governor today, at once."

Drake glared at him. Having no choice, he went to Tarcher's worktable and grabbed the first of the papers the magistrate held out to him—the betrothal contract. It was predated six months earlier. He was grateful. It protected him, "proved" he'd come to the Caribbean as a bridegroom, not a pirate. He signed it.

He read the marriage contract next. Under its terms, he was not to be a husband at all, but a puppet. By signing it, he would relinquish his right to rule his wife's property. Further, under threat of being retried for crimes of piracy, he was not to set foot off the island of Barbados without his wife's permission.

"This is no marriage contract," he snapped. "It's little more than a bond slave indenture."

The woman panicked. "Mr. Tarcher, my plantation!"

Tarcher calmly held out the quill pen. "You have a choice, Mr. Steel."

A wonderful choice—sign or die. He wrenched the pen from Tarcher's outstretched hand, stabbed it into the ink pot, and scrawled his signature.

The marriage license came next. As he took pen in hand and held it poised above the document, a memory pierced him—Anne, bubbling with excitement, clinging to his arm as he purchased and paid for their marriage license in the city hall at Cornhill, London. He glanced at Edwinna. *She* would never cling to a man's arm. She wouldn't need to. She looked to be as self-sufficient as an Amazon.

He scrawled his signature and pushed the license down the table to her, parchment rustling. She took pen in hand and signed with as little emotion as if she were ordering a shipment of tools for her plantation. Her signature was as bold and upright as a man's. Anne's signature had been dainty, feminine. She'd taken pride in her pretty penmanship.

The marriage rite immediately followed the signing. It was simply a matter of standing side by side—she was almost as tall as he—and giving heed to the words as the magistrate read from his leather-bound, insect-chewed book of civil ceremonies. The vows they were required to repeat were mere lip service, and Drake spoke his tightly, with a grim jaw.

"I, Drake William Steel, take thee, Edwinna Charlotte Crawford . . . forswearing all others . . . with my body I thee worship and with all my earthly goods I thee endow . . ."

Edwinna felt a qualm as Drake Steel spoke his vows. He had a magnificent voice—full-timbered, mellow, resonant. She wondered what it would be like to have that magnificent voice say those vows to her and mean it.

She glanced at his profile. He was tired and upset. Well, she was upset, too. She wanted this marriage no more than he. When it was her turn, she said her vows in a soft voice, faltering twice, but managing to finish. Simon Tarcher pronounced them man and wife, and she realized with a jolt that they were married. Her plantation was safe!

CHAPTER

* 3 *

Supper that night was tense. At least it was for Drake as he sat at the table with Edwinna and Tarcher, dining by the meager light of one candle in Tarcher's dark cottage. Candles, evidently, were in short supply in the Caribbean and were burned sparingly. Beyond the table, in the darkness, Tarcher's manservant was already asleep on a pallet on the floor. Edwinna's servants were also—an Irish peasant bondsman and the boy, Jeremy. He drew a breath and contemplated his situation: He was in a dark cottage on a darker island on an even darker, moonless sea. England and home were thousands of dark, watery, distant miles away.

The trade winds wafted in the open windows, bringing the scent of jasmine. The surf hummed and whispered, rhythmic as a lullaby. He wanted to sleep for a month. He glanced around the table. They made a ridiculous trio: Edwinna wary and silent, Drake weary and spent, Simon Tarcher bearing the brunt of the conversation, optimistically marching in with topics like a soldier marching in to shore up a breach in a wall.

Drake was too tired to think, let alone talk. He couldn't believe the trap he found himself in. He couldn't stop brooding. William and Katherine doubtless thought their father dead. In the morning, before traveling to Crawford Plantation—wherever in hell *that* was—he would write Verity and then ask Tarcher to send the letter for him. Tonight he was too tired, too emotionally spent to take pen in hand.

A brief spate of conversation hit the candlelit silence like buckshot. Sugar again. Drake swung his gaze to Edwinna. Sugar seemed the only subject that interested her. She felt his gaze, looked at him, then swiftly looked away. She seemed afraid of him. Why? He'd done his best to convince her he was not a pirate. He'd done his best to appear civilized. Courtesy of Tarcher, he'd managed to bathe, shave, and dress himself in clean clothes. He'd expected his civilized appearance to lessen her wariness; instead, it had heightened it. He didn't understand her.

He continued to gaze at her. She had fabulous hair and knew it. She wore it like a sexual banner. Combed out now, loosened from that ridiculous braid, it was a light sunny brown in color and as thick and curly as sheep's wool—hair a man would want to touch. Her sexuality confused him. Sometimes she looked at him with interest, and sometimes as if she wished he would drop dead.

"Might I inquire, Mr. Steel," Tarcher tried optimistically, "as to your political persuasion? Are you Royalist or Protectorate?"

"Royalist," Drake answered without hesitation. He saw displeasure on Edwinna's strong, candlelit features and squared his shoulders, eyed her steadily, and deliberately said it again. "Royalist, Mr. Tarcher. Royalist yesterday, today, and tomorrow. I am implacable in that sentiment and I do not apologize for it."

He looked at her disapproving profile. If she didn't want a Royalist husband, send him home. He'd gladly go.

Tarcher's eyes bore the suspicion of amusement. So he and Edwinna amused Tarcher, did they? Damn the man. Tarcher helped himself to another piece of fried fish, flipping it from platter to plate with the flat of his knife, saying, "Then life in London must be difficult for you, Mr. Steel."

Drake looked directly into the man's eyes. "I was ten when the civil war broke out, seventeen when Oliver Cromwell beheaded the king. My father was one of the few London merchants brave enough to label Cromwell for what he was: a regicide, a murderer. For his honesty, my father was incarcerated in the Tower of London, despite his advanced age and fragile health. In that damned dungeon, he fell ill with 'Tower cough' and died. Yes, I *am* pro-king, and I intend to remain so. What was good enough for my father is good enough for me."

Edwinna had stopped eating to stare at him, her expression arrested, her spoon hovering midway between plate and mouth, its pewter glowing in the candlelight. She had alluring hair. He wanted to touch it. Drake took a deep breath to calm himself and went on more quietly.

"And if you perceive, Mr. Tarcher, that my life in London is difficult, you are quite right. My ancestral home, Highgate Hall, has been seized and sequestered by the Lord Protector. My wine business suffers constant harassment. Vandals regularly break my shop windows. More the Lord Protector cannot do to me. I am an Englishman, and I have an Englishman's inalienable right to live. At least I *did* before I was Barbadosed."

Pointedly he used the scurrilous term in vogue in London drinking houses to signify persons who were kidnapped off the streets and transported into forced labor in the Caribbean. It was a common practice in these lawless times. Lawlessness had prevailed in England since the civil war. Highwaymen ruled the highways, robbing every traveler. Pirates commanded the seas.

Tarcher smiled wryly. "Come, come, Mr. Steel. Your political persuasion makes no difference in Barbados. You will find Barbados planters amiably divided on the issue—some pro-Royalist, some pro-Protectorate. I myself am elderly and sentimental enough to long to have the monarchy back, the king."

"And you?" Drake said to Edwinna. Not that he cared. He was only being polite.

"Protectorate," she said bluntly. "The Protectorate does not enforce the Navigation Acts. Under the Cromwell government I am free to sell my sugar anywhere, at the best price it will fetch." Her manner was as forthright as a man's, challenging, looking him straight in the eye, her shoulders as squared as his. He'd never met a woman so sure of herself.

It provoked him, yet he knew he was being irrational. The woman had a right to her own opinions. A realization struck. In his first marriage, he had been the protector, the provider. In this marriage—if it *was* a marriage—Edwinna was protector, provider. It pierced his vanity.

He felt building in him the urge to lock horns with her.

"Then your allegiance can be bought—at market price."

That brought sparks to her eyes.

"Nonsense. My allegiance is to Barbados."

"You are an Englishwoman. Your allegiance belongs to England."

"My parents were English, yes. But I was *born* in Barbados. I am Barbadian first, English second. I care little who rules England—king or Lord Protector—so long as I can market my sugar unhindered."

"A specious, self-serving attitude."

"Specious, self-serving? And how does England serve us? Our waters teem with pirates. Does she send help? No. Instead, she sends us all manner of undesirables whom she sells to us as indentured servants. What allegiance has England ever felt for us but to clamor for our sugar, slap a high tax on it, and then rub salt in our wounds by sending greedy governors to rule over us? England deserves and gets no allegiance from me, nor from any sensible-thinking planter on Barbados.'' She slanted a hostile chin at him. ''You find that an unnatural attitude?''

He speared a piece of fish from the platter. ''Not,'' he said caustically, ''in a colony that sees fit to traffic in black slavery.''

''You object to slavery?''

He laughed. ''With all my heart. Every decent-minded, Christian Englishman objects to it.''

''What nonsense. Slavery has always existed in the world.''

''*Not* in the world as God designed it. *Not* in Eden.''

''You do not know what you are talking about.''

''Nor do you.''

''In the first place, most of the slaves we buy were already enslaved by other black tribes in Africa. In the second place, the slaves are treated better here than in Africa.''

''Ah, you beat them less, do you?''

She gave him a look that had fire in it. Evidently two topics could fire her up: sugar *and* slaves.

''We do not *beat* slaves on Crawford Plantation. Only fools beat and abuse their slaves. Sensible planters do not. Slaves cost thirty pounds sterling each. They're a considerable investment.''

''Human life is an 'investment,' then?''

''You know nothing!''

Flatly dismissing him and his argument, she returned to her eating. Drake gazed at her in mild astonishment. He'd never met such an outspoken woman in all his life. *She is a totally unfeminine female*, Drake thought, eating his fish, eyeing her.

An idiot, Edwinna thought, picking at her fish, eyeing him.

A dried up spinster.

A rogue pirate.

As charmless a woman as ever I've met.

Probably a drunkard and a woman beater.

She baffles me.

He frightens me.

Still, she has a right to her own opinions.

Still, he has a right to his own opinions.

She has . . . fine, erect posture. I like that in a woman . . .

He has . . . a magnificent voice. It rings with the passion of his convictions. I like that in a man . . .

Their eyes lifted and met across the table at the same moment. Edwinna was first to look away. During their crisp exchange, Magistrate Tarcher had sat eating, his eyes bright and watchful and amused. Drake resented it. Tarcher behaved as if he were a matchmaker and pleased with the match he'd made. It was about as much of a match as yoking an ox with a donkey and expecting them to pull in unison.

Now Tarcher injected a mild statement. "Mr. Steel, you are unaware that Edwinna is one of the few planters in Barbados who manumits her slaves. They are granted their freedom papers at age thirty-five, and they are free to go, or they can stay on and live free of charge."

Drake was unimpressed. One year was too long to be enslaved. Thirty-five years? Impossible. But for the sake of peace he kept his tone neutral and nodded at Edwinna.

"Admirable, I am sure."

"Thank you," she said, accepting his remark at face value. "It is no more than they deserve. I love my slaves."

Drake's lips parted slightly in surprise. While he opposed slavery on principle, he had never actually known a black person, had never thought of them as individuals one might come to know and like and even to love. He frowned, studying Edwinna in the candlelight, more mystified by her than ever. She was, he decided, an enigma.

A diplomatic man, Tarcher adroitly took the conversation

away from slavery, refilling Drake's wine cup as he did so. He didn't refill Edwinna's cup. She drank no wine, no beer, no alcoholic spirits of any sort. *She ought to*, Drake thought caustically. *It might mellow her*.

"You have children, Mr. Steel . . ."

Edwinna reacted to the refilling of his wine cup with a look of alarm that vexed Drake. What did she think he was—a drunkard, as well as a pirate? Besides, the wine was of such poor quality a man would need a wooden palate to bear getting drunk on it. A taste of it had told Drake it had been poor to start with and had further deteriorated in the tropical heat. Wine didn't belong in the tropics. Only the Madeiras improved in a warm climate. Wine was his business; he knew it inside out, from top to bottom.

Ignoring her, he gave his attention to Tarcher.

"Yes, two," he said, unable to quell the pride in his voice. "A son, William, who is six, and a daughter, Katherine, who is three. They are in London, living with my sister, Verity." It felt good to speak of his children again. Aboard the pirate ship, he hadn't let one mention of them escape his lips for fear some insane, murdering bastard might take it into his head to go to London and hunt them down.

"A fine family, Mr. Steel," Tarcher complimented.

"Thank you. Yes, they are."

"And your wife died a year ago?"

Drake leaned forward and doubled over slightly, the question slamming him in the gut. She'd been dead eleven months, and still he could not get used to it. He rested his hand on the edge of the table and drew a steadying breath.

"Yes. About a year ago."

"Did she die in childbirth?" Edwinna asked bluntly. His narrowed gaze shot to her in anger. What a question. But when he saw genuine sympathy and not morbid curiosity in her eyes, he answered her, first drawing two steadying breaths.

"No . . . she died . . . at sea—a shipwreck during a storm

in the English channel. She was traveling to visit her sister in France, who was ill. I was abroad in Holland at the time, on a wine-buying trip.'' He did not add what was none of their business—that his trip had been coupled with a mission for the Sealed Knot, the secret society within England dedicated to restoring the monarchy.

Both Edwinna and Tarcher murmured appropriately. Drake felt drenched with relief when the subject went no further. He didn't want to speak about Anne's death—he couldn't. Her death had shattered him. It was his own private tragedy—not something to be bandied about at someone's supper table.

Alert and sensible, perceiving he'd trespassed, Tarcher took the conversation back to sugar. He and Edwinna talked; Drake ignored them. He scarcely listened. Physically exhausted, mentally drained, he tried to think about how to get out of his situation and get home to England, but he was too tired. His thoughts went around in circles. Now and then, when the surf hummed and whispered, he saw in his mind's eye the chained bodies washing back and forth in the dark water, and a chill shot through him. How near he'd come to death. God in heaven. But for Edwinna making him her husband, he would be out there . . .

He looked at her. She felt his eyes upon her, tossed her hair in that sexual way, and glanced at him—a lightning-swift glance full of emotions he could not read. She confused him. She was a mix of sexuality and stiff, hostile primness.

Entrapped by those blazing blue eyes, Edwinna swiftly looked away. He terrified her, with his handsome good looks, his careful grooming. His shoulders were so broad, she hadn't been able to find a shirt in the storehouse to fit him. The one he wore strained the seams. He was so clean he glistened—black hair, mahogany skin, neatly pared nails.

Did he suppose this to be a conjugal marriage?

Well, it wasn't!

Drake wondered if this was to be a conjugal marriage. On

the far side of the one-room cottage, out of the range of candlelight and in the shadows, stood the cottage's only bed, a mosquito net cascading down from the tester. As guest, Edwinna surely would sleep in it. Would he be expected to join her, perform a bridegroom's function in this less than private setting? He grew uneasy. He was a private man.

He was relieved when Tarcher broke off droning about sugar and addressed him. "I will string sleeping hammocks from the ceiling beams for you and for me, Mr. Steel. You have no objection, I hope, to sleeping in a hammock?"

"None," Drake said quickly. "None at all."

A little later, exhausted and spent and too tired to even think about his predicament, Drake climbed into his hammock and fell into instant sleep. He slept like a rock, dreamlessly and deeply.

He awoke before dawn the next morning, refreshed and with only one thought in his head—escape. He lay in the darkness in his hammock and considered his options. They were damned few. Make his way to the capital of Barbados—Bridgetown—and try to get passage on a ship? Impossible. He had no money, and by the law governing English colonies no captain could take a passenger who did not have a ticket of departure from the governor's office.

Stow away on some ship? He grimaced. Stowaways could be hanged. Escape to the hills? Live in the wilds until such time as he could make his escape to England? Ridiculous. He was a wine merchant, not a farmer or hunter or fisherman. Forced to grow or catch his own food, he would likely starve to death in a month.

Frustrated, he climbed out of his hammock in the darkness, made his way through the sleeping cottage, went out to the privy, and then, haunted by yesterday, walked through the silent hamlet to the beach. Gently buffeted by the fragrant trade winds, he stood alone in the pink sunrise, looking down into the cove and meditating on his narrow escape. The tide was out and the swollen, bloated bodies hung from their chains in ankle-deep water. Crabs had already begun to feed on them. Drake shuddered. There but for the grace of God . . .

When he turned to go back to Tarcher's, he saw Edwinna loping toward him. She made an intriguing sight with the bright pink sunrise at her back, setting her aglow as she ran along as graceful as a man, braid swinging. She reached him breathless.

"Where have you been?" she demanded. "I thought you'd tried to escape."

"Tried! Had I meant to escape, I would have done it. And I would *not* be standing here now with my hands in my pockets."

"And that would have been the height of foolishness. They would hunt you down and hang you."

He narrowed his eyes. "By your order?"

She was genuinely taken aback. Her expression showed it.

"No, I would never set the authorities upon you. I—I do not wish death for you, Mr. Steel. I am only saying that I am responsible for you."

"I am *your* responsibility?" he asked. "Like a cow you own, or a slave?"

"Don't be foolish."

"Believe it or not—" He halted in frustration. He didn't know what to call her. By rule of courtesy he should address her as *wife*, but he revolted against it. Anne had been that. No one could replace her. He settled for *Edwinna*—the bold name that suited her. "Believe it or not, Edwinna, I have been responsible for myself since the age of fourteen."

"Then you have not done a very good job of it, have you —getting captured by pirates and almost executed as one?"

He flushed and swung a look out at the sea.

"I want a compromise."

She grew quiet and wary. "What sort of compromise?"

"You need me to stay in Barbados three more years, until your brothers are twenty-one."

"Yes."

"I have children. I damn well will not stay here three years without the chance to see them. Grant me leave, one year from today, to sail to England, and I pledge to you that I will come back. Do you hear me? I pledge it! I also pledge that in the coming twelve months I will do everything I can to help you hold on to your plantation."

Men were liars. Edwinna knew that. Especially handsome men. They thought the world their oyster. Likely this pirate did, too. But given a year, her position as guardian of Crawford Plantation would be secure and unquestioned, especially if she had a good harvest. God willing, Thomas and Harry would be back. That would keep her uncle at bay. Besides, what was her alternative? If she refused to agree, he would escape. She could see it blazing in his blue eyes. He would be caught and hanged. She didn't want that! She didn't want him to die.

"Very well. Agreed."

Drake had just been warming up for the fight. He'd expected they would argue, haggle like a couple of fishmongers in a London fish market. He hadn't expected capitulation. He wondered if she were lying. No, she wasn't. Edwinna Crawford might be many things he disliked—overbearing, bossy, mannish—but she was not dishonest. He was a merchant and he'd long ago learned how to sift the dishonest from the honest at a glance. He didn't know what to say, so he said what was in his heart.

"Thank you."

It seemed to undo her, rattle her. What would she rather do—fight, slug it out? She walked swiftly toward Tarcher's cottage. He walked with her. She had a long stride, but his was longer. Breeches. They were damned unfeminine, but he couldn't complain of the view, that twitch of hip and thigh.

"I'm grateful to you, Edwinna. I am well aware that you saved my life. I'm not a fool—I know I owe you a debt."

This rattled her, too. She seemed more comfortable with strife than with gentleness.

"Yes, well, never mind," she said, and fled to an errand at her sugar storehouse. He went on to Tarcher's alone and entered the cottage feeling less burdened of heart. A year was not an impossible length of time. He could stick it out. And he owed her. He prided himself on being a man of honor, a man who paid his debts.

Edwinna being Edwinna, she clashed with him again not an hour later when she came back from the storehouse and found him sitting at Tarcher's worktable, writing Verity.

"What are you doing?" she demanded.

"Obviously, I am writing a letter."

"You cannot do that now. You can do it later, at Crawford Plantation."

"I intend to do it here and now."

"We have to leave."

"I will leave when I'm finished with the letter."

She brushed a hand at a strand of hair that had worked loose from the braid. "You fail to understand. Harvest begins soon."

He looked up angrily. "*You* fail to understand. I have two young children and a sister who believe me dead. I mean to rectify that situation at once."

Her eyes softened. So did her mouth. She had a good mouth, wide and smooth, with a natural cleft in the center of her upper lip that formed two pretty peaks. On a woman less bossy, he would have found it stirring.

"I did not mean you cannot write your children."

"Thank you!"

"I only mean it is imperative that I go, that I get back to my plantation, to my work."

"Then go. Give me directions. I can find my way."

Edwinna considered. "I will leave the boy, Jeremy, to serve you. Also, three of my bond slaves should be coming down from Crawford Plantation with a string of burros, to pick up supplies from my storehouse. You *must* wait and travel back with them. It isn't safe to go alone. Runaway slaves—''

Drake flexed his shoulders in frustration. "Edwinna!" He'd settled on calling her that. Besides, he found a slight pleasure in the way she flinched every time he said her name. "I am so damned frustrated with my situation that I'd like nothing better than to be attacked. I'd welcome the chance to tear someone limb from limb." He went back to his letter.

Edwinna grew vexed with him. She was only taking sensible precautions. What did a London wine merchant know about the Caribbean and its dangers? Nothing.

"I will leave a pistol for you."

He nodded without looking up. Dipping pen into ink pot, he concentrated on his letter, but said, "Don't worry about the boy, Jeremy. I'll take care of him."

That, at least, was decent. Edwinna lingered in the doorway, aware that she'd handled things poorly, but uncertain as to how to make it right. She wished he would look up, exchange a civil nod with her, but he didn't. She left.

Drake finished his letter and penned a copy. The copy would go on a second ship. That would assure that one arrived. Letters were chancy things. Some got to their destination, some did not. This one must. In the letter he'd been brief and succinct. He'd assured Verity and Arthur that he was alive and well, asked them to send money, and gave them an abbreviated account of his past six months, including the preposterous charge of piracy.

He'd been deliberately vague on the subject of Edwinna Crawford. He'd given her credit for saving his life and had admitted this obligated him to be of service to Crawford Plantation for the coming year, but he did *not* tell them he'd had to marry her. He was too damned chagrined by it. Further, and more serious, he didn't want Katherine and William to know. They were so young and vulnerable. They would think he'd abandoned them in order to start a new family.

He absolutely refused to distress his children. This so-called marriage would have to remain his own private secret.

CHAPTER

* 4 *

A string of eighteen miniature burros, dainty little creatures, picked its way down to sea level from the green terraced
hills of sugar cane, and plodded gracefully into Speightstown's dusty street by midmorning, as Edwinna had promised. For a moment Drake forgot his troubles and watched
the delicate burros with pleasure, wishing Katherine could
see them. She would clap her chubby hands in delight. They
were as charming as any stuffed toy in her nursery, their faces
rabbit-sweet, their eyelashes swooping and silky, their ears
long and floppy, inviting touch.

Affingoes, the boy Jeremy called them when Drake reached
out to pet them. Spanish bred, Drake supposed. They had
amazing strength. They carried loads twice their size, and
they knew the route so well they scarcely needed the three
drovers who accompanied them. Of their own volition they
plodded straight into Edwinna's storehouse yard. Faithful
little beasts.

He could say less for their drovers. They were Newgate

trash, if ever he'd seen any. Shoulders hunched, they slunk to their chores, dog-sly, furtive. He disliked them on sight. Joining Drake in the storehouse yard, Tarcher identified the three men, pointing them out.

"That small one is Jacka. He's a sly son of a bitch. Watch him." Jacka was slim as a whippet with a face full of smallpox pits and a cocky way of snapping orders at the others. "The big one is Yates. He's a half-wit, but likely to do anything Jacka tells him to do, so watch him, too." Yates was so filthy Drake could smell him twenty feet away. He had the greasiest, longest hair Drake had ever seen on a man. It straggled down his back to his waist. The third was a bond slave whom Tarcher called Hastings. The three had the look of ruthless ne'er-do-wells who would cut your throat for a penny.

"Why in hell does Edwinna buy such bond slaves?"

"She has no choice," Tarcher said crisply. "Nor does any planter on the island. What she said last night was true. This is what England sends us to work our plantations: felons, pickpockets, murderers." He gave Drake a tart look. "Is it any wonder planters prefer to use African slaves?"

Drake had no answer. He hated slavery, but if the alternative was to use men like Jacka, Yates, Hastings? Good God. It made his blood run cold.

A few hours later, sitting on the stiff-legged, plodding mare Edwinna had sent down for him, following the heavily loaded affingoes and their drovers up a cane path to God knows where, he'd found no reason to change his mind. Jacka, Yates, and Hastings were a sullen, surly lot, skulking along, shoulders hunched. Drake was glad Edwinna had provided him with a pistol.

Although he hated the company he was in, he reveled in the beauty he saw all around him as they climbed, heading for the plateau. The island rose lush and green under him. Cane fields rippled like green silk, mile after mile of it. Far below, the sea sparkled like a blue jewel. A necklace of surf encircled the island, and here and there, crescents of white sand beach shimmered. Overhead, exotic birds soared: golden plovers, blue heron, pelicans, wild parrots. Butterflies flew up in clouds of brilliant yellow, fluttering into the blue sky. Beautiful.

And he could fall in love with the trade winds. Blowing night and day without ceasing, blowing with the same mild constant velocity, the trade winds seemed the only "constant" in a chaotic, inconstant world. He was a man who prized constancy, and God knows, he'd had little of it in his thirty-two years. There'd been the war; the loss of home, father, mother; and then the hardest blow of all—Anne. He was still reeling from it.

"Sir? Do you be a *real* pirate?"

His chain of thoughts broken, Drake glanced down at Jeremy, who bobbed along on the path beside his mare, staying closer than a shadow, and smiled.

"No. I was a prisoner aboard that pirate ship."

The boy's shoulders slumped in disappointment. *He's plainly disenchanted, just as I would have been at thirteen,* thought Drake. Still smiling at the romantic notions of youth, Drake stood in the stirrups and looked back down the path to survey his surroundings. His smile faded. Where in hell was he? He felt edgy with the sea disappearing behind him and tall cane fields swallowing him up.

"Even so," Jeremy persisted, "she must have been excitin' bein' aboard a real pirate ship, wasn't she, sir?"

Drake gave the eager boy his attention. He wasn't about to tell a boy of thirteen the truth—that pirate ships were hotbeds of sodomy, where men paired off with other men, coupling like husband and wife.

"It wasn't exciting; it was disgusting," he said firmly, shutting the door on the subject. The boy dared ask no more. But when his young shoulders sagged again, Drake leaned out and gave him a paternal pat on the back. He liked children.

"So, Jeremy. How did you come to be a bond servant in Barbados?"

"I was spirited, sir," Jeremy offered cheerfully.

"Spirited?"

"Ay, sir. Grabbed right off Cheapside Street in London, I was. Shoved in a sack and throwed aboard ship."

Drake had heard of such things. He knew unscrupulous sea captains made a practice of seizing children on the streets of London, spiriting them to the Caribbean, and selling them as bond slaves. He looked at Jeremy askance. The boy seemed remarkably cheerful about his fate.

"You don't mind being here?"

"Nay, I likes it. Back 'ome, sir' in London, there was a passel o' us 'round the table board. I ne'er could grab fast enough to get me fill. Here, sir? I fills me belly. Bone meat twice a week. Salt fish. Plenty o' beans and cassava bread."

Drake made a mental note that Edwinna fed her bond slaves well. It surprised him. She'd struck him as stingy, withholding.

"Then you are fond of . . . Mistress Crawford?" He balked at calling her Mrs. Steel.

"Mistress Edwinna? Oh, ay, sir," Jeremy said enthusiastically. "A fortnight ago, when I lost m'cap in the cow pond, Mr. Plum, he were goin' t' thrash me—it were the second cap I lost in a fortnight. But Mistress Edwinna, she wouldna let 'im. She made Mr. Plum go t' the storehouse and give me a new cap."

Jeremy liked Edwinna. That, too, came as a surprise. It roused his curiosity. He wanted to ask more about this woman he'd married, but he refused to stoop to pumping a child. Instead he asked, "Who is Mr. Plum?"

"The head overseer, sir," the boy said with awe, as if he couldn't imagine anyone not knowing. Plum, evidently, was God on Crawford Plantation. Already Drake was prepared to dislike him.

The mare plodded along, rocking him in the sun-warmed saddle. Ahead on the trail, the little affingoes scrambled up the slope, diligent, obedient, carrying their loads without complaint. The drovers were a different story. They slunk along, paying the affingoes no attention except to yank roughly at their harnesses when a load slipped. Drake watched them with hearty dislike. Jacka was their leader, despite his smaller size. When he barked, the others jumped. He looked to be a cunning man, as trustworthy as a fox. Once, when Jacka whirled as if to bark an order at Jeremy, Drake glared at him, and the man shut his mouth and skulked on. The look he gave Drake in the split second before turning was not that of a passive bond slave. It was bold, glittering.

"I got me a girl . . ."

"Have you?" Drake stood in the stirrups and looked back to get his bearings. He hated the company he was in and hated like hell to let Speightstown slip out of sight. No wonder Edwinna had insisted he carry a pistol in his belt.

"Ay. 'Er name's Marigold. She be twelve. She be a bond slave, like me—a kitchen maid to Mistress Edwinna. 'Course, she don't know that she's me girl. I ain't never talked to 'er yet. But once I waved."

Drake had to smile. "A wave is nice."

"Ay." Jeremy screwed up his face and looked up at Drake, solemn. "What d'ye think I should do next, sir—grab 'er and kiss 'er?"

Drake wiped a hand over his mouth to hide his amusement.

"That might be rash. Why don't you start by smiling at her?"

"Ay. But . . . what if she don't smile back?"

What, indeed? Drake could remember thirteen—the age when an unreturned smile could wound deeper than a sword thrust. He reached out and tousled the boy's shaggy hair.

"Well, she might and she might not. But we're men, and that's the risk we take. It's up to us to smile first, isn't it?"

"Ay, sir!" Jeremy beamed, and Drake had the impression

he'd just become the father of a thirteen-year-old. Suddenly embarrassed, or perhaps just tired of striving to be manly, Jeremy sprinted ahead on the path to walk beside his favorite affingoe, whom he'd named Sugar.

Drake's worries came surging back. He stood in the stirrup and squinted into the sun to get a glimpse of Speightstown. It was growing smaller with every step his mare took. Where in the devil *was* Crawford Plantation—at the end of the world?

The path sloped upward, cutting through a field of mature cane that rustled in the wind and towered a good foot above his head. He felt as if he'd been swallowed up. Speightstown disappeared. There was only sky above, cane behind him, cane ahead of him, cane on either side of him. It gave him a panicky feeling. London bred, he preferred to be surrounded by houses, people, streets, noise, cart traffic. Paths trailed into the cane, but only a small animal would use them. He'd discovered the hard way—by reaching out and grabbing at a tuft of cane as he rode past—that the foliage on mature cane was as sharp as a razor. He'd cut his palm.

Nevertheless, he loved listening to the wind in the cane. He was a sensual man and he loved sensual things. The wind rustling through the cane sounded like silk petticoats slithering to the floor, a woman undressing for love—an altogether lovely sound.

Mesmerized by the sound, he didn't hear the commotion developing uptrail until violent shouts rang out, and the tops of the cane whipped wildly as though something large was running through the field.

"Catch the bastard. Don't let 'im escape. The reward!"

Drake loosed his pistol, slung himself out of the saddle, and sprinted toward the uproar, worried about the boy. But it wasn't Jeremy. He found Jeremy standing scared-eyed and rooted to the path, clutching Sugar's halter.

"Stay here," he ordered and sprinted on. If this were London, he would know what to do. He'd dealt with footpads and robbers who'd tried to break into his shop. This was so alien. Shouts and curses rang. Something squealed in agony. Human? Animal? He couldn't tell. Blocking the trail, spooked affingoes milled, brayed, bumped into each other, the wooden boxes and barrels on their backs clunking.

In the few moments it took Drake to reach Jacka, the commotion was all but over. Hastings and Yates came lumbering out of the cane as Drake ran up, their bodies scratched and bleeding. They dragged a black man behind them. A vicious kick in the kidney sent him flying to Jacka's feet, where he cowered, shaking and bleeding from cane cuts.

"Who is he?" Drake demanded.

Jacka smiled with vicious satisfaction and savagely looped a rope around the black's thin neck. "Runaway nigger. There'll be a reward o' thirty shillings."

If this was a runaway, he'd been months on the run. He looked starved—his belly was so taut, so concave, it appeared to be affixed to his backbone—and his ragged loincloth, the only article of clothing he wore, hung from hipbones that were as sharply peaked as buzzard beaks. His frizzy black hair was long and wild and matted, sticking out in all directions. Thick white callouses caked the bottoms of his bare feet, and his chest was so thin his ribs stuck out like the wooden frame of a dinghy. Drake pursed his lips grimly. The poor devil had been badly mistreated. His back was a patchwork quilt of cat-o'-nine-tails scars.

"How can you be sure he's a runaway?"

Jacka all but sneered. "He ain't carryin' no ticket. No nigger can leave his plantation wi'out a ticket signed by his master, spellin' out where he's goin'. 'Tis the law."

Drake narrowed his eyes at Jacka in disgust. Since when was the law so bloody damned revered by a Newgate convict? It was the reward driving Jacka, not the law.

"Does he belong to Crawford Plantation?" He hoped not. He didn't want to believe Edwinna Crawford could order a slave flogged half to death.

"Nay, not Crawford Plantation."

Drake watched the shaking black man and felt a surge of sympathy. A damp spot suddenly appeared on his ragged loincloth and spread wetly. Yates chortled and pointed at it. Drake glared at him. Yates was a simpleton—a huge, filthy, brainless brute.

Drake nodded at the black man, ignoring Yates, but unable to ignore his foul body stench. Hastings was sucking on his cane scratches and spitting the blood at the black's bowed head. Drake glared at him.

"What will happen to him?"

Jacka shrugged. "Be burned alive in Bridgetown, likely."

"Burned alive?"

"Ain't half what the nigger deserves, hidin' along the sugar path, makin' ready to grab that cask." Jacka jerked a thumb at a keg that lay askew in the trampled cane, then at the affingoe who'd carried it and still milled in circles in alarm, pivoting on its hind legs, braying softly. Jacka laughed mirthlessly. "The jest's on him. Weren't no food in that cask—were only Ireland caps."

Drake needed just an instant to make up his mind.

"Let him go," he ordered crisply. For a moment the men looked at him as if he'd lost his mind. Jacka's surly mouth went slack. Hastings stopped sucking his scratches and stared. Even slow-witted Yates blinked, his mouth hanging open.

"Let 'im go?" Jacka exploded. "Are ye daft? There be a reward o' thirty shillings, and it rightfully be mine—mine and Yates's and Hastings's."

Drake brought the pistol up and pointed it straight at Jacka's heart. "Do it!"

Jacka's eyes blazed. Drake cocked the pistol. Then, with a string of curses, Jacka yanked the rope noose off the black's neck and challenged, "The planters o' Barbados ain't gonna fall in love with you fer this."

Drake could not care less. He didn't know any planters, but he knew his own conscience. He pointed the pistol at

Hastings. "Now, unload a keg of dried fish. Break it open with your musket butt and leave it here on the path."

Jacka had a fit. "Mr. Plum'll have our heads!"

"*I* will have your heads. Thwart me again, and so help me God I'll blow you to kingdom come. I've done it before to your sort—thieves breaking into my shop in London . . ."

Jacka glowered at him but snapped his fingers, and Hastings jumped to carry out the order. Hastings unloaded a barrel from an affingoe's back. Five hard thrusts with the oak butt of a musket split the keg wide open. The overpowering aroma of dried smoked fish curled into the air. Curious, Jeremy had crept up the path. Drake ordered him to go on up the trail and calm the affingoes. He didn't want the boy witnessing Jacka's humiliation, or the boy would surely pay for it later. Jacka looked the vengeful sort.

The black wretch continued to cower on the ground, his terror-stricken eyes following every move of Drake's pistol. Poor devil. He hadn't understood a word. He expected to be shot.

Drake let his pistol arm go limp and gestured with sign language that the man was free to go. At first the slave didn't comprehend. Drake made signs again. Suddenly, a fierce hope transfused the fear in the slave's eyes. He swung his matted head toward the others who stood there, sullen, angry, muttering under their breath. He turned a fierce, piercing look at Drake, then leaped up and dove into the cane, disappearing into its green thickness as expertly, as silently, as a wild animal. Drake couldn't even follow the slave's passage with his eyes. Now and then the tops of cane moved contrary to the wind. That was he.

When the sullen, angry bond slaves had reloaded the barrel of Ireland caps on the burro, they started out again. This time Drake took charge of the party's musket, not trusting them, and kept it on his own saddle. He hadn't a doubt that given the opportunity, Jacka would kill him and likely tell Edwinna that runaway slaves had done it. He wasn't going to take that chance. He rode at the tail end of the burro train, keeping the three bond slaves in sight.

When they reached the top of the next hill, Drake stood in his stirrups and looked back down the cane path to where they'd left the open barrel of fish. He saw with satisfaction that it was gone. Someone had scooped it up and carried it away. He drew a grim breath. At least the poor wretch would have something to eat for a few days.

CHAPTER

* 5 *

"You should not have done it," Edwinna said angrily. The only answer she received was a glare from blazing blue eyes. It was night and dark. She and Drake Steel were in Crawford Hall's dining chamber, partaking of a silent, mutually hostile meal lighted by only one tallow candle that smoked in the chandelier above the table and cast a dingy glow. The shipment of candles from the colonies of New England had not arrived, and all Barbados was dark.

Night sounds drifted in through the open windows. Palm fronds rattled in the trade winds. Tree frogs whistled. A drum beat softly among the slave huts, and she could hear the faint answering beat from Dinny Fraser's plantation. No doubt the slaves were telling what Drake Steel had done. By morning all Barbados would know it. The fool! He was a well-meaning fool, but a fool nevertheless.

By cautious design, she had put herself at one end of the dining table and Drake Steel at the opposite end, a long, safe sea of polished mahogany between them. It had been a mistake. That place had been her father's, and Drake Steel's broad shoulders and angry glares filled the space as effectively as if her father had sprung back to life. She gave him a hot look. She didn't want to be reminded of her father. She wanted to forget she'd ever *had* a father.

In truth, she was more upset and worried than angry. He would yet put his neck in the noose. When the governor heard, and the governor *would* hear, she would have to make amends. Her spirits sank. She could ill afford to part with sugar for bribes, but she would have to. Someone would have to pay for what he'd done.

Discouraged, she pictured her uncle hearing the news. He would crow and run straight to the governor. It was one more mark against her—proof she was unfit to govern Crawford Plantation. She sent him an angry look. How dare he put Thomas and Harry's plantation in jeopardy!

Still, her sense of fair play would not allow her to damn him completely. In all fairness, she admired what he'd done. He'd said he hated slavery, and at first opportunity he had acted on it. At least he was no false-face. She gazed at him. There was much to admire in a man who lived by his moral convictions. She tore her gaze away. He was such a dominating man that he rattled her. She didn't *want* him in her house. He scared her.

Drake eyed Edwinna with deadly calm—a calm which, if she had been his sister Verity, would have sent her quickly tiptoeing out of the room, leaving him carefully alone. He was not a man who lost his temper often; but he was hot, wilting, and in no mood to be lectured by an overbearing woman who wore her hair like a sexual banner and flaunted it at him, yet behaved in every other way as if bed were the last thing on her mind.

He pointed at the chandelier, at the single candle burning there. "Hold your hand in that flame for one minute, damm it. Then multiply the pain by a thousand, and you will gain some *slight* idea of the agony of being burned to death."

"I would *not* have allowed him to be sent to Bridgetown to be burned."

"Ha!"

"What do you think I am?"

"A slave owner."

"I may be a slave owner, but that doesn't mean I have no compassion for a poor beaten runaway. I do. There are other ways to handle these matters. If you had brought the slave to Crawford Plantation I would have discovered who his master is, written him, and purchased the slave myself."

He didn't believe her. She was a slave owner. He was completely willing to tar her with the same brush. He withdrew his attention from her hair and her mouth, and gave it to his meal. There was sugar on everything—the carrots, the turnips, the potatoes, sprinkled on the salad greens. Even the roast of pork bore a crust of blackened sugar. Was there nowhere on this island he could escape sugar?

He didn't seem to like his meal, Edwinna noticed, craning her neck to see what he was picking at. She'd hoped he would like it. Despite her anger with him, part of her had hoped he would like Crawford Plantation and like *her*. But those hopes seemed remote. The only looks she got from him were caustic ones. She watched him flick the sugar crust off his pork with the point of his knife.

"Is the meal not to your liking?"

"Must sugar be put on *everything*?"

"Speak to Honor. She will cook it as you wish."

"I would sooner speak to a dim-witted cow."

"She is not that bad."

"Yes, she is." Drake thought about Honor. Her name was a joke. She was Edwinna's fat trollop of a cook, a bond slave straight out of Newgate Prison in London. Edwinna's entire household was an inefficient bunch of misfits—elderly, deaf, infirm, half-blind. There was a cute little black boy called Tutu who had the run of the house. Drake liked him. He liked children running about a house, but Edwinna's abominable pet monkey, a vexing creature called Priscilla, also had the run of the house. She'd jumped on Drake the moment he'd arrived, scaring him out of his wits, and when he'd tried to shoo her away, she'd bitten him. Bitten him! And Edwinna acted as if it were nothing, insisting it was his own fault for scaring Priscilla. Scare the monkey? He'd like to barbecue her.

There were only two servants of any worth—Jeremy's little friend, Marigold, who was so shy Drake couldn't even glance at her without causing her misery; and Kena, who seemed sensible. All in all, Edwinna's household was a royal hodge-podge. Speak to Honor, indeed. He would get better results speaking directly to the sugar barrel.

"Is there any wine?"

"No."

"Wonderful."

He glanced around the dimly lighted room, discontented, wondering how long he would be stuck here. A year? That seemed too long by three hundred sixty-five days. Here, too, as in Tarcher's cottage, legs of furniture stood in saucers of water to thwart ants. Out of the corner of his eye, he spied Priscilla slipping into the room, strutting on her knuckles, tail straight up, tipped like a shepherd's crook. She was a tiny ball of white fur. Her brown eyes were amazingly sweet and human. She settled in the shadows and contemplated him with her earnest monkey stare. He wondered where he would be bitten this time—shin, wrist, ear?

"I must insist on having your word that you will never again interfere with a runaway slave."

"No," he said flatly.

"You do not understand—"

"*You* do not understand. I did what I felt to be right. I followed my conscience."

"Your conscience? Your conscience will be of small use to me when I am asked to defend your actions to the governor."

"I can defend myself."

"Just as you defended yourself in the sea yesterday, chained to the boulders."

He put down his eating utensils, rested his forearms on the table, and took a hot breath. The look he slanted at her would have sent Verity backing rapidly out of the room, and Verity was the boldest woman he'd ever known—until now. But Edwinna was not fazed by it. She went barreling on.

"You didn't stop to think of the trouble it could cause my plantation! No. Did you stop to think that my uncle could *use* this trouble to take my plantation? No. You didn't even stop to think about the consequences your actions may have brought down upon the head of every English man, woman, and child on this island."

He became acutely alert. "What consequences?"

"You didn't stop to consider that by freeing the runaway you might have encouraged other slaves on the island to revolt, to rise up against their masters and murder them—English men, English women, English children. It happens, you know! Not often, thank God. But it can happen. And the slave revolt does not stop there. The blacks go on to murder their own kind. They slaughter their tribal enemies —every man, woman, and child of them."

The skin on the back of his neck crawled. Though she was probably exaggerating, there was enough truth in what she said to give him pause. He stared at her in quiet, intense thought.

"I didn't know," he said. "I'm sorry."

Edwinna had opened her mouth to say more, but she was taken aback by his quiet confession. She gazed at him, bewilderment filling her. She was unused to honesty in handsome men. She didn't know what to say. His hair, clean and wet from the bathhouse, glistened like fine black oil. She liked the plain way he wore it, combed straight back and tied with a black ribbon at the nape of his darkly tanned neck.

He added a caveat. "But if I *had* known, I am not sure I would have acted differently. Nor can I guarantee I will act differently in the future if the occasion—damn it to hell!" Leaping to his feet, his chair crashing, he clutched his shin. Priscilla bounded into Edwinna's lap, cowering there, chittering at him.

"You needn't have scared her!"

"Scared her! She bit me."

"She only does that because she likes you. Though *why* she likes you I cannot fathom."

Drake swore under his breath and rubbed his shin. If ever he managed to get off this island and out of this woman's house, he would be the happiest man on earth. He would celebrate by never eating another grain of sugar for as long as he lived.

Alerted by the noise, Marigold and Kena came rushing in. They saw the situation at once, and Kena ran to get him a cold, wet napkin for his ankle while Marigold mopped up the spilled water from the ant saucers. When he curtly demanded they cage the beast or he'd kill it, Marigold gently took Priscilla and ran to the kitchen with her. This won him daggers from Edwinna.

"You don't *mind* if I have your beast caged while I eat, do you?" he asked caustically.

"No. If you're afraid of a tiny monkey, by all means do."

"Thank you!"

They settled down to finish their supper, silent, wary, eyeing each other, thinking separate thoughts. Drake was keenly aware this was their wedding night. He wondered what she would be like in bed. She was so dominating, *she* would probably mount *him*. He wondered if Priscilla shared her bed. If so, the wretched creature would probably bite him on the balls and put him out of commission for good.

Edwinna grew uneasy at the gleam in Drake's eyes. Maybe it wasn't a gleam at all, but a trick of candlelight. Still, he made her uncomfortable, and she grew stiff. As a consequence, what she said next came out stiff. She hadn't meant it to be. She'd meant it to be nice, conciliatory.

"It is my wish that you will be happy here on Crawford Plantation."

"You jest." He went on eating in his picky way. "Everything that makes me happy is out there." He pointed with the handle of his spoon. "Out there beyond that savage sea. Back home in England."

"Nevertheless, if there is anything you need . . ."

"Money," he said flatly. "The loan of it, if you will. I've written my sister Verity to send money. Until it arrives, I would appreciate a loan."

"You don't need money in Barbados. We pay for everything with sugar. You simply go into a shop and the shopkeeper tells you the price of the item in pounds of sugar, and he puts it on Crawford Plantation's account. When the account reaches thirty pounds, he sends me the bill and I send the sugar down to him."

Sugar again. Drake looked at her in frustration.

"Nevertheless, I want money in my pocket. I'm accustomed."

"That is foolish. You'll lose it in the cane fields."

Drake raked a hand through his hair. He couldn't believe her. She had Verity beaten in spades.

"What do you want it for?" she went on, tactlessly. "What do you wish to purchase?"

"Clothing, for one!"

"There are plenty of clothes in the storehouse. You have only to ask my overseer, Matthew Plum. As to a suit of dress clothes, there are my father's good suits upstairs in a trunk. They should fit tolerably well. Except—" She looked at him uneasily. "Except in the shoulders. But Marigold can alter them for you. The child is clever with a needle."

Drake squinted at her. He could hardly believe his ears. She expected him to wear bond servant clothes and hand-me-downs? He had to bite his tongue to keep his reply halfway civil.

"I do not wear bond slave clothes or hand-me-downs."

"Clothes are clothes."

His glance raked over her, taking in shirt, breeches.

"To you, perhaps. Not to me."

Edwinna flushed. She was woman enough to feel the sting. She knew she wasn't pretty. Most of the time she didn't care, but once in a while, she did. Sometimes she even wished she could be like Dinny Fraser, so outrageous and charming and bawdy that every male on the island from the age of six to sixty adored her. Well, she wasn't Dinny, and that was that. She lifted her chin.

" 'Tis vanity."

"Some people could *use* a little vanity."

They ate in silence, wary of each other.

"If you wish to buy clothes," Edwinna said after a few moments, relenting, breaking the silence, "the tailor shops are in Bridgetown. Matthew Plum will be going there soon to buy slaves. You can go with him."

"Thank you," he said frostily. Even when she conceded a point she rubbed him the wrong way. She had a damned bossy way of putting things. "As for the cost of the clothes, I will repay you."

"It isn't necessary."

"It is to *me*. I pay my debts."

They ate, thinking their separate thoughts—Drake's hopeful, Edwinna's disheartened. *Bridgetown*, she thought, discouraged. *Ships come and go in its harbor every day. He will escape. He will flee to England. He won't keep his word and stay.*

Bridgetown, Drake thought, hope surging. *If I could work out some arrangement with a ship captain* . . . His conscience stabbed him. *I pay my debts*. Steel, you hypocrite. You owe her your life. You gave her your word you would stay a year and damn you, you will stay. He gritted his teeth and wondered for the hundredth time if this was to be a conjugal marriage.

Supper mercifully came to an end. The house was hot, the climate wilting. After supper he went outside to cool himself in the blowing trade winds. He stood in the darkness, inhaling the fragrant wind, hands thrust deep into his pockets, head back, eyes on the stars. It struck him that this was his first truly private moment in half a year, and he used it to mourn Anne. He ached for her.

When he went back into the house, the servants were shuffling about, preparing for bed. He could hear the commotion in the kitchen as they strung hammocks and hauled out pallets. He could hear Tutu giggling as his mother bedded him down. It was a sweet sound. It reminded him of Katherine.

He watched the lockup process. An elderly black called Scipio went out and locked the front gate and stuck a lighted pitch torch in its sconce on the high coral wall, then shuffled back in, locked the doors, and closed and bolted the wooden shutters on the first floor. The house instantly grew as hot as an oven.

"You had best bring a candle," Edwinna said.

He looked at her. Did she mean they were going to bed? She'd tossed her hair when she had said it. He was surprised at how his groin sprang to life. He was a sexually starving man. He took a candlestick from the sideboard, lighted it from the dining room candle. Edwinna led the way, striding along in her breeches, hips switching. A deep, wide hall stretched across the front of the house. It was big enough to hold a banquet in. To the rear of it, a wooden staircase led to the second floor, presumably the family sleeping floor. He followed her up.

Upstairs, she strode briskly down the hall and turned into a bedchamber. Drake was just two steps behind her when, to his amazement, her door closed in his face. He stood there dumbfounded. Was he a bridegroom, or merely a boarder?

He took a breath. *Well, find out, Steel.* He rapped on her

door. Several moments passed. The door opened one wary inch.

"Yes?"

"Am I to sleep here . . . or where?"

Her fine eyes filled with such shock that he was thrown off balance. Lord, what was wrong with the woman? Hadn't she ever heard of the marriage bed? The look passed so swiftly he was unsure if he'd truly seen it, for when she spoke she was her usual self—stiff.

"Honor did not give you your room?"

"Honor has given me nothing but a sugar headache."

"Your room is there." She pointed at the room at the top of the stairs, the one farthest from hers, said good night, and shut her door. He heard the bolt shoot across.

He frowned, perplexed. That answered his question.

He found his room and went in. Wilting in the tropical heat, sweating, he left door and window shutters wide open, but it did little good. The house had been built with no regard for the climate. With its front facing south and its back facing north in the traditional fashion of English houses, it failed to catch the cooling east trade winds. He wondered briefly about the nature of Edwinna's father, Peter Crawford, who could ignore so basic a factor. Then, weariness overtaking him, he forgot the late plantation owner.

Stripping nude, he got into bed, loosed the mosquito netting, and pulled the sheet to his waist. Drifting to sleep, he thought of Edwinna. What was wrong with the woman? Had the island sun driven her mad? He could half believe it. He fell asleep puzzling.

The gate bell clanging woke him in the middle of the night. He sat up in the darkness and saw Edwinna steal past his room in the shadows and go silently down the stairs. A few seconds later he heard the front door open. He reached for his timepiece and peered at it. Two of the clock. Where in hell was she going? Curious, he pushed the mosquito netting aside, got out of bed, and went to the window.

The torch still burned in its sconce in the locked gate. Two blacks waited there. Edwinna spoke briefly to them, unlocked the gate, and vanished into darkness. Drake's scalp prickled. Was she crazy, trotting off into the night with slaves? He had the urge to throw on his clothes and go after her. His sense of responsibility demanded it. But which way had she gone? He'd likely end up lost in a cane field. He went back to bed and slept uneasily.

The sound of the gate opening woke him. He grabbed his timepiece. Half past three of the clock. He pulled sheet to waist, waited, and when she came stealing up the stairs, he called out, "What's wrong? Trouble?"

She started at his voice. Either she'd forgotten he was in the house or she'd hoped he was deep in sleep. The latter, he deduced, for she was carrying her shoes as if to make no noise. She halted at his door.

"No trouble," she answered. "Something quite wonderful—a birth."

"Why did they come for you?"

"My slaves consider it a good omen if the mistress of the plantation sees the birth and is first to hold the baby and name it."

Drake propped himself on one elbow, intrigued. "*All* Barbados Englishwomen trot off in the middle of the night to attend slave births?"

He sensed her smile and wished he could see it. He had yet to see her smile, but her voice in the darkness was soft and gentle. He liked it. Evidently, holding a newborn gentled her.

"No, but I want to, for the child's sake. Africans are superstitious, and omens mean much to them."

Drake quietly absorbed it. It was dawning on him that she was as devoted to her plantation as he was to his wine shop—a shop that had been handed down in the Steel family for six generations. To him, wine wasn't a business—it was a sacred trust. He hoped with all his heart that his son William would feel the same zeal when he inherited it.

"Nevertheless, it must be difficult, seeing women in their travail."

"I've seen worse—boiling house accidents. Grinding mill accidents. They are the worst. During harvest I live in dread of accidents. Once harvest begins, we make sugar twenty-four hours a day. The slaves work in shifts. Once the cane is cut, we must grind it within forty-eight hours or it spoils."

"I see." She seemed inclined to talk in a friendly, normal manner—a surprise. He credited it to the darkness and to his being flat in bed, a disembodied voice in the dark. "Nevertheless, you should have awakened me. I would have escorted you safely there and back."

"That would have been the very worst omen—a man coming to the birth hut."

He had to smile. "Ah. I see men have the same importance in the birth process the world over: none."

"None," she agreed good-humoredly. Then she sighed. "Tomorrow I will record the birth in the plantation books, and likely, a month from now, I will have to record it as a death. So few of the babies live."

"It's like that everywhere," he assured her. "In England, too."

"Is it?" she said with interest. "I didn't know that."

"Even in England a man can father a dozen children and not be assured that even two will survive to adulthood." Drake lay back on his pillow, lost in memory for a moment. He laced his hands under his head. "My wife and I lost a four-month-old son. He was born between William and Katherine."

"I'm sorry. One could never forget a thing like that."

Drake glanced at her shadowy outline in surprise. "I never forget," he admitted. "Even now I stop and I think, 'He would be four years old this year, if he'd lived.' Or, I will think, 'He would be just the right age to enjoy coming to the wine shop and playing hide-and-seek among the wine barrels in the cellar.' ''

"Yes. I imagine it would be just that way."

He gave her a grateful look. He wouldn't have guessed she was a sympathetic person. He lay back, thinking about his son's death, thinking about Anne.

Edwinna's thoughts were spinning around, as well. "My wife," he'd said, that magnificent full-timbered voice tender, reverent. His wife had been greatly loved. What would it be like to be loved by a man like Drake Steel? She swallowed tensely.

She gazed at him in the darkness, knowing she should go, but wanting to linger and talk. She was starved for talk, for friendship. Surrounded by slaves and bond slaves, she was lonely. She had no one to really talk to on the plantation—no one except Kena and Matthew Plum.

Her eyes adjusted to the dark room and she saw his big-shouldered figure delineated behind the mosquito net. He politely kept the sheet pulled to his waist, but she presumed he slept naked. The climate was too warm for him. She'd noticed his discomfort, his sweat. As for nakedness, she was used to it. She'd lived her life among naked slaves and bond slaves toiling in loincloths in the fields, but somehow the thought of Drake Steel's nakedness stirred strong feelings, some pleasant, others not pleasant.

"Good night," she said hastily. In the safety of her room, she shut the door and locked it. She pressed her forehead hard against the door, pressing out the old, dark memory, casting it out.

Drake gazed at the empty doorway, startled. Good night? He'd thought they were having a conversation, and a good one at that. He shook his head, then lay back, tantalized, remembering the glow of her hair in the darkness. She stirred him.

* * *

"Mr. Steel? I am Matthew Plum, Edwinna's overseer. Edwinna thought you might like to accompany me on my rounds today, to see the plantation."

Already hot and sweating in a bright tropical morning, Drake unsmiling, descended the front steps of Crawford Hall, and went to the man who waited below. He'd already had an irritating start to his day. He'd awakened to find Priscilla perched on his pillow, pawing through his hair, grooming him. With a yell that was part shock and part curse, he'd scooped her up, shoved her outside his door, and slammed it. She'd stayed in the hall, chittering and scolding.

The corners of his lips twitched. In retrospect it *had* been funny. Lord, she'd adopted him for her mate.

The morning's second irritation had been Edwinna herself. He'd come downstairs to find her long gone, God knows where. She hadn't done him the courtesy of breaking her fast with him. Further, she'd left a purse of coins at his place at the table, as if he were a salaried lackey or a schoolboy being given his allowance. He wanted to wring her neck.

He scrutinized Plum. Prepared to dislike the man, he was taken aback. Here stood a pleasant, middle-sized, slope-shouldered man of about fifty who had brown, leathery skin and twinkling, good-humored eyes. To the overseer's credit, Plum gave Drake the better of the two horses that waited at the gate, taking the swaybacked mare for himself—a sign that he respected Drake's position as Edwinna's husband.

"You'll not find much good horseflesh here in Barbados, Mr. Steel," he apologized. 'Tis the climate. Horses do not fare well here."

"Nor do I." Drake swung up into the creaking saddle, drew off his hat, and mopped his brow with his sleeve. His arm pits were already wet with sweat, and his shirt clung damply to the small of his back, whereas Plum looked dry as toast.

Plum's eyes twinkled. "You will acclimate, Mr. Steel."

"That I doubt." Further, he didn't want to acclimate. He wanted to be gone.

Tall mahogany trees lined the dirt path, granting merciful shade for a few hundred feet as the horses plodded down toward the millworks. As they rode along, Drake couldn't help but be aware of Plum's intelligent eyes assessing him. Did Plum think him a pirate, too? Overhead, the leaves in the trees whipped about and he cringed, spotting Priscilla's raisin brown eyes and tiny white face.

"Don't you do it," he muttered darkly.

"I understand Priscilla likes you, Mr. Steel."

"If *biting* me means she likes me, yes."

Plum chuckled. "Edwinna found her half-starved and cowering in a cage in Bridgetown. Edwinna tends to rescue all of God's helpless—animals, children, pirates . . ."

The dry way he said *pirates* told Drake that Plum did not consider him one, and he almost smiled. But he was too frustrated to smile. Plum's view of Edwinna as a "rescuer" surprised Drake. He slanted a curious glance at Plum. The runaway slave incident had to be uppermost in the overseer's mind—in any overseer's mind—but Plum tactfully avoided it and led conversation in more pleasant directions.

"So, Mr. Steel. Edwinna tells me you are a wine merchant."

"Is that so? I thought I was a pirate. At least, in her opinion."

Again Plum chuckled. "She believes you, though she will never tell you so. That is her way. She also tells me you have two children—a son, William, who is six, and a daughter, Katherine, who is three."

Drake gave him a look of guarded surprise. He hadn't thought she'd listened that night at Magistrate Tarcher's cottage, let alone remembered details such as names, ages.

"Yes, I do."

"If William is past five, then he's had his Breeching Day,

eh? Ah, it's a proud day for a father. I've a son of my own, grown now and living in England. I well remember his fifth birthday—taking him out of gowns and putting him into his first pair of breeches. A proud day.''

"Yes, it was." It *had* been a proud day. Drake's thoughts drifted back to it. To celebrate, Drake had given a party in his small house on Thames Street that stood next to his wine shop and warehouse. There'd been friends, relatives, feasting, drinking, merriment. His mouth tightened as a shadow clouded the memory. Midway in the festivity, going out to the privy, he'd found Anne and his best friend, Charles Dare, in the garden, kissing. He'd exploded in a jealous fury while the pair of them, tipsy with wine, had only giggled at him. Charles had accused him of having no sense of humor, and Anne had called him "foolish." He'd had to clench his fists to keep from knocking Charles's block off. For the sake of the party he'd curbed his temper and let the incident pass, but it had ruined the day for him.

Anne had been right, though she couldn't have known it. He'd been a fool to worry about a drunken kiss in the garden. But that was before he learned how short life can be, how little time there was for kissing.

He managed to ride out from under the mahogany trees without having Priscilla land on his head. That was one minor blessing at least, he thought tartly.

From the vantage point of Crawford Hall's hilltop, he could glimpse the whole plantation. Cane fields undulated in the wind as far as the eye could see. They rolled on—five hundred acres of them, according to Plum—covering the land in all directions. Drake hadn't realized Edwinna was so rich. A merchant, he couldn't help but be intrigued by the potential profit the cane represented. He knew the price sugar commanded in the London market.

He looked out with immense interest. The plantation was laid out like a wheel, with the millworks at the hub and cane paths spoking out from it. The wheel design was deliberate,

Plum explained. The spoking paths allowed the cut cane to be brought to the mill rapidly, so that it could be processed quickly after cutting.

Built into the hillside, the millworks consisted of a half dozen buildings that descended down the hill in stair-step fashion so as to use the force of gravity to let the cane juice flow down pipes to the boiling house. The mill rang with noise. Although the main harvest would not begin for two more weeks, according to Plum, a ten-acre field that had ripened early was under harvest now. It was Edwinna's decision, Plum told him.

Drake looked at him askance. "You mean it was your decision, but you let her think it was hers."

Plum smiled in amusement. "No, Mr. Steel, I do not mean that. Edwinna was born with a green thumb. She knows more about planting by instinct than I have learned in a lifetime. I've learned to trust her judgment. Cane juice runs in her veins."

With the small harvest underway, the rumble of the grinder dominated all other noises, and he could see a dainty affingoe coming up a path, loaded with cut cane. At the end of the path she headed up the hill to the millworks, toward the topmost building, the grinding platform. The faithful little creature plodded along without a drover, unerringly knowing the way. Drake smiled. He wished he could take an affingoe home to Katherine.

He and Plum rode to the mill and walked uphill to the grinder. Its rumble assaulted Drake's ears, growing louder with every step he took. Plum didn't seem to notice. The grinding platform was a fifteen-foot-square wooden structure built into the hillside just under a huge stone windmill. Plum explained they sometimes used wind to power the grinder and sometimes oxen. Edwinna preferred oxen. It was safer.

Drake and Plum mounted the steps to the platform, which shook from the vibration of the grinding. The grinder consisted of four vertical rollers, each as tall and thick as a robust man. Two black slaves worked at the grinder, buck naked. Drake's scalp prickled when he saw the danger involved. No wonder Edwinna preferred ox power. Oxen could be stopped quickly, wind could not. He watched. One slave fed the cane stalk into the rollers, and the other caught it coming out on the other side and fed it back into the roller to return to the first slave. Cane juice spurted and ran down the rollers into a catch basin beneath the platform. The air smelled sugary.

"It looks damned dangerous," Drake shouted to Plum above the noise of the grinder.

"It is," Plum shouted back. "That's why we use our best, most alert slaves at the grinder, and we work them short shifts—only four hours. They work naked lest their clothing get caught in the roller and they be pulled in and crushed before we can stop the grinder."

Good lord. Next they went downhill to the boiling house. Drake took out his handkerchief and clamped it to his nose. He'd never smelled anything so vile as boiling cane juice. The stench filled the air, rising from six steaming kettles of graduating size that were set flush in the boiling house floor. The place was hot as Hades. The heat came from the furnace room beneath the boiling house floor, where each kettle had its own oven. Fire feeders kept the fires burning at graduated temperatures.

Drake watched the boiling process. Sweating like horses, four glistening black slaves wielded heavy, gallon-size dippers that had handles as long as their bodies. As the cane juice boiled and thickened, it was transferred from kettle to kettle, each kettle a little smaller and hotter than the last. They also skimmed the boiling juice and cast the skimmings into a cistern. From the cistern the skimmings ran down pipes to the distillery at the bottom of the hill. There the skimmings were distilled into kill-devil rum—a drink so potent that it would burst into flames if a candle were brought anywhere near it.

Plum introduced Drake to the boiling house overseer, a

Cornishman named Alvis Nansellock, and they stood watching as a batch of boiling, thickened juice crystallized into sugar in the final and hottest kettle.

"Strike," Nansellock said.

The boiler swiftly dipped into the kettle, scooped out the sugar, and cast it to the floor, where it steamed and sizzled in a brown heap. A second boiler quickly scooped thickened cane juice into the empty kettle so the kettle wouldn't burn. It was an exacting, arduous process, and Drake was impressed.

He and Plum finished their tour of the millworks, peering in at the dark, windowless curing house where the triangular wooden sugar pots would hang drying in their racks for a month as the molasses dripped out of them and the sugar hardened. They took a moment to look in at the knocking house, where cured sugar was knocked out of the pots, sorted for quality, and prepared for shipment.

Then they rode out to the cane fields, passing through a village of slave huts. He saw slaves everywhere. Edwinna had an empire—a shabby empire, to be sure.

"How can she afford to run this place?" he asked Plum.

"She can't," Plum answered frankly. "Crawford Plantation is deeply in debt, Mr. Steel. However, it is *not* Edwinna's doing. Her father, Peter Crawford, was, shall we say, a trifle self-indulgent? Edwinna is doing her best, and a very good best it is." The bitterness that crept into Plum's voice at mention of Peter Crawford surprised him, and he wondered again about Edwinna's father.

By the time he'd spent two hours in Plum's company, he knew he and the overseer would become friends. Plum reminded him of his own father, a gentle, dry-witted man who'd been astute and intelligent. Plum even handled the runaway slave incident as his father would have, making no mention of it until the guilt weighed so heavily upon Drake that he wanted to clear the air of it.

"As to the runaway slave, Mr. Plum . . ."

"Yes, Mr. Steel."

"I won't deny it. I did what my conscience bade me do, and, given the same set of circumstances tomorrow, I would likely do it again."

Plum eyed him sternly as their horses plodded down the cane path side by side. "Plainly spoken, Mr. Steel. Thank you. I shall be plain also. I admire a man who follows the dictates of his conscience. But *not* if it brings harm to Edwinna or her plantation. My allegiance is first and foremost to her."

"And *my allegiance* is first and foremost to my conscience."

"Then we understand each other, Mr. Steel."

"We understand each other, Mr. Plum."

The air having been cleared between them, the two men rode on, and a feeling of mutual respect flowed between them. He could grow to like Matthew Plum.

Drake had never seen so many blacks in his life.

"What keeps them from running away, revolting? God in heaven, they outnumber the whites ten to one."

"Seventeen to one," Plum said dryly. "Planters maintain a ratio of one white bond slave for every seventeen slaves. As you can see," he gestured at an open field where black slaves were trenching the soil and planting cane, guarded by just one bond slave, "the bond slaves serve as overseers and are armed with muskets."

"The likes of Jacka and Yates with muskets? Wonderful."

"What choice have we? As for the blacks running away, we do our best to prevent it. We give every black his own wife. The boiling house and grinder slaves are given two wives. This makes them happy, less likely to run away or revolt. Also, we buy only a few blacks of each tribe. The African tribes are natural enemies. They fear each other more than they fear us. They do not even speak the same language, and that is how we control them."

"Disgusting."

"This is Barbados, Mr. Steel, not Whitehall Palace in London."

Plum explained that women did the most important work on the plantation—weeding. This was a tropical island where growth was lush and rapid. Without weeding, a newly planted cane field would be swallowed up by the rain forest in a week. The women weeded each new field until the cane was six months old and the plants so thick and well established that weeds were no longer a danger.

He took Drake to a young cane field to show him the women weeding, and here Drake began to sweat in earnest, and not from the heat. Caught mopping his brow by Plum, he smiled.

"All those bare breasts."

"You will get used to it, Mr. Steel."

"That, Mr. Plum, I doubt."

"We give them tunics to wear, but they refuse to cover their breasts. African women consider it shameful to do so. They use the tunics we give them to make head turbans."

As they rode on, the women gestured and shouted.

"Papa—no loblolly, no loblolly . . ."

"Are they talking to me?" Drake asked in astonishment. More than twenty women were shouting, gesturing, smiling at him.

"They are, Mr. Steel. The plantation mistress is 'Mama.' That makes you 'Papa.' They know you are Edwinna's husband. There are no secrets on a plantation."

"Papa." Drake had to smile. "What are they saying to me?"

"Loblolly is cornmeal mush. Africans loathe it, but sometimes the provisions ships do not come in and we must feed them loblolly. They are asking you not to."

Out in the field the rest of the women took up the chant —even the old ones who, with their flaccid, stretched breasts, looked as if they had six legs as they stooped to their weeding.

"Papa, no loblolly . . ."

"You'd best answer them, Mr. Steel. They put great store in what the master of the plantation says and does."

"I'm not master and don't want to be."

Plum smiled indulgently. "You've no choice, Mr. Steel. You can go out into the field and talk your antislavery philosophy at them until you are blue in the face, and they won't understand a word of it. They have always been slaves, here and in Africa. Now, make them happy, Mr. Steel. They ask so little."

Drake flushed but waved a hand at the women.

"No loblolly," he called. The women cheered.

Plum's eyes twinkled. "There you are, Mr. Steel. A proper slave owner."

"To hell with you, Plum."

Plum chuckled. They spent the morning together, easy in each other's company. Drake kept looking for Edwinna. Was she avoiding him? Why? He'd thought they'd achieved a rapport of sorts in that middle-of-the-night talk. Was she frightened of him? The thought offended him. How could she still judge him to be a danger?

Plum found Edwinna's absence derelict, too, for as they rode along he made up unlikely excuses for her. "Edwinna is probably tied up with her bookkeeper." Drake didn't answer, which was answer enough. He didn't believe it.

Toward the end of the morning, they stopped at Plum's cabin, sat on the shady porch, and thirstily drank tankards of cold water from the coral drip, brought to them by Plum's black slave woman. She also brought them pipes to smoke, which she lighted in her own mouth, sucking at them to get them properly started. Plum took his and smoked with relish. Drake took a puff or two to be courteous to the woman, then set it aside. He disliked Barbados tobacco—it had an acrid, bitter taste.

As they sat on the porch, three little mulatto children, naked as jaybirds, came shrieking across the yard and threw themselves at Plum, hanging on his neck. Plum kissed and hugged them. Drake watched in astonishment. When he'd sent the tots back to their play, Plum gave him a twinkling look.

"Yes, Mr. Steel, they're mine. I won't deny it—not before God or man. I have grown children in England and a wife there, too, but I'll be deviled if I'm not fonder of these rascals than of the whole lot back home in Yorkshire."

"As for my woman," Plum sent a fond glance into the house where she'd shyly retired, "I bought her off a slave ship ten years ago, and she was the best thing I ever bought in my life. She makes me happy, Mr. Steel. She fills my home and my heart. Now I ask you, can more be said of any woman, black or white?"

Drake smiled in bemusement. "I daresay not." This island and its conventions were as strange to him as if he'd gone to sleep one night in his bed in London and awakened to find himself in another world. He couldn't imagine siring a child on a black woman. Then, mentally jabbing himself, he had to admit he could easily imagine it. The island was damned beautiful and sensual—bare-breasted maidens, undulating cane, flowers, sun, trade winds. Yes, he could easily picture a lovely black maiden in his arms.

He nodded at the yard where the children played, running and shrieking happily. "What will happen to them when you return to England? You'll surely go home someday."

Plum didn't deny it. "I've made provision. If I should leave or die, my woman and my children will be freed. Edwinna knows what to do. She keeps a copy of my will in her strongbox. I've put money aside for the woman to open a small business in Bridgetown—an inn or drinking house. As for those little rascals . . ." He glanced at them fondly. "I have purchased a ten-acre farm plot for each of them. They will able to hold their heads high, knowing they are property owners."

"Edwinna sanctions all this?" He couldn't imagine it.

Plum smiled indulgently. "You are an Englishman, Mr.

Steel, and you think like one. Edwinna is Barbados born, and she thinks like a woman of the island. Plantation life is normal to her, *including* slavery." Plum paused, his eyes narrowing, assessing Drake. "You don't much like her, do you, Mr. Steel?"

Taken aback, Drake drew a careful breath. "She is . . . unusual."

"Ay, Mr. Steel, unusual in that's she's a fine, decent woman. There's no finer to be found in all Christendom."

Drake sat in thought. The noon bell clamored, ending the conversation. Slaves and bond slaves drifted out of the fields, heading to their huts and their food. They stood. According to Plum, midday meal at Crawford Hall was a work session, with Plum's chief overseers gathering to eat at Edwinna's table. David Alleyne, the young, fair-haired plantation doctor whom Drake had met earlier, came bounding from the hospital huts, his step jaunty, his face as joyful as if he were going to a feast.

Plum winked at Drake. "David Alleyne is in love with Kena."

"Kena. What will come of it?"

"Who can say? I only know this. It is true love that shines in that young man's eyes, not lust, else Edwinna would not permit him in the house."

"Edwinna seems to be very fond of Kena, and Kena of her." Drake had noticed the bond between them at supper as Kena served.

Plum smiled humorously. "With good reason, Mr. Steel, with good reason."

It was a cryptic response, and Drake's eyebrows lifted in curiosity. But Plum chose to say no more on the subject.

"Let's go eat, Mr. Steel."

CHAPTER

* 6 *

Evading Priscilla, who waited for him like the plague, perched atop the coral water drip in the front yard, ready to pounce, Drake slipped into the house through a side door.

A hallway led past the plantation office. The door stood open. Drake stopped and glanced in. Ledgers stood neatly on shelves. A large map of Crawford Plantation covered one wall. He saw each cane field, provisions field, pasture, cattle pond, fruit grove, and building precisely labeled. He itched to take a look at the books, but they were none of his business.

He went upstairs, into his room, and stopped, startled. His bedchamber was decked out like a tailor's shop. Suits of clothes lay everywhere. For a moment he didn't know what to think. Then he remembered Edwinna's offer of her father's suits. This was Marigold's work. He smiled. With surprising flair for so shy a child, she'd arranged each suit scarecrow fashion, as if someone were in it, shirt tucked into waistcoat, waistcoat in coat, shirtsleeves in coat sleeves with lace cuff neatly showing.

He examined the suits with distaste. They were a gaudy lot, bright and ostentatious. Who but a peacock would wear such garb? Peter Crawford's taste certainly hadn't rubbed off on his daughter. Edwinna dressed as plainly as a mud hen. He found only one suit he would be willing to wear—a black wool serge with a waistcoat of gray silk. He scooped it up, along with the shirt and breeches he'd worn yesterday, and went to the open door.

"Marigold?" he called, certain she was out there somewhere. She materialized instantly, as if out of the woodwork.

"Thank you for laying out the suits. It was very kind. I want this one, none of the others. You can alter it by using my breeches and shirt for measurement."

"Yes sir." She was so timid he could hardly hear her voice. Poor Jeremy. He deposited the suit in her arms. "Wait, Marigold."

From the nightbox where he'd stowed the money purse lest he prove Edwinna right and lose it in the cane fields, he fetched a coin.

"Do you know the young bond servant called Jeremy?"

Her answer was eloquent. She blushed red as a ripe autumn apple. Puppy love, in all its glorious agony. She nodded.

"Good," he said matter-of-factly. "Then please go find him this afternoon and give him this coin. Tell him it is my thanks for accompanying me yesterday. Will you do that?"

She nodded, her blush deepening to scarlet. She took the coin, curtsied, and ran off. Drake smiled. *Well, Jeremy, the rest is up to you.*

He was about to wash when the pleasant sounds of a mother and baby playing drifted in. He followed the sounds to the hall window and looked down into the kitchen herb garden.

It wasn't a mother, it was Edwinna. She sat cross-legged on the ground, Tutu in her lap. They were playing a singing game in which Edwinna lifted Tutu's hands a peg higher with each line she sang. Tutu chortled happily.

Give her a bucket and she couldn't carry a tune. Her soft,

husky voice was perilously flat. He thought of Anne's fine singing voice, which had charmed everyone who heard it. But somehow the effect here was . . . touching. Like her concern for her slaves, this was an unexpected side of Edwinna.

The game came to an end in happy laughter. This was new, too. He'd never seen her smile, let alone laugh. Tutu threw his arms around her neck, and they hugged, kissed. As he watched, her eyes closed. An expression of such *need* molded her features that he felt like a Peeping Tom. He left the window and went quickly to his room to wash, but he couldn't forget that look.

Shorn of their sweat-stained hats, Matthew Plum and his overseers gathered at Edwinna's table for midday meal. They smelled of the sweat of their day's labor. It was a party of diners most women wouldn't have put up with for an instant, but Edwinna seemed content in their company.

They were indentured bondsmen, but decent men, not convicts. There was Valentine O'Brien, a big, brawny young Irishman who was in charge of the mill; his brother, Sean, in charge of the provisions fields, the plantain groves, fruit groves, and the livestock; James McCarran, a Scot in charge of the cane fields; and Alvis Nansellock, from the boiling house.

The talk was sugar and nothing else. Edwinna gave orders as readily as Plum. Sitting opposite her at his end of the table, Drake found it irritating that a woman should give orders to men. Still, he had to admit she listened to each man's say, and while doing so, looked him straight in the eye. Her manner wasn't charming, but it was forthright.

"How many sick as of today, Mr. Alleyne?"

Drake hid a smile as David Alleyne was jolted out of his woolgathering. He'd been lost in a young man's daydream, his gaze on Kena as she served. David had to fumble through his pockets to find his list. He blushed furiously as he read it. Listening, Drake heard the names of strange sicknesses:

dengue fever, mosquito fever, yaws, sleeping sickness. The young doctor's genuine concern for all his patients, white and black, impressed Drake.

Edwinna's briskness softened during this discussion.

"And the baby born last night?"

"Not well, ma'am. I doubt it will live."

"Oh, no."

Drake spoke up quietly. "Do your best for the infant, Mr. Alleyne. I know what it's like to lose a child. The sorrow won't be any less in a slave hut."

David Alleyne gave him a polite, "Yes, Mr. Steel; of course, Mr. Steel."

Edwinna looked at him in surprise. She smiled, but it was so fleeting and done in so flustered a manner that she'd looked elsewhere before he could even return it.

Talk at the table returned to dengue fever, and Plum tasked Valentine O'Brien with the job of inspecting the slave huts for signs of standing water. Stagnant water bred mosquitoes. Mosquitoes bred fever. Conversation had just turned to a shipment of firewood for the boiling house, which had failed to arrive and was badly needed for the harvest, when a commotion broke out in the front hall. Footsteps stomped toward them and burst into the dining chamber. The men swung about in their chairs. There in the doorway stood a fancily dressed man, clenching a silver-tipped riding crop. He was angry and plainly drunk, unsteady on his feet.

Edwinna half rose from her chair. "Uncle, you have no business coming here!"

Plum rose, putting his napkin down. "Now, Mr. Crawford—"

A sixth sense warned Drake, too, for he was halfway out of his chair when the man charged across the room.

"You scheming wench. Trick me with a pirate marriage, will you!" Lifting his riding crop, he smote Edwinna so hard across the breast that she staggered backwards, clutching herself.

Drake's chair crashed. He sprang around the table, grabbed the man's wrist as the crop went up to strike again. He looked up to see Edwinna with a table knife in her hand, ready to defend herself. Drake slammed the man into the wall and held him there by the throat. Reeking of rum, the drunkard cursed and writhed and swore and kicked. Plum sprang to help. Drake threw the man forward and clamped an arm around his neck.

"Who in hell is this, Edwinna?"

"My uncle, George Crawford." She put her hand to her breast. "He's drunk. Get him off my plantation."

"With pleasure. Mr. Plum." Plum snapped an order at the stunned table. First to react, the two O'Brien brothers, Valentine and Sean, sprang up. Big, brawny men, they easily subdued Crawford, each grabbing an arm with a bearlike grip. Drake stepped back, his shins aching. Crawford went on kicking and cursing, railing at Plum.

"Plum, I'll see you dismissed for this, without a stipend for your old age. I'll see you run out of Barbados. The governor listens to me!"

"Now, now, Mr. Crawford," Plum said. "You're drunk. Go along home. You have no authority here."

"This is rightfully my plantation!"

"This is Thomas and Harry's plantation, Mr. Crawford, and until they return, I'll take my orders from Edwinna and from Mr. Steel."

George Crawford scalded Drake with a look. "You. You're the pirate. I'll see you hang, I promise you. The governor listens to me!"

"Take him off the plantation, Mr. Plum. If he sets foot on it again, put him in chains."

"Ay, Mr. Steel."

The drunkard roared in fury. "I'll see you hang, pirate."

Plum jerked his thumb, and Valentine and Sean dragged Crawford off, Plum following. He went kicking and cursing, his violent noise echoing through the house in counterpoint to Plum's calm, "Come, come, Mr. Crawford. You're drunk. You'll see things more sensibly in the morning."

Drake glanced at the stunned men still sitting at the table. "Dinner is over," he said quietly. The men rose instantly and stole away. Only David Alleyne waited.

Edwinna had vanished. Drake wiped the sweat from his brow, left the room, and went upstairs, taking the steps two at a time. He didn't find her in her bedchamber or in any of the other rooms. He went downstairs, strode past the kitchen, where servants stood in scared, whispering clusters, and went to the plantation office. The door was closed. He knocked softly.

"Go away."

"Edwinna, it's Drake."

"Go away!"

He waited a moment, then lifted the latch, went in, and shut the door quietly behind him. If he'd found her crying, as would be natural in the circumstances, he couldn't have felt more compassion than he felt now. What he saw touched him to the quick. She sat at her worktable, ledger open, quill pen in hand, bravely working as if nothing had happened.

"I want Doctor Alleyne to have a look at you."

"No."

"Kena, then."

"No."

She wouldn't look up at him. She went on working, copying figures and entries into the ledger from the notes that lay beside it. As she worked, her right arm moved gingerly. He winced for her. He couldn't imagine hitting a woman in the breast.

"That was a vile thing your uncle did to you."

"What do you expect?" she said viciously. "He is a man. All men are alike."

Uninvited, he took a chair, turned it around, straddled it, and studied her. He said gently, "No, they are *not*. Most men do not strike women."

"Men do as they wish. Since the beginning of time, they always have and they always will. Please go away." He watched her. She worked swiftly, now and then brushing a wrist at the corner of one eye. "Please!" It touched him.

"What do you want me to do about him?"

"Nothing."

"He was drunk, but that is no excuse. He shouldn't be allowed to get away with assaulting you. I could go to Bridgetown, report it to the governor, have him arrested."

"Do nothing," she said viciously, then, more softly, "Do nothing, Mr. Steel. You already are in enough trouble. I won't have more trouble brought down upon your head."

He breathed softly. She did not want him to interfere. He watched her work on her ledgers. Guilt pricked him. If it had been Anne or one of his children the drunken son of a bitch had touched in violence, he would have strangled him with his two bare hands. But all he'd offered to do for Edwinna was to report him to the governor. Guilt pricked him that he felt so little for her, when she'd saved his life. He owed her more.

"Nevertheless . . ."

"Mr. Steel," she burst out angrily. "This is a private work closet. Please get *out*."

He'd let her remarks about men pass; they'd been natural, under the circumstances. But this stung. He was a private man himself. And to be accused of violating privacy?

"Very well." He got up, went out the door, and slammed it. He didn't know what he was supposed to be in this marriage, husband or flunky. David Alleyne hovered there, a dish of medicinal-smelling salve in his hand. He was flushed and breathless, as if he'd run all the way to his apothecary and back. Kena hovered, too, her doe eyes scared and worried.

"Does she need me?" Alleyne asked.

Drake strode straight on down the hall. "She doesn't need me, she doesn't need you, she doesn't need Kena, she doesn't need anyone."

Alone in her plantation office, Edwinna sat with her head in her hands, tears trickling down her cheeks.

Clive Crawford came in the afternoon to apologize for his father's actions. Edwinna had half expected it. Clive had always been a smooth one.

When he ambled into the dimly lit windowless curing house where she was taking a count of sugar pots, she instinctively grabbed one of the pots. It was a foolish gesture. They were no longer children. He could no longer bully her. But whenever Clive came around, she felt safer with a weapon in her hands.

Clive looked at the sugar pot and smiled.

"That doesn't show much cousinly love, Edwinna."

"What do you want, Clive?"

"Now, now. I came to bring my father's apology, Edwinna. He told me to tell you he is truly sorry he hit you. He'd had a wee bit to drink—"

"He was drunk."

"A wee bit to drink, and he'd begun to worry about Thomas and Harry's inheritance and got worked up, that's all."

Worry about Thomas and Harry? She didn't believe it for an instant. Strong, quick footsteps sounded on the outer stairs. Drake Steel burst in and swept them with a glance.

"Plum said Crawford rode in. I thought your uncle . . ."

"This is my uncle's son—my cousin, Clive Crawford. He's come to bring his father's apology. Clive, this is my—husband, Mr. Drake Steel."

The two men looked at each other. Edwinna felt a surge of satisfaction. Drake was twice the man Clive was—bigger, stronger.

"He owes her more than an apology," Drake said, his full-timbered voice echoing in the empty curing house. "If he'd struck her temple with that hard-tipped cane, he might have killed her." Drake saw the sugar pot in her arms. His eyes flickered. She set it aside.

"So this is your husband," Clive drawled. "I must say it was a remarkably convenient marriage for both of you—almost unbelievable in its convenience. Edwinna retains Crawford Plantation, Mr. Steel saves himself from execution as a pirate. The governor should look into it."

She clenched her fists. "We planned it for a year, Clive!"

Drake strolled to her side and slipped an arm around her waist, as a husband might, and said calmly, "We signed the betrothal papers seven months ago. The piracy charge was ridiculous. I was traveling to the Caribbean to wed Edwinna when I was captured by pirates."

"That's right, Clive."

Clive smiled in disbelief, nudged the sugar pot with his toe, and ambled to the door. "Anyhow, my father sends his apologies."

When he was gone, Drake let go of her waist.

"Can he make trouble for us?"

"No. He's nothing but wind."

"Let's hope to hell you're right. I don't relish being shackled to a boulder in the sea again." He glanced at the sugar pots and her open ledger. "Do you want help here?"

His arm around her waist had stirred the old fears.

"No. I like to work alone."

His lips tightened. With a nod, he left.

Drake wanted to write Edwinna off his books, the way he would write off a bad barrel of wine at his wine shop and take the loss. She plainly had no need of him. Their needs had been served. She had saved her damned plantation, and he had saved his life. Beyond that? Nothing. It had been ridiculous to even warm to her. Well aware that he owed her a year, he made himself a small calendar, a grid of twelve months at a glance. He nailed it to the wall of his room and crossed off each day as it finished, glad to be done with it.

As the plantation geared up for harvest, he spent most of his time with Plum. Against his will, he found his fascination with sugar increasing. He longed to see the books. A merchant and an astute man of business, he had some ideas for cutting costs and boosting profits—not at the farming end in Barbados, but at the London market end, which he knew so well. But he'd be damned if he'd offer unsolicited advice to Edwinna, and he'd be damned if he'd step uninvited into that "private" work closet again.

Over the next couple of weeks, visiting planters came to have a look at "Edwinna's pirate," some of them friendly, some hostile. The hostile got under his skin by lecturing him on the slave laws of Barbados. All of them, friendly or hostile, proved to be monumental drinkers. It seemed the way of the island. Drake was astonished. They drank kill-devil rum morning, noon, or night and rode home soused, slipping about in the saddle, the despair of their body slaves, who ran alongside, trying to hold them upright. As irritated as he was with Edwinna, he sympathized with her, having to entertain drunkards.

Then Lady Dinny Fraser came to call, and Drake's life grew sunnier. He fell under her spell at once. She exploded onto the plantation like a keg of gunpowder, a woman past forty with garish, red-dyed hair and a smile as bright as a sunflower. He and Edwinna had just finished midday meal with the overseers when Dinny came striding into the dining chamber wearing a loud red gown, her plump hips and bosom jiggling, but with eyes so merry that the whole effect was charming. She came forward with hands outstretched for him to take.

"So you are Edwinna's pirate! Lord, but you are a handsome thing. Your name is Mr. Drake Steel, is it? Well, Mr. Drake Steel, I ain't seen shoulders like yours since Irish Nick was pirating these waters. If you're as good in bed as you look out of it, Edwinna likely lives in glory."

Drake couldn't believe his ears.

"Dinny," Edwinna said hotly, rattled, flushing. Drake could only gaze in astonishment.

Grabbing Edwinna and hugging the life out of her, she crooned, "Dearling! I'm so happy for you. I always said there was naught ailing you but that you needed a man."

Scarlet now, Edwinna struggled out of Dinny's hug and tried to salvage her dignity. "Mr. Steel, this is my very best friend, Lady Dinny Fraser. Dinny's plantation is adjacent to mine."

"Lady Fraser?" Drake took her plump hand and kissed it. It smelled, charmingly, of the horse she'd ridden.

"Poo! Call me Dinny. Everybody do," she said generously, her smile bright and wide. "I wasn't born no lady. I come to this island a bond slave and married up." She whirled. "Jumbo!" she said to the Negro who had followed her in—a gigantic, well-built young man attired in the flashiest livery Drake had ever seen, bright red trimmed with purple and green. "Jumbo, you behave in the kitchen. Don't you be trying to kiss Edwinna's kitchen maids. She won't have it. Nor will I." Unfazed by his mistress's threat, he grinned at her fondly and went to the kitchen.

She swung back to them and whispered in a confidential manner, "They say he's got him a cod *this* long. Would you believe, Mr. Steel, eighteen inches?"

"No, I would not." He couldn't stop smiling. She was outrageous. He felt the laughter building. It felt good to want to laugh again.

Edwinna was beside herself. "Dinny, I'm glad you came, I want to talk to you, but we're very busy. Come to the boiling house. I have a new kettle I want to show you."

"Damn the boiling house. I came to feast my eyes on your pirate, dearling, not your boiling kettle." A trifle nearsighted, Dinny stepped closer and looked him up and down. Particularly down.

"Dinny," Edwinna tried desperately. "Would you like something to drink?"

"Rum, dearling," Dinny said sweetly. "And don't go watering it down. It ain't healthy. If God had meant rum to be watered down, he'd have caused it to grow in a pond like rice, not dry in a field.''

Drake wanted to laugh. ''I'll get the drink,'' he said to Edwinna, and she threw him a grateful look—her first. It caught him by surprise. Her eyes were lovely when she looked at him like that, needing something of him. He liked it, and smiled to show her so.

He went to the kitchen, got the rum closet key from Kena. Rum was kept locked in Crawford Hall. The Newgate convicts, including Honor, would swill it down until dead drunk otherwise. When he went back to the dining chamber, Dinny was still cheerfully chirping, but Edwinna's face had gone brick red. He wondered what Dinny had been asking her.

''*Thank* you, dearling!'' She whirled around with plump grace, took the cup, and polished off the rum in two swallows. He stared in amazement. Kill-devil rum could peel the lining off a shark's throat. Ridding herself of the cup, she gave them an enormous sunflower smile and linked her arm with Drake's.

''Now, dearlings, let's sit and talk. I want to hear *all* about your life, Mr. Steel—every single detail. My goodness, you're handsome. Are those shoulders real?'' She felt them. ''They are.''

Something flashed in Edwinna's eyes—something he'd never expected to see there. Jealousy. For a moment, he was mesmerized. So, she was enough of a woman to be jealous when someone flirted with her husband, was she?

''I do adore pirates,'' Dinny chirped on. ''Did you know of the pirate, Niles Goforth, Mr. Steel? Alas, they hanged him in Bridgetown five years back. 'Twas the greatest loss of my life. We were lovers, you know. But he went in style, my Niles did, laughing at the hangman.''

Enchanted by that jealous flash, he smiled at Edwinna while Dinny rattled on, and wondered if this would be a conjugal marriage after all.

Dinny Fraser! Edwinna wanted to shake her. *How dare*

she paw my husband! Leaving the two of them on the pretext that she had work to do at the boiling house, Edwinna stormed out of the house through the kitchen, stopped at the bath shed, went in, shut the door, doused a towel in a water bucket, and held it to her flaming cheeks.

All that charming banter. All that flirting. Sometimes she hated Dinny. Men were taken by her. She'd seen that sizzle of interest in Drake's eyes, the way he'd lowered his beautiful black lashes to look at Dinny. She held the towel's cool wetness to her cheeks until her skin ceased to burn, then tossed it down. Her spirits grew calmer.

It wasn't true that she hated Dinny. She didn't—she loved her. Dinny had been a second mother to her when her own mother had broken her heart by running off with a lover, abandoning her, Thomas, and Harry. She'd gone to Dinny whenever she'd needed a hug or a sympathetic ear. She told Dinny many things, but not the terrible ones. Those she hadn't been able to speak about and still couldn't. She rubbed the goose bumps on her arms. Nevertheless, Dinny had better leave Drake Steel alone or Edwinna would scratch her eyes out!

Drake spent an entertaining afternoon with Dinny, and when she rode off, he genuinely missed her. He wouldn't for an instant put up with a wife like her, but somehow, she'd been the perfect antidote for his suffering. She'd made him laugh again, and he was grateful. He hadn't laughed in a long time. Not since Anne. He felt . . . almost lighthearted.

He stood on the hill near the boiling house and waved as she rode off. She made a ludicrous and utterly charming sight, bobbing like a plump cork on her mare, her dyed red hair aflame in the sun, her servant Jumbo in his flashy livery, trotting on foot in her dust. He watched until the cane fields swallowed her up. She'd roused the deviltry in him. She hinted in every way possible that she was curious about his and Edwinna's wedding night. He told her, in strict confidence, that he'd given Edwinna *eight* trips to glory on their wedding night. She had stared at him in outright awe. "God help me, Mr. Steel! You put Niles Goforth to shame."

With Dinny gone, the luster wore off the day and his mood. Evading Priscilla, who'd jumped on his shoulder in jealousy while he'd sat talking with Dinny, he slipped into the house, got ink and paper, settled at the dining table, and wrote a letter to Arthur—in the main, a business letter. Drake hated not having control of his business affairs, leaving things at sixes and sevens. He was a man who chafed to be at the helm, in command.

When darkness fell, he and Edwinna supped alone, as usual, by the meager light of one candle. They'd both fallen silent. Edwinna, stiffly so. Drake, sexually so. Dinny's flirting had aroused him more than he'd realized. He felt . . . eager. He ate and gazed at Edwinna. His eyes found the exact spot he would want to kiss first if he were making love to her—that delicate, pulsing hollow at the base of her slender throat.

"Is something wrong?" she demanded.

"No. Nothing at all. Is something wrong for you?"

"No!"

He looked down at his plate smiling, feeling pleased. She was jealous of Dinny being with him. He could see it in her eyes.

"I enjoyed Dinny's visit," he said, "but not overly much. She can be a trifle overbearing."

"Oh?" Edwinna felt a surge of lightness in her chest. "Most men are taken with her."

"I am not most men."

Drake glanced as Priscilla came stalking into the dim room on her little curled knuckles, her question mark tail held high.

"If she bites me, I swear she is monkey meat tomorrow."

Edwinna glanced down at her plate and hid a smile. He would do no such thing. He'd been in her house two weeks, and she was beginning to know Drake Steel's nature. He was not a mean man. Priscilla had vexed him in every way imaginable—nipping him, hiding in his room, snatching a letter he was writing and running with it—yet he'd done nothing cruel to her. In fact, Edwinna had once caught him holding her, petting her. An interesting thought came to her. *If he is not cruel to Priscilla, he would not be to you, either.* The thought was so unsettling she didn't know where to look.

Drake frowned, puzzled. He'd thought he was making progress, but Edwinna suddenly went silent as a stone, not responding at all to his efforts to make conversation. Well, to hell with her. He couldn't figure her out. Nor was he sure he wanted to bother to try. He gave up and ate in silence.

Kena broke the stillness, quietly entering the dimly lighted room to bring a letter that had come by slave. Edwinna took it, broke the seal.

"It's from Dinny," she said wonderingly. "She invites us to dine with her tomorrow. We cannot go, of course," she said. "Dinny has no concept of the importance of harvest." She went on reading, and as she read in the meager candle-light, her face grew brick red.

"I was only teasing her," Drake said, watching.

"How *dare* you tell her something like that?"

"I'll retract it. I'll tell her it was only six times, not eight."

"Don't make sport of me!"

"I'm not." He looked up, genuinely surprised, serious. "I was not making sport of you, Edwinna. I was making *sport.* There is a difference. Life is a damned hard journey without some sport in it. It is full of knocks and blows. If a human being can't take time for a bit of fun on the journey, then he—or *she*—might as well turn up their toes and die."

"You needn't lecture me on *life*, Mr. Steel."

"Drake. My name is *Drake.* We've been married two weeks. The least you can do is learn my name. It's *Drake.*"

"Drake, then!" She said his name awkwardly, as if it cost her emotionally. Flushed and angry, she exuded an interesting femininity, breeches, braid, and all. He wondered what she would be like in bed. Soft clouds and thistles. Fire and ice.

"We could make it true."

"What do you mean?"

"You know what I mean. You understand it well enough when it concerns slaves—you give each one a wife. What do you think they do each night in their huts—weave baskets?"

"I do not *like* this conversation, Mr. Steel."

"Drake."

"Drake."

"Then suffer," he said bluntly. "There are things I want to say. May I ask you a frank question?" Priscilla leaped to his lap. He scooped her up, set her on the floor, then wiped his hands on his linen napkin and went on eating. Edwinna gave him a fiery look that told him she wanted to leave the table, but had too much pride to do so. It was her table, her house.

"Yes."

"Is this ever to be a conjugal marriage?"

"No."

"Why not?"

Edwinna was dumbstruck. She hadn't expected him to persist. Her throat grew parched, dry. She felt as if someone had raked all the flesh out of her throat.

"Because I . . . I don't wish it."

"Why not? It seems to me we are two normal people, sexual beings, created so by God. We both have sexual needs. We are both lonely people—at least, I am. I . . . I'm very lonely, Edwinna, and I sense you are, too. There would be no sin in it. The law says we are wed."

Her heart pounded. "I—I am not one of your tarts, Mr. Steel."

"Drake. My name is Drake." He went on eating.

"Drake."

"And I don't have a tart. I've never had a tart and never shall. Tarts don't interest me. I have no use for them." He looked at her quietly, his eyes as blue and clear as the waters of Carlisle Bay. "To me . . . the thrill of the sexual is in fidelity—a woman's body reserved for me alone. Mine reserved exclusively for her and shared with no one else. Her kisses on my lips only. My lips pledged to hers. A clean, faithful bed . . . chaste . . . committed . . . pledged. To me, that is the ultimate sexual thrill."

Edwinna felt as if someone had wrapped wires around her chest and pulled them tighter and tighter, cutting her lungs in two. She couldn't breathe. This handsome man, with his black, glistening hair, and beautiful blue eyes, and his breathtaking speech.

"I . . . I do not wish it."

"I see." He cooled visibly and nodded. "Then I assume you wish me to meet my needs elsewhere."

"Yes. No, I don't know. Just . . . do it *off* my plantation. Leave my slave women alone!" It was a mean, unjustified thing to say. Drake Steel had done nothing dishonorable on her plantation. He'd made no advances on any of the women; intuitively, she knew he would not. He was a proud man.

His blue eyes blazed with indignation, anger.

"Mr. Steel, I didn't mean—"

"Drake. The name is Drake. Until you can remember it, eat alone." He tossed down his napkin, pushed back his chair, and stood. "Thank you for supper." He strode out.

Edwinna forced herself to finish her supper. It was a lonely meal. She had supped alone and lonely for years, but tonight's meal seemed the loneliest of all.

CHAPTER

* 7 *

As the days went by, Drake Steel seemed to intrude upon Edwinna's mind, her senses. Not that he was overbearing; he was not. He was a private man who went his own way and kept his own counsel—just as she did! Whatever thoughts he had, he kept to himself. He did nothing to disrupt her household. When he gave an order to a servant, he did so with courteous firmness, and to her amazement, the servant jumped to obey. His voice carried an authority no one dared dispute, not even Honor. Edwinna began to admire him. She liked the way he was with Marigold and Jeremy. Tutu loved him. Priscilla adored him.

It flustered Edwinna that she should be so . . . *aware* of Drake Steel. It flustered her that she knew the cadence of his step and that she found herself listening for it. Suppers with him had become the high point of her day. It flustered her that when she went on the plantation and glimpsed him in the saddle, his black hair glistening in the sun, she felt as if her lungs had suddenly become weightless.

How foolish! She was acting as silly as Marigold over Jeremy. Such behavior was excusable in a twelve-year-old girl, but Edwinna was twenty-six.

She was confusing Drake. She knew it. His perplexed glances at supper told her so. But she was confused herself. She didn't know what she wanted or did not want of Drake Steel.

A reserved man, a man of pride, he neither made his sexual offer again nor referred to it. The issue stood closed. She told herself she was glad, relieved. Nights, she tossed and turned in her bed. *To me, the thrill of the sexual is in fidelity*, he'd said. But all men were alike, were they not?

Three nights after their uncomfortable discussion, the gate bell clanged at two of the clock. Hastily dressing in the darkness, she stepped into the shadowy hall to find Drake there, tucking shirt into breeches.

"What are you doing?" She brushed a strand of curly hair off her brow. Her braid was disheveled, working its way loose.

"I'm going with you."

"Why?"

"Because I cannot let you go alone. It's unsafe."

"What nonsense. I am as safe as a babe in cradle on my own plantation. I know every inch of it. I could find my way blindfolded, in black darkness."

"Edwinna," he said with vexation, "that well may be. However, I am not a man who can sleep peacefully while the woman of this house trots off into the night to God knows where. Now, let's get started. I want to retrieve one or two hours of sleep out of this night."

Outside the gate, they followed a young Ashanti into the velvety darkness. A million stars twinkled overhead. Here and there, starlight silvered the fields of blowing cane. The balmy trade winds caressed Edwinna's skin. She loved her plantation passionately—loved it by night almost more than she loved it by day. She glanced at Drake, wondering if he thought it beautiful, but he strode along beside her, his face impassive. No doubt for Drake all beauty lay in England— his wine business, his children, the memory of his wife. He would not come back after his visit to England. She knew it with absolute certainty.

"What is the trouble? I didn't understand his gibberish."

"Macaw."

"The boiling house slave?"

"Yes. A domestic dispute between his two wives. Valentine O'Brien is there, but he cannot calm them down. The women want Mama to decide the matter. They threatened each other with bill-cane knives."

"Good lord," he said, frowning. "You should leave such things to Matthew Plum."

"I've given orders that Mr. Plum is not to be called out, except in dire emergency. Mr. Plum doesn't know this. Please do not tell him. You see, he suffered heart trouble two years ago, and I worry. I want him to have his sleep."

"So, instead, you lose *your* sleep."

"I like being out at night." She often woke at night anyway. Going out was better than lying in bed and remembering sad things. They walked along. The wind rustled the cane fields.

"You don't think it immoral that a slave should have *two* wives?"

"No. Boiling house slaves always have two, sometimes three wives."

"Yet you would object if a planter took two wives."

"Certainly! What a question." Her voice grew bitter. "Anyhow, Barbados planters have no need of *one* wife, let alone two. They have their slave women. Witness the mulattoes all over the island, Mr. Steel."

"Drake," he said.

"Drake." She found it difficult to use his name, as if using it would be a commitment.

"Mulattoes like Kena," he summed up.

She looked at him. If he touched Kena, she would kill him!

"What about Kena?" she said aggressively.

He gave her a puzzled look. "Only that she's mulatto."

"Yes, she's mulatto."

They found the women in a royal row that could rival any fishwives' squabble. They shrieked at each other in their separate, incomprehensible languages. They spat and kicked. Valentine O'Brien held one, Alvis Nansellock the other. The noise was enough to wake the dead. Slaves stood outside their huts shaking their fists at the women, shouting at them. In the midst of the melee stood Macaw, cocky as a rooster, with his ear-to-ear grin and gleaming white teeth. Drake wanted to pop him in the mouth. He hadn't the slightest doubt what had started this fight—the marital bed.

He stood back, exasperated, to watch Edwinna deal with it. She marched right into the center of the melee, which died the instant the slaves saw her. The women stopped fighting and cried out, "Mama, Mama?"

"Shall I whip 'em, Mistress Edwinna?" Valentine offered.

"You are not to whip my female slaves *ever*, not for *any* reason," she said sharply. "Do you understand?"

"Ay, mistress."

Getting to the root of the problem proved difficult. The first wife, Juba, did not speak the language of the second wife, Kitta; neither wife spoke the language of their husband, Macaw; and certainly, Edwinna spoke none of their languages. But with patience and sign language she sorted it out, dealt out their punishment, and made them understand it. First, they would forgo their weekly ration of kill-devil rum, a Saturday night treat that every slave waited for all week long. They wept. Second, their food ration would be cut in half for one week. Third, they were to get no ticket to leave the plantation for one whole month.

Drake added a suggestion. "Make Macaw understand he is to have no day off this week. Instead, on the Sabbath he is to get wood from the carpenter and build a separate hut for Juba. If he cannot keep peace in his own hut, he must build two.'' An intelligent scamp, not overly fond of work, Macaw understood perfectly and his face fell.

''That was a sensible order,'' Edwinna complimented him as they walked back to Crawford Hall under the starry sky, the cane fields whispering in the wind. ''I didn't think of two huts.''

He smiled. ''Comes of experience. Two women rarely get along living in the same house. Arthur and Verity lived with us for a time. Anne and Verity used to scrap like a pair of cats.''

''I wouldn't know about that. I've always lived among men. My . . . father, my brothers.''

''Your mother died when you were young?''

''She . . . was gone when I was ten.''

It was a peculiar way to put it, he thought. He looked up at the unfamiliar stars of the southern hemisphere. The night was as balmy as July in London. He remembered a starry summer evening he'd taken Anne boating on the Thames. They'd made love on a blanket in the privacy of a grove of willows on the south shore. He liked to believe Katherine had been conceived that night, out there under the stars.

''I was a grown man when my mother died. Even so, I felt somehow that a part of my world had fallen away, irretrievable, gone forever.''

''I felt that way, too. As if the world had ended.''

He glanced at her. He felt a stirring. The starlight was lovely on her hair. Almost as if she'd sensed his thoughts, she increased her speed, striding faster, as if to put safe space and distance between them. What was wrong with her? Didn't she have a woman's normal needs? Striding faster, he caught up, and they said little on the way back.

When they'd let themselves in the gate and into the house, Drake led the way upstairs in the cavelike darkness. He let her pass, then leaned a shoulder against the frame of his door, crossed his arms, and said quietly, "By the way, what *was* the trouble between Macaw's wives?"

"A domestic dispute."

"Exactly what?"

She hesitated. "If you must know . . ."

"Yes, I must. I didn't take that two o'clock trot for my health, Edwinna."

"They were fighting over whose turn it was to—to sleep with him."

Drake sighed. "Lucky devil. No one ever fights to get into *my* bed."

She went into her room and shut the door smartly. Drake uncrossed his arms, ambled into his room, stripped, and got into the bed. One minute later he heard the bolt shoot across Edwinna's door. He sighed. Evidently she'd decided he was a randy son of a bitch and wasn't taking any chances. He lofted his arms, laced his hands under his head, and lay looking up at the tester.

Word came from Simon Tarcher in Speightstown that an English slaver had rounded the northern point of the island and was heading for Carlisle Bay. She had signaled by flag that she had a full load of slaves to sell.

The men left at once for Bridgetown, Matthew Plum and Drake on horseback; Valentine O'Brien, David Alleyne, and Jeremy on foot; the affingoes gracefully plodding behind, loaded with barrels of sugar that would be used to purchase the slaves. Jacka, Yates, and Hastings brought up the rear.

Edwinna watched them go. She couldn't keep her eyes from Drake. She wondered if he would break his word and escape. He would be tempted in Bridgetown, with so many ships setting sail for England.

When he'd stepped up to bid her a courteous farewell, she'd tried to think of something nice to say—something to make him want to come back—but everything had come out stiff.

"Is there anything you'd like me to purchase for you in Bridgetown?" he'd offered.

"Mr. Plum does that. He has the list."

"I see. Any messages you wish me to deliver?"

"No. None."

They'd parted without a smile, and when the last of the affingoes had trotted off, she quickly hiked up the grassy hill to the windmill. From the hill she could see the ocean, Dinny Fraser's plantation, her uncle's plantation, and the cane paths that crisscrossed the island, eventually leading to Bridgetown. She watched Drake Steel's figure grow smaller and smaller, until the cane fields swallowed him up.

The distance to Bridgetown was only eight miles, but the travel took half a day. No roads existed on the island—only cane paths that cut through plantations and descended into and out of ravines.

Drake despised being in Jacka's proximity. The little weasel harbored a deep grudge about the runaway slave. But to hell with him and Yates and Hastings. He concentrated on enjoying the beauty of the island and Plum's company. He liked and respected him more with each passing day. Drake had also brought Jeremy along, and the boy didn't walk to Bridgetown, he bounced. He had never been to town, and he was excited. Also, Jeremy had carefully tied his coin in the handkerchief around his neck. He intended to buy something pretty for Marigold. Drake had to smile at that. This was true love—a boy willing to spend on a girl the only coin he'd ever owned.

Drake was hot and sweaty and unimpressed with Bridgetown by the time he rode out of the cane fields and down into it. True, the harbor was excellent. Crescent-shaped and sheltered by a spit of land, its defensive location was superb. Any foreign ships meaning to attack the colony would have to tack into the trade winds, making themselves sitting ducks for shore cannon. But the town itself was a joke. Of the three hundred buildings that comprised the town, one hundred fifty were drinking houses and brothels. A few decent homes clustered at the tip of the crescent harbor where the governor's house stood, but the mud flats of Bridgetown stank to high heaven with the tide out.

Edwinna had a sugar storehouse near the wooden bridge from which Bridgetown took its name. They drove the affingoes there, left them with Jacka and his cronies, and found a drinking house that let rooms. Drake hoped his bed would be free of lice, but hadn't high hopes of it. The place was slovenly, but the best Bridgetown offered, according to Plum. They ordered a roasted goose and fresh fish for their supper later that night, then he and Plum rode down to the harbor.

They counted twenty-two ships at anchor, the slave ship among them. It would not unload until morning, and the moans and wails that drifted from the ship made his hair stand on end.

"For God's sake!"

"A slave ship is an unpleasant place, Mr. Steel."

"Unpleasant? It's vile!"

"Ay. Well, poor things. They'll be off the ship by morning."

"And into a lifetime of slavery."

Drake listened a while longer, then rode into Bridgetown to hunt a tailor's shop. He found a decent one on Swan Street, where he selected fine quality, lightweight black serge cloth and had himself measured for a suit. Next he hunted a shoemaker, then a linen draper's shop, where he bought three shirts of fine soft cotton—shirts that were finally roomy enough for his shoulders. He also bought soft, expensive drawers, silk stockings, and two linen shirts of the best quality the shop offered. He liked quality in clothes and wine. He would sooner go without than settle for less than the best.

As he signed the voucher to Crawford Plantation, he felt a ripple of irritation that Edwinna should pay for these things.

He was a man who liked to take care of a woman, not vice versa. He sent the purchases to his inn and bought a cup of wine in a drinking house. Newly arrived, the claret had not yet succumbed to the tropical heat, so Drake was able to enjoy it. He had a second cup and mellowed.

He fell into conversation with a sea captain who sailed to the Orient. When the man invited him to his ship to see his collection of erotica, Drake went. He was interested in sensual things.

Aboard the ship, he spent a pleasant, arousing hour looking at the man's treasures—in particular, an exquisite hand-painted scroll of a sloe-eyed, black-haired beauty in the throes of pleasuring her lord and being pleasured by him. He studied the positions foreign to his knowledge. Sweat broke on his forehead. He was a fool to do this to himself. He hadn't a prayer of having a woman in his bed, and he refused to chance a prostitute. He came to the most beautiful picture of all— the delicate beauty on her knees before her lord, her hair unbound and flowing like black silk, her head bowed, the nape of her neck exposed, her mouth eagerly taking her lord's erect, swollen root.

"Is the scroll for sale?" he asked reverently.

"Nay. Wouldn't part with it for the world."

"I can understand that."

Reluctantly he returned the scroll and thanked the man for a pleasant visit.

He was about to climb down into the captain's boat to be rowed back to shore when he spotted a tarp shading a row of cages. Raisin brown eyes like Priscilla's stared out at him. An idea came to him.

"Are the monkeys for sale?"

"Ay. Three shillings each."

"Do you have a male?"

"Got a fine one. His name's Jocko."

The captain pulled out the cage. Drake chuckled. Jocko proved to be a bored, complacent little fellow who looked patient and long-suffering enough to put up with anything Priscilla might do.

"He doesn't bite, does he?"

"Wouldn't harm a flea."

Drake tested him—put his finger into the cage and scratched the underside of Jocko's chin. Jocko leaned into the scratch, as blissful as an old house cat.

"I'll take him. Send him to the Crawford Plantation storehouse at sunrise, day after tomorrow."

"Done."

The slave sale the next morning proved to be a wrenching experience. Shackled and terrified and many of them sick, five hundred Africans were rowed to shore in longboats that went back and forth. Brandishing whips and cudgels, slavers drove them into herds, the females in one mass, the males in another. All were young. Drake judged them to be no younger than fourteen, no older than twenty-five—prime slavery material.

When all were ashore, the slavers ordered them to strip off what little clothing they wore—loincloths for the males, bark-cloth skirts for the females. It was plain that their tribal customs forbade showing themselves in public. The women wailed, covered their faces with their hands, and wept copiously. None was spared—not even pregnant women with their bodies gently swollen with child.

"For God's sake!" he said to Plum.

"Ay, Mr. Steel. 'Tisn't pleasant to watch."

Some of the young black males refused to strip, and the slavers fell upon them with cudgels, beating them into obedience. Incensed, Drake started forward, but Plum grabbed his arm.

"Mr. Steel, there are thirty of them, and only one of you."

He breathed hotly, but accepted Plum's wise advice. Plum was right. There was nothing he could do. What came next was worse. When the young people stood stripped and humiliated, the women weeping, the men terrified, the slavers signaled and slave buyers swarmed into the mass to select what they wanted to buy. They prodded and poked at the slaves, male and female, pulling their hair, thrusting fingers into their mouths.

"Damn it to hell! They shop as if they are buying cattle."

"Ay, Mr. Steel, let's be done with it. I'll make my selection. Mr. Alleyne?" The young, fair-haired doctor stepped forward, his gentle face constricted with shock. David Alleyne, had never before attended a slave sale, either.

They stepped into the hot, fetid mass of humanity, Drake with them. The air reeked of unwashed bodies. Here and there, a sick or weak black fainted. Alleyne went down on one knee quickly, but what could one doctor do among so many?

Plum made his selections swiftly and humanely. He didn't prod or poke. He examined the eyes. "Health is in the eye, Mr. Steel." He chose four strong young field hands, and, examining the terrified men gently, Alleyne corroborated the choice. Plum signaled a slaver and made his purchase. As Valentine O'Brien led them off, a wild cry erupted from the women's side of the beach. A young pregnant woman lunged in her shackles, her arms outstretched and begging, and one of Plum's new slaves whirled in his shackles, a guttural cry bursting from his throat as he tried to go to her. Valentine jerked the shackles tight, preventing him.

"I will take her, also," Plum told the slaver, then went to arrange payment.

Drake didn't go with him. He'd seen enough. Putting the stench and the noise behind him, he strode to the nearest drinking house and ordered a brandy. It came with a clump of sugar in it, dissolving in trails of bubbles. Sugar again. He shoved it aside and ordered another *without* sugar. This time, the sugar clump came served on the side, in a dish. Drake shoved it away, took a mouthful of brandy, let it burn like fire on his tongue for a moment, then swallowed it down. He breathed deeply, cleansing his lungs. God in heaven, what devils men were.

When Plum came in and joined him, Drake shoved the sugared brandy at him. Plum added the dish sugar, swirled it until it dissolved, and tossed the brandy down in a swallow. Evidently he, too, needed cleansing from the morning's event. Drake signaled for two more brandies, and they tossed them down before they sat back and began to talk.

"That was a decent thing you did out there, Plum, buying the man's wife."

"Nay." Plum denied it, shaking his head. "'Twas common sense. If a slave's wife is taken from him, he will run away to find her, first chance he gets. If his wife is with him, he will stay. I was merely protecting my primary purchase."

Drake gazed at him. "You're a lying son of a bitch. You did it out of the goodness of your heart." Plum's smile as much as acknowledged it. Drake signaled for a third round of brandy. This time when it came, they sipped it slowly, companionably.

"Edwinna would have wished me to do it," Plum said. "She objects to breaking up families." To which, Drake raised a skeptical, sardonic eyebrow. "You don't think much of Edwinna, do you, Mr. Steel?"

Drake glanced away impatiently. "She's a slave owner. Right now, I've no inclination to like any slave owner."

Unwinding with the brandy, Plum settled mellowly into his chair, his eyes on Drake. "I think it's time I told you about Edwinna, Mr. Steel."

"What about her?" He glanced as the drinking house began to fill with loud, noisy slave buyers. They brought the stench of the slave market with them. Drake wanted to torch the place.

"Did she tell you about her mother?"

"Little. I only know her mother is dead."

"She's not dead, Mr. Steel." Drake swiveled his gaze to

Plum. "Lydia Crawford ran away with her lover. Edwinna was nine or ten when it happened. Thomas and Harry were two or thereabouts, too young to miss their mother for long. But Edwinna took it hard—very hard."

Drake stared at him. He tried to imagine his own mother abandoning him when he was ten, and he couldn't. His family had been close-knit, loving, his parents devoted to each other and to him and Verity.

"Nobody blamed Lydia Crawford for running. I'm not one to speak evil of my employer. I don't hold with that. But Peter Crawford was a difficult man. Overfond of kill-devil. When he drank, the whole plantation shook in its boots. Drunk, he could rage like a madman."

Drake's thoughts expanded. So *that* explained it all—Edwinna's flash of wariness every time he took a drink, her abstemious habits, her avoidance of even a drop of wine. He'd chalked it up to prudery. It wasn't. It was outright fear. She feared what men could do under the influence.

"That must have been hard on Edwinna, growing up with a drunkard for a father."

"Hard?" Plum smiled bitterly. "I remember a time when she was ten or eleven. She came to my cabin in the middle of the night, running scared through the darkness, clutching her wrist, sobbing and crying, her face bruised, her lips white with pain. Her wrist was broken, Mr. Steel."

"An accident?"

"She would not tell us. I only know that after the plantation doctor and I splinted her wrist, I held her in my lap the whole night long. She sobbed and sobbed. Not from the physical pain, Mr. Steel, but from a broken heart."

Drake stared at him. "Her father beat her?"

"I'm not saying that," Plum hedged. "I'm only saying Edwinna had more than her share of bruises and broken bones as a child."

"Why didn't you do something?"

"I did. When I made my complaint to Peter Crawford he

threatened me with dismissal. I thought it better to bite my tongue and stay on Crawford Plantation for Edwinna's sake. There I could help her, gone I could not."

"Why didn't she go somewhere, get help?"

"Loyalty, Mr. Steel. She loved Thomas and Harry. She was a regular little mother, bringing them up proper after Lydia Crawford ran off, though she was but a child herself and in need of mothering. She stayed for Thomas and Harry's sake. But I'll tell you this. Not one tear was shed on Crawford Plantation the day Peter Crawford took that fall from his horse and broke his back. He spent his final years a cripple in bed, unable even to wield his cane. Edwinna got no more broken bones or bruises." Feeling his brandy, Plum said, "Add George Crawford and Clive to the picture, and you can understand why Edwinna is the way she is with men. She don't trust a jack one of 'em."

Drake uttered a healthy curse. He got out of his chair, paced to the open window, and breathed in a deep draught of the trade winds. Plum's story bothered him more than he wanted to admit. He'd not been prepared to feel anything for Edwinna. Until now, she'd been an enigma, a challenge. But now he felt different. He felt outraged, angry on her behalf.

Drake couldn't sleep that night. The air was sultry. Plum snored away next to him in the bed they shared. Mosquitoes abounded, finding their way through the holes in the window netting. The day weighed too heavily upon him. The brutality of the slave sale. Edwinna. Her father.

What sort of island *was* this? Englishmen were not Englishmen here. They were slave keepers and depraved drunkards who beat their own daughters!

Abandoning his attempt to sleep, he rose quietly and dressed. Valentine, Sean, and David Alleyne snored blissfully in the other bed. Stepping over Jeremy, who slept on a pallet on the floor, his grubby fist clutching the pink silk ribbon he'd purchased for Marigold, Drake carefully made his way out and quietly shut the door behind him.

A sailor's port, Bridgetown never closed. Well past midnight the torches burned brightly in sconces on the coral water drips outside the drinking houses, and drunken revelry echoed through the town. Drake went into a drinking house, ordered a cup of Madeira, drank only half, then left. The place stank of rum and whores, who doused themselves with jasmine toilet water.

He walked the town in the darkness, killing time. He went to Edwinna's storehouse to check on the new slaves, the affingoes, the bond slaves. The affingoes stood patiently in the yard, sleeping on their feet, occasionally kicking out at a mosquito. He peered in the open window. Clothed and fed, the new slaves slept in pathetic huddles, their shackles catching a stray bit of moonlight and gleaming. Three additional women Plum had purchased slept curled together, shackled to each other. Drake rubbed his wrist in sympathy. He still bore the scars of his Speightstown shackles.

Candlelight flickered dimly from a window at the far end of a storehouse across the alley. Curious, Drake quietly moved to it and peered in. His scalp tingled. Held fast to the floor with its own melted wax, a single candle burned under a shield as two dozen men—bond slaves, judging by their muslin clothing—crouched around it, arguing in low, furtive voices. Drake recognized Jacka, Yates, and Hastings. The others were strangers. What were they doing? It struck him as wrong. He pressed flat to the wall and listened. The argument ensuing was a duel for power between two men. He recognized Jacka's surly snarl, not the other man's. Their quarrel was so hot and furtive, he caught only stray words.

"You'll do as I say . . . the twenty-sixth."

"You fool . . . too soon! Let 'em get the harvest . . ."

The quarrel went on hotly for several minutes, then stopped dead. Frustrated at how little he'd heard, Drake eased close to the window and peered in. He watched as one of the men took out his knife and thrust the blade into the candle flame to heat it. What in hell were they doing?

A twig crackled under Drake's foot. "What's that sound?" someone snarled. "Go see." Drake dashed to the shadows nearby, and watched as the door of the storehouse opened. Two men came out, looked, shrugged, and went back in. Drake kept watch. Perhaps an hour passed. The men slipped out in twos and threes, looking about before they slipped off into the darkness. Drake waited until all were accounted for—twenty-seven bond slaves, including Jacka, Yates, and Hastings. When the street was clear, he stole quietly back to the inn.

"I don't like it," Plum said in the morning when Drake took him aside privately and told him.

"Nor do I."

"We'd best keep a close watch on Jacka, Yates, and Hastings. And we'd best not mention this to any of the other bond slaves—not even to Valentine or Sean or David Alleyne. There's no telling who's involved or what is intended."

"I agree."

Plum scowled in anger. "Bond slave revolts are not unknown. I'd dearly like to sell them bastards, Mr. Steel, but I can't short myself three trained bond slaves during harvest."

"I understand. There is one thing I want to do."

"What's that?"

"I want to write a private letter to all the large planters on the island, telling them what I saw and heard, warning them that a conspiracy may be afoot."

"Ay, Mr. Steel, do it."

Drake hesitated. "Should Edwinna be told, or would it only worry her?"

Plum ruminated on it, then looked at him.

"She is your wife, Mr. Steel. You decide."

"I'll tell her."

"Good," Plum approved. "I hoped you would." Plum smiled. "She's no shrinking violet, Mr. Steel. She loves her plantation. Likely you'll have to hold her back from murdering Jacka.''

Driving the shackled slaves before them, their party left Bridgetown before the sun was fully up. On the last high hill that afforded a sweeping view of Carlisle Bay and the ships rocking at anchor, Drake halted his horse and let the others pass on. He looked down at Bridgetown for a long time, feeling torn. There were a dozen London-bound ships he could stow away on. Yet Edwinna had saved his life. How much did he owe to himself and his children and how much to her?

A quarter mile up the trail, Matthew Plum looked back and watched Drake Steel, a distant, broad-shouldered figure sitting his horse, poised motionless on the hill above Bridgetown. "What will it be, laddie? Honor and decency? Or will you hightail it to England, eh?"

Plum kneed his horse and rode on. A few minutes later, he looked back again and smiled. The distant figure had turned his horse and was coming up the trail.

CHAPTER

* 8 *

The journey back to Crawford Plantation took all day. They traveled slowly. The exhausted slaves needed to rest often. The males trudged along in heavy chains, shackled hand and foot. The shackles incensed Drake. He knew firsthand the pain, the humiliation, the terror of being in shackles. He demanded that Plum unshackle them, but Plum overruled him.

"Not a chance, Mr. Steel. Every new male is a high risk. There's no telling what he'll do. I know of a ship captain who made the mistake of pitying his shipload of slaves and unshackled them. Before the ship even got out of the Gambia River, the slaves overran the crew and cut their throats. I don't mean to have that happen to me."

Jaw tight, Drake had to defer to Plum. Still, he detested shackles on anyone, black or white. At least the women wore none. They stumbled along, spent and scared. His heart went out to the young pregnant woman. She ought not walk—she looked sick. But when Drake had taken her arm and had tried to lead her to his horse, meaning to let her ride, she'd shrieked in terror and recoiled, and her husband had lunged in his chains, his eyes blazing. Drake couldn't make them understand. They'd never seen horses before and feared them.

He'd given up and had ridden on. But it went against the grain to ride while tired, sick females walked. Sugar and slavery. He hoped to hell he would never set eyes on either one of them again, once he left this island.

His thoughts drifted to Edwinna and grew gentler. What Plum had told him had touched him, roused his protective instincts. He couldn't shake it out of his mind. A little girl, only a few years older than Katherine, running through the darkness, sobbing, her little wrist broken, her heart, also.

He had plenty of time to think as the party slowly plodded through the windy fields, following the cane paths. Edwinna stayed central in his thoughts. Knowing what he knew, he felt a new tenderness for her. He saw her in a new light. He resolved to befriend her, to be patient and gentle with her. He would court her, if she would let him. If it ended in bed, well and good. If not? He uttered a helpless laugh. He was so damned randy he didn't know what to do about it.

Riding along the plateau that formed the spine of the island, breathing the fresh, sweet air, listening to the cane rustle in the trade winds, he had to admit the island was as sensual a paradise as ever he'd encountered—sea, cane, trade winds, bare-breasted women. No wonder he was such a horny son of a bitch.

Edwinna was in the boiling house with Alvis Nansellock when a slave brought word that the affingoes were returning. She ran down the hill and waited for them to emerge out of the cane fields. When Strussie, one of her favorite slave children, came toddling to her, Edwinna scooped her up and held her.

Had Drake Steel come back, or had he escaped?

David Alleyne and the eight new slaves came into sight

first, David helping a pregnant female to walk. Everyone trusted David—even terrified, new-bought slaves took to him. Next came the affingoes, heavily loaded with supplies purchased in Bridgetown. Then the bond slaves. Then Jeremy, happy and bouncy. Then Valentine O'Brien. Then Matthew Plum on his horse. She gripped Strussie tightly. Behind Matthew Plum? Glistening black hair, broad shoulders.

He'd come back. She released the breath she'd been holding, drew another, and smiled hugely. It was ridiculous to feel so happy, but she did. Drake glanced her way and lifted his hand in greeting. She kissed Strussie's warm head to hide her feelings. She didn't want him to think she'd been worried about him.

A courteous man, he dismounted, gave the reins to Jeremy, and quickly came to see her in that loose, masculine way, hands draped on hips. He was feeling the climate. His shirt clung damply and she smelled his sweat. There was something different about him, a gentler expression. The glittery criticism she was used to seeing had left. His eyes were kind.

"We're back," he said.

"Yes." She wanted to add, "I'm glad you're back," but it stuck in her throat, and all that came out was a stiff, "Was the trip tolerable?"

"Barely. The slave sale was an abomination."

"I know," she admitted. "I never go."

"I can understand that." He was looking at her in an odd, tender way that made her fidget. She fussed with Strussie's hair.

"I had best check on the new slaves."

"I want to clean up. We'll sup together?"

"Yes."

"I've invited Plum. We need to discuss something with you."

A wave of disappointment washed over her. How ridiculous to feel disappointed that they weren't to sup alone.

"That's fine," she said. Hoisting Strussie higher in her arms, she strode off to Matthew Plum and the new slaves.

Drake watched her. She looked lovely with a child in her arms. It softened her. She should have one of her own. Her voice drifted back to him as she asked Plum about the mail he'd picked up at the Planters Council room in Bridgetown. Had there been a letter from Thomas and Harry?

"No. I'm sorry, Edwinna," Plum responded gently.

"Well . . . they will surely write next month."

"Of course they will."

The poignancy in her voice roused Drake's ire. The ungrateful bastards. Didn't they know their sister was living her life on their behalf, tending *their* plantation, protecting *their* inheritance? The least they could do was write.

Drake's resolution to be patient with Edwinna received a sore testing even before he'd been back two hours. Just before supper, bathed and freshly clothed, he'd gone down to the bond slave quarters and carried Jocko's cage up to the house. He set it on a chair in the dining room.

"What is *that*?" Edwinna asked.

Priscilla reacted even more hysterically. Shrieking in her tiny monkey voice, she fled from Jocko's cage, bounding up onto the dining table, scattering cutlery. She leaped up among the unlighted candles on the chandelier, where she swung back and forth, scolding as if Drake had brought the devil himself into the house. Jocko sat in his cage, a perfect gentleman—composed, complacent, blinking calmly.

"A head, two arms, two legs, a tail. It's a monkey, Edwinna."

"I can *see* that," she said. "But what is it doing here?"

"I bought him for Priscilla—to be her mate."

"Mr. Steel, that is absolutely ridiculous. Priscilla doesn't want or need a mate."

"Drake," he said patiently.

"Drake."

"Of course she does. All normal, healthy females want and need a mate." He gave her a smile. "It's the nature of things, Edwinna—or haven't you heard? Male, female, the desire to mate? Besides, I'm tired of being the object of her affections. You know how she pesters me."

"She doesn't even like him."

As if to corroborate it, Priscilla leaped down from the chandelier and into Edwinna's arms, where she huddled, making a royal fuss, peering out at Jocko and making monkey screams.

"Certainly she does. She's just putting on a show for him." Lightly, Drake added, "Besides, how can any female resist a handsome, sensible fellow like this?" Sticking a finger into the cage, he scratched the underside of Jocko's whiskery chin. Jocko leaned into the scratch, bored, complacent. Drake smiled. "I admit he's short on charm. But then, a female can't expect everything, can she?"

"I don't *like* this. He might hurt her."

A few days earlier Drake might have chuckled. But in the light of what he now knew, he answered soberly.

"He won't hurt her, Edwinna. No sensible male of any species hurts the female he wants to mate with."

"Well, I don't like it. Take him out, Mr. Steel."

"Drake."

"Drake," she said with exasperation.

"Let him stay the night, in his cage. Let Priscilla get used to him. Tomorrow, we'll see."

"She won't like him any more tomorrow than she likes him right now," Edwinna insisted. "Which is not at all."

"That is your opinion, not mine."

"You're a wine merchant. What do you know about monkeys?"

"Nothing. But I *do* know about mating."

"Mr. Steel—"

"Drake! Edwinna, the name is Drake. Drake, *Drake*."

At this juncture, Plum walked in. Caught in a spat, Drake and Edwinna both flushed. Plum ignored the spat with benign good nature and nodded approvingly when he spotted Jocko's cage.

"Ah, Edwinna, you've bought a mate for Priscilla. Good. I meant to suggest it long ago. 'Twill cure her of her biting, I'm sure. A monkey that bites can best be cured with a mate."

"Let's eat," Edwinna said with disgust, and Drake grinned a little.

After supper, at Plum's request, they took a candle and went to Edwinna's office, shutting the door for privacy. The request made her uneasy. What was it about? Had Drake asked Matthew Plum to intercede on his behalf so that he could leave Barbados?

She listened with alarm as Drake described what he'd seen and heard in Bridgetown. She believed him. In the past eight years there'd been three bond slave uprisings on the island. All planters feared them. When he finished his ominous story, she took a key from her table drawer and unlocked the cupboard where she kept the house pistols and took two out. Drake should have one for his room, and so should she.

"What does it mean?"

"We don't know," Plum put in.

"We'd best sell Jacka, Yates, and Hastings at once. Harvest or not, get rid of them. Get them off the plantation."

"That might be a mistake," Drake said, leaning against the wall, arms crossed. "If we sell them, we lose the opportunity to watch them, to discover what they are up to. And there is no assurance that their plot, whatever it is, will end even if we sell them. It may proceed as planned. It's better if we can keep them under our thumb. Besides, we don't know who else might be involved, if anyone."

She rubbed her arms, anxiety rising. "We." He'd said "we." Perhaps he was growing to like her plantation. Perhaps he wouldn't leave, even when the time came.

"What do you suggest?"

"First, I suggest we check your gun closet," Matthew Plum said, "against your inventory, to see if anything is missing."

Her eyes widened, but she rose immediately, pulled down the plantation inventory ledger, and flipped through to the munitions page.

"Thirty-eight muskets. No, thirty-seven. We discarded one for rust two months ago. Thirteen pistols."

They took a candle and a key and went outside to the gun room, a stone room built against the outer kitchen wall. Edwinna unlocked it. They went in, scattering lizards. They did a careful count against Matthew Plum's list of muskets issued to bond slaves, as well. Two muskets and one pistol were missing.

Edwinna felt shaken but determined when they reentered the office. "You had best do a search of the bond slave quarters tomorrow, Mr. Plum."

"A casual search," Drake amended. "We don't want to alert anyone. Don't be scared," he said to her with a smile. "We've the advantage. They don't know we know."

"I'm not frightened," she said staunchly. "I can shoot, and I will if I have to."

"Good." He reached out and gave her braid a playful tug. It was a friendly gesture, but she stiffened. She hadn't meant to. It put him off. He looked at her oddly. She wished she could tell him that she . . . just wasn't comfortable being touched.

"I'll search," Plum agreed. "But if it's Jacka behind this, I won't find a thing. He's as sly as they come."

"We must alert Valentine, Sean, some of the others—"

"No," Matthew Plum and Drake said in unison. "Edwinna, Mr. Steel and I have discussed this at length. We are in agreement that no one must be told. There is no way of guessing how large this conspiracy may be or who may be involved in it."

She looked at one, then the other.

"Surely David Alleyne, Alvis Nansellock—"

"No one," Plum said firmly. "Not Nansellock, not David Alleyne, not anyone. Edwinna, not even Kena. It might be dangerous for her to know."

It took her breath away. "But the other planters *must* be told. I insist. They could be in danger."

"We agree," Drake said. He told her about the letter he wished to write to each of the large planters on the island, warning them that mischief may be afoot, swearing them to secrecy, asking them to check their gun inventories. "The letter will have to come from you, Edwinna," he finished. "The planters have no reason to trust me."

"It will come from both of us," she said firmly. "I want you to have credit for this. They think you a pirate, and you are *not*."

"Since when?" he asked with a smile. "I thought you believed me one."

"Don't be silly." They shared a smile. It was a lovely, rattle-headed moment, but it filled her with anxiety. She wasn't ready for what she saw offered in his eyes.

A chair scraped and Matthew Plum rose to his feet.

"I'll leave the letter writing to the two of you."

"There are forty letters. Aren't you going to help?" Edwinna asked.

"Nay." Thanking her for supper, Plum strolled out. Drake hid a smile. He was an observant man, Matthew Plum.

Edwinna got the pots of ink, the paper, and the quill pens, and settled opposite Drake at the writing table. "That was peculiar." She frowned. "He is usually so helpful."

Drake didn't think it peculiar at all. He thought it sensible. Plum was a man who'd just recognized that a courtship was springing into bloom.

They worked long into the night, the glare of the candlelight straining their eyes. Edwinna fell asleep in the middle of a letter, quill pen still in hand, cheek cradled on arm, her silly braid wrapped around her neck like a fur collar. Drake noted it with a smile.

He let her sleep. He finished his letter, then silently lifted his chair back, got up, and went around the table to her. He squatted on the balls of his feet, balancing lightly, elbows on knees. He should see that she got to bed. But how? If she were Anne, he would simply pick her up in his arms and carry her. If she were even a normal woman, he would touch her shoulder to wake her. But he couldn't touch Edwinna. In a thoughtless moment earlier that evening he'd given her braid a tug, and for a split second, fear had glinted in her eyes.

He gazed at her. She wasn't pretty. She couldn't hold a candle to Anne. But she was handsome. The lashes on her cheeks swooped gracefully, thick as silk.

While assembling the list of planters to write and warn, she hadn't hesitated to include her uncle. Had Drake been the one George Crawford had hit with a riding crop, he'd have skipped the bastard and hoped he would be killed by his own bond slaves.

She slept on, her lips slightly parted.

"Edwinna?" he said. "You had best wake up and go to bed."

Her lashes flickered. Though her eyes opened slightly, he could see by the distant look in them that she was not awake. She was still asleep, though gazing at him.

"Drake . . ." she whispered. "Drake . . ."

Unprepared for the passion in her voice, his scalp rippled. She blinked, then came fully awake. She looked at him in shock and sat up, erect.

"Did I fall asleep?" she said in her usual brisk voice.

"You did."

"How foolish. I'll just finish this letter."

"You'll finish nothing." He took the quill from her hand, then took the snuffer and snuffed the candle. "Can you find your way in the dark?"

"Yes, of course."

He let her lead the way upstairs, then waited at his door while she made her way to her room. She went in and locked it. He sighed and went to bed. He wondered if he was bashing his head against a brick wall trying to court her.

Drake slept soundly until the six o'clock bell clamored in the morning trade winds. Knowing Edwinna would rise quickly to tend harvest matters, he rose, too, and got down to the dining chamber before her.

He'd forgotten about Jocko and Priscilla. They were crouched side by side atop the livery cabinet, looking like an old married couple. He grinned. Priscilla was industriously grooming Jocko, pawing through his fur. Jocko leaned into the grooming. Priscilla glanced at Drake and chattered.

"Don't worry," he said, "I'm not the least bit jealous."

Clever Priscilla. Evidently she'd figured out how to unlatch Jocko's cage and had let him out. Jocko certainly wasn't smart enough to do it. Drake sat at the table to eat the morning bread and cheese Kena had set out.

"See?" he said, gesturing at the happy couple as Edwinna entered the room. As Edwinna stood there, hands on hips, Priscilla scampered down from the livery cabinet, went to the dining table, snatched a banana, and scampered back. She gave it to Jocko, then sat back and watched him complacently eat it.

"The ideal wife," Drake quipped. "At least *Priscilla* knows how to serve her lord and master."

The corners of Edwinna's wide, pretty mouth twitched. Striding on through the dining chamber with her swinging braid and hips, she detoured to the table, snatched up a banana, plunked it on his plate, and sailed on her way.

He sat there looking at the banana and chuckling.

They finished the letters by morning light, sealed them, and dispatched them all over the island by bond slave. There was nothing unusual in this, nothing to alert Jacka and his cronies. Planters regularly consulted each other by letter.

Dinny's plantation was nearest, and she wrote back at once in her charming, illiterate hand. *Eye am mising no muskit nor pistal, butt three bill-kain knifes are gone*. Drake shuddered. Given the macabre choice, he'd rather be killed by a musket shot than a bill-cane knife. Responses from the other planters came in quickly, too. Bond slave uprisings were not taken lightly in Barbados. Every major planter was missing weapons and expressed concern. One of the leading planters, a Mr. Drax of Drax Plantation, wrote to urge Drake to attend a meeting of the Planters Council, scheduled in Bridgetown in six weeks, at midpoint in harvest season.

"I think I'll go," he told Edwinna.

"I think you should, Drake," she agreed.

She had finally taken to calling him Drake. It was a small step forward in their odd marital arrangement, but a crucial one, Drake thought. If she could call him by name, she was losing her fear of him.

But he was no nearer her bed. She still kept him at arm's length. She confused the hell out of him, flaunting her gorgeous hair at him and wearing a shirt that exposed bosom on one night, and on the next night coming to supper in a shirt buttoned to the neck and hair in a tight braid. He didn't know where he stood or what was expected of him.

Evenings were lonely for him. Edwinna habitually stayed shut in her damned office, working. Left to himself and lonely, Drake walked, wrote letters home, counted the days until he could expect his first letter from Verity and Arthur. Sometimes he went down to Plum's and they played chess. The odd looks Plum gave him said Plum wondered about their marital arrangements, but Drake remained silent on the matter. He was a private man. But he was so ripe for a woman he wanted to howl at the stars!

Sundays were dull. Drake sat at a table in the great hall and played "Papa," writing tickets for slaves who came and went, asking permission to go off the plantation. It was a tedious business, made more so because he didn't understand a word of their language and had to resort to sign language. But only a heartless man would refuse them. Their desires were so simple. Two wanted to go crabbing at the seashore. Three more wanted to go to the mangrove swamps to gather hemp, which they could sell to merchants in Speightstown to gain a little money. One had a cousin in slavery on a nearby plantation and wished to go see him. Women wanted to go gathering herbs and grasses for their bush teas.

Jeremy came in to ask, with big, scared eyes, if he could take Marigold walking. Drake pretended to deliberate.

"Only if you treat her like a lady," he warned sternly.

"I will, sir."

David Alleyne came in, hat in hand, fair hair carefully combed, clothing fresh and clean, to request permission to take Kena walking to the seaside.

"If she's willing," Drake said, glancing to where Kena stood with her eyes modestly lowered, Tutu in her arms. She looked very pretty in a fresh blue cotton gown. She wore her long, curly hair combed straight and flaring over her shoulders like a soft black shawl.

"She is," Alleyne said happily.

"Then I'll write her a ticket."

Drake watched them stroll off. They would be an odd sight in London—David with his blond hair, a black baby riding on his shoulder, a young, pretty black woman strolling at his side. But here in Barbados it seemed sweet and right.

When the petitions ended, Drake wandered into Edwinna's office, where she sat working at her everlasting ledgers. She didn't look up. She had a maddening ability to concentrate. He fully believed she could sit there working on her ledgers as the house burned down around her. He planted a hip on the edge of her worktable and sat there. She wore reading spectacles, which made her eyes huge.

"What do you do for sport?" he asked.

She looked up. Her spectacles slid down her nose.

"What do mean, sport?"

He drew a deep breath and sighed. He slid his hip off the table and headed for the door. "Edwinna, you wouldn't recognize sport if it jumped up and bit you. I'm going for a ride."

"If you're going to Speightstown, check for letters."

"I'm not." He stopped at the door and gazed at her. "Come with me, Edwinna."

She looked up and he saw her swallow hard.

"I cannot. Harvest starts tomorrow. I am busy."

He gazed at her a moment, acknowledged her decision with a nod, and left.

Edwinna listened as his footsteps rang through the house and vanished out the front door. She knew what sport was —it was what other people had. Even the bond slaves and the slaves had sport on Sundays. But she had never had it in her whole life. She didn't know how.

She wondered where Drake was going. Her cheeks flushed. She had a very good idea of what he wanted, or he wouldn't have sat on the edge of her table like that, his manly crotch displayed right before her eyes.

She thought of Dinny's visit and the sizzle of interest she'd seen in his eyes. She wondered if he would visit her. She was surprised at how upset she felt at the thought, how envious, how . . . jealous.

Drake ended up at Dinny's house by accident. At loose ends, drifting toward the Atlantic coast and its wild, rugged beauty, he'd taken a wrong path. He'd spent an anxious hour lost in the cane on paths that crisscrossed. Heading for high ground, he'd finally ridden out of the cane on a hilltop and found himself before a large, white frame planter's house.

He hoped to hell it wasn't George Crawford's, then smiled in relief as he spied a familiar, red-dyed head bobbing in the yard. He rode forward. Dinny was out in front of her house, loudly berating Jumbo for some misdemeanor. Head and shoulders taller than she, Jumbo grinned down at his little owner with fondness and took his scolding. She broke off haranguing Jumbo when she saw him and bellowed happily, "Mr. Steel!"

He dismounted, and she came to him with both hands outstretched, her sunflower smile shining like the sun. She wore a green linen gown that revealed she was much too plump, and her garish red hair was no color that God ever designed, but her warmth made up for every defect.

"Mr. Steel, you've come to visit me, at last!"

"I have, but I must apologize. It's accidental—I'm lost."

She laughed merrily. "Jumbo will guide you home. But first, you are just in time for midday meal. Are you hungry?"

He was, he discovered, and said so.

Her eyes gleamed and her smile bounced even brighter. He had a momentary qualm, Edwinna at its center. This was not a sound idea. Seizing his arm, she led him along to the house, bellowing over her shoulder, "Jumbo! Our best wine for Mr. Steel and a tiny drop of rum for me. Then see to Mr. Steel's horse."

When he'd washed, they settled down to eat in her charming, breezy dining chamber, at one end of her long, polished table. She knew how to coddle a man. He'd been seated no longer than two seconds when he had a drink in his hand and a pillow at his back. His free hand rested on the table. Dinny gave him a big smile and covered his wrist with her plump little hand.

Her touch rippled all the way through him. It had been a long time since he'd felt a woman's touch—a year.

"So, Mr. Steel," she demanded, beaming. "Where is our Edwinna? Why isn't she with you?"

"She is busy with her ledgers."

"Ledgers?" She drew small circles on his wrist. The ripples went all the way to his groin. "What is wrong with that girl, working on ledgers on a beautiful Sunday when she could be out riding with her handsome pirate!"

"I'm not a pirate, Dinny."

She fluttered her eyelashes prettily. "Pray, do not disillusion me, Mr. Steel."

He had to smile. "As for pirates, I fear Edwinna has little interest in them, handsome or ugly."

She patted his wrist, then traced the blue vein on the back of his hand. He felt it all the way to his toes.

"Now, now, you must be patient with Edwinna. I love that girl, Mr. Steel. She's like a daughter to me, and I'll simply ask this of you. Be patient. You don't know what Edwinna's been through, what with Peter Crawford and all."

Drake looked at her somberly.

"I know he beat her."

"Did she tell you?"

"No."

"Well, she wouldn't. Peter Crawford was a drunken sot, Mr. Steel. You can be sure I was happy as a fool when he took that fall from his horse and broke his back. He couldn't do no more to that sweet girl." Then she beamed. "But let's not talk of unhappy things. It's such a lovely day . . ."

"Yes, it is."

Dinny chirped on, leading the conversation to merrier subjects. When he could politely manage it, he removed his hand and put it in his lap. She was wonderfully entertaining. She plied him with wine and told him story after story. She was so honest about herself that he laughed in delight.

She'd been a London pickpocket as a young girl, she told him. She'd been caught and thrown into Newgate Prison and then been transported as a bond slave to the Caribbean, where she'd set her cap for a rich planter. She's seen one the instant she'd stepped off the ship—Lord Fraser. She'd given him the biggest, sunniest smile she had, and he'd bought her indenture at once. A month later he'd married her. The marriage had been happy but short. When he'd died, she'd found herself not only Lady Fraser, but a woman of wealth.

She sighed. "To tell you the truth, Mr. Steel, sometimes I miss the adventure of picking a pocket."

He chuckled, and she looked up, beaming. She ran a hand up his sleeve. "Would you like to see the rest of my house, Mr. Steel?"

He drew a sharp breath and shifted in his chair uncomfortably, but her hand lingered on his sleeve. This was not a good idea. He felt guilty. Nevertheless, he found himself touring her house, first downstairs, then upstairs.

"And this is my bedchamber, Mr. Steel . . ."

He'd intended to make do with a hasty glance, but Dinny put her small palms on his chest and sensually traced the muscles there. Already warmed by wine, he felt the sensation like fire.

"My, but you're well built, Mr. Steel."

"Dinny, this isn't a sensible—"

She stood on tiptoe and put a kiss on his lips. It was the softest thing he'd felt in a year. He suddenly ached for Anne.

"Dinny, this isn't honorable. I try to be an honorable man."

"Of course you do, Mr. Steel," she crooned. "Of course you do."

She kissed him again, her hand gliding to his crotch, and he was lost. He bulged like a schoolboy. She looked up and smiled, and he didn't lift one finger to protest when she took his hand and led him to her bed.

The sun was setting by the time he started for Crawford Plantation, and the cane fields already lay in darkness. Jumbo loped ahead on the cane path, lofting a torch, guiding him. Each time Drake thought of Edwinna, guilt washed over him.

When he reached home, he looked for her, hoping to sup with her, but she remained shut in her office. He wondered uneasily if she'd seen the torch out in the cane paths, coming from Dinny's. He hoped not. He didn't want to hurt her.

CHAPTER

* 9 *

Harvest day dawned at last. Long before the sun came up, Edwinna rose, dressed, and took a bill-cane knife out to the dark, windy fields.

Had she selected the right field? Was the cane truly ripe, or should it grow another week or another month? Underripe cane meant less juice. Less juice meant a ton less sugar per ten-acre field—a shortage she could ill afford.

She ran through the darkness, wind whispering in the cane. She reached a field marked with a red flag and felled a cane stalk. Juice spurted. She tasted it. It was sweet. She hadn't made a mistake.

Satisfied, she hurried to the mill. She found Valentine O'Brien there already, although they couldn't possibly begin to grind until noon. The cane had to be cut, stripped, and cleaned before it could be put through the grinder. She conferred with Valentine on a last-minute decision. Use the mill or cattle to drive the grinder? She decided cattle. It was safer. She lingered at the grinder with Valentine, checking everything. This was the most worrisome place on the plantation, the most dangerous.

She found Alvis Nansellock already in the boiling house, rechecking his cisterns, pipes, kettles, sugar pots. A loyal bond servant, he was there although he could not hope to start boiling until sundown, when the cistern would be full of cane juice. Surely Alvis Nansellock was not involved in Jacka's mischief! Matthew Plum and Drake had warned her she must suspect everyone.

She had seen Drake's torch coming through the cane the evening before. Earlier, worried that he might be lost, she'd sent slaves looking. They'd come back to report he was at Dinny's. Jumbo had told them Drake and Dinny had dined and then gone upstairs to spend the afternoon. She seethed whenever she thought of it.

Thrusting Drake and Dinny out of her mind, she concentrated firmly on harvest. Everywhere she went on the plantation, she found things ready. She trembled with the familiar excitement of harvest. She was a planter. Her entire year rolled forward to culminate in this day. She didn't need Drake. She didn't need Dinny. She didn't need anyone. She had her land and her planting. She had her brothers. And she had harvest!

Drake felt the excitement in the air, too. He arose early— well before the six o'clock bell. When yesterday came surging back, he felt a stab of guilt. His interlude with Dinny had not been worth wronging Edwinna. In bed Dinny had been as cheerful and experienced as a courtesan, but the physical satisfaction had been fleeting—gone in an hour. He wished he'd never set eyes on her.

He went downstairs to look for Edwinna and found her already out, which meant she'd gone trotting off into the darkness, a thing they'd agreed she would *not* do, in light of the Jacka problem.

So he left the house at a run. Kena, who was devoted to

Edwinna and who could be counted on to be awake if Edwinna was, told him she'd gone to field twelve to test the cane. He ran down the rutted, uneven cane path in the murky gray of predawn, cane towering over him, swaying in the wind. Anyone could be hiding there. Anything could happen. Something scuttled across the path. The red, feral eyes of a cane rat flashed at him, then vanished as the animal scurried into the cane.

When he reached the harvest field, marked by its tall bamboo pole with red flag fluttering high above the cane, he found no one there. But she'd been there. A freshly cut cane stalk lay on the path.

He ran all the way to the mill and, breathless, found her where he should have looked in the first place—in the boiling house with Alvis Nansellock. He was relieved, but with the worry gone, quashed, anger welled up. She'd scared him.

As he entered the echoing, barnlike structure, his footfalls left no doubt as to the state of his temper. Nansellock quickly found something else to do and somewhere else to do it, but Edwinna went on checking a sugar pot, her back to him.

"Do you know that I have been running all over this plantation searching for you?" he demanded. "We agreed you would not go off alone in the dark. We agreed you would let me escort you."

She turned around and hit him. He took a step back in astonishment. She hit him again, eyes afire with harvest tension and fury. These were not slaps, but hard blows to his chest with the flat of her strong hand. He caught her wrist.

"Edwinna!"

She blazed at him. "You and your fine talk about commitment, fidelity! How dare you go to Dinny's? How dare you make sport of me in that way? Don't you know the whole plantation knows of it, and likely the whole island?"

He flushed. His guilt deepened. He hadn't thought of the humiliation he might cause her. She struggled to free her wrist. He held it tightly. Guilty or not, he didn't want to be battered to death.

"Edwinna, I was at Dinny's by accident. I got lost in the cane. By the time I rode out of it I found myself at her house. She invited me in to dine and I did so."

She wrenched her wrist free and rubbed it, then gave him a scorching look. "Did you sleep with her?"

He riffled a hand through his hair and looked away. There was no point in lying. She would find out later and be doubly hurt. He didn't want that.

"Yes. But that was an accident, too—one that will not be repeated. You have my word."

"I don't believe you!"

If he could have looked ahead and known this would wound her, he would have run like a rabbit the instant he'd spied Dinny's red hair bobbing about in her yard. Jealousy burned in Edwinna's eyes. He was taken aback. He hadn't expected that. It gave him hope.

"You have every right not to believe me. I will have to prove myself. And I intend to. Edwinna . . . I'm sorry I hurt you. I apologize."

She glowered at him, indecisive.

"Oh, do go away, Drake. Just go. I'm busy." She turned and went on with the work she'd been doing, checking and stacking sugar pots. He worked beside her.

"Edwinna, we've enough worries with a possible bond slave uprising. Let's put this behind us and be friends. Give me work to do. Let me help you with harvest."

"It isn't necessary for you to work."

"It is to *me*. I am accustomed to work. I hate idleness."

"You're a wine merchant. What do you know about sugar—nothing."

She was so damned blunt.

"I'm not without intelligence. I can learn."

She looked dubious, jealous, angry.

"Do you think you can learn sugar?" she challenged.
"Easily!"

Easily? Drake ate the word a hundred times a day during his first week of learning sugar. It proved to be a brutal taskmaster. Plum put him in charge of the cane cutting, which was backbreaking, dangerous toil for the slaves who did it. They stooped all day, working their way down the endless rows of cane, swinging their bill-cane knives, blisters rising in their calloused palms. David Alleyne treated their hands in the field with ointments and mercifully prescribed a dram of kill-devil rum at the close of each workday.

Harvest proved to be an orgy of work, such as Drake had never in his wildest dreams imagined. The rumble of the grinder echoed night and day. The gate bell clamored in emergency at least once every night, and because Edwinna rose up, Drake doggedly rose, too. He tried to prove himself to her, but he despaired of ever succeeding.

Matthew Plum saw what was going on between them and grew downright irritated with Edwinna's attitude toward Drake, her unwillingness to include him in business matters. He took her to task for it.

"Edwinna, Drake should be consulted," he chided in her plantation office one day after the midday meal as she sat with her head in her hands, overwhelmed by the latest financial blow. Her London sugar factor had raised his commission charge from five percent to seven. "Drake is a merchant, Edwinna. He knows London, he understands business. He could advise you."

"I don't want him interfering in Crawford Plantation business."

"He is your husband."

"In name only."

Plum sat back and looked at her gently. *Ah*, he thought. *So there's the rub. There is no bed in this marriage.* He'd suspected as much. He'd heard the foolish rumors about

Dinny Fraser. They should be discounted. Dinny seduced everyone. A man hadn't a chance. But even before that, Edwinna hadn't the look of a bride. Drake hadn't the look of a happy bridegroom.

Yet, if ever two people were a match, it was Drake and Edwinna. Both were private and deep—they thought deeply, felt deeply. Both were passionately dedicated to their chosen work—Edwinna to her plantation, Drake to his wine business.

"Nevertheless, Drake should be included in plantation decisions. I insist."

She took a ledger and began entering yesterday's harvest figures, which she'd compiled at midday meal from the overseers' reports.

"No. He cares nothing for Crawford Plantation."

"Caring comes with responsibility, Edwinna. Give him responsibility and he will care."

"There is no point in it. He will leave when his year is up and he will not come back. I know he will not."

So, he thought. *She doesn't want him to go. She is falling in love with him.*

"He might. If he thought he had a nice wife to come back to."

"This is not a *love* match, Mr. Plum," she said scornfully.

Plum was not so sure. He'd observed the way her eyes followed Drake. When he was around, he was the only man she saw. He'd seen the way Drake looked at her—frustrated, interested.

"Nevertheless, you should let Drake help you."

"I don't need him. I have you."

He crossed one leg upon the other, sat back, and carefully considered his words.

"I will not always be here for you, Edwinna."

Her head shot up and her eyes widened.

"You are not ill again?"

"Nay. I'm fit as a fiddle. But I'm getting older, Edwinna.

As a man gets older, his thoughts turn more and more to home. I have lived in Barbados twenty-five years, most of them on Crawford Plantation. But each year the yen to see England again grows a bit stronger.'' He twinkled at her. "I've even a yen to see my wife. And who knows, after all these years *she* may have a yen to see me. It might be pleasant for my wife and me to spend our sunset years together, sitting on the stoop of our cottage in Leeds, watching our grand-children play at our feet. I'm not saying I'll go this year or next, or even the year after. However, the day will come when I *will* go.''

She looked utterly shocked. "But . . . I count on you.''

"Then you should not. Count on your husband. Depend on him. It is the proper order of things.''

"My—earliest memories are of you. You, carrying me all around the plantation, letting me ride on your saddle, cutting small pieces of cane for me so I could pretend to plant and grow my own cane field. I never thought you would leave. It never occurred to me.''

"Well, I will!''

Now she was truly alarmed. She looked about the room in a distracted fashion, more distressed over this news than that of her dastardly London sugar factor.

"Edwinna,'' Plum said calmly. "Let Drake into your life. He will prove worthy. I am certain of it.''

Boots shucked, Drake was lying on the bed catching a noon rest before the next round of cane cutting resumed, when he heard Edwinna's step on the stair. He glanced at the doorway. To his surprise, she didn't pass by, but stopped.

"Drake? I—that is, Mr. Plum and I wondered if you would come down to the office and help us with a business problem.''

He sat up with alacrity and hauled on his boots, surprised.

"Gladly. If it's in the area of my competence.''

"It is. It concerns our London sugar factor.'' They discussed the problem on the way down the stairs, crossing through the dining chamber where Priscilla and Jocko were blatantly robbing the fruit bowl.

"I presume it isn't a simple matter of dismissing your sugar factor and hiring another?"

"No. Crawford Plantation is deeply in debt to him. You see, a sugar factor extends credit until harvest comes in. In the meantime, he orders and sends the supplies we need— tools, clothing, bond slaves, parts for the mill, food—"

"And charges another five percent for that."

"Yes."

"How much is the total indebtedness?"

"About four thousand pounds sterling."

Drake gave a low whistle. "How did it get so high?"

"My . . . father was a trifle careless in business matters."

He glanced at her. A trifle? Four thousand pounds was not a trifle. Peter Crawford had left his plantation in a mess.

"Do you think you can advise us?"

"That would be rash without studying the ledgers. But I will do one thing immediately. I'll write my brother-in-law Arthur to inquire at London banks about a loan to cover what you owe your sugar factor. The loan likely will cost you less by one or two percent than what you are paying him. Arthur can also inquire about hiring a new sugar factor. There are good ones to be found in London who will work for less than five percent. As for the ledgers, I'll study them in the evenings, if you'll sit with me and explain entries."

"Yes, of course."

Matthew Plum smiled to himself as the pair came into the office talking earnestly. Edwinna was flushed. Drake's eyes shone with interest. Plum rather doubted the interest had anything to do with a sugar factor.

Drake couldn't account for Edwinna's new willingness to admit him into the center of plantation business, but he was grateful for it. He was a man who needed responsibility.

Without it, he was like a fish out of water. Sharing the sugar factor problem and also remaining alert for any bond slave trouble, he and Edwinna drew a little closer. Sometimes, working late at night by candlelight in her office, they would glance up at the same moment and, surprised by it, smile; and he would think going to bed with her possible. But that was a false hope. If his hand even brushed hers in passing her a quill pen, she grew tense. He didn't understand her.

Harvest went on relentlessly. The work never stopped. The only respite came late Saturday afternoon when the boiling fires were allowed to go out in preparation for the Sabbath. By law no planter could make sugar on the Sabbath. The strident grinding ceased. Peace descended, and the sudden shock of it almost deafened the ear.

Enjoying themselves, the slaves plunged into the cattle pond to bathe and swim and play. If the week's work had gone well and Plum was pleased with them, he provided a duck for their sport. They all had a merry time—except for the duck, Drake noted wryly.

Plum clipped the duck's wings to prevent flying and tossed it into the cattle pond. Swimmers would vie to capture it. For all of their brawn and strength, the men rarely won this contest. Usually, one of the quick, slender maidens carried the duck home to her stewpot.

These afternoons were lovely. As the sun slanted into the Caribbean, coating the cane fields with a wash of gold, the slaves lined up at the provisions storehouse to receive their week's supply of food. Drake found it a beautiful sight to watch the firm-breasted maidens glide off into the sunset with their provisions balanced gracefully on their heads. It was also stirring and put him into a sweat.

By tradition, the black male slaves had the right to come into the planter's front hall on Saturday night to receive their allotment of rum, which they shared with their wives. The "papa" of the plantation dispensed the rum by his own hand, and that meant Drake did it. The rum tradition was one Ed-

winna despised, but he saw the sense of it. If he were enslaved, he too would want to get drunk every Saturday night,
giving not a thought to Sunday's headache.

"You should not have given David Alleyne permission to
take Kena walking," Edwinna said sharply.

Drake looked up, curious. They were alone in the dining
chamber sharing midday meal on the Sabbath after Drake
had spent the morning granting slave tickets and reading the
obligatory Sabbath prayers to bond slaves, who were required
by law to gather for prayer each Sabbath morning. Praying
over the likes of Jacka, Hastings, Yates? A joke.

Granted her ticket, Kena had left with a joyful David.
Planning a long walk, they'd left Tutu behind. He perched
happily in Drake's lap, chomping the bread sops Drake fed
him. He used to feed Katherine this way.

"Why shouldn't David take Kena walking?"

"Because I don't like it, that's why. It's not safe. He—
he might hurt her."

Drake went on feeding Tutu, but in his mind's eye he was
seeing a little girl running through the night, sobbing, her
wrist broken.

"Edwinna," he said gently, "David Alleyne would never
hurt her. I think you know that. He is one of the most decent
young men I've ever met."

She backed off from her extreme position, but insisted,
"Nevertheless, I do not want Kena leaving the plantation
with him. In the future, please do not grant permission."

"And if Kena insists?" He popped a bread sop dipped in
honey into Tutu's open mouth. He chewed and grinned.

"She won't. She listens to me."

Tutu had had enough. He scrambled down and ran to Edwinna, his bare feet pattering on the floor. Edwinna picked
him up and kissed him. He settled in her lap exactly thirty
seconds, then wriggled down and ran off to play. Drake
resumed his own eating.

"Where did they go? Where did he take her?"

He failed to understand this.

"I did not think it necessary to put David on the rack and torture the information out of him."

"Don't make sport of it, Drake," she warned.

He looked at her, amazed. "I'm not. I just do not understand this overconcern for Kena, this protectiveness. Has something happened to her before?"

"I just don't want her with David Alleyne."

"Why not?"

Heated, agitated, she ate her food, then put her spoon down. She looked up fiercely.

"She is my *sister*, that's why!" Then, more quietly, "My half sister."

Drake sat back in his chair. He was speechless, shocked. He shouldn't have been. He'd lived in Barbados long enough to know that planters commonly forced themselves upon their slave women. Most of them kept black mistresses—even the planters whose English wives lived in Barbados. He should have guessed. Kena was devoted to Edwinna, and Edwinna to Kena.

He shook his head, scarcely knowing what to say.

"Then, Tutu . . ."

"My nephew."

He was at a loss for words.

"It is not so surprising," Edwinna said bitterly, "men being what they are."

He took a deep breath. "And what *are* men, Edwinna? Tell me. I'd like to know. Since the day I came here, I have done my best to repay you for saving my life. I've worked for you. I have tried to befriend you. I have offered, with a sincere heart, to be a husband to you, though God knows we are ill-matched. Yet you reject my every overture. So tell me, exactly. I would like to know. What *are* men?"

Her eyes filled with bitterness, as if at some memory he could not even guess at.

"Animals."

It was enough. With a single smooth movement, he folded his napkin, pushed back his chair, and rose. He headed for the door. Her voice followed him.

"Where are you going?"

He paused in the doorway and looked at her. He was beginning to understand what made her the way she was, but that didn't mean he had to forgive her or even like her. She crossed the bounds far too often.

"I'm going to eat in the kitchen. Far be it from me to force you to eat with an animal."

His footsteps rang through the dining chamber, and then he was gone. Edwinna sat and forced herself to finish her meal, her chest constricting. How could she say such a terrible thing to Drake? It was terrible, but true.

The food was suddenly tasteless without Drake sitting at the table, sharing it. She reminded herself she preferred dining alone. She'd dined alone most of her life. She liked it. A tear spilled down her cheek.

Drake remained incensed with her and she knew it. On Monday, he did not come to midday meal with the overseers. His empty place at the table was a reproach. Matthew Plum glanced at it several times during the meal and gazed at her quizzically, but it was none of his business. She gave him no explanation, and he asked for none.

Drake didn't sup with her that night, either. Where he supped, she didn't know. Probably down at Matthew Plum's. The two had become good friends. As for herself, she ate in the large, dark dining chamber, alone.

It was up to her to apologize. Going up to bed in the dark house after midnight, she paused at his open door. His room lay in shadows, the mosquito netting like a white cloud.

"I'm not asleep." His unhappy voice came quietly from within the netting.

She drew a breath. "Drake, I am truly sorry I said those things."

"I'm sorry you said them, too. I'd thought there was the possibility we might become friends. Now I see it's not possible."

"I want to be friends, Drake."

He sighed. "Do you? Somehow, I doubt that. I do not understand you, Edwinna. I try. But the truth is I do not."

She was glad for the darkness. He couldn't see the emotion she was feeling. "Sometimes . . . there are many things I do not understand myself. But I'm sorry if I offended you."

She went down the hall to her door.

"Edwinna?" he called gently from his bed.

"Yes?"

"Good night, sleep well."

"Thank you." She went into her room, closed and locked the door. She sat on the bed and wrapped herself tightly in her own arms, for lack of anyone else to hold her. Dear God, did she want to be held and comforted in Drake Steel's arms?

Edwinna was standing in a cut cane field in the dazzling morning sun, holding the rein of her mare and trying to reach a decision as to whether to let a crop of rattoon cane spring up from the stubble for a third year or to dig up the stubble and plant new cane, when a slave came running down the path from the mill, gesturing wildly.

"Mama, Mama, come!"

She dropped the reins and ran out of the field as he came toward her, the whites of his eyes showing in his fright, the sweat on his black body catching the sunlight and gleaming like beads of gold.

"Jehan, what is it?"

"Mama—" Deserted by the few English words he knew, he could only make beseeching gestures and point frantically in the direction of the mill. Helpless to explain, he imitated the sound of the grinder, "Garooooom, garoooom —Papa—"

"The grinding platform? Papa Drake? He's hurt?"

He nodded so hard the sweat beads flew.

"Oh, dear God." Fear gripped her. For a moment, she stood rooted, unable to move for the terror of it. Then, with only one thought in her head—Drake!—she bolted and ran like a wild woman, arms flailing, braid coming loose, hair flying wild. The mill was a quarter of a mile away. She forgot she had a horse and simply ran, but the faster she ran, the slower she seemed to move. It was like running in one of her terrifying nightmares in which Thomas and Harry needed her, called to her, and she couldn't get to them. Oh, not Drake, not Drake.

She came to the end of the cane path, gasping and breathless. The familiar rumble and squeal of the grinder had stopped. She ran uphill to the mill, past the distillery, the curing house, the boiling house, the affingoes heading toward the loading platform with cut cane.

Under the grinding platform, men clustered around a lax, booted figure who reclined on the ground, propped against the platform post. Dark hair, broad shoulders. Drake! The cluster of men parted for her as she ran to him and fell to her knees.

"Drake, Drake—"

Terrified of seeing him lying dead or dying or maimed, she was struck by a sudden blinding headache and could scarcely see him at all. She groped for his large, tanned hand and clutched it.

"Drake, Drake—"

"Edwinna." He squeezed her hand. Getting his second wind, getting over the initial, astounding shock of the fall, Drake still saw stars. The back of his head, where he'd struck the edge of the platform when he'd slipped and fallen, felt as if it had been whacked by the flat of an axe. It throbbed in rhythm to his heartbeat, goose egg rising. But the real bitch was his shoulder. It had separated. He'd felt it go. Low and humming, seductive as a siren, pain crept toward him, coming for him. The sound of it filled his ears.

But it was Edwinna who concerned him. Wild-eyed and scared, she was shaking as if chilled to the bone. Her pretty lips were blue, and fear had constricted the pupils of her eyes to velvet pinpoints.

"Edwinna." Babying his shoulder, he gripped her hand. It was as cold as ice, and he could feel the force of her shaking all the way up his arm. "Edwinna, I'm all right."

"Drake—"

David Alleyne squatted, his fair hair catching the sunlight.

"Mistress Edwinna, Mr. Steel will be all right. I'll see to it. He has had a knock on the head, but 'tisn't serious. His shoulder will be an agony for a week or two, but I'll bind it well."

"Help him!"

"I will, ma'am, I will. Now, please move aside. Let go of his hand. Let go. Come now, let go."

Drake had never seen emotion so strong. He was stunned by it. He hadn't thought she had so much passion in her. He hadn't thought she cared. But she did. It was plain in the violence of her shaking.

"What happened?" she demanded.

Drake tried to smile, for her sake, but the tide of pain was coming in. "I was up on the platform, estimating the amount of cane that needed to be cut tomorrow. My foot slipped on cane juice and I fell off the platform, that's all."

Her eyes were so luminous he could see all the way into her heart. What he saw shocked him. She cared about him!

"I thought—the grinder."

"I know," he said gently, reaching out to touch her hair. It was wild, disheveled. Her face was flushed, her forehead sweaty. How far had she run? "I know."

Alleyne injected, "I had best bind him *now*, Mistress Edwinna. Before the pain starts."

"Do it! Do it at once."

"Before it starts?" Drake smiled raggedly at Alleyne. "You jest." David Alleyne smiled back and went to work binding him—an agony. Drake tried not to cry out. For Edwinna's sake he gritted his teeth. She watched like a hawk, her lovely eyes scared, an occasional tremble still rippling through her body. He closed his eyes, panting to keep the pain at bay, watching her through his drooping lashes. He thought: *When pain is great enough, it is almost sexual.* Watching her, he thought about going to bed with her. Her braid had come undone. Loosed from that unattractive prison, her sunny brown hair fell thick and curly to her shoulders. It wasn't the lovely color of Anne's hair, but he liked it. It . . . suited her. The tide swept in and covered him. He closed his eyes and gritted his teeth. David worked, binding him tightly. When the pain ebbed, he opened his eyes again and looked at her. She was watching him intently. He smiled a little, to show her the pain was bearable. She smiled, too, eyes intense, lips trembling. He'd never seen such emotion.

Plum showed up. Noting Edwinna's shaken state, he made nothing of Drake's injuries, even joked a little. Drake was relieved. A man of common sense, Plum ordered the gawking slaves and bond slaves back to work. The grinder began to rumble overhead, the day returning to normal.

David Alleyne helped him walk up to the house. Drake had rejected Edwinna's insistent offer of a litter or a horse. Riding would be excruciating. A bouncing litter would be worse.

Edwinna felt foolish hovering over Drake, so as soon as David Alleyne and the servants had made him comfortable in bed, she forced herself to go back to her work, leaving him in the hands of Kena and Marigold, who stayed near, seeing to his every wish and need.

Still shaken, she went to the curing house and for an hour forced herself to check sugar pots that hung from their racks, the molasses slowly dripping out of them into the pans below. She marked the pots of sugar that were not hardening and would have to be reboiled.

But Drake was in every breath she took. What if David Alleyne was wrong about Drake's "mild" head injury? What if it was worse than that? She abandoned all pretense of working, ran back to Crawford Hall, and breathlessly climbed the stairs to his room.

The door stood open. To her relief, she found him sitting up in bed in a nest of pillows, his deeply tanned chest bare, his shoulder muscles straining against the tight bindings. He looked in great pain.

"How are you feeling?" she asked from the doorway.

He managed a smile. "I've a grandfather of a headache, but it's the shoulder that's a bit of a bitch."

"Yes." More than a bit. She could see a white pain line that outlined his brow where his deeply tanned forehead met his black hair. His hair was neatly combed and clubbed back. Even in pain, he kept himself tidy, neat. "Can I get you something? Is there anything you want?"

"Company." He smiled painfully. "Other than simian." With his good hand, he gestured toward Priscilla and Jocko, who perched on his dresser. Priscilla was brushing Jocko's head with Drake's hairbrush. Jocko endured it stoically, eyes closed, head ducked, blinking every time the hard wooden back hit him. "Come in. Sit with me, Edwinna."

She hesitated. The room was not one she ever entered willingly. It had been her father's. She'd never known what to expect here—a kind word, a cross word, a drunken rage, blows. The unpredictableness had confused her. She'd lived her childhood confused, terrified. But there had been good years, too—the years before he drank, before her mother ran off.

She forced herself to step across the threshold. Drake kept his room as tidy as he kept his person—boots and clothing put away in the wardrobe, shaving tools put away in the shaving box, towel folded and hung square on the towel rack. He'd made himself a small, neat calendar grid, which hung on the wall above his writing table. She winced. With neat strokes, he'd crossed off each day as it had passed, as if he wanted to be done with the year.

"Bring a chair to the bed. Sit with me."

She did so, but she was uncomfortable with his near-nakedness. She was used to it in the field, in the boiling house. But Drake's bothered her. He was so . . . big. His chest was tanned to the dark color of mahogany, and it was sprinkled with crisp black hair that descended in a dark T into his breeches. She flushed, imagining it descending lower, into a soft black bush.

"Shall I put on a shirt?"

Her eyes flew to his.

"It's not necessary."

"Good. Barbados is so damned hot—hot and bright."

"Is it? I wouldn't know. I have never lived anywhere else."

"I have and I *know*. Believe me, it's hot."

"I could have Scipio come up and fan you."

He smiled wryly. "Like an Oriental potentate. Send up the harem girls, too. They can pop grapes into my mouth."

She smiled. *You are falling in love with him, Edwinna*, she thought. She quickly looked away, and, flustered, rubbed her hand.

He gingerly settled his head against the pillow.

"Does your head hurt badly?"

"Let's put it this way. I would sell my soul for a piece of ice to put on my goose egg."

"What is ice?"

Drake lifted his head and stared at her. Their two separate worlds slid into juxtaposition, colliding so loudly he could almost hear the crash. He was a man who knew what ice was, a man raised in England, with enough morality to know that slavery was wrong. She was a slave owner, a woman who didn't know what ice was, who thought it natural to have a black half sister. Never before had their differences been so clear to him. He was wrong to blame her.

"Ice," he said "is water that becomes solid as rock and very cold when the temperature drops low enough."

"How strange."

"In England in winter some ponds and rivers become solid ice and people take sleds and go sliding on them."

"I would like to see that."

"I would like to show it to you." He meant it.

Priscilla swung down from the dresser and stalked to the door, tail a straight, high crook. When Jocko failed to follow, she turned and gave him a piece of her mind, chattering. Jocko obediently swung down and followed her.

"It's plain to see who rules the roost."

"This is not yet mating season," Edwinna said. "In mating season he will likely become aggressive. If he becomes mean and starts to bite, you will have to get rid of him, Drake."

"Edwinna." He smiled gently. "Only stupid males mate aggressively. Most males mate gently, out of consideration for the female."

That bothered her and she stared at her hands. Gazing at her through a veil of pain, Drake wished he were mating with her right now. She'd forgotten to rebraid her hair. It was long and lovely and as thick as sheep's wool. The tide came in. He breathed deep and braced himself for its onslaught. Eyes closed, he dog-paddled in a sea of pain. It was a powerful aphrodisiac. He gazed at her through his lashes. He wished she were astride him right now. Shoulder or no, he would let her ride to her heart's content, and when she had, he would take his turn. He wondered what it would feel like, being intimate with Edwinna Crawford.

"Drake, do you want kill-devil for the pain?"

He had to smile. He was in bad shape if Edwinna was willing to offer rum.

"No. I'll wait until I need it." His smile grew wry. "Alleyne tells me the second to the fifth day will be the worst, though I hope he's joking. I can't imagine worse."

He lay his head back, closed his eyes, and floated on the tide.

"Drake?" Edwinna said, moving her chair closer. "David Alleyne said you must not fall asleep the first few hours after a head injury. It can be dangerous."

He gingerly pulled himself up, and with his good arm, he reached back, captured the goose-feather pillow, and dragged it to the crook of his neck. "Well, then, let's talk. It will keep me awake."

"Yes. We'll talk. About what?"

He wished he could talk about bed, about touching each other, but instead he said, "Tell me about your brothers. What sort of young men are they?"

It was a subject she liked. Her eyes glowed. She wasn't a beauty, but she appealed to him. He liked the cleanness of her features, the decency in her character. The passion he'd seen displayed today, on *his* behalf, had knocked him silly. He felt as aroused by it as if he were in a harem full of scantily clad nymphs and not merely sitting with a spinster who wore breeches and shirts. He slid a knee up, lest his arousal become obvious.

"They are wonderful young men—handsome, high-spirited, adventurous. I remember the day they were born." She smiled, her expression soft. "I thought they had been brought to the house as a gift for me. I thought they were mine. I remember taking a pallet into the nursery and sleeping there because I knew they were mine." Her gaze shifted away for a moment, and a stressful line formed on her brow. "After my mother . . . was gone, they truly *were* mine. I raised them."

"They ran away to sea at sixteen?"

"Yes. They—they'd had a quarrel with my father. But they'd always yearned to go to sea," she added quickly. "They'd begged to go, even as children."

So, Drake thought, Peter Crawford had destroyed all his

children. The drinking fool. The ignorant jackass had been too big-headed to see that a man's real treasures were his children, not his rum barrel or his damned cane fields. Drake treasured his own children above everything else on earth.

"Then they are not fanatic planters like you?"

She smiled at the word *fanatic*. "No. They think it dull. But I'm sure," she said, "that when they're older they will settle into it and be very happy as planters."

Drake was sure they wouldn't. From what he'd seen, planting was not an occupation, it was a calling, like that of priest or nun. It required complete dedication, night and day. You were either born to be a planter, as Edwinna plainly was, or you hated it, as the Crawford twins likely did.

"Tell me about your children, Drake. What are they like?"

He smiled despite the tide that was coming for him again. He wanted to ease out of the bed and pace.

"Well, they say William is my image." Edwinna smiled, picturing him, a sturdy, handsome boy with midnight black hair and eyes as blue and clear as the waters of Carlisle Bay. "Though where he gets his aggressive nature from is beyond me."

"From you," she assured him with a nod. "You could not have survived six months on a pirate ship without an aggressive nature."

He smiled. "Is that so?"

"Yes, that's so."

"Perhaps. But Katherine is totally her mother—blonde, petite, very pretty. It is too early to say for sure, but I think she may have inherited Anne's singing voice, too."

The description brought unexpected pain. She'd already guessed Drake's wife would have been like that—very pretty and accomplished—but now she knew for sure. "Katherine sounds wonderful," she said firmly. "William, too."

"They are." He glanced at his writing table. "I wrote each of them a separate letter last night." He smiled. Edwinna watched him anxiously. His smiles were taut curves now laced with pain. "Of course, Katherine is too young to read. Verity will have to read it to her. But it will still be her own letter. I wrote William about the cane fields and the mill, and Katherine about Priscilla. I wish I could draw."

"I can draw," Edwinna offered. "When I was young I used to spend a lot of time alone with paper and pen and ink, drawing. I would go into the cane fields, to the boiling house. I could draw Priscilla in the margins of your letter if you like."

"That would be excellent."

She fetched letter box, pen, and ink and set to work. Drake watched her as the tide came for him. He tried not to sink; he tried to stay above the water. God! He reached for the flask of kill-devil David Alleyne had left on his nightstand, popped the cork out, and took a sip. Edwinna looked up. He managed a half smile.

She went on drawing for a long time. He floated in the tide. God! He panted. When she finished, she gave him Katherine's letter and he studied it.

"This is wonderful, Edwinna." Her talent surprised him. She had caught Priscilla perfectly—the mischievous, haughty little imp. She had caught him, too—the humorous look of outrage on his face as Priscilla bit him. There was another of Priscilla waiting in ambush for him on top of the water drip. Had it not been for the throbbing in his head and shoulder, he would have laughed.

Flushing in pleasure, she worked on William's letter. Drake watched through eyes that grew heavy with pain. A cane field sprang up, so real Drake could almost hear the cane rustling. Cane cutters bent to their work. Drake himself stood in the cane field, arms crossed.

When she was finished, he sat with the two letters in his hands, admiring them. "These drawings are superb, Edwinna."

Mesmerized by the pain and the clear shine of her hair, he reached out and touched it.

She drew back.

"I—I had best take your letters downstairs and seal them and send them to Speightstown."

She left the room as quickly as she could. Drake watched her go, touched by her distress, but suffering with his own.

CHAPTER

* 10 *

The pain grew unbearable for Drake that night. Warned by David Alleyne that it would, Edwinna slept lightly, listening for him, and when she heard the rhythmic creak of a floorboard in his room, she knew he was pacing. She rose, used flint and tinder from her tinderbox to light a candle, and swiftly dressed. She carried the candle to his open door. Worshipful of Drake, eager to be of help, Jeremy had brought a pallet to the hall floor. But he was a child and slept, deep and blissful, oblivious to Drake's wakefulness. Drake's room lay dark.

"Drake, shall I fetch David Alleyne?"

"No." He uttered a small laugh, a harsh, ragged edge to it. "Don't bother to wake him. There's nothing to be done." He came forward into the candlelight, casting a long, dark shadow, his handsome face haggard. He managed a smile. "I'm sorry if I disturbed you with this confounded pacing."

"I was listening for you. Can I get you anything?"

"No." He gestured with his good arm at the nightstand.

Everything he needed stood there: a rum flask, a pitcher of squeezed juices, a crock of cold water from the coral drip, laudanum drops.

"Then, can I do anything for you?"

"Yes. Tie this damned sling tighter, if you will."

"Of course." Taking a deep breath, she forced herself to step into her father's room, hearing the echo of her father's voice in the darkness. *You whore's daughter. I'll flog the living daylights out of you, lest you grow up to be what your mother is—a sea captain's whore. Father, please! Please don't hit me again.* Heart pounding, she went in and set the candle on the livery cabinet.

Drake painfully lowered himself to a footstool and sat. The knot had slipped to his chest. She knelt before him to work on it. It was a peculiar sensation to be so close to him. Her heart thundered, causing her hands to tremble as she worked on the knot.

"Don't be afraid of me."

"I'm not."

"Good."

He smelled of sweat and rum and pain. He had a fever, too. Even through his bandages his skin radiated intense heat. While he cradled his shoulder and arm, she retied the knot, pulling it tighter. She worked gently. Even so, he gritted his teeth.

"Drake you have fever."

"I'm also slightly drunk."

She drew back.

"Don't be afraid of me!" he reiterated harshly, seizing her hand and bringing it back to the knot to finish the work. "I will not hurt you. I have never hurt a female in my life and never will. I will not hurt you or any other female on this plantation."

"I know that, Drake," she said softly. And she did. She had only to think of the way he was with Jeremy and Marigold and Tutu and even Priscilla, to know that. She finished the knot then sat back on her knees, wishing she could ease his suffering.

He smiled, his blue eyes, usually so clear, smoky now with pain and rum.

"Do you know what I like about you, Edwinna? I like the cleanness of your soul. And don't ask me what that means, for I'm too drunk to know what I'm thinking."

Afraid that he might kiss her with his hot, feverish mouth—he was looking at her lips so intently—she got to her feet and tended to the candle, which was burning too fast in the breeze. She put a perforated tin candle guard over it. The light grew dim, speckles dotting the walls. The ceiling looked like a field of fireflies. Drake rose with a groan and began to pace. She sat in a chair, anxious. From the mill came the sound of the grinder rumbling.

"It's not necessary for you to keep me company, Edwinna."

"I don't mind."

"I'm poor company tonight."

"I've known worse."

Drake halted and gazed at her. Raggedly he said, "Well, then, let's talk. It will keep my mind off the pain. What would you like to talk about?"

"Tell me about your wine business."

Drake retrieved the rum flask from the nightstand and carried it with him while pacing. It was a vile, hellish drink. He loathed the taste, the way it burned a hole in his gut, but it did the job. Tonight the kill-devil was a mercy.

He paced and talked wine for an hour. He talked himself silly. It kept his mind off the agony. Edwinna sat listening, rapt, her eyes shining in the candlelight. He talked and talked. He told her the Steel family history—how the wine shop had been in the family in the same location on Thames Street for one hundred fifty years, how it had prospered in some eras, gone begging in others. It was now at its lowest ebb—the penalty imposed upon the Steels for allegiance to the king.

Because she was a good listener and he was in so much pain, he went beyond the wine business and told her of his hopes and plans for the future, how he longed to reclaim the Steel family home—Highgate Hall—for William's inheritance.

Then, to keep the pain at bay, he talked wine simply for the sake of talking wine, expounding on the different properties of burgundy, claret, Madeira, canary. He told her of his wine-buying trips to France and Portugal, his small adventures there. He did *not* tell her he'd had a double mission, delivering messages from the Sealed Knot to exiled cavaliers. He was not that drunk, nor that trusting. She was pro-Cromwell.

She listened to it all—truly listened. Her occasional comment or pertinent question proved it. He was surprised and said so.

"You don't seem a damned bit bored."

"Bored?" Her eyes widened in surprise. "Why should I be?"

"Most women I've known find business boring."

"I find it interesting. I like business."

"My wife," Drake said, taking a sip from the flask, "did not. Anne used to say 'wine, wine, wine—it is meant to be drunk, Drake, not talked to death.' "

"She sounds clever and witty," Edwinna offered softly.

"She was."

"And beautiful, like Katherine."

"That, too," Drake admitted. "Tell me about your life," he said sharply. "What do you do besides sugar?"

She smiled a little. "Nothing. What do *you* do besides wine?"

Despite his agony, he had to smile. "Nothing." He toasted her with the rum flask. "We've that in common, then. We are both working maniacs. What about friends? Who are your friends here in Barbados?" He'd never thought to ask the question before. *Barbarian*, he thought. *You've never even tried to get to know her. You want to bed her, but you don't want to know her.*

"I haven't many," she admitted, her eyes aglow. "There are not many women in Barbados. Only planters' wives. I have little in common with them. They dislike life here and talk of nothing but returning to England. I suppose my closest friends are Matthew Plum, Simon Tarcher in Speightstown, Dinny." He winced, feeling like a traitor. "And Kena, of course," she added.

He paced. "David Alleyne is in love with Kena."

"I know."

"What will you do if he asks to marry her?"

"Marry her?" Her eyes widened in surprise.

"Yes, damn it, marry her! I'm sure he intends it."

"I want the best for my sister. And for Tutu. I'm not sure that marriage to a white man . . ."

"Look at the heart, Edwinna, not at the color of the skin. David Alleyne is trustworthy."

"I don't trust many . . . people," she admitted. He gazed at her. *Men, you mean, darling. You don't trust men.* "Do you have many friends in London, Drake?"

The pain made him terse, made him talk in clipped sentences. She didn't seem to mind. "Many acquaintances. Few true friends. Only two close to my heart—my brother-in-law, Arthur, and my best friend since boyhood, Charles Dare. I've lost track of Charles. He went to Holland about the same time my wife died. I miss him."

He paced quietly and groaned. He couldn't hold it back. The sounds of Barbados filled the night. The grinder rumbled, palm branches rattled in the trade wind, tree frogs whistled shrilly, fruit bats flapped their large wings as they settled into the guava and paw-paw trees in the yard.

"Life is full of loss, isn't it, Drake?"

"Yes, it is. That goddamned savage sea." He lifted the rum and drank deeply. He wondered if William and Katherine would like her for a mother. He decided they would. *Lord*, he thought, *I must be truly inebriated.*

He changed the subject to the harvest. They talked on, until the kill-devil finally got on top of the awful pain and he could stop pacing. When he did, he eased his sweaty, trembling body onto the bed, into the nest of pillows, and shut his eyes.

Edwinna kept watch until his breathing evened out, until he was asleep. Then she took the candle and went to her room, stepping carefully around Jeremy, who slept with an arm sprawled on the floor.

Loss? Yes, she'd suffered loss, and she already knew what her next one would be. She would lose Drake Steel. When this handsome London wine merchant returned to his complex life in England, he would not come back, despite his promise. He would cease to remember a small, insignificant Caribbean island where trade winds blew through cane fields and where the weather was ever the same, warm and balmy, in winter and summer, spring and autumn, year upon year. If he ever gave her a passing thought as years went by, it might be with some slight gratitude—she had once saved his life—but nothing more. Unhappy over the inevitable loss, she got into her bed and fell asleep, missing him already.

Drake suffered intensely three more days. Then, he began to mend. A strong-bodied man in his prime, he came strolling down to the cane fields by the end of the week—gingerly, to be sure, and with shoulder tightly bound and arm in sling—but he came! Seeing him out and about, Edwinna smiled.

Drake had been waiting for a letter for weeks. It finally arrived on a sunny harvest afternoon, sent up from Speightstown. Knowing how dearly it was wanted, Edwinna took it and ran out to the cane fields, braid swinging.

"Drake, a letter!"

He came bounding out of a field of cane stubble, careless

of his shoulder. He seized the letter, sat in the cane path, and patted the ground beside him for her to sit, too. She knelt quickly, anxious for him. His hand trembled undoing the leather packet. She understood. Letters could bring bad news as well as good.

He gave her a quick look and considerately asked, "Any letter from Thomas and Harry?"

"No. Perhaps next time."

"Surely."

He yanked his thick, multipaged letter out of the packet. "It's from Verity." He took a deep breath, scanned the opening page, expelled his breath, and gave her a quick, dazzling smile. "William and Katherine are well and sound and healthy."

"Drake, I'm so glad."

"Listen to this: 'My beloved brother. First, the news you surely crave. William and Katherine are hale and hearty and in the best of health and spirits. Katherine took the measles this winter, but I do assure you they left her none the worse. She remains sound in every faculty—eyesight, hearing, heart, and her quick little brain. The only calamity your William suffered this winter is the loss of his baby teeth. The new are coming in—great, huge, manly teeth that will do him proud—and he looks for all the world like an adorable chipmunk. Your children are a joy. They love us and we love them, and I do assure you their only complaint in life is that they want their papa.' "

Drake touched a finger to the corner of his eye. Edwinna watched. "Drake? Let's send for your children. Bring them here. I would gladly pay."

"No, Edwinna, but thank you for offering," he said, excitedly returning to his letter. "I've already lost a wife to that goddamned sea. I won't risk my children."

"No, of course not." She was disappointed. She would have liked Drake's children in her house, mothering them, loving them.

"Listen to this. 'Now, my great fool of a brother who set sail on a ship ill equipped to fight pirates, shall I endeavor to describe how Arthur and I felt when your letter came? Impossible. Let it suffice to say we shouted, we wept, we laughed, we fell to our knees in thanks to God who saved you alive. Your precocious William grew much vexed with us, saying, "Of course my papa is alive. You said he was, Aunt Verity!"'

" 'For in truth, though we heard nothing of you in eight months, we staunchly refused to believe you dead and forbade your children to think it. We clung fervently to our faith in the Almighty, that he would restore you to us, which, praise God, he has done. I sternly admonish you, Drake, to tell Mistress Edwinna Crawford that she has earned my undying love and my everlasting devotion for her rescue of you.' "

"She's wonderful, Drake. I like her."

He glanced at her with an excited smile. "So do I. We've had our battles royal, but Verity is Verity."

A physical man, he needed physical release for his high excitement. She knew that. So when he impulsively reached out and squeezed her hand, she made nothing of it. To him, it was a mere release. He would have touched anyone who'd brought him the letter.

In a state of excitement, he went on reading, but for her the touch was stirring. He had a big, strong hand, darkly tanned, the back of it sprinkled with black hair.

Drake went on reading aloud, a courtesy to her. Whenever he glanced at her, she smiled. But in truth, the more he read of Verity's letter, the more distant she felt. Drake's world was as separated from hers as the moon from the earth. What did she know of a sister called Verity and of a wine shop on a street called Thames in a city called London? She only knew of sugar cane and Barbados. Hearing him read, hearing the bits and pieces of his life, she felt unhappy. But she smiled boldly each time he smiled, wanting him to be happy.

And he was. In addition to joyful family news—after seven years of childless marriage, Verity and Arthur were expecting their first child—the political news excited Drake, sent him into raptures. She listened politely, understanding little of it. Oliver Cromwell's son and successor, Richard Cromwell, was proving an inept leader. Dissatisfaction had spread. All England was now clamoring for the restoration of the monarchy. King Charles's loyal General Monck was said to be poised in Scotland with his army, ready to ride down upon London to force Parliament to bring the king back from exile in Holland.

Rejoicing, Drake strode back to the house in a euphoric state. Striding along beside this tall, handsome man in his sweaty work clothes, she gazed at him and knew with sorrowful certainty that he would not come back once he left Barbados.

The twenty-sixth of February, the date Drake thought he'd overheard in Bridgetown while spying on the bond slaves' midnight meeting, had come and gone without incident. Edwinna had been tense about that. She'd worn a pistol whenever she was out on the plantation, night or day. Matthew Plum and Drake each wore one, too.

There was undercurrent on the plantation that worried and angered her. Other planters reported the same thing. The field slaves and bond slaves seemed spooked, as if someone were intimidating them. When she questioned them, they insisted they knew nothing. Drake and Plum tended to believe them, but someone or something was frightening them.

Incensed, she'd done something headstrong and rash. She'd marched into the cane fields and harshly questioned Jacka. She'd learned nothing. Jacka had been insolent, demanding the thirty shillings reward that was rightfully his for the runaway slave Drake had freed. Also, he'd denied that he or Yates or Hastings had been at any so-called midnight meeting in Bridgetown. She'd wanted to flog him. Only the thought that she would be following in her father's and uncle's footsteps stopped her.

When Drake found out what she'd done, he came bounding into the boiling house where she was training a new slave. Blue eyes blazing, he grabbed her by the elbow and walked her out of the place.

"What is it?"

"Not here."

He walked her rapidly up the hill, past the loud, noisy grinding platform and up to the stone windmill. Not until they stood behind it in privacy did he free her elbow from his angry grip.

"What in the devil do you think you're doing, Edwinna, confronting Jacka like that? Are you crazy? Jeremy was out there with the affingoes and he told me."

"I won't have my slaves and bond slaves intimidated, Drake! I'm sick of this. Crawford Plantation is my responsibility. I want to get to the bottom of this."

"Well, so do I! But not like this. Good lord, Edwinna, if there *is* a conspiracy underway—if Jacka or any other bond slave on this plantation *is* involved—you could be killed just for knowing about it. You could be left slain in a cane field with no one able to figure out what happened."

She felt herself grow pale.

"I didn't think of that. I may have endangered you, too —you and Matthew Plum."

The heated intensity went out of him. His shoulders relaxed.

"There's likely no real harm done this time. But don't, for God's sake, do it again. Let it be, Edwinna. Don't precipitate anything that we can't handle."

He looked at her with grim tenderness.

"I don't want to mourn another wife. I can't take it, Edwinna. Especially a wife that I am just getting to know and like—a wife I haven't even kissed yet. So be careful. Please.''

Her mouth went dry. So did her lips. She touched her tongue to them. His clean black hair glistened so in the sun. She gazed at him. Strong feelings stirred. She wanted his kiss, wanted it fiercely, but the old fears came surging. With Drake, a kiss would be the beginning of other caresses, intimate caresses. She wasn't ready for that.

''I'll be careful.''

He nodded.

''Good.''

She whirled and strode swiftly down the hill to the boiling house, but her thoughts that afternoon were bewildering ones. Drake Steel would care if she died. She hadn't known that.

Edwinna waited impatiently for Planters Council. To be absent from harvest as short a time as possible, they traveled to Bridgetown the day of the Planters Council, starting out at three in the morning. Riding under a sky full of sparkling stars that seemed close enough to touch, they followed dark, silent paths into darker cane fields that rustled in the trade winds like heavy black silk. She wore a pistol in her belt. Drake did, too, and kept a loaded musket in the saddle sheath, a precaution not against runaway slaves, but against Jacka, Hastings, and Yates, who led the affingoes, with their burdens of molasses kegs and rum that gurgled in casks. Drake and Matthew Plum had convinced her to take the three convicts along. Not to do so would arouse suspicion; the task of taking the affingoes to and from her Speightstown and Bridgetown storehouses had always been theirs. Also, given the freedom of Bridgetown, they might tip their hand. But she was glad for Drake's company and for that of Sean and Valentine O'Brien. She'd also brought Jeremy and Marigold along.

Excited and unaware of trouble, Jeremy's and Marigold's voices rang in the darkness as cheerfully as cane sparrows.

Adventure-bound, they tramped along, heads bobbing. Parts of their conversation drifted to her ears.

"Are you truly going to be a wine merchant when you grow up, Jeremy?"

"Ay. Pro'lly in London. On Thames Street."

"That sounds grand, Jeremy."

"Ay. And after we're married, Marigold . . ."

They liked Drake. Well . . . so did she.

They reached Bridgetown by midmorning, and rented two rooms at the Nancy Belle—one for her and Marigold, the other for Drake and Jeremy. They hurriedly washed and dressed.

In her room, Edwinna unbraided her hair and brushed it out. It fell past her shoulders, long and thick. She felt a ripple of excitement while brushing, knowing Drake's gaze would be on her hair in that sensual way. She pulled on a gown, wishing she'd paid more attention to style and fabric and color, but those things had always bored her. Now she suddenly wished she had a fabulous gown.

She arranged the cracked looking glass so she could see herself and tugged the neckline down. She had good breasts, firm and full on a slender frame, and she had a sudden fierce urge to show them off. She tugged the green silk fabric lower. Dinny would be at Planters Council, all breasts and charming smiles. She still seethed whenever she thought of what Dinny had done with Drake.

There was a tap at the door.

"Ready, Edwinna?"

She took one last look in the glass and wrenched the door open. Washed, closely shaved, his hair carefully combed and clubbed back to the nape of his neck with a black velvet ribbon, Drake stood before her. He looked elegant in a new black suit, impeccably tailored to fit his wide shoulders and slender waist. He wore a white silk shirt, black silk stockings, and shoes of fine black leather. He looked like a London wine merchant.

She waited uneasily for his reaction to her.

"Well . . ." he said. She smiled at the admiration in his voice. A slight flicker of his black-lashed eyes made her guess her gown wasn't London fashion, but the warmth of his smile made that thought unimportant.

"You look lovely."

She smiled proudly.

The stairway of the Nancy Belle was narrow, in disrepair, and creaky. Drake went down first and at the street door gave her his arm. She took it. She'd never walked holding onto a man's arm before.

The Planters Council met six blocks away in another hastily erected Bridgetown building that served as both city hall and the island's jail. To enter the building, they had to pass through the jail—a stifling-hot place that clamored with noise and reeked with odor. White prisoners were locked in crowded cages. Blacks suffered worse. Stuffed into cages not three feet high, they crouched on hands and knees like animals, their tall bodies cramped in agony. Their eyes wore the hopeless glaze of death, for they had nothing to anticipate.

Edwinna's steps slowed in sympathy. Drake put a hand on her back and pushed her on. About to follow her through the doorway, he swept the jail with a last disgusted look, then started.

"Edwinna." He pointed at dark eyes filled with pain that gazed at them from a low cage. "It's the runaway I freed."

Uneasiness rippled through her. "Don't say anything. Don't tell anyone. It will stir up trouble for you and for Crawford Plantation."

"Poor bastard."

The Planters Council room was loud and noisy. Planters milled about, talking energetically, puffing on long clay pipes, swilling down kill-devil punch that they dipped from huge bowls set on the long meeting table. Of the twenty-five planters assembled, two in addition to Edwinna were women. Edwinna pointed out Lady Maud Locksley, who had a booming voice and smoked a pipe. Then there was Dinny, who spotted them at once and waved exuberantly from the opposite side of the room.

Edwinna didn't wave. She wanted to scratch Dinny's eyes out.

"Do you wish us to sit with her?" she asked stiffly, unable to keep the jealousy out of her voice.

"No. I've had enough of Dinny's company. I've no wish for more of it. Let's sit elsewhere."

Edwinna was gratified when the largest landowner on the island and council president, Mr. Drax of Drax Plantation, came immediately to meet Drake. Deeply worried about the bond slave situation in Barbados, he intended to address that issue first and asked Drake to speak to it.

Taking their seats at the table, Drake whispered to her, "I want to buy that runaway slave. Can that be done?"

Her eyes widened. "Yes. But why?"

"Poor devil. I feel a responsibility to him."

"I'll arrange it during dinner break. I'll find out who owns him. But . . . we'd best not make the offer ourselves. It might bring trouble down upon our heads."

"Can you ask Dinny to buy him for us?"

She wanted to say no, but she knew Dinny was the best choice. She could trust her to keep Drake's secret. She hesitated only an instant.

"Yes. I'll talk to Dinny. I know she will buy him for us. She can take him to her plantation. Then we can buy him from her. No one need ever know it was the runaway you freed."

"I like you."

It startled her. She felt the pulse flutter in her throat.

"I like you, too, Drake."

They shared a smile and she felt oddly breathless.

Drax called the assembly to order just as her uncle strode in. She gripped the edge of the table, prepared to do battle with him. Drake calmly covered her hand with his. Blistering them with a look, George Crawford seized a chair at the table's opposite end and sat, a hot, angry man. Wasting no time, he interrupted Drax.

"I refuse to sit at table with that—that pirate!" He indicated Drake with a jab of his thumb. "Crucial matters are decided here—matters of harvest, shipping. He will spy on us, send word to his fellow pirates, and we will lose everything we ship."

Edwinna jumped to her feet. "Drake Steel is not a pirate. He is a London wine merchant. He was a prisoner aboard that pirate ship. We are legally wed, and no one here can dispute it. Drake Steel is my—my—"

"Your husband, dearling," Dinny trilled, staunchly in her camp.

Edwinna rounded on her. "Dinny, you be quiet! He is my husband, not yours."

Drake yanked her to her seat, his face red. "Edwinna, shut up," he whispered angrily. "This is no place for a cat fight. Shut up, or so help me God I'll march you to the Nancy Belle and lock you in your room."

"I am only trying to defend you."

"I'll defend *myself*, speak for *myself*."

Edwinna sat back, put out with him. Her uncle was barreling on in his blustery way.

"A marriage of expedience," George Crawford accused. "So that *I* should be deprived of governing Thomas and Harry's plantation."

Lady Maud Locksley barked with laughter, pipe smoke snorting out of her nostrils. "And what marriage is not expedient? A man weds because he finds it expedient to hump a woman every night. A woman weds because it is expedient to have children. Go drench your head in the bucket of killdevil you crawled out of, George Crawford. I did not ride my rump sore traveling all the way to Bridgetown to listen to you wash Crawford family linen in public. Be done with it. I want to hear what Mr. Steel has to say to this bond slave trouble.''

Mr. Drax pounded his gavel on the table for order. "As do we all,'' Drax said. "Mr. Steel, will you speak to the issue?''

"Gladly."

"Here, here,'' the others said approvingly.

Her uncle seethed and sent dark looks everywhere, but no one cared. "That pirate freed a runaway slave. 'Tis against the law!''

"He did not!'' Edwinna burst. Drake gave her a warning look. She shut her mouth, but it was hard. She was used to giving orders, not taking them. A rumble went through the room. "Runaway slave? Freed a runaway?'' This was not liked. Edwinna wanted to strangle her uncle, making trouble like this for Drake. She couldn't hold her tongue.

"The slave had been badly tortured,'' she burst again. "Mr. Steel showed compassion freeing him.''

"Of course he did, dearling,'' Dinny trilled loudly, foursquare on her side of the issue.

"Edwinna!'' Drake snapped. She sat back.

Drax banged on the table to restore order. When the room grew quiet, Drake calmly addressed the assembly.

"First, Mr. George Crawford is correct. I freed a runaway slave. I will not apologize for it, and I will do it again if ever I come across a runaway in such a sorry state.'' Edwinna gasped, but he swung her a look. The rumbling undercurrent started again. "Second, I am *not* a pirate. I am a man of business, like yourselves—a London wine merchant. I was a prisoner aboard that pirate ship, not a pirate. Third, to the business at hand. Edwinna, her overseer, Matthew Plum, and I believe there may be a bond slave conspiracy afoot on this island.''

The room grew utterly silent. Small wonder. Convicts accounted for almost half the population of Barbados. The other half consisted of black slaves. The planting class was a slim, precarious minority and lived in daily danger of uprisings.

Taking his time, Drake described the midnight bond slave gathering he'd witnessed his last trip to Bridgetown, telling what he'd seen and heard. He reminded them of the letters he and Edwinna had sent, though they needed no reminder; they'd been worried for weeks. He took a list out of his pocket. "From your letters, the total number of weapons missing on the island are: ninety-six muskets, fifteen kegs of gunpowder, thirteen pistols, thirty-five bill-cane knives."

There was an uproar, everyone talking at once. Drax banged his gavel. Maud Locksley spoke above the noise in her rough, booming voice, "Then we can presume bond slaves are amassing weapons to fight against the governor's troops in an uprising."

"That is a logical assumption, yes."

Talk burst out all over the room. Still seething, George Crawford raised his voice louder than any. "Lies! This pirate merely wishes to ingratiate himself with us, worm his way in, become one of us. He wants to take over my nephews' plantation. He wants to become a wealthy planter, like us!"

"Maybe that's true," someone else shouted.

Edwinna had to bite her tongue to keep from leaping into the fray. Drake drew a breath that made his coat seams strain.

"You think I want to become one of you slave owners? God help me! I would not be one of you for anything in this world. Trafficking in human flesh. Sucking the life's blood out of human beings so you can get rich on sugar. Become one of *you*? I'd sooner be dead." Edwinna waited, breathless, scared for Drake.

Mr. Drax said sternly, "Your opinion of us, Mr. Steel, is neither here nor there. To the matter at hand . . ."

Drake drew a breath to calm himself. "I think," he said, "it is likely the conspirators will gather tonight. The date of

Planters Council has been set for months. It is likely the ringleaders are among the bond slaves you brought with you."

"Nonsense," Crawford blustered. "Tricks, lies."

"Ah, shut up," Maud Locksley boomed.

The meeting erupted with loud, hot talk. Everyone had something to say to the issue. When they'd talked heatedly for an hour, it was decided the planters would patrol Bridgetown that night, after midnight, searching for any clandestine bond slave gatherings.

A big blustery planter from St. Michael's Parish said, "Then let's march out and find 'em. All of us, with musket and pistol. Gather 'em up and string 'em up."

Drake smiled a little. "If we come marching through town like an army, they'll scatter like cane sparrows. Let's just a few of us go—say, a committee of ten. Ten men, paired off, won't be noticed. Twenty or thirty would be."

The planters agreed to it, and the morning session ended.

Edwinna was fiercely proud of Drake, but devastated for herself. *You think I want to become one of you slave owners? God help me! I would not be one of you for anything in the world.* When Drake Steel returned to London, he would not come back. She knew it.

CHAPTER
* 11 *

At midnight Drake slipped out of the Nancy Belle and into the dark street. Bridgetown lay black as a tomb except for several drinking houses where a candle burned and drunken seamen caroused. A rising moon hovered over the bay, its pale light reflected in a skimpy necklace of surf far out on the reef. Keeping to the shadows, he walked swiftly to the city hall to meet with the planters. He wore a pistol.

When he'd gone to Edwinna's room to tell her he was off, she was up, dressed in breeches, hair braided, pistol in her belt, ready to go with him. He'd had to argue with her to get her to stay behind. Reluctantly she'd agreed, but only after he'd pointed out that someone had to protect Jeremy and Marigold in case of trouble.

The door of the dark jail stood open. No one saw any point in locking it, evidently. There was no official jailer in Bridgetown, only a magistrate who, when he thought of it, sent his slaves to the jail with food. Drake had felt extremely proud at the end of the lavish council dinner when Edwinna had stood and bluntly ordered the serving men to collect all of the leftover food, take it to the jail, and dispense it to the prisoners.

He strode silently through the jail. The cage of his runaway stood empty. Edwinna had been faithful in that. She'd talked to Dinny, Dinny had talked to the owner, and, soused to the gills, the owner had readily sold the runaway, no doubt considering himself a clever businessman since the sick slave would surely die. Drake knew it, too. The smell of death had clung to the poor creature. But at least he would die on Crawford Plantation, in whatever slight comfort David Alleyne could provide.

Nine men assembled in the darkness of the council room. Drake had expected eight. To his irritation, George Crawford had come. He reeked of rum and began ranting the moment Drake walked in. "'Tis trickery. I see no conspiracy but this pirate's "

"Shut up," Drake snapped, "or by God, I'll knock you silent. You'll alert every bond slave in this town and give us away, if you have not already."

"Ay, Crawford," the others growled. "Shut up."

He glowered in silence. The men quickly paired off, deciding which sector of Bridgetown each would search. Crawford insisted on accompanying Drake and his partner. "To keep an eye on you, pirate."

"Then do it, but do it quietly," Drake warned, and Crawford reluctantly held his tongue.

They set off quickly, Drake and John Monyford, a husky planter from St. Michael's Parish. They strode toward the waterfront, heading for the sugar storehouse where Drake had seen the bond slave meeting.

Aside from Crawford's presence and his rum stink, the night was as lovely as any Drake had ever seen. Moonlight lay upon the entire crescent of Carlisle Bay. The surf rolled in with a murmur, whispering up onto the sand. The trade winds caressed his face. It was a night for love, not for hunting convicts. He thought of Edwinna and the softness of her hair.

In contrast to the moonlight on the sea, the narrow, smelly waterfront alleys and the storehouses lay dark as the bottom of a wine barrel. Rats ran underfoot. Bats swooped, hunting gnats and mosquitoes. A fruit bat with a wingspan a yard wide, swooped so close that it stirred the air in front of his face, then alighted in a papaya tree, folded its huge wings, and began to eat.

The planters searched the waterfront futilely. They saw nothing amiss—in fact, saw nothing moving but a horse that had managed to break free of its hobble and was munching tussocks of salty beach grass. It was a frustrating expedition. Drake had been so sure the conspirators would gather tonight.

"You see?" Crawford crowed to Monyford. "I told you we'd find nothing. Nothing, that is, but *pirate* trickery."

"Ah, Crawford. Be still," Monyford said.

Drake held his temper. "Let's go back." They strode to city hall, and in the dark council room compared results with the other returning pairs. Nothing.

"We represent nine major plantations. Let's each of us go to our own sugar storehouse and make sure every bond slave we've brought along is accounted for," Drake proposed. "We can report to one another in the morning when Planters Council resumes. If all of our bond slaves are where they should be at this hour of the night, well . . ." Drake raked a hand through his hair in frustration, "then, I'm at error, gentlemen."

"'Twas trickery from the start," Crawford charged. "A plot by my niece and this pirate to ingratiate themselves with the governor so that I be deprived of ruling my nephews' plantation."

"Stop it, Crawford," Monyford snapped. "We're sick of that old song. Let Edwinna be. We are all of us missing weapons on our plantations, and if that don't worry *you*, it damn well worries *me*."

Another said in the darkness, "I am missing three fifty-foot coils of rope from my supply house. 'Tis worrying. To what purpose would rope be stolen?"

"To hang someone," Monyford suggested.

"A dead chicken with its throat cut was left at my door," said another. "The blackguard who killed it took the blood and painted an X on my door."

"An X?" Drake said. "That might be significant. An African wouldn't make an X, would he?"

The man shook his head in the darkness. "Africans like to dabble in chicken blood and make their black magic—*if* they think they can get away with it, which they can't. I hanged a slave for making black magic last year, for it can turn the whole plantation upside down. Slaves fear magic. But they would not paint an X. It ain't a African symbol."

The planters talked a bit longer in frustration, then each headed for his own sugar storehouse to count heads. Drake loped the dark distance to Edwinna's storehouse, and when he got there, rapped on the bolted door. Two minutes passed, then Sean O'Brien's rough voice challenged, "Who's there?"

"Drake Steel, Sean."

Sean opened up at once. "What is it, sir?"

"I merely want to look about. Don't bother lighting a candle." Faint disappointment made Drake's shoulders droop when he saw the three most likely conspirators—Jacka, Yates, and Hastings—sound asleep on pallets near the door. It mystified him. He'd been so damned sure! He went farther into the storehouse, past huge, shadowy hogsheads, each capable of holding a ton of sugar. He found everyone accounted for. He went back to the Nancy Belle with a frown on his brow. It had been a wasted night's work.

The moment Drake Steel left, Jacka opened bright, feral eyes and smiled in satisfaction. George Crawford's drunken afternoon and loud yapping in the taproom at the Golden Anchor had easily alerted every bond slave in town. Waiting until Sean Valentine's lusty snores once more echoed through the storehouse, he viciously kicked Yates and Hastings in the leg to wake them.

"'Tis time," he whispered.

Rising, the three crept to the door. They eased the bolt and slipped out into the darkness, gliding through the shadows to the meeting at the bridge.

Dim candlelight spilled out from under Edwinna's door. Drake tapped softly.

"Yes?" she said warily.

"It's Drake, Edwinna."

She opened at once. "What happened?"

He put a finger to his lips and nodded at the youngsters sleeping in happy exhaustion in her room, Marigold in Edwinna's bed, Jeremy on a pallet on the floor. He gestured toward his room. She came at once, bringing the candle. She was still dressed, alert, ready, but she'd unbound her hair. It cascaded down her back, curly and thick. It gave him an indecisive moment. Did she want him or didn't she? He never knew what moves to make with her.

He took the candle from her and set it on a tottering, musty-smelling highboy that had seen better days, then motioned her to sit on the bed. She sat, her back stiff as a ramrod, knees together, hands clasped in her lap.

"What happened?"

"Nothing." He described the night in detail, including her uncle's interference. He told her about checking the storehouse and finding everyone and everything exactly as it should be. "Along about now, I doubt there's a planter who believes I saw what I saw last month in Bridgetown," he concluded.

"*I* believe you."

He smiled. "You're likely the only one."

"Never mind. What should we do next?"

He told her about the planters' plan to do the same search tomorrow night. Then he gazed at her.

Edwinna knew the instant his thoughts drifted. His long, swooping black lashes flickered, and he drew a deep breath. She got up from the bed quickly.

"It's late, and you're tired. I'll let you get to sleep."

"Edwinna . . ." he said gently.

Her rib cage heaved. She tipped her head back and to the side in an attempt not to look at him, not to see his desire.

"Edwinna . . . it would not be sin. We are legally wed."

"Drake—"

"We are two mature people. We are not children. We have a right to seek physical happiness."

"Drake—"

"Life is short, Edwinna. You of all people, know that. You see it on your plantation daily—birth, death. Life is so brief, the moments of joy so few. Why not take joy together? We respect each other. In these few months we've lived in the same house, we've learned to like each other."

He took a step toward her, then halted as she jerked back in fear, her elbow striking the bedpost.

"Edwinna? I would never hurt you."

"I know that."

"Then . . . why? Is there something else?"

Her heart thrashed.

"No!"

"I see." He drew a deep breath, composing himself, then looked at her.

"Drake, I know I owe you an explanation."

"Yes, you do," he agreed. "I am not a mind reader. My understanding goes only so far. Then it abandons me, and I stand here understanding nothing." He uttered a husky laugh. "If you want the truth, I feel foolish offering what you do not want."

"Drake, I'm sorry."

"Tell me," he urged. "I am an understanding man, Edwinna. I can understand."

"I—" She tightened. "There is nothing to tell."

He drew a breath. If she didn't wish to speak of it, it was her right. Again, that peripheral thought shimmered. Had she been raped? He thought of the day Clive Crawford had come to the plantation, how Edwinna had defensively held the sugar pot like a weapon.

"Take the candle," he said. "I'll see you safely into your room."

He found Marigold and Jeremy still asleep in their separate beds. Exhausted from their happy day, they'd hardly moved a muscle. Jeremy had flung a hand off the pallet. Drake squatted and tucked it back inside the sheet.

When he left, Edwinna went with him to the door.

"I'm sorry, Drake."

"So am I. It might have been wonderful, but you needn't worry. I won't bother you on that issue again. You have my word." She looked troubled, sad. He would give anything to know what kept her locked inside her sexual prison. He sighed, reached out, and touched her hair. She stiffened, but did not pull back.

"Braid your hair, Edwinna. Don't tease me anymore. Bolt the door."

"I—I will."

In the darkness of his room Drake pulled off his boots, then his shirt. With his head full of Edwinna and the futile attempt to find a bond slave conspiracy, he couldn't sleep. He planted a hip on the sill of his open window and let the trade winds cool and calm him. The window looked across the alley into an upper hall window of an inn.

As he sat there, a candle flame appeared in the dark hall, popping out of one of the sleeping chambers. Dinny's blatant red hair accompanied it. Wearing her chamber robe, she stole down the hall, carrying her candle, and disappeared. He supposed she was going out to the privy, but a few moments later she reappeared, tiptoeing down the hall with Jumbo in tow.

Drake's eyebrows shot up to his hairline. Looking furtively

to the right and the left, she took Jumbo into her room. The candlelight disappeared, the candle extinguished. For a moment he couldn't believe his eyes. He drew a horrified breath. For God's sake, she was sleeping with her slave!

The second day of Planters Council duplicated the first, and Drake grew impatient, bored. Planters swilled rum, argued sugar, drafted letters to Parliament that would never be read, and made lists of demands the governor of Barbados would never grant. Edwinna spoke boldly to every issue, as was her right. George Crawford tried his pirate nonsense again and made fun of last night's empty search.

Drake clenched his fists but did not raise his voice to argue. A business meeting was no place to air quarrels. He'd not done so in his business, nor would he in Edwinna's. It was all he could do to hold Edwinna down. She was angry enough to fly at her uncle.

That night Drake and the planters again patrolled Bridgetown. Again, they found nothing. Drake began to feel like a fool. Even the men who believed his story now eyed him askance. But one fact remained, and no one was willing to overlook it. Weapons were missing on every plantation on the island.

Drake, Edwinna, and their group left the next morning, reached Crawford Plantation by noon, and plunged into the round-the-clock work of harvest. For the next month, they labored in sun and darkness, in fair weather and foul, and even when migrating birds landed so thickly upon the cane fields that one could hardly see the green of the cane, let alone harvest it.

As Drake had expected, his runaway slave died, but at least he'd died in David Alleyne's kind care. Drake had no reason to be as upset as he was by it. He'd neither known the slave nor been able to communicate with him. They hadn't understood each other's language, but for a few moments on a cane path, they had shared an epiphany. Their eyes had met in brotherhood, and in that instant they'd become part of each other.

Edwinna had done a lovely thing for Drake as the slave lay dying in the hospital, breathing his last. She'd come in and put a sympathic hand on Drake's shoulder, and she'd left it there for him to reach up and pat and take comfort from. That evening, they'd gone for a walk together, their first. It was a bizarre walk, with each of them wearing a pistol, alert for bond slave trouble; but they strolled under the enormous starry sky, wandering far, talking gently, peacefully. Drake wondered whether to consider it the start of courtship.

Sitting at supper one night, the candle pulled near, he read Edwinna his latest letter. "Listen to this, from William: 'Dearest Papa. Send me a slave at once. He shud be like the one in Mistruss Edwinna's drawing. He shud be very tall and very black so as to put Aunt Verity into a fright. Then she will not make me eat groats or go to school. I hate school. Papa, come hom. Your luving son, William Drake Steel.' "

Edwinna laughed.

He read on, from Verity's letter. " 'Your Katherine, dear brother, adores Mistress Crawford's drawings of Priscilla. She insisted we mount the drawing on the nursery wall, where she kisses Priscilla good night before we put her to bed. Of course, she kisses the drawings of you, too.' "

Again Edwinna laughed.

He glanced up and smiled. He returned to his letter, but did not read the next part aloud.

As for Mistress Crawford, dear brother, she is in love with you, of course. It shows in her drawings. You have ever been a handsome man, but never so handsome or so noble as rendered by Mistress Crawford's pen.

Taken aback, he glanced at Edwinna. In love with him? He returned to his letter.

As to the nature of your feelings for Mistress Crawford, I can only speculate. You are a vexingly private man, brother mine. Your letters reveal precisely what you wish them to and not one iota more. You never have welcomed my advice in the past, nor will you welcome it now. Nevertheless, I give it. You will do well to cherish your Mistress Crawford. She sounds like a sensible woman who would never give you problems or grief.

His mouth tightened. The last was an unsubtle echo of Verity's dislike for Anne that even Anne's death had not tempered.

"Bad news?" Edwinna asked.

"No. It is only that my sister can be a vexing woman." Engrossed in receiving his own letters, he'd given no thought to Edwinna's. "Any letters from Thomas and Harry?"

"No. Next month. They will surely write next month."

"Surely," he agreed, but he wanted to knock Thomas and Harry's ungrateful young heads together.

Still worried about a possible bond slave insurrection, the planters kept in touch with one another by letter. Believing Drake's story about what Drake had seen and heard, Mr. Drax had alerted the governor.

At the Planters Council, the planters had devised a means of rapid communication. If an insurrection seemed imminent on any plantation, that planter immediately would write to his three nearest neighbors; those three immediately would write to their three nearest neighbors, and so forth, until all the plantations on the island were covered.

Meanwhile, disquieting reports came in. There had been a fire in Dinny's boiling house that had had no explicable cause. A grinder on a St. Lucy's Parish plantation had been chopped to pieces. Worse, a bond slave had been found mysteriously slain in a St. Michael's Parish cane field, an X carved in his chest.

The insurrection worry heightened. At Crawford Plantation the house pistols were kept loaded but locked in drawers safely away from Tutu, Priscilla, and Jocko. Meanwhile, the hard work of harvest ground steadily on. The mill rumbled night and day. Drake learned to deal with calamities, great and small, on a daily basis. The gate bell clanged every night. Some of the calamities were humorous. To spare Edwinna her sleep, Drake went down to answer the gate bell one night. He returned upstairs and whispered, to her inquiry, that the problem was nothing. Macaw's wife had given birth to twins.

She sprang up as if shot from a cannon. "Drake! If an African's wife gives birth to twins, he will hang her. He views twins as a sure sign that she has slept with some other men of the village."

"You jest."

"No!"

Edwinna threw on her clothes, and they ran through the dark, starry night to the slave village. Plum was already there, trying to reason with the big, ebony-skinned slave, but Macaw stood adamant. He intended to hang Juba, and that was that. No amount of talk by Plum, Alvis Nansellock, or Edwinna could persuade him she'd been anything but unfaithful.

"If he doesn't hang her now, he'll do it later when we're not around," Edwinna confided in Drake, worried.

Drake picked up the confiscated rope and gave it to Macaw with an approving nod.

"Go ahead, hang her. Do it." He turned to Nansellock. "Get another rope. As soon as Macaw hangs Juba, we'll hang *Macaw*."

Macaw's eyes grew enormous. He shook his head frantically. "I no hang her."

On the way back to the house, a sound suspiciously like a giggle came from Edwinna's throat.

Drake slanted a look at her. "You found that funny, did you?"

"Yes."

"And you're laughing at me."

"Yes."

They strode along in the fresh blowing trade winds, a heaven full of twinkling stars overhead. Now and then he caught a whiff of fragrant jasmine.

"So. How does an African punish his wife for laughing at him?"

"He refuses to sleep with her."

"That is your punishment, Edwinna. I refuse to sleep with you." He lifted a hand. "No, don't get down on your knees and beg. I'm adamant. I absolutely will not sleep with you."

"Drake!" She smiled. She wasn't a prude; he knew that. She wasn't a virgin; he sensed that, too. But the when and the who? Lord knew. Whatever had happened had left her emotionally wounded. He smiled gently. They had a pleasant walk to the house.

Upstairs, in the darkness of the hall, he said, "There is one more punishment for laughing."

"What's that?"

"A kiss."

Edwinna's heart began to pound. She wanted to kiss him. She suddenly wanted it more than she'd wanted anything, ever, in her whole life. She looked at his strong mouth. She felt as if a herd of affingoes were clattering through her chest. She couldn't breathe.

"Don't be afraid."

He took her hands and drew them to his chest, cradling them there. Her mouth trembled.

"Edwinna . . ." With a stifled moan, he leaned forward and took her mouth in his own. It was so sweet, so shocking a kiss, she felt helpless to move, didn't want to. Her eyes fluttered closed. He lifted his mouth and kissed each lid.

With a gentleness that threatened to undo her, he ran his tongue back and forth in an erotic rhythm over her lips. His body pressed along the length of hers, he began to move in the same way. Kissing her, he gently put his hand on the pulse on her neck, then trailed his hand down to her shoulder, down her arm.

"The conjugal bed," he whispered into her mouth. "Chaste . . . clean . . . committed . . ."

She drew back and shivered violently. The shiver started at the crown of her head and coursed all the way through her body. Trembling as if palsied, she crossed her arms and rubbed them fiercely.

"We had best get some sleep."

She went down the hall and into her room, shutting the door and locking it. Drake watched her go, touched again by her distress, yet suffering with his own unmet needs.

CHAPTER
* 12 *

Drake, Edwinna, and Matthew Plum were in the plantation office late one night when a wild, scared cry came from the backyard, just outside the kitchen door.

"It's Marigold!" Edwinna said. Drake wrenched open the desk drawer and grabbed a pistol. Edwinna grabbed the other. They ran. The kitchen lay dim and shadowy, lighted by the usual single tallow candle. They ran through it, out the open door, and into the backyard. Eerily lighted and cast with shadows by the candle old Scipio held high overhead, the house servants bunched close together, trembling. Drake ran forward, Plum and Edwinna following. Marigold stood in the eerie candlelight, red-eyed, sobbing, her mouth open, her flat chest heaving.

At Marigold's feet lay Jocko, his throat cut, his sweet little monkey face in repose. A bloody X had been carved on his small torso, from hairy chest to smooth belly.

Edwinna grabbed Marigold and pulled her close.

Marigold stammered, "I–I be goin' out to the privy. I stepped on 'im." She began to cry.

"It's not your fault, sweetheart." Edwinna crushed her close. Marigold buried her face in Edwinna's breast. "Scipio, Augustus," Drake said, "go inside and shut and bolt every storm shutter on every window." The old slaves nodded, their eyes large and scared. A glance convinced Drake that none of the servants had had anything to do with it. They all stared in utter horror. Big, fat Honor had tears in her eyes. Jocko had been her favorite—a placid fellow who never gave her a bit of trouble. Jeremy tried to be brave, but he was only thirteen. He mashed at his eyes with a grubby fist. Drake hated to speculate on what had happened to Priscilla. "Jeremy, go inside and help Scipio and Augustus." The boy nodded and gave him a throat-clogged, "Yes sir."

"Everyone inside," Plum ordered sensibly. "No one uses the privy tonight. The doors stay locked. Use a chamber pot."

"Where is Kena?" Edwinna demanded. "And Tutu?"

"Here, Mama." Wide-eyed, Kena stepped out of the shadows, rocking Tutu, keeping his fuzzy little head averted from the awful sight. Edwinna reached out and hugged them. Drake and Plum shepherded everyone inside, and Edwinna sent Kena upstairs with Marigold and Tutu, to put them to bed in the safety of her own room.

Edwinna rejoined the men, pale but calm, her eyes somberly on Drake's. She didn't ask about Priscilla; larger things were at stake than a beloved pet. They went into the office to confer in private as storm shutters were banged shut all over the house. With each shutter that clunked closed, the noise of the grinder grew more distant.

"Edwinna," Drake said tensely, "I want you to make sure that the pistols and muskets in the house are loaded. Keep them ready. Keep the doors and windows locked. Let no one in except David Alleyne. I will send him up to you. If there is any trouble, fire a musket. We'll come at once."

"Yes. And you?"

"Plum and I are going to take Jocko's body down to the mill, roust the slaves and bond slaves out of their huts, and question them."

"Can it wait until morning?"

"No."

"Strike while the iron is hot," Plum put in. "Mr. Steel and I agree. There's no telling if this is a scare tactic or if it's the start of an uprising."

Edwinna grew paler, but nodded. Already a St. Lucy's Parish planter had been scared into leaving his plantation and going to Bridgetown. He'd left his harvest in the hands of his overseer. "Shall we shut down the mill for tonight?" she asked sensibly. "Stop boiling and close down the grinder?"

"No," Drake and Plum said in unison. Drake went on, "It would only prove they'd managed to scare us, whoever 'they' are. The question now is which of your bond slaves are trustworthy enough to be armed. What about your overseers, Plum—Nansellock, the O'Brien's, McCarran?"

"Give 'em a keg of rum and they'll drink themselves stupid. Let 'em spot a guinea lying in a street and they'll not overstrain themselves seeking the owner. They're no more criminal than that."

"Then you say arm them."

"Arm them."

"Edwinna?"

"Yes. They should be armed. Their lives may be in danger, too."

Drake looked at her with admiration. Even at a time like this, when her plantation and perhaps her own life were in danger, she had consideration for bond slaves.

"Then let's get busy." While Edwinna ran through the shadowy house to get toweling to wrap Jocko's body, Drake and Plum checked shutters, carrying a candle from dark room to dark room. Drake had a private moment with Edwinna when she came running back with the bundled sheet.

"Drake, take care."

"You, too. Look after yourself and the children."

"I will." She looked so numb that he took her in his arms and held her for a moment. She nestled in his embrace and he brushed her hair with his lips.

"Steady as she goes."

"I'm all right, but I'm glad you're here."

"So am I. There is nowhere else I want to be at this moment. I want to help you through this mess. We'll solve it."

Her strong hand curved around his wrist. Then she went to prepare her firearms.

Jeremy waited at the door. He'd manfully conquered his tears, but didn't know his dirty face was streaked with them. "I'll go wi' you, sir. T'help find them what killed Jocko."

"You're needed here, Jeremy. I want you to take care of Mistress Edwinna and Marigold and the rest."

"Ay." He straightened proudly. "I'll take care of 'em, sir."

"I also have a task for you. It might be scary."

Jeremy nodded bravely. "I'll do 'er, sir."

"Good. I'm going to lock the front gate and take the key with me. Mistress Edwinna has another key. When Doctor Alleyne comes to the gate and calls out and you're certain it's he, I want you to run to the gate, unlock it, and let him in. Then lock it again and get back into the house as fast as you càn. Can you do that?"

"Ay, sir, I can," Jeremy said emphatically. "Mr. Steel? Where d'ye think Priscilla is?" A tremor shook his voice.

"She's a smart little thing," Drake said gently. "She likely took off into the trees the instant she got scared. Jocko was slower, that's all." Jeremy nodded, swallowing.

A few minutes later, he and Plum grimly wrapped Jocko's body and hurried down the dark path. Drake cast one last, worried look at Crawford Hall, its windows tightly shuttered.

"Don't worry. Edwinna can shoot," Plum said. "I taught her myself when she was but a girl."

"But *will* she shoot?"

"She will. She loves Kena and Tutu mightily. She'll protect them if she has to shoot every bond slave on the plantation."

"Let's hope so," Drake said tightly.

At the millworks, they laid Jocko on the ground in torchlight and made the slaves, who shook in fright, and the bond slave convicts, who stared with hard sullen eyes, come forward one at a time to look at the body and be questioned. They raked Jacka, Yates, and Hastings with questions. The three swore they'd been asleep all evening, and Sean Valentine, whom Drake and Plum tended to trust, verified it. It was frustrating.

Drake left Jocko's burial to a slave and returned to the house in the darkness before dawn. Moonlight lay upon the tops of the cane as beautifully as it had lain upon Carlisle Bay a month earlier, but tonight he saw only ugliness.

Kena and David Alleyne let him in—Kena with a slender finger to her lips. Everyone was asleep, including Edwinna, she said. He quietly climbed the stairs and went to Edwinna's room. The door stood open. Marigold and Tutu slept in Edwinna's bed. Jeremy slept on a pallet on the floor. Edwinna had nodded off sitting up in a leather armchair, legs drawn up and curled under her. Her pistol lay on a table at her elbow, her musket on the floor.

He hesitated. He'd never entered her room before. But she would want to know what had happened. He quietly went in and squatted beside her.

"Edwinna," he whispered. Exhausted from her vigil, she slept on. He touched her arm. "Edwinna."

She woke like a crazed woman, lunging away from him. "Don't!"

Astonished, he whispered, "Edwinna. It's Drake."

"Don't," she begged. "Don't do it to me. Don't!"

It stunned him. "Edwinna, it's me, Drake—Drake."

She was still asleep. "Drake?" Her lungs pumped violently. Then, by degrees, she seemed to waken. "Drake," she whispered, lucid. She brushed at her hair with a trembling hand.

"I wanted to tell you about our night," he said gently. "Let's go down to the kitchen and have Honor make us some of that Brazilian coffee. You look as if you could use it."

"Yes."

He drew her to her feet and held her lightly in his arms for a moment, his lips in her hair. *Don't do it to me. Don't.* What had she meant? He was afraid to speculate—afraid he didn't want the answer.

Exhausted himself, he went to bed and slept until noon, then rose, washed, dressed, and went out to the fields. He and Plum had agreed they must carry on as usual. Jeremy came with him, staying so close that Drake almost tripped over him every time he turned around. The boy had been thoroughly frightened.

They were out in a freshly cut cane field with Jacka and Hastings, who were loading cut cane on the affingoes, when Jeremy remarked, "Y'know that there X, Mr. Steel? What was carved on Jocko? I seen it somewheres."

Drake looked at him with interest. "Where?"

"I dunno. Somewheres. I can't r'member."

Drake's interest, which had risen, waned. An X was a common signature among bond slaves who could neither read nor write. That's where Jeremy probably had seen it. "If you remember, tell me."

"I will, sir," Jeremy said enthusiastically. Jacka and Hastings stared at the boy.

Two days and two nights passed without repetition of the bloody incident, but Plum, Drake, and Edwinna didn't relax. The situation was too damned scary. They had taken the overseers into their confidence, and the men now wore muskets in slings over their backs by day, and slept on pallets in Plum's small house, weapons at hand.

Tensions ran high. Although Priscilla failed to come back, Edwinna continued to hold out hope that she would. Drake thought her optimism about as futile as her hope of receiving a letter from Thomas and Harry. The strain of it all ran so deep that Edwinna grew haggard-looking and Drake worried about her.

Trouble started unexpectedly and from a direction no one could have predicted. Washed, shorn of his sticky, juice-spattered cane field clothes, and freshly changed, Drake came down the stairs to supper in the already darkening dining chamber. The sun had just set, and with rain clouds gathering in the sky all day long, the sunset's afterglow blazed spectacularly. He was at the window watching the end of it, appreciating the savage beauty of the island, when Edwinna came striding from the kitchen.

"Drake. Marigold and Jeremy have not come back to supper."

"The scamps. They were told to be back before sundown. I don't want them out after dark—not with all this going on."

"I know. I sent Kena down to the millworks to inquire, and it seems they haven't been seen all afternoon."

Drake frowned. Determined to find Priscilla, the two children had been granted permission to search for her, so long as they did not set foot off the plantation and so long as they finished their daily duties first. Positive they would find her, they'd bolted through their chores by noon and had run off hand in hand.

"I'll look for them."

"I'll go with you."

"No. It's going to rain. There's no point in both of us getting soaked. They're likely in the fruit groves. Jeremy was sure he'd find Priscilla in the fruit trees. You stay here—in case of other trouble. The house guns are loaded?" She nodded.

Out of doors, Drake took off at a lope, using what was left of daylight. Now and then an isolated raindrop spattered the ground. He glanced at the sky. It was going to pour in an hour or two.

Moving faster, he loped down a cane path through a ten-acre field of ripe cane. Now and then, a fat, heavy raindrop hit the tough cane tops with a loud crack. It sounded like a musket ball. The path emerged at the cattle pond. He ran past the pond to the fruit groves—five acres of plantain, banana, paw-paw, guava, breadfruit. Thick, impenetrable castor bean hedges fenced each fruit grove, deliberately planted to keep cattle and pigs out.

Darkness had already gathered in the groves. He stopped to catch his breath and shout their names. "Jeremy, Marigold?" Nothing. He moved on. He saw raindrops hit a silken ribbon that was caught on a castor bean hedge, and when he yanked it out of the hedge and saw that it was Marigold's pink ribbon—the ribbon Jeremy had bought her in Bridgetown—he grew scared.

Go back for help? No time. Wild boars sometimes roved here, attracted by the fruit. Frightened for the children, he leaped over the wooden stile into the next grove. A frustrating hour passed before he'd covered all the groves. By then the sky was black, and the rain fell steadily. His hair, his shirt, his breeches clung to his skin, cold and prickly.

It was going to be a tropical deluge.

He could scarcely see through the curtain of falling rain, so he ran toward the mill, his feet slipping and sliding on the slick, muddy cane paths. He'd almost reached the mill when a barrage of gunfire split the air. For a moment he froze, disoriented in the rain, unable to tell where the shots had come from. Then he knew—the mill.

He'd brought neither pistol nor short sword. He'd been so sure he'd find the children in a matter of minutes. A second barrage of gunfire cracked in the air, again from the mill. He veered in the opposite direction, back toward the house. Edwinna! Plum and the O'Briens and Nansellock would have to defend themselves at the mill. God help them. He strained to hear the grinder over the sound of the pounding rain and couldn't.

The gate of Crawford Hall stood open, which made his chest pound. Stormy gusts of wind could have blown the gate open if Edwinna had left it unlocked for him. The house lay dark, sensibly shuttered from the inside. He ran through the puddled yard to the front door and banged on it. It was locked. Rain drumming on the roof drowned out his banging.

He ran through the mud, past wind-whipped trees, to the back of the house. There, too, all lay dark, shuttered. Weak light from the kitchen candle outlined the seams of the shutters. The upstairs windows were dark, not even a glimpse of candle showing. He found the kitchen door bolted. He banged on it and shouted, identifying himself. "It's Drake—let me in, Edwinna." He waited, hunching his shoulders against the rain, water drizzling down his neck. Odd they should take so long.

Finally, the door swung inward as Scipio opened it. He plunged inside. "Get Mistress Edwinna. There's shooting at the mill." He shook the rain off, then looked up and into the barrel of a pistol. His heart stopped. Pointing the pistol was Jacka, arm outstretched, thin, slack hair wet and plastered to his head, eyes gleaming.

"Come in, Mr. Steel."

His heart surged with fear. He swept the room with a look, taking in everything in an instant. The kitchen was dim and cavelike, and beyond it the house lay dark. A candle guttered on the kitchen table, casting moving shadows. Yates stood at the fireplace, his musket barrel held to Kena's temple. Huge-eyed, she stood absolutely still, Tutu clutched to her breast, wrapped in her shawl. Tutu began to wail. The other servants stood with backs to the wall, frozen in fear: Honor with her fat mouth open and rounded in shock, Scipio blinking, Augustus shaking. When Augustus moved, his old knees buckling, Yates swung the musket at him, then back at Kena.

Everyone gasped. Drake held his breath. A bead of water trickled down the musket butt. The powder in the pan was probably wet and wouldn't fire. Even so, Kena, Tutu! The men hadn't been in the house long. Rainwater still dripped from their clothes and hadn't had a chance to puddle on the floor.

"What do you want?"

"Your life, Mr. Steel. And Mistress Edwinna's."

"She's gone."

Jacka gave him a vicious look. In the dim candlelight Jacka's eyes gleamed as red as a cane field rat's at night. "Search the house," he snarled at Yates.

Honor piped up, "'Tis true. Mistress Edwinna be gone ter Lady Fraser's. Left b'fore supper."

Drake sent her a swift look. Truth or lie? Maybe Edwinna *had* gone looking for Jeremy and Marigold. He'd told her to stay in the house, but it would be like her to go anyway.

Drake's muscles tensed. Doglike, Yates waited for Jacka's decision. Jacka threw Honor a fierce, indecisive look, then snarled at Yates, "Stay here. Keep your musket on that black bitch sister o' Mistress Edwinna's. She's the one we'll kill if anybody makes one false move. Her and her brat." Kena was crying now and gripping Tutu, trying to cover him with her arms, protect him. Tutu wailed. "Shut 'im up," Jacka snarled, "or I'll have Yates shut 'im up wi' a musket butt." Tears flowing down her cheeks, Kena frantically patted him.

Drake trembled with the urge to spring, but the musket barrel rested on Kena's temple. Jacka's wet sleeve bound his pistol arm. He yanked at the sleeve with his teeth, and at that instant Drake saw it—a scar on the inside of his forearm, a perfectly carved X.

"Now, me luvs." Jacka cast his rat eyes over the shaking servants. "Yer going ter watch me kill yer master. B'cause he ain't yer master no more. *I* be yer master. This be *our* plantation now, *ours*. It belongs to us bond slaves. This be *our* island. All over this island, bond slaves be risin' up. Throw in yer lot wi' us and you live. If not . . ." He smiled cruelly.

"I'm wi' yer," Honor said promptly. Jacka growled, "Then go stand at the other wall, you fat bitch." Honor jumped to obey—all three hundred pounds of her. Scipio and Augustus jumped, too, and cowered near Honor, shaking.

Kena stood alone, weeping, clutching Tutu.

"Kena," Drake said quietly, his tension rising so high the blood beat in his head. "Go with Honor." If he could get the musket barrel off her temple, he would take his chances and spring.

She didn't understand.

"Well?" Jacka demanded of her. "Are y' with us or not? You'll be a pretty thing in my bed . . ."

She stood there weeping. A soft cry broke from her throat. "No!"

"She's had her chance," Jacka snarled at Yates. "Shove 'er to that other corner. We'll keep 'er alive until we tire o' spreadin' her legs. Then you can kill 'er." Brutal and dumb, Yates salivated at the prospect. Fury ignited in Drake as Yates gave Kena such a vicious shove that she fell to her knees, Tutu with her. Tutu screamed and wailed. She clutched him and crawled into the corner, crouching over him, protecting him with her own body.

"Now, Mr. Steel. Rob me of me runaway slave reward, will yer?"

Drake counted his own heartbeats. Jacka slowly cocked his elbow, relishing, preparing to take better aim. Dying a thousand deaths, Drake waited to spring. Suddenly a loud crack split the air. A pistol shot reverberated through the kitchen like thunder. The sulfuric smell of burnt gunpowder filled the room, thick and gritty. Kena screamed and covered her ears. Jacka's face froze in utter surprise. He rocked forward for a moment, then fell and crashed to the floor. He lay unmoving, blood welling from the back of his shirt.

Stunned, Yates hadn't time to react. Drake sprang at him and grabbed the musket with both hands, slamming him into the wall, ramming the length of musket barrel into his Adam's apple. Yates clawed at the musket, choking, strangling. Honor came rushing, grabbed an iron cook pan from where it hung on the wall among her kitchen utensils, and, putting all of her three hundred pounds behind the blow, bashed it across his face. Blood flew. Yates's nose moved to the side of his face. He uttered a choking scream. Drake threw him to the floor.

"Sit on him, Honor."

She didn't sit—she dropped her weight upon him like an anchor dropped from a ship. A kneecap snapped. Yates screamed in agony.

Drake sprang to Edwinna, who stood in the dark hallway, the pistol barrel still smoking, her face white, her lips an ashen blue. She held a second pistol in her left hand. With a look of primitive fury, she sprang across the room to Yates and leveled a pistol at his head. Drake had to grab her wrist and wrench the pistol out of her strong grip. He set it aside and shook her by the shoulders until sanity flowed back into her wild eyes.

"Edwinna, reload the pistol. Bring the other loaded pistols. We don't yet know what is happening."

"Yes."

"You're all right?"

Her ashen lips had to work to form the answer. "Yes. What is happening at the mill?"

"I don't know. Shooting."

"I must go at once." She lunged for the door and he had

to drag her by the shoulders and swing her around into his arms. "Edwinna! Do as I said. Get all the house pistols." It was hard to get through to her. She was shocked, numb. Finally, she looked up at him and nodded.

Drake returned to Yates, who moaned under Honor, while Kena wept in relief, rocking Tutu in her arms. Tutu was wailing inconsolably, understanding none of this. Scipio and Augustus still stood at the wall, stunned. Drake grabbed Yates's left arm and wrenched the sleeve back. Nothing. He grabbed the right and found a scar—an X carved deep into the skin.

"Yates, what does the X mean?"

"Tain't nothin'. Git 'er off'n me."

"Honor, bounce on his knees." She did.

Yates shrieked. "The X is a sign of them what's takin' over the island. Me knees are broke. Git 'er off me!"

"How many on this plantation?"

"I dinno."

He nodded. "Honor?"

"Nay," Yates shrieked. "'Tis Jacka, Mule, Slay, Hastings 'n' me."

"Who else?" There was too much gunfire in the heavy rain for it to be only three others.

"I dinno."

"Honor?"

"Nay! I dinno," Yates begged in a shriek. "Jacka, he kept it secret. We met at night, wi' hoods over our heads."

Drake sat back on his heels, inclined to believe him. It corroborated what he'd seen in Bridgetown. "But they will all carry an X on the forearm?" Yates nodded. "What about the other plantations? Are they all linked?" Yates was moaning now, shaking in intense pain. He nodded. "Is it the plan to strike on every plantation tonight?"

"I dinno!"

"Honor?"

"Nay! Git 'er off'n me," he begged, shrieking. "'Tis the

plan t' strike tomorrow night. But Jacka, he had t' strike t'night b'cause the boy, Jeremy, he seen the X on Jacka's arm 'round midday t'day and he were goin' t' tell."

Drake closed his eyes and drew a ragged breath that shuddered all the way through him. God. "Jeremy and Marigold—where are they, you son of a bitch?"

"I dinno," Yates screamed. "Jacka took 'em off somewheres. I dinno where—I swear to God. Git 'er off me!"

Drake sprang to his feet and grabbed the musket. Yates would not be able to crawl, let alone walk, but he intended to take no chances. "Scipio, Augustus. Spread his hands out on the floor, palms down, and hold his wrist tightly." The scared, shaking old slaves jumped to.

Yates shrieked. "Don' shoot me! What're you goin' to do?"

Drake hefted the musket overhead like an ax and brought it smashing down on Yates's hand. Bones shattered. Yates screamed in agony and tried to roll away. "Hold his other hand." Scared to death, Scipio and Augustus jumped to do his bidding. Drake lifted the musket and smashed the second hand. "You can get up now, Honor. He'll go nowhere." She did so heavily, rolling off his knees, and Yates's screams rent the roof. He rolled away in agony.

Edwinna came running back to the kitchen with the loaded pistols and placed them on the table. White-faced, she averted her eyes from Jacka's body. It was beginning to dawn on her that she'd killed a man. The blood pooling around the body had formed a small lake. It smelled sweet, sickish.

He took her gently by the shoulders. "Edwinna, you'll have to be in charge here."

"I'm going to the mill."

"No! I'll go to the mill and help Plum and the others. You stay here, locked in. Guard the others."

"Yes. All right." Amid the gripping tension, his frazzled mind strayed. Anne never would have been able to do this. He quickly told all he'd learned from Yates—the incriminating scars, the general uprising that was planned for tomorrow.

"You'll have to gather your wits, sit down, and write the planters at once—the three neighbors who are in our chain to notify. Put the letters in waterproof cases, for they must go tonight, storm or no."

"Yes."

He turned to the slaves. "Scipio, you will take the letter to Mr. John Monyford's plantation. Don't be afraid. Keep to the edge of the cane path and no one will see you. Augustus, you will carry two letters—one to Lady Dinny Fraser, which you will deliver first, and the second to George Crawford's plantation. I want them to sign a note that they have received it, and you will bring the note back to me. Do you understand?"

They looked scared to death, but nodded.

His jaw tightened. "If you fail to do any of this—" He glanced at Yates. "I will do to *you* what I did to him. Do you understand?" They nodded.

He turned back to Edwinna. Unmindful of the servants, he took her face in his hands and gave her a hard kiss on the lips. She'd saved his life. He felt so much for her at this moment he could scarcely contain it.

"I'll be back."

"Yes. I know you will, Drake."

He stayed off the main path and ran to the mill by a circuitous route that took him first up to the windmill on the hill, then down to the millworks. Rain continued steadily, but the high winds had eased. The shooting had ceased by the time he got to Plum, and he found the competent, unruffled overseer patrolling the mill area with the Valentine brothers, Nansellock, McCarran, and David Alleyne—all of them armed with musket and pistol. He quickly told them what had gone on at the house. Covering the grounds by torchlight, they found abandoned weapons on the ground. The convicts had not taken rain into consideration. With the powder wet and useless and the muskets unable to fire, they had panicked. They'd abandoned their shooting pieces and run away. Some no doubt had fled the plantation, but Drake and Plum thought it likely the others would duck into huts and pretend they had been there all along, totally uninvolved.

Plum immediately ordered torches lighted in the boiling house. He sent his overseers to roust out the bond slaves, hut by hut. They were brought in one at a time, nervous, most of them frightened from the shooting and frightened of Plum. Whenever Drake and Plum and Sean Valentine discovered an X carved into a man's forearm, they clamped him in shackles—hand irons, leg irons, and an iron dog collar— and threw him into the furnace cellar beneath the boiling house floor.

Many begged pitifully, claiming Jacka had threatened to kill them if they did not join him. Drake and Plum believed them, but had no pity. Guilt was guilt. The bond slaves had their chance. They could have reported Jacka. In all, the patrollers found thirteen men with X's gouged into their forearms. The hair on the back of Drake's neck prickled. Good God, the family had been in even more danger than he and Plum had suspected.

Up at the house, Drake and Plum dragged Jacka's body out of the kitchen and dumped it in the yard like garbage. Thoughtful of Edwinna, Kena immediately took bucket and brush and scrubbed away every trace of blood, while David Alleyne tended to Yates—not with his usual compassion, but with a savage roughness Drake had never seen in the young doctor. Incensed that Yates had held a loaded musket to Kena's head, David did nothing to alleviate Yates's pain and bound the splints to the screaming man's knees with wrenching jerks that made even Drake wince.

Plum, Alleyne, Edwinna, and Drake sat up the night in the plantation office, drinking Brazilian coffee, waiting tensely for whatever else might happen. Drake held Edwinna's outstretched hand on the table. Outwardly she seemed composed, sitting erect, her head high, her lips pale but untrembling. Now and then, she threw Drake an acute look to reassure herself he was alive. Her eyes bore a glaze, as if they were made of pottery, as she maintained an artificial calm, containing by force of will the utter shock of having killed someone. He brought her hand to his lips and pressed a kiss to her palm. She scarcely noticed.

Plum and Alleyne and he avoided the subject of Jeremy and Marigold. Edwinna would disintegrate. She'd loved those children. Drake was in anguish himself.

The night passed slowly while they waited for the dawn, and for Scipio and Augustus to return. Plum kept things on an even keel, speaking in his calm voice, suggesting the millworks be closed down until the crisis passed, that search parties of slaves and bond slaves be sent out at the crack of dawn. Tactfully, he refrained from saying for whom or what they would search. Drake's chest tightened.

Scipio returned in the midst of the downpour, and they rushed to the kitchen to hear his report while Kena gave the elderly slave a warming dram of rum. Scipio's note said Monyford was dispatching word to his nearest three neighbors at once and also to Magistrate Tarcher, who would notify the governor in Bridgetown. According to Scipio, Monyford, his three tall, grown sons, and his overseers had armed themselves at once, then taken torches and shackles and marched for the bond slave huts to search out and chain up any man with an X on his arm.

Augustus returned an hour after Scipio, and they listened to his alarming report in the kitchen while Kena fed him rum. Dinny Fraser's house had been set afire by three bond slaves, but the rain had put out the blaze, and Dinny's overseer had caught the bond slaves in the act. Under torture, the bond slaves had confessed and named others involved. They'd been shackled hand and foot and thrown into the pit under the boiling house, but no one could find Dinny.

"Dinny," Edwinna whispered. "We have to search for her!"

"We will." Worry knifed Drake, too. Dinny was outrageous, a bawdy wench, but he liked her. Everyone on the island liked her.

Augustus reported that at George Crawford's plantation, Clive Crawford had laughed at the note and George Crawford had been so drunk he'd come weaving across the floor as though he were walking in a cane field furrow. He'd taken the note, read it, and torn it up. "Tricks," he'd shouted. "Another trick by my niece and that pirate. Get out of here, get out!" Augustus had been glad to go. He'd run, scared of George Crawford.

"The blind fool," Drake said.

"He's my uncle," Edwinna said, worried.

"He's chosen his course, Edwinna," Plum said firmly. "So has Clive. Let them bear the consequences of it. You have warned them. You owe them nothing more."

The rain stopped just before dawn. Equipping themselves with pistols and muskets, they went down to the millworks to organize the search for Jeremy and Marigold. Drake and Plum both had urged Edwinna to stay home. She was exhausted. She refused with fire in her eyes and insisted on joining the search. Scared for her—she looked to be at the breaking point—he and Plum conferred and decided it best to let her come along. Concentrating on another problem might push Jacka from her mind.

Search parties of slaves and bond slaves set off at dawn through the wet, dripping cane paths. Drake, Plum, and Edwinna went by horse, riding up to Cherry Point, where they could look down over the rough, white-capped Atlantic. They searched for hours along every likely path. Edwinna would not give up.

At noon they spied the two children, sitting roped to the trunk of a tree. Their arms were wrapped around each other. Their throats were cut. They were dead.

CHAPTER

* 13 *

Plum and Drake buried the children at the foot of a sunny, flower-covered wall in the yard at Crawford Hall. Edwinna wanted them near. Drake, fearing for her sanity, agreed. He lifted the bodies into hastily built coffins—young children, once so full of bright, lively promise, they now lay ashen, unmoving.

He glanced at Edwinna with worry. She stood watching every step of the burial process, stiff, white-faced, silent.

When the last shovelful of dirt had been mounded on the graves and when Kena, weeping, had drawn down some of the cerise and purple flowering vines and spread them over the graves, Edwinna said in an unnatural voice: "I want a whip."

Drake felt the hair on the back of his neck prickle. He looked at Plum, whose expression was grimly flat, leaving the matter to him. Drake leaned his shovel against the garden wall and moved toward her.

"Edwinna," he said gently.

"I want a whip," she demanded, fists clenched, expression wild and fiery. "Get me a whip. I'm going to flog every one of them until they're dead."

Kena backed away, weeping, her hands clenched to her mouth.

Drake put a hand on Edwinna's shoulder. She slapped it away.

"I want a whip!"

"Edwinna, the bond slaves will be punished for what they've done. They will be sent to Bridgetown in shackles, tried in a court of law, and punished."

She scorched them all with a look of fury.

"If you won't get me a whip, I'll get one myself. My father kept them in the windmill."

Kena wept. Edwinna whirled and bolted. Drake ran with her, trying to no avail to take her elbow, dissuade her, calm her. He could easily have stopped her, but not without strong measures, and he was afraid that in her fragile state she would shatter if he used force. So he ran beside her as, with the speed of a deer, she took a path uphill through a field of young cane.

When she reached the towering stone windmill, she wrenched the wooden door open and lunged inside. The windmill was a tall cone of solid stones with slits in the stone facing for windows. Enormous beams and pipes lay across the circular dirt floor. Old, dank cupboards and storage chests lined the walls. She searched through them like a madwoman, throwing open doors and sending storage lids crashing. The stone walls reverberated with the noise.

"Edwinna . . ." His heart pounded.

She paid him no heed. Finally, she found what she wanted in a tall, upright cupboard, the door of which she sent crashing into the wall. She reached in and pulled out a whip. It was a cat-o'-nine-tails, a vicious instrument with nine braided leather strips, a pellet of lead embedded in each tip. A shadow fell across the sunshine that streamed in the door. With gratitude, Drake looked and saw that Plum had followed them.

Edwinna held the whip in her hands, panting, looking at it. Then, as though it were a snake, she dropped it with revulsion, and backed away from it, her fists clenched to her mouth.

"Oh my God, I am like my father, I am like my father."

"No, Edwinna," Plum said calmly, his voice echoing in the stone chamber. "You are not like him. You are different. The difference is that he would have used the whip, you will not."

She gave them a frenzied, exhausted look. Drake reached for her, but she pushed past him, ducked out the door, and ran toward Crawford Hall, more slowly now, wearily. Drake started to go after her. Plum stopped him.

"Let her be, Mr. Steel. She was like this when her father died. Near broke my heart. But let her be. She needs to be alone to grieve."

"Needs it? It's damned lonely grieving alone. When my wife died . . ."

"Edwinna is used to being alone." He tapped his heart. "In here she is alone. She always has been."

Sorrow pierced Drake. He wanted to comfort her. He needed comforting himself. He felt so guilty about Marigold and Jeremy.

"Damn it to hell! You once suggested putting the torture iron to Jacka and getting the truth out of him. If only I'd let you."

"Nay," Plum said bluntly. "'Twasn't just you, 'twas Edwinna, too. You've that in common, the two of you—overmuch respect for human life. As for me? I've no respect for it. It's my experience that most of humanity—black *and* white—isn't worth the powder to blow them to hell. Now, uprising or no, Mr. Steel, we've a plantation to run."

* * *

The planters of Barbados crushed the insurrection in two weeks. They did so ruthlessly. A St. Lucy's Parish planter rounded up the guilty on his plantation, locked them in a windowless hut, nailed the door shut, chopped a hole in the roof, poured in two barrels of kill-devil rum, and tossed in a torch. The hut went up with a roar, flames incinerating the rebels.

The instant the news of the insurrection reached Bridgetown, the governor dispatched troops and militia. They swept the island, hunting down escaped rebels. In all, 259 bond slaves, a dozen of them women, collected from plantations all over the island, were marched into Bridgetown in shackles, put on trial, found guilty, and condemned to death by public execution.

Drake worried about Dinny. He and Plum sent out search parties and searched themselves. Her overseer had put down the uprising on her plantation, but she'd vanished. Everyone worried that she'd been killed. Drake did not, however, waste a moment's worry about George and Clive Crawford; and when news came that they'd been slain, Drake felt a savage satisfaction that he hadn't realized he was capable of.

Edwinna remained his worry. She stayed shut in her room for two days. "Let her be," Plum continued to counsel. Drake did so, but unwillingly. She'd saved his life. The least he could do was comfort her.

The uprising left the plantation in chaos for those first two days. Terrified of "boom sticks," frightened first by the shooting and then by the armed troops and militia marching across the plantation, the Africans cowered in their huts.

Drake and Plum set to work bringing order. They sent the women out into the cane fields to resume their weeding. Everyone pitched in to clean up the mill. After three days on the grinding platform in the rain and then in the hot sun, a ton of cut cane had rotted, and stank to high heaven. It had to be shoveled off the platform, carted away, and buried.

The boiling house had suffered, too. The cane juice standing in the cisterns had spoiled, and the cisterns had to be drained and cleaned. All six of the bronze boiling kettles had suffered damage the night of the shooting, when frightened boilers had run off, leaving the sugar to boil into a hard black crust until the fires under the kettles went out by themselves. The kettles had to be taken outdoors and scoured—not a minor job. The smallest weighed a hundred pounds, the largest five hundred.

The only light spot in all of this was Macaw, who plagued Drake at every opportunity for a third wife. Scouring a kettle, his seven-foot-tall ebony body folded into a squat, the wily slave grinned up at him.

"Papa! When get Macaw wife?"

"Never," Drake snapped.

"She be this many old." He held up ten fingers, then two.

"Over my dead body."

"She be pity." It boggled Drake for a second. Then he interpreted. *Pretty*.

"Anything else?" he asked sarcastically.

"New. Not used."

Drake chuckled. It was a relief to chuckle after days of tension. He rubbed the back of his neck as tight muscles relaxed. "Clean that kettle, you fornicating black devil, or I'll have Mr. Plum buy you the oldest, ugliest, most "used" wench he can find in all Bridgetown."

The third day after the insurrection, they sent the cane cutters back into the fields, and by nine on that bright, sunny morning, Drake and Plum stood on the grinding platform and watched with satisfaction as the grinder began to rumble and squeal.

"This racket will bring Edwinna down," Plum shouted over the noise of the grinder. And it did. A half hour later they spotted her coming down the path from Crawford Hall. In her breeches and shirt, hair blowing in the wind, she made a lovely sight. Drake wondered how he'd ever thought her plain. He didn't wait for her to reach the mill—he loped up the path to meet her.

"Feeling better?"

"Yes."

She looked so thin! Kena had told him how little she'd eaten.

"Kena said there's been no news of Dinny."

"No. I'm sorry." He told her of their search efforts, then hesitated. She looked so fragile. "Your uncle and cousin. You are aware. . . ."

She nodded, swallowed. "Kena told me. I wish I could have helped them."

"You tried. You sent the letter. They disregarded it. They wanted no help. You couldn't force them to accept it."

Again she nodded, swallowed. He wanted to take her in his arms and hold her, comfort her, but he knew better than to touch her.

"Is someone taking care of Uncle George's plantation? Feeding the slaves and such?"

"Yes. The governor appointed a neighboring planter to oversee the plantation until your uncle's will is read in a London court."

"The other planters—Lady Maud Locksley?"

"Only one planter, Rubin Vincent, was killed in the uprising. As for Lady Locksley, she's fine."

This was no time to tell her Lady Maud Locksley had behaved like a veritable Viking during the uprising. Snatching up a musket as if it were a feather and not a thirty-pound weight, she had marched with her overseers to the bond slave huts. She'd put her musket barrel to the throat of the first bond slave who bore an X on his forearm, demanding to know the names of the others. When he'd failed to say, she'd blown his head off.

Scared to death, the guilty had fallen to their knees, begging. She hadn't killed them; she'd turned them over to the governor's troops, but she'd given every slave and bond slave on her plantation a memorable lesson.

"We have to keep searching for Dinny!" Edwinna said. Drake nodded.

They walked down the path, trade winds blowing through their hair. Drake talked to Edwinna of small, unimportant things, avoiding the larger—Marigold, Jeremy, Jacka. A true planter, she drifted toward the noise of the grinder.

Drake stayed at her side that morning as she went about checking everything she'd neglected for the past few days. She seemed to want his company, to need it. The only time he left her, ducking out to the privy, he came back to find her looking for him with panicky eyes.

"I'm right here, Edwinna," he said calmly. "I'll stay with you."

Her eyes grew crystal bright. "Yes, please."

When the noon bell rang, signaling the end of the morning's work, he took her elbow and steered her up to the house. He'd told Honor to resume the usual schedule, producing midday meal for the overseers.

Edwinna felt overwhelmed when she sat at the table with the overseers. Everything seemed loud, a roaring in her ears: the voices, the noise of cutlery and plates, a chair scraping. She felt as if someone had taken her by the hair and jerked her upward, pulling every muscle taut and tight. Drake alone gave her peace. She kept her eyes on him, and when he rose in midmeal to go to the kitchen to ask for something, her chest pounded with panic until he came back. She was glad when dinner ended and the men rose and left. She rose, too, and looked down at her plate in surprise. It was still full. She thought she'd eaten.

Drake came to her. "You had best take a nap. We'll go down to the mill later."

She nodded. "Where will you be?"

"Right here," he assured her. "In the office. I'll wait for you. Then we'll go down to the mill together."

"Yes."

Drake watched her go upstairs, worrying.

"If you want my opinion," Plum said later as the two of them sat in the office, "she's behaving normally for the first time in her life. She's leaning on someone—you. She's never done that before, Mr. Steel. True, she leaned on me as a child. But since she has grown up, she has leaned on no one. If she needs you, Mr. Steel, I call that healthy, not sick."

Drake sighed and flipped a pen onto the worktable.

"What will happen to her when I go back to England? For I *am* going back. My life is there—my children, my work —not on this island. What will happen to her then?"

Plum eyed him. "You tell me, Mr. Steel."

Drake shook his head. He had no answer.

Edwinna seemed better in the afternoon. She even stopped in the kitchen to eat fruit before they went down to the mill. That night after they'd supped, Drake proposed they play backgammon. He'd found a board in the livery cabinet in the dining room.

"Backgammon? Why?"

"Because it's fun." He smiled. "You do remember how to have fun, don't you?"

"Yes."

They set up the board in the office because it was cool and private. The balmy trade winds wafted in through the open windows. They played by candlelight—a shielded candle that diffused the light, sparing their eyes the glare. The board sat in light, the rest of the room lay in shadow and darkness, the atmosphere intimate, pleasant.

They played, wooden pieces clicking on the board, Drake calm, Edwinna tense. Her tension grew as they played, but her mind was not on the game. He knew where it was.

Keeping his eyes on the board, he said softly, "Edwinna,

you had to shoot Jacka. He would have killed me and he would have killed Kena and Tutu.''

She nodded, stiff, tense, her eyes on the board.

"Of course, it's hard. You feel guilty. God knows, I understand. I've never killed a man, but I feel guilty as hell about Jeremy and Marigold. A few days before the insurrection, Plum wanted to torture Jacka and Yates and a half dozen bond slaves selected at random with a red-hot iron, to find out what they knew—if anything. I wouldn't allow him to do it. If I had, Jeremy and Marigold would be alive right now.''

She looked up, eyes bright.

"Drake, don't think that. Please. Matthew Plum asked me and I forbade him, too. I couldn't let him do it. After . . . my father had his accident and could no longer oversee the plantation, I took over, and I vowed to myself that no one ever again would be tortured on Crawford Plantation.''

"Your father was a harsh man?''

She looked down at the board and resumed her play, swallowing several times, finding it difficult to admit. "Yes.''

They played on for a few minutes longer, then Drake gathered up the pieces, put them in the board, and closed it. He looked at her gently.

"Get some rest, Edwinna.''

"Yes. Yes, I will.''

He snuffed the candle. They made their way through the dark house that was becoming as familiar to him as his own small house on Thames Street. The memory of that house was fading, perhaps because Anne no longer was in it. Without her, he didn't even want the house. In fact, when he returned he intended to give it to Arthur and Verity and find some other small house near the wine shop to live in with his children.

"Look what I found," Drake said jubilantly, striding into Edwinna's office the next afternoon. Sitting at her ledgers, wearing her thick magnifying spectacles, she at first failed to see what he carried in his arms, but when she heard the indignant chatter, she wrenched off her spectacles and leaped to her feet.

"Priscilla!" Drake watched with satisfaction as Priscilla bounded into Edwinna's arms, wrapped her tiny, white-haired arms around Edwinna's neck, and chattered up a storm, scolding, no doubt chronicling her adventures.

Edwinna's eyes shone. It warmed his heart. She was better today, but not healed.

"Where did you find her?"

"She jumped on my back from atop the coral drip and bit me on the ear, the little wretch."

"Priscilla, that was naughty. I wonder why she didn't come into the house? The windows are open, and the kitchen door always stands open."

"She probably was frightened to come in. Jocko . . ."

"Yes." She look at him tensely, then smiled at Priscilla.

"Priscilla, where have you been?" Her eyes grew dark and bruised, as if struggling against tears. She threw him an apologetic glance. "You must think me foolish, growing emotional over a monkey."

"I would think it unnatural if you did not."

"I was thinking of Marigold and Jeremy. It was Priscilla they'd gone searching for that day. That's mostly why I'm —a little undone by this."

"I know."

Unwilling to display tender emotions in front of him, she settled Priscilla in the crook of her arm and said in a throaty voice, "Priscilla, you are as dirty as—as Tutu when he plays in mud. I'm going to take you to the bathhouse and scrub you."

She went out the door, and Drake suspected the bath would take a long time.

More good news came. Word arrived that Dinny was home, safe and sound. It seemed that on the night the rebels had slipped into her house to loot it and set it afire, Jumbo had helped his mistress climb out a second-story window. They'd run into the cane fields, heading for Crawford Plantation. Hearing gunfire there and unsure of what was happening, Dinny and Jumbo had sensibly headed north to the caves of St. Lucy's Parish.

Edwinna insisted on visiting Dinny at once. Drake went with her. Riding over, he worried that his indiscretion with Dinny had driven a wedge into Edwinna and Dinny's friendship. He needn't have been concerned, Edwinna went flying into Dinny's arms, and they embraced as lovingly as mother and daughter.

"Dinny, you're safe."

"Dearling! I heard about your trouble. About your Marigold and Jeremy." Dinny threw him a glance, and Drake shook his head in warning. "Now, now, we shan't talk about it. And of course, I'm safe. I was with my Jumbo. He kept me safe. Oh, wait until I tell you about it. He was grand, marvelous. Heroic, in fact. He fed me with fish he caught. He carried me through swamps. He killed a wild boar, and with naught but a sharp stick. Come in, dearlings, and I'll tell you all about it."

She swept them into the house with a shout, "Jumbo, juice of orange for Mistress Edwinna, wine for Mr. Steel, and I've a mind to sip a wee bit o' kill-devil." Garbed in fresh scarlet livery, grinning, his white teeth on display in a face as black as coal, the young man jumped to do Dinny's bidding.

When they'd had their drinks (Dinny's "wee bit" a full cup cheerfully tossed down in a few swallows), and after she'd mournfully showed them her burned dining chamber and its charred furniture, she sat them down and made them listen to her adventures.

Drake listened, astonished, incredulous. He didn't believe a word of it, beyond the bare bones: Jumbo had helped her escape and they'd lived on wild fruit until they'd dared come home. With flamboyance and flair, Dinny spun them a tale of adventure that rivaled that of Sinbad the sailor. The story was absurd. Even Edwinna glanced at him, eyebrows raised. He winked at her. It was a nice moment.

But what Dinny said next stunned them.

"And that, dearlings, is why I mean to wed my Jumbo. We're going to tie the knot this coming Sabbath, and I want you both here to witness it."

"Dinny," Edwinna gasped.

"Now, loveling, hush. There's no law against it, and my mind's made up. Jumbo's the husband I want, and Jumbo's the husband I mean to have. Ain't you, Jumbo!" Jumbo grinned at her affectionately. "And I mean to wed him proper and legal, which is why I want the two of you here when Simon Tarcher ties the knot. I don't want *nobody* telling my Jumbo he ain't my legal husband, because he *will be*."

"Dinny," Edwinna said, "you cannot marry a slave."

"He ain't a slave no more. Jumbo! Stick out your foot." Obedient, Jumbo did. The silver ankle bracelet worn by manumitted slaves glittered on his ankle. "Now, I won't hear a word against it. Jumbo's my man. He saved my life. And as for bed?" She leaned forward confidentially. "If you took you a measuring stick, you would see he's got him a—"

Drake lifted a hand for mercy. "We know. You've told us."

Dinny gave them a sweet, confused look. "Ah, did I? I don't remember." Courteously, she added, "That is not to say the other gentlemen on this island are not well built."

Drake drew an embarrassed breath. He wanted to choke her.

"Dinny, be quiet!" Edwinna said, ruffling.

"We'll come," Drake said quickly, to put an end to discussion of the subject. "We'll come to your wedding, Dinny. Edwinna and I will be glad to."

"Dearlings. I'm so happy!"

* * *

The wedding was the most bizarre event Drake had ever witnessed. Dinny invited the whole island, and many of the island people came, including Lady Maud Locksley, who smoked and chuckled throughout the entire ceremony.

The bridegroom wore footman's livery, a gaudy suit of silver-trimmed burgundy velvet, and never stopped grinning. The bride, who never stopped talking, was radiant in scarlet silk and freshly dyed red hair that had gone slightly purple. Jumbo grinned at her in adoration. When the marriage license and certificate of marriage had to be signed, the bride guided the bridegroom's hand as he made his mark, a wavy J. Simon Tarcher's white eyebrows remained inverted in an incredulous V throughout the ceremony and the noisy feast after it.

Because she truly loved Dinny, Edwinna had dressed in her best, a gown of forest green silk. Again, Drake noted that neither the style nor the color suited her. In fact, Anne, with her fashion sense, would have laughed. The thought bothered him. He didn't want anyone laughing at Edwinna.

"You look lovely," he told her as she sat next to him at the wedding table during the loud, riotous feast. She smiled.

"Thank you, Drake. You look very handsome."

"Thank you." Their eyes held intimately for a moment.

The wedding feast was a great success, if the amount of kill-devil punch consumed was any criterion, and when Jumbo, still grinning, slid from his chair onto the floor like a seal into water and passed out, Dinny trilled cheerfully, "Ain't he sweet? Can't drink no more than a two-year-old babe. Well, it's certain I shan't have much of a wedding night . . ."

Her eyes went speculatively around the table, and came to rest on Simon Tarcher, who instantly rose to leave, remembering a judicial function he had to tend to in Speightstown in the morning. Lady Maud Locksley bellowed with laughter and slapped her knee.

Drake and Edwinna left soon after, neither of them caring

for drunken revelry. Because she rode sidesaddle in her gown, Drake helped her dismount, taking her thin waist in his hands. When he'd lifted her down, he didn't let go. She was so slender his hands could trace the individual ribs.

"You stir me."

Her breathing grew ragged, and her bosom rose and fell visibly. "Drake, please don't ask anything of me." The stable smelled clean, of well-kept horses and fresh cane toppings that were strewn on the floor, used in place of straw.

"I'm not asking for anything. I just want you to know you stir me. Sometimes I lie in bed at night and I know you are down the hall and I ache in need. Tell me, Edwinna. Do you ever ache in need?"

She looked at him.

"Yes."

"Then . . ."

"Drake, I must go up to the house!"

"Of course." He reluctantly let go of her waist, and she picked up her skirts and walked rapidly out of the stable and up the path toward the house. Now and then her hand went tensely to her hair, tightly smoothing it back, controlling it in the same tight way she tried to control her life.

The gesture filled him with despair, because he did not know why she was the way she was, and so had no hope of changing her.

CHAPTER

* 14 *

On the day of the Bridgetown executions Edwinna awoke sick at heart. Thirteen of her own bond slaves would be executed. Guilt flooded her. If she had managed the plantation better, differently, would they have rebelled?

She knew that to be foolish thinking. They were convicts, men who lived on the edge. It was their way. Still, she felt she'd failed. Unable to sleep, she rose and dressed in the darkness. For days planters and the curious from all over the island had been traveling to Bridgetown to watch the public burnings. She was glad Drake had been as repelled by the thought of going as she. She could not have continued to . . . to feel for him if he'd shown interest in it. And she did feel for him. Her feelings grew stronger every day.

Dressed, she went quietly down the dark hallway, pausing at Drake's open door. His room lay shadowy. Only the distant sound of the grinder disturbed the quiet. Mosquito netting cascaded around the bed. Through the netting she could see his dark head on the pillow, the outline of shoulder and chest. She drew a deep breath, remembering the one kiss they had shared.

It had been a mistake to put Drake Steel in this room, her father's room. The memories here loomed too darkly. Yet perhaps that was to the good. One day he would leave Barbados, and when he had left she could come to this room and remember that a handsome London wine merchant had once lived here. It would cancel the other memories.

"Edwinna." His voice came from the bed. "Try not to feel too bad about today."

She hadn't thought he was awake. The unexpected tenderness in his tone, the intuitive understanding, made her throat fill with emotion.

"I'm trying not to," she said. "Still, I cannot but feel if I had run the plantation differently . . ."

"Today is *not* your fault. The men brought it down upon themselves. There is nothing you could have done to prevent it. Believe me, the world is full of such people. They set a course for their own destruction and follow it to the end."

She nodded, her voice too thick to respond.

"Are you going to the mill?"

"Yes. To the curing house."

Drake lifted up on one elbow and gazed at her in the darkness. He was beginning to understand. She used work to keep her own personal demons at bay. Work could be measured and controlled and predicted. She could knock on a sugar pot and predict if the sugar was going to cure, but she could *not* knock on the head of a bond slave and predict whether he would someday rise up against her.

"I'll go with you."

"It isn't necessary. You have hours yet to sleep."

"I want to."

Concerned for her, filled with a fierce fondness, he stayed with her throughout the morning. As the hour of the scheduled executions drew closer, she grew so pale that he took her firmly by the elbow and marched her up to the house to eat something. Then he sent for the horses.

They rode east to the wild, savage beauty of the Atlantic coast, tethered their horses in the shade, and sat on a cliff looking out over miles of rugged coastline. They watched the whitecaps roll in and batter the shore. The trade winds blew fresh and clean. Speaking little, they waited for noon. Edwinna was closed in her own private thoughts as a clam is closed in its own shell.

He felt helpless, unable to aid her. She lived behind a barrier and he couldn't get through. He longed to take her in his arms and comfort her, but he knew better than to do that. He would scare her.

"What time is it?" she asked.

He brought out his timepiece and looked at it ruefully.

"It doesn't work anymore. The humidity."

"Why do you carry it?"

"It was a gift from my wife."

She gazed at the timepiece, touched it with one finger, tracing the scrollwork, the English birds and flowers, the rich embellished silver case. He was glad she didn't know of the engraving inside the case—his and Anne's names linked with a heart. She held the watch for a long time, as if absorbed in it.

"She must have loved you very much to give you so fine a gift."

He drew a careful breath. "That is the whole point of marriage, Edwinna, isn't it? To be loving to each other?"

She looked into his eyes, tense, intense. Caught in the wind, unbraided wisps of sunny brown hair blew around the edges of her face. The wind molded her shirt to her breasts. He ached to touch her there, in the gentlest way.

"Yes."

As the sun neared its zenith, her lips grew tight. She sat

with her knees up, her arms locked around them, head on knees. The sun passed its zenith. She seemed not to want to notice, as if by not noticing she could prevent the executions. When an hour had passed, he grew worried and gently prodded.

"It's over, Edwinna."

She nodded. Pale but staunch, she got to her feet. When she hesitated and glanced south toward Bridgetown, he put a hand on the small of her back and walked to her horse.

"It was a matter of justice, Edwinna, and justice was meted out. Justice has been served."

She nodded. "I know."

"Then don't grieve. It was not your fault."

Two evenings later, he and Edwinna were working by candlelight in the office, entering the day's harvest figures into ledgers, when David Alleyne and Kena appeared in the open doorway and hovered there expectantly.

Glancing up, Drake knew their mission at once and smiled. Kena was radiant, her eyes shining and her dusky skin flushed with happiness. David fairly shone. Joy emanated from every pore, from his fair, suntanned skin, from his blond hair, his eyes. He held Kena's hand as if it were a fragile treasure.

Edwinna knew instantly, too. Drake saw her stiffen, go pale.

"Mistress Edwinna?"

"Come in, David," Drake said, since Edwinna was silent. He put down his pen. The pair stepped in, glancing at each other with excitement and uncertainty.

"Mistress Edwinna?" Alleyne said respectfully. "Kena and I have come to ask your permission to wed. I love your sister with all my heart, and she loves me. We wish to be man and wife. If you will grant me permission, I will wed her properly and with all honor, saying our vows before a minister of God, kneeling at the altar in St. Lucy's Parish Church. And I *swear* to you," he finished, voice trembling with emotion, "I swear to you I will love and honor her, cherish and protect her, to the best of my ability for the rest of my life on this earth."

It was a moving speech. Drake was touched by David's sincerity. All eyes swung to Edwinna. She sat gripping the table edge. She looked as if she'd been assaulted. Oblivious, blinded by their own happiness, David and Kena waited eagerly.

"Mistress Edwinna?" David said.

"No." The word broke deep in her throat. "No!"

Kena's happy look disintegrated. David's eyes grew huge. Drake leaped to his feet to usher the stunned, crestfallen young couple out the door.

"David, take Kena to the dining chamber and wait there." David nodded, blank with bewilderment. Putting his arm around Kena, who wept softly, David led her away. Drake closed the door, then went around the worktable and squatted beside Edwinna's chair. She sat with elbows propped on the table, her head in her hands.

"Why, Edwinna?"

"She is my sister!"

"That is a fact. It's not a reason."

"You don't understand."

"Maybe I do. I have a sister. I remember how I felt when she wed. Arthur had been one of my best friends, yet I felt he wasn't good enough for her."

"No, you don't understand!" Seizing the finished ledgers, she leaped to her feet, went to the wall shelves, and started shoving them into their slots, roughly, one by one, with noise and banging. "You *don't* understand. Six years ago my father gave Kena to a boiling house slave as wife. To a *boiling house slave*. His own daughter!"

Drake slowly got to his feet. He raked a hand over his brow. "God, Edwinna, God."

"I begged him not to. Kena begged, too. She was only fourteen and frightened. She didn't even speak the slave's language. He was a bush slave out of Africa. But my father and uncle thought it funny. Funny! The boiling house slave used her so brutally she miscarried her first child and nearly lost her own life."

"And you think David Alleyne would be like that?" Drake said, incredulous. "You can watch David Alleyne doctoring on this plantation and you can believe that of him?"

"He's a man, isn't he!"

Drake breathed quietly. She went on shuffling her ledgers, banging them about on the shelves, putting them in a new order, needing something to do with her hands.

"Yes, he's a man, Edwinna. A good man."

"There aren't any." When he took that, when he calmly let the insult pass, she glanced at him. "He'll take her away from me," she burst. "And he'll take Tutu away," she added intensely. "I don't want to lose them."

Now they were nearing the truth. He gazed at her with understanding. Thomas and Harry were gone. Kena and Tutu were all she had left.

"He hasn't said so."

"David is from England. He'll want to go back someday. All Englishmen do. He'll take her back there. Drake, she's mulatto! How many mulattoes are there in England?"

"Few," he admitted.

She banged the ledgers around. "She's my sister. I love her. In England she would be a curiosity, something freakish for people to stare at. It would break her heart. I won't let that happen to her. She has to stay *here*—where mixed blood is accepted, where I can take care of her."

"Edwinna, David Alleyne loves her. Surely, he has thought of this. If you could listen to what he has to say, hear him out, discuss his plans . . ."

"No."

He didn't know how to deal with her, help her. He sensed the matter went even deeper than Kena and David; it went to themselves. If she couldn't let go and trust and give Kena to a fine man like David, she would never be able to give herself to him.

"Edwinna?" Upset, she moved to another shelf, rearranging the ledgers there. "You say you love Kena, then think of Kena. She's not cut out to be a spinster widow all her life. She's a normal young woman with a normal woman's wants and needs. She wants a husband to love, children to love. She wants . . . sexual love, the marriage bed." He added, "Think of her. Perhaps she wants to take the risk. Perhaps she's not like you, Edwinna, neither wanting or needing any sort of love."

She looked over her shoulder, eyes glistening.

"I need love."

He drew a breath and shook his head helplessly.

"That, I sincerely doubt. To get love, you have to be willing to give it, Edwinna. And you are unwilling. I know you feel something for me. I see it shining in your lovely eyes every day. Yet you won't take me into your confidence, you won't share a bed with me, though I have offered until my heart is bruised from rejection. Granted, in a sense I am still a widower and in mourning. I can't offer you blazing, glorious love. But I can offer you fondness. Fondness is a form of love . . ."

He eyed her gently. "What do you do for your sexual needs? You're a mature woman, Edwinna. Passions run deep in you. Do you meet your physical needs alone in bed at night?"

Her face went dead white, then scarlet. She snapped her head around to the wall and rested her hands high on the bookshelves, her breathing ragged, her head bowed. She was incredibly silent.

He was ashamed. He stepped forward and put his hands on her shoulders in apology. "Edwinna, I'm sorry," he whispered into her hair. "I shouldn't have said that. I had no right to say it—no right at all. I meet my own needs that way."

He rested his cheek against her thick, curly hair. "And it's lonely. Very lonely. Isn't it?"

She nodded stiffly.

"Of course it is. We're both lonely, Edwinna. I'm going to put my arms around you and hold you tightly for just a little while. Only hold you, nothing more. This arm goes across your chest to your shoulder, my hand gripping your shoulder." He could feel her heart pounding. "There, that's lovely. This arm crosses it to your other shoulder. There. Lean against me, Edwinna."

She did so, breathing rapidly, eyes closed. He could feel her heart thudding against his chest. He pushed her hair aside with his mouth and rested his warm cheek against hers.

"There," he soothed. "Only this . . . nothing more."

With Edwinna's permission, David Alleyne and Kena rode to St. Lucy's Parish Church two days later and were married. Glowing with joy, they returned an hour before sunset.

Edwinna had to brace herself for their return. She smiled to welcome them back. She kissed David to congratulate him, to welcome him into the family as her brother-in-law. She kissed and hugged Kena. But inside she was devastated. She'd lost her sister. She saw it in Kena's eyes—eyes that saw only David.

The four of them ate a wedding supper by candlelight in the dining chamber that night. Edwinna put on her best gown and tried to make the supper a special occasion. Drake made the event celebratory, too. He dressed handsomely and toasted the young couple with wine. Edwinna even sipped a little wine and smiled to show her goodwill, but inside, her heart was breaking.

Drake understood. His glances told her so. But that made her feel . . . oddly violated. She wasn't used to sharing her feelings. She was used to guarding them, keeping them tightly closed inside her, where she could control them. Yet, when she thought of how he'd held her—just held her in his strong arms—she was filled with longing.

As the supper party went on, she saw gentleness in his eyes, but another, more basic interest, too. The old anxiety rose; the dark memory came flooding back. When supper ended and David had to go check on his patients, he and Kena parted with a soft kiss, David reluctant to leave her even for a moment. Edwinna watched with fierce envy. When she glanced at Drake and found him looking at her, his blue eyes smoky with desire, her heart pounded.

Inviting David and Kena to live with her had been a mistake. How could she stand it, knowing they were in the room across the hall, consummating their marriage night after night while she lay alone and lonely? She felt as if a war were being fought inside her body, inside her head. She wanted Drake! But then memory took hold of her with its sharp talons.

When they rose from the wedding supper, Drake came to her in the candlelit dining chamber and said gently, "It's a lovely evening. Shall we go for a walk?"

Her chest tightened. "No."

"Edwinna, what's wrong?"

"I don't want a walk, that's all."

She pushed past him, went to the office, and locked herself in. Trembling, she groped for the tinderbox on the table in the dark room, lighted a candle, took ledgers down from the shelf, opened them, and began to work. She could cope with facts and figures. What she could *not* cope with were wedding nights and loving Drake Steel and losing her sister. When a tear ran down her cheek, she brusquely brushed it away and concentrated on the day's harvest.

A candle burned in Kena and David's room nearly all night, its light spilling under their door and flowing to hers, settling under it as a faint glow. It made her breathless, restless. She slept poorly.

David and Kena's wedding night had been a strain on Drake, too. She saw it in his sleepless eyes the next day, in the shortness of his temper. He was testy. They quarreled about inconsequential things, the stacking of the cut cane on the loading platform, for one. They quarreled so foolishly on the platform that the slaves stared, and even Matthew Plum lifted an eyebrow in disbelief.

"You should stack the cane crosswise, Drake."

"I will have it stacked the way I want it stacked."

"If you stack it lengthwise it will roll into the grinder."

"If I stack it crosswise, it will roll off the platform."

"We always stack it crosswise on Crawford Plantation."

"Then you do it, and I'll do your job, hopping around in a dark curing house all day, banging on sugar pots."

"I do not bang on pots, I knock on them."

"Fine, then I'll knock on them. You stack the cane."

It was so foolish a quarrel, even to their own ears, that they both stepped back and looked at each other. Drake wiped sweat and cane field grime from his forehead with his sleeve.

"Edwinna," he said, "we're both upset with that damned honeymoon going on in the house right under our noses."

She nodded and swallowed tightly.

"Let's try not to be."

"Yes."

"I'll have the cane stacked crosswise."

"You needn't. It can be stacked lengthwise."

He smiled, reached out, gave her braid a tug, and went back to his work.

Nevertheless, the newly weds were a strain on the nerves. They were so happy, they floated on air. Edwinna felt a fierce stab of envy every time she looked at Kena. Kena went about her duties with the flush of happiness on her face, her eyes shining.

David was just as bad, and a thorn in the side for Drake. Drake felt that if he saw one more happy smile, he would put his fist through it. Exuberant, full of zest, David was all over the plantation, doing the work of ten doctors. Beaming cheerfully, he willingly sewed up bill-cane cuts out in the cane field, dug painful chiggers out from under slaves' toe-nails, lanced boils, treated boiling house burns, helped in a lengthy, difficult breech birth, and even found time to treat the mill oxen's yoke sores.

It was a damned imposition, all that happiness by day and a candle burning in their room down the hall all night every night. Drake wanted to wrench open their bedchamber door and dash a bucket of cold water on them.

In truth, it made him ache to have some happiness of his own. It made him ache to have Edwinna in his bed.

They'd worked late one night in her office. When they finished, they snuffed the candle and went through the dark house to the stairs, Edwinna leading. As she started to mount the stairs, he put his hands on her waist and gently turned her to face him. Again, her body heat startled him. She was a hot-blooded woman, certainly capable of passion. She stiffened.

"Drake?"

"Just a kiss. To tide us over. To get us through one more damned honeymoon night." He glanced at the top of the stairs. David and Kena had gone to bed hours earlier, but the candle still spilled its glow into the dark upper hall.

"Drake—"

"Edwinna, I don't know what happened in your past—what happened to make you so fearful of this. I cannot even guess, but—"

She grew rigid. "Nothing happened!"

"—but I do know we cannot carry the past on our shoulders forever. The burden is too heavy. There comes a time one must lay the burden down, leave it behind, and walk on. God knows, I'm trying to do that with Anne's death. I'm trying to leave it behind and walk on. Help me, Edwinna. I need help, and I sense you need help, too."

"Drake—"

"Just a kiss."

He ached. He could hear her heart pounding in the darkness. He drew her near. She remained stiff but didn't refuse him. He took one of her arms, pressed a soft kiss to the wrist, to the throbbing pulse point there, and draped it behind his neck, then the other. Even the skin of her wrists burned him.

He brought her nearer and molded her body to his, thigh to thigh, waist to waist, chest to breast. He panted a little.

"Just a kiss."

She began to tremble as his erection swelled against her.

"Drake—"

"Don't be afraid of my body, Edwinna. It means you no harm. May I kiss you? Just a kiss?"

Her heart pounded against him. "Yes."

"Oh, Edwinna." He dipped his head and began to kiss her mouth, then pulled back for a startled moment. Her mouth was so hot. Stirred by her heat, he kneaded her shoulders and took her soft, hot mouth in his. Unaccustomed to kissing, she knew only his way of doing it—with mouth bold and open—and it utterly thrilled him.

"Edwinna." He drew her closer, dipping his tongue into her mouth. To his surprise, her tongue responded. He sucked on it, worshiped it, plucked at it with his lips while her hands clutched his shirt, her scared heart beating so hard he could feel it.

Then, overstirred, on the brink of doing something that might truly scare her, he broke the kiss and held her close, panting against the pulse point in her temple, kissing it. A whimper came from her throat. He kissed her ear, tongued it, whispered hoarsely, "Let's be together as we should. Come to bed."

Her heart pounded so wildly he thought she might surrender to her desire and take pleasure with him. But her eyes were wild, too—wild and wounded. They were old wounds that he could not heal for her. Only she could heal them, for they went deep, into places he could not see or understand or even guess at. Even before she pushed him away, he sensed that she would and released her. He didn't want to scare her, only to make love to her.

She stepped back, touched his cheek, then turned and rushed up the stairs. He followed her up. She went into her room and closed the door, but she didn't bolt it. Didn't bolt it! He drew a hoarse breath. She was ready. To give her a few minutes privacy, he went to his room in a state of sexual excitement and washed, shaved for her, put on fresh breeches, nothing else. He went to her room in anticipation, touched the latch. It was unlocked. Drawing an eager breath, he went in and closed the door behind him.

The room lay in darkness, lighted only by the moon. She stood at her dressing table in a white night rail, brushing her hair. When she saw him, she dropped the hairbrush.

"No—no!"

Astounded, he stopped in his tracks. "Edwinna, I thought—"

She backed away in a panic. "Don't touch me. Don't. Don't. You're just like him."

"Who?" Her reaction stunned him.

"You're no different from him. I thought you were, but you are not. You're the same—you're like him!"

She was so wild she scared him. "Edwinna . . ." he said gently, becoming scared himself.

"No," she cried out. Her cry was wild, primitive, ringing. She backed away, toward the window. That and her unearthly cry made his hair stand on end. She'd gone insane. The window. She would not . . . good God!

Scared, he moved toward her. The window shutters stood open. The drop to the ground would be a full twenty feet. "Edwinna, it's Drake. Drake."

"Don't," she cried out, "don't."

"Edwinna."

"Don't!" With a cry of agony, she flung herself at the window. He leaped for her, caught hold of her. "No," she screamed. "Don't do it again. Don't." She fought him tooth and nail, like a tigress, hitting him, clawing him, scratching him. He felt blood rise on his cheek. He had to struggle with all his might to hold her. He feared to let go.

"Don't let him do it to me again—don't!"

He shook her ferociously. "Edwinna, who raped you—who? Was it Clive?"

She raked her nails across his face and lunged back and forth, trying to get free. He held her in a vise, swinging his head away to avoid the worst of her violence.

"Who raped you, Edwinna? Say it. You need to say it."

With a scream of agony she beat on his face with her fists.

He wrenched his head away. He was getting battered. She was as strong as a demon. "Say it, Edwinna, say it."

"No!"

"Say it." He shook her fiercely. "Say it."

"My father," she shrieked. In an agony of spirit, she gnashed her teeth and threw her head back and forth. "My father. My father raped me. My father, my father, my father, my father!" She beat on his chest with her fists, the blows gradually subsiding, growing weaker. He gathered her in his arms and held her close. She collapsed against his chest, breathing in agonized rasps that wouldn't stop. Her breathing was so loud and horrible it sounded like a death rattle, that graveled breathing so penetrating it can be heard all over a house when someone is dying. "My father," she said over and over again. "My father raped me. My father."

"Oh, sweetheart." He stroked her hair, her warm skull. A trunk stood at the foot of the bed. He helped her to sit, turning her to lean on him, holding her, letting her breathe against his chest, those deep, shuddering breaths. Lord. It was worse than he'd suspected.

"Tell me, Edwinna. Talk about it."

"Drake."

"You have to get it out. Say it."

Weary as death, she forced out the words. "Drake. It was when I was thirteen. He was drunk. He came to my room.

He—did it to me. He told me if I told anyone, he would hurt Kena—he would hurt Thomas and Harry. I couldn't let them be hurt, Drake—''

"No, of course not."

"I couldn't let him hurt Kena and Thomas and Harry."

He tenderly crushed her close. God in heaven. Her agonized breathing went on as if it would never stop. He wished she would cry, but she held it in. He brushed the hair from her flushed cheeks with his hand.

"The worst part was, he didn't like me after that. He wouldn't talk to me, he wouldn't eat with me. He was—so cold to me."

He rocked her. "He felt guilty, Edwinna. That's why."

"When I was young, he used to hit me. I was glad when he had his riding accident and couldn't walk. I was glad when he became an invalid. I was glad—"

"Of course, you were," he soothed, rocking her back and forth in his arms.

"I was glad when he died. I was glad—"

The heartbreak in that agonized breathing broke his own heart. Her father should have been the one man in the world she could trust.

"Of course, you were glad he died. Don't feel guilty."

She clung to him so desperately that he expected to find bruises in the morning. "I used to think it was my fault—something I'd done to make him hate me and hit me. And then later, to cause him to—"

He rocked her. "Rape. Use the word, Edwinna. For your sake, not for his. You need to say it."

"—to cause him to rape me."

"It wasn't your fault."

"I know. I know that now—"

"Sob, rant, rave. Get it out, Edwinna."

"I don't know why I slapped you that day in the boiling house. I felt—bad, after."

"You were slapping your father, not me."

"I—I wanted him to love me and he didn't."

Drake rocked her. "Maybe he didn't know how to love, Edwinna. Maybe he didn't know how."

He held her as she gasped herself into exhaustion with loud, rasping, hollow breaths. A long time passed before her breathing grew calmer and she slumped against him.

"Now that you know the truth, you will think me ugly." Her voice was hoarse.

He rubbed his cheek on the top of her head, her hair soft and curly. "I think you are lovely," he said. "There is goodness and kindness in everything you do, and I find that lovely."

A choke caught in her throat. "Drake—about bed, I cannot."

He kissed her flushed forehead. "I know that. I know that now. And I give you my word, Edwinna. I will never approach you on the matter of bed again. Never. I swear it. You have my word."

He moved on the trunk seat so as to cup her face in his hands. In the moonlight it looked ravaged. "But if the time should ever come when *you* want me as much as I want you, you need only come to my room. For I would love to make love to you. And I promise you this. It will *not* be rape."

She began to shake now, the aftermath of it all. He helped her to stand. Her knees buckled in exhaustion. Supporting her waist, he helped her to her bed. "Now let's tuck you in. Then I'll get you drops—something to make you sleep."

"The servants. They've probably heard me."

"I'll take care of it."

She nodded, too emotionally exhausted to protest. When he'd put her to bed and she began to shake even more, he hunted a blanket in her livery cabinet and covered her warmly.

When he stepped outside the door, he found the whole household aroused. Kena stood in the doorway of her room, stiff and scared. Clustered at the bottom of the stairs around a candle that Honor held stood the other servants, their eyes round and frightened, shining in the candlelight.

He calmly addressed them. "Mistress Edwinna has had a nightmare, a bad dream. She's fine now. You can all go back to bed. Kena, go down and fix her a juice drink. Put a couple of drops of David's laudanum in it." Nodding, clutching a shawl over her night rail, she swiftly flew down the stairs, and when she came back with the drink a few minutes later, Drake took it in.

He found Edwinna sleeping peacefully. He left the drink on her nightstand where she would find it if she woke up. He leaned over her, watched her for a long time, then kissed her forehead.

"Sleep well, Edwinna," he whispered, stroking her hair. "Sleep well."

CHAPTER

* 15 *

Edwinna slept until noon—through the six o'clock bell and the eleven o'clock bell. Unaware, she also slept through the two visits Drake made to her room to make sure she was all right.

She awoke with a heart full of misery, her thoughts centered on Drake. Now he knew the sordid truth. He'd been kind last night, but by now he'd had time to think and become repelled by it.

She wanted to curl into a ball and stay in her bed forever, but that was childish. She was not a child, she was an adult with a plantation to run. Thomas and Harry were counting on her.

She dragged herself out of bed. A piece of paper lay on the floor, half under the door. She picked it up and recognized Drake's strong handwriting. Likely, he'd gone to Bridgetown to find a ship to take him to England. Her chest tightening, she read:

Stay in bed, Edwinna. Rest. I shall be out in cane field six all morning and would welcome your company if you are able. If not, I will see you this noon when we dine with the overseers.

He hadn't left her! That and his kindness of last night gave her the courage to wash, dress, and go downstairs.

As she went down, midday meal was already in progress. She could hear it—cutlery clattering, chairs scraping, platters clunking on the table board as Honor served in her rough, indifferent fashion. Men's voices blended, discussing harvest. She knew each by heart: Matthew Plum's dry, good-humored twang; Alvis Nansellock's high-pitched tenor; James McCarran's soft Scots burr; Shawn and Valentine O'Brien's Irish brogue; David's bridegroom voice laced with happiness and vigor. She knew Drake's voice best—so full-timbered that even when he spoke quietly, his words echoed for a moment, like the resonance of a fine bell.

She halted at the dining room door, heart thrashing. She felt suddenly vulnerable, naked, as if everyone could look at her and know her father had raped her. Drake leaped up and came to her the instant he saw her. At the table, talk went on normally. Matthew Plum and Sean O'Brien were discussing the planting of a new provisions field. Drake reached out and took her cold hands in his warm ones.

"Feeling better?"

"Yes."

"You're sure?"

"Yes." She looked into his eyes, dreading what she might see there. Disgust? Dislike? She saw nothing like that—only gentleness and warmth. His interest still burned in the blue depths, unabated, unchanged, unaffected by last night. He knew the worst, yet he was not repelled. She felt dangerously close to tears.

"Did—you start cutting number six?"

"Yes. I estimate three days to finish."

"I think we'll cut field eighteen next."

"We'll take a bill-cane knife and go out this afternoon, together. You can check it."

Then, with his hand firmly on the small of her back, he guided her to her chair, seated her, and went to his own place at the opposite end of the table.

Dinner talk went on loud and vigorous, but she heard none of it. Drake filled her senses. Oh, dear God. He knew the worst, yet he still liked her, wanted her. Amid the cacophony of harvest talk, she sat silent and still, her eyes on him, everyone else fading from sight, the din of their voices fading until she heard nothing but the singing of her own soul. A tranquil feeling seeped into her—a feeling so sweet she felt close to tears. For a moment she couldn't identify it. Then she knew. Peace—it was peace. Deep in her soul, the old, painful wound was mending.

The next few days and nights were hard on both of them. Sexual tension crackled between them whenever they glanced at each other. The candle burning nightly in David's room didn't help matters. Drake wanted to take David and Kena and knock their heads together.

He dealt with his frustration as best he could. He felt an overwhelming tenderness for Edwinna, but he was a man, not a woman. He couldn't begin to guess what she might be feeling. But he could take a stab at it. Shame. Relief. Desire. Terror of anything sexual. Distrust. Most of all, distrust.

He watched Edwinna struggle with her demons for a week, his heart full of sympathy. She wanted to come to him. He saw it in her eyes. They never lied about anything, and what he saw in them when she looked at him was desire. But he saw terror, too, and there wasn't a thing he could do about that. That demon was hers to subdue. He couldn't help. Only she could do it.

He prepared himself for her each night, washing, carefully shaving, sleeping in breeches lest his nudity frighten her. He even brought a dish of aloe to his nightstand, should she prove eager but so frozen with old terrors that her body's honey refused to flow. For he didn't want to hurt her, not even a bit.

He left the door of his room ajar each night and burned a candle to show her that he was waiting and that she was dearly wanted. Covered with a perforated tin shield, the candle flame sent hundreds of dots of light spinning across the ceiling as he lay there watching, night after night.

He'd almost given up in despair when, two nights into the second week, she suddenly appeared in his doorway, exhausted, spent, as if she had done battle with a hundred demons.

He got off the bed, went to her, and cupped her face in his hands. "Edwinna, you've come to me."

"Yes, I—I've come to you, Drake. I want to be a woman. I don't want to be afraid anymore."

He drew her inside and softly shut the door. She wore a plain white linen night rail, but to him, at this moment, it seemed lovelier than sheerest silk. Her hair was unbraided, loose, long, lovely.

He rested his hands on her shoulders. Her skin scorched him. He could feel the heat of it through her night rail. Yet, she shook like a wind-battered tree limb in a storm.

"Don't be afraid of me."

"I'm not. Truly, it's not you I'm afraid of."

"Don't be afraid of my bed."

He drew her close. She braced her hands on his chest— whether in fear or desire, he didn't know. He buried his face in the lush thickness of her hair and inhaled deeply. It smelled of sunshine and trade winds. He burrowed with his lips until he found her ear. "Don't be afraid. It's going to be sweet and good. I promise you. And I promise you this: If at any time you wish me to stop, you need only say so. I'll stop. God help me, it won't be easy for I want you. But I will stop. Do you understand?"

She nodded. "Thank you, Drake." Her heart was pounding

so hard it jarred his chest. He let his hands slide up her shoulders to her lovely neck. He cupped her face and put a kiss on her mouth. It opened, hot and willing under his, but she was shaking so badly their teeth met and clicked. He drew back with a gentle smile.

"If you don't stop shaking, we'll hurt each other."

"I know." She tried to smile, too. It was the bravest effort he'd ever seen in man or woman. This tall, decent woman, trying to put an ugly past behind her. Though her body was hot, her hands were ice. He took them, chafed them, tried to rub warmth into them.

"Let's sit you on the bed, Edwinna."

She began to pant in terror. He gazed at her in worry.

"You only need sit there, Edwinna. Edwinna?"

She nodded and allowed him to lead her to the bed. He sat her on the edge of it, then knelt below her on the bed step and gently opened her nightrail, taking a long time untying each of the sets of ribbons down the front. His hands brushed her chest. Her heart pounded against his fingers.

"I—I'm too thin."

"You're beautiful."

"Drake?" He looked up at the edge of panic in her voice. Tense, the sexual sweat was already rising on his brow, his erection swelling in painful need.

"Do you want me to stop, Edwinna? I'll stop."

"No."

Slowly he drew the night rail down from her shoulders, baring first one arm, then the other. He pooled the night rail around her bare hips. Her eyes were huge. He could see her heart pounding in her breast.

"You're lovely," he said in an awestruck voice. Despite her slenderness, she had full breasts, beautifully curved on the underside, white and soft as the breast of a dove. He touched them. Her heart pounded. Below her taut, flat abdomen her curly nest was soft, the sunny brown color of her hair. He longed to put his mouth there, taste the sexual musk from the curls, touch his tongue to her pink pretty place. But he must not frighten her.

As it was, she stiffened when he tried to make her comfortable, tried to lay her back on the pillow. So he took a few minutes just to kneel on the bed stair and hold her against him, whispering reassurances. "Edwinna, this is Drake. I won't hurt you. Never. I swear it."

"Drake, I'm sorry I'm so stiff—"

"It doesn't matter. I don't mind. Truly."

"I'm not—afraid of you, Drake. It's the bed—"

"I know . . . I know."

He gently drew her night rail down to her feet and discarded it. It slid to the floor with a soft plop. She had beautiful legs. He touched them. They were long and shapely. She shivered.

He kissed her mouth. Her eyes leaped with fear as he rose and went to the opposite side of the bed and shed his breeches. Aroused, his erection was a blatant fact, nothing he could hide, so he didn't try. He eased into bed and lay on his side, facing her, hoping he wasn't scaring her. He knew what she saw, for he knew what he looked like. Shoulders too damned broad to fit in a shirt without splitting the seams. A chest matted with black hair. A trail of black hair descending to a black bush, his erection florid and throbbing there.

"Drake!"

"Don't be frightened," he whispered. "My body means you no harm. Don't be afraid of it." Her hands had stiffened into fists. He took the nearest one and brought it to his lips, kissing each tight knuckle, kissing her thumb, gently raking his teeth over the nail. Gradually, her hand relaxed, grew pliable and willing. He pressed his lips to her palm. She trembled, not entirely from fright. She desired him. His erection surged fuller. Her eyes grew large and dark and bruised. She breathed through her mouth—scared, shallow breaths that made her lovely breasts rise and fall. Poor darling.

To show her there was no harm in his body, he took her soft hand on a tour of it. He pressed her palm to his cheek, letting her feel the smooth-shaven skin with its underlying promise of tomorrow's beard. He took her hand and drew it across his brow, his eyes, his nose, his lips. He held her palm to the hot, pounding artery in his neck. She watched, breathless, eyes huge, as if the hand were a disembodied thing and not her own.

He pressed her palm to his chest, letting her feel his heartbeat, learn his rhythm. Here, her strong hand came to life, moving of its own accord. Eyes scared and huge, she touched his nipples. Propped on one elbow, he let his head fall back and closed his eyes, rejoicing, sweat breaking. He watched her through sensually drooping eyelashes. Her gaze flickered between his chest and his eyes.

"Dear God, that was sweet," he whispered.

Watching her eyes, he took her hand lower. He drew it to his waist, then guided it down the lean, hard muscles of his belly. Here he began to pant. Her hand trembled and curled up into a tight claw.

"Don't be afraid," he said hoarsely. "My body means you no harm."

"I—I know." Her breath was shallow, labored. He shook her hand a little, to relax its tenseness, and brought it to his mouth to kiss. When it uncurled and became willing again, he gently took it to his groin. When she trembled but didn't pull away, he let his head fall back and gasped with joy. He pressed her palm to his testicles. She touched his silken scrotum with gentle wonder.

"Am I hurting you?"

"God, no."

Needing to feel her hand there, he seized it and pressed her palm to his erection. His erection stood up like a post, its color vivid, its heart-shaped head bulging, the slit stretched. He was so aroused that a drop of translucent liquid rose from the slit and shimmered in the muted candlelight. He watched her eyes.

"It's my seed, Edwinna," he whispered raggedly. Then,

too close to going off, he abruptly ended the exploration. He kissed her hand, sat up, threw his legs over the edge of the bed, and planted his feet on the bed stair. Gently he reached for her and gathered her into his arms.

"Sweetheart, face me. Sit on my lap." He didn't want her in the submissive position—it might scare her, revive memories of her rape.

She came into his lap shaking, but hot and willing. He breathed hoarsely as her nest met his. He took one lovely leg and gently wrapped it around his hip, then the other. He put her hands on his shoulders and drew her close. Her breasts burned against his chest, and the heat of his erection seared both their bellies. They both panted: he in ecstasy, she in fear and desire.

"Don't be afraid, Edwinna."

"I–I won't."

Her mouth opened even before his reached it. He kissed her in every way he knew to kiss a woman—tonguing her, sucking her, nibbling, gently biting, giving her his tongue to suck and nibble. She clung, trembling, her body hot as fire, her mouth sweet and generous, returning like for like.

He trailed kisses on her shoulder, her neck. He cupped her breast and suckled hungrily while she gripped his head, her hands clawing his hair. Her heart beat like a hammer. He slipped a hand under her taut, firm buttocks. She was wet. He gloried in it. Gently he found her love hole and slipped one finger in, spreading her honey, preparing her for entry. She gasped. Her muscles gripped his finger so tightly he nearly came, imagining his rod there.

"Oh, Edwinna. Hold tight to my neck, Edwinna." He drew her forward, lifted her buttocks, and positioned her over his throbbing erection. Breathing raggedly, he gently coaxed her down on the head.

"Drake—" she cried out in fear.

He kissed her mouth. "Little by little. Take what you can. Don't hurt yourself."

"Drake, I'm frightened!"

"I'll stop, but, God, don't ask me to!"

He groaned, sucking on her shoulder while she took him, gasping, inch by scared inch. He encouraged her, whispered words of praise, fragments of love words, sex words, and when he was fully in her, he gently began to move. She clung, her forehead hot and moist against his. Their musk rose like thick perfume. With one hand around her hips, supporting her, he licked his other hand and slipped it down the front of her soft belly and found the spot where a woman needed to be touched. He caressed it.

A deep, shuddering cry erupted from her. "Drake—"

"Yes, it's my gift."

"Drake!" She arched, breasts thrusting into him.

"Edwinna, yes!" If he hadn't wrapped his arms tightly around her, she might have thrown herself to the floor. Her thick, curly hair tumbled. He gripped her, holding her close and safe while she panted wildly and came. It was a thrilling moment. Her muscles gripped his erection so tightly he started to come himself. When she'd finished, he crushed her close, thrust once, and stiffened as if he had been struck. The ejaculation tore out of him. He nearly blacked out at the force of it, and when he finished, they held each other, shaky, sweating, gasping.

"Oh, Edwinna." He panted. "Edwinna."

When his erection went down and he could move without hurting her, he lifted her onto the bed, put her dazed head on the pillow, and lay beside her, an arm possessively draped over her.

She lay there pleasantly exhausted, all the muscles of her face relaxed, eyes closed, lips kiss-stung and parted. He smiled. She looked as if she were adrift in a lovely dream. He watched her for a long time. When her silken lashes flickered, he buried his face in her neck, kissing her softly there.

"You thrilled me."

It took her so long to respond, she might have been on another planet. He smiled, pleased that he'd given her this.

"As to that . . . I don't know."

"I *do* know. You're a thrilling woman, Edwinna Crawford." He kissed her neck, softly, languidly, enjoying her glow. "I will need to do this to you every night and every morning. Can you bear it?"

She smiled drowsily, eyes still closed. "Only . . . twice a day?"

He smiled into the slender column of her neck and kissed her there. "I have an idea. Let's drive David stark raving mad. Let's burn the candle all night long, every night."

She smiled in drowsy amusement. "Let's."

He kissed her bare shoulder, then licked at the spot he'd kissed. "You are a passionate woman, Edwinna Crawford."

"Am . . . am I?"

"Absolutely."

Her lashes parted. She opened her eyes and gazed at him with so much love it startled him. He felt a stab of guilt. He didn't love her. He was fond of her, delighted with her in bed, but he didn't love her. His conscience stung.

He gathered her into his arms. Carefully. He wasn't idiot enough to think one session of bed had cured her. She probably would carry the scars from her rape the rest of her life. Tenderly he kissed her eyelids, her nose, her chin, then rubbed his face in the cleft of her breasts, licking the salty moisture there.

"I like the way we smell together. Our sweat. Our musk."

"I like it, too."

"Why did we wait so long?"

"I don't know."

They gazed into each other's eyes. Hers were smoky, bruised. To his amazement, desire shot through him as strongly as if he'd not just sated it.

"Edwinna," he whispered. "I fear I need you again."

He made love to her again, very gently, before they fell asleep. As he'd fearfully anticipated, she'd suffered a flash of terror when he started to mount her in the traditional way, and he instantly stopped and swept her into his arms, rocking her, soothing, petting, whispering words of assurance while she clung to him in fear, whimpering.

"It's all right, Edwinna."

"Drake—I'm sorry."

"Shssh, shssh, I understand, I do."

"I don't want to be like this."

"I know, I know, shssh."

When he'd calmed her, they'd lain in each other's arms and talked gently. Later, he'd made love to her in an unorthodox position, but one he found arousing and erotic, and they'd both found satisfaction. He thought it a blessing she knew nothing of common sexual practices, aside from her father's brutal attack. For she was a tabula rasa—his blank slate. He could write on her, teach her.

They fell asleep side by side, letting the trade winds caress and cool their bodies, lying on their backs, hand in hand, fingers companionably twined. As he drifted off, he realized he'd not felt so content in years, if ever.

Edwinna awoke before dawn, well before the six o'clock bell. There was the initial shock of the unfamiliar room, the bed, and Drake asleep beside her, his broad shoulder and black hair strikingly dark against the pillow. It passed, and she lay quietly watching him, listening to the sound of the grinder, remembering the splendor of the night.

She hadn't known he'd be so gentle. Instantly she contradicted herself. Yes, she had. She'd known it from the moment she'd met him in Simon Tarcher's cottage, else she wouldn't have found the courage to marry him. Taking care not to wake him, she eased out of bed. The cool floor planks met the soles of her feet. Everything felt different this morning.

She fished about on the floor to find her night rail and pulled it over her head. She felt sore from his lovemaking, but pleasantly so.

"Where do you think you're going?" he asked, his voice husky with sleep. She jumped. He'd rolled to his back, arms under his head, tufts of black hair glistening in his armpits. He was watching her.

"To the privy."

"Not without giving me a kiss."

She smiled a little, brushed a hand through her tangled hair, and leaned over the bed. He reached up with gentle hands and drew her down on top of him. His breath smelled stale, of last night's endless kisses. So did hers. Neither cared.

"There is a cardinal rule in this marriage, Mrs. Steel. Neither of us leaves the bed in the morning without giving the other a kiss. It's rude."

Mrs. Steel. Joy filled her. "I don't want to be rude."

"Good." They kissed—a sweet, warm kiss. Sleep-warmed, Drake's shoulders were smooth and muscular to the touch. They kissed again, softly, until their heartbeats quickened, but then the six o'clock bell clanged in the trade winds.

Drake loosened his grip and gave her a rueful smile. "We'll have to start earlier if we intend to do this every morning and harvest, too."

"Yes."

He smoothed back her hair, an affectionate gesture.

"Edwinna, I'm fond of you."

Fondness wasn't love. She knew that. His love was buried with Anne Steel. But she could make do with fondness. She could! She would rather have fondness from this gentle man than love from any other man in the world.

"I'm fond of you, too, Drake." Then, stabbed by the dishonesty of it, she said, "That isn't true. I love you."

She pushed off the bed and hurried out of the room. Drake watched her go with worry. He felt a stab of guilt again. He wished he loved her. But the truth was, he did not.

* * *

Love her or not, he was surprised by the surge of pleasure and well-being he felt when she came out into the cane fields to visit him that morning. Perhaps this *was* love, of a different sort. It was not the possessive, fiery love he'd felt for Anne. This was more peaceful, pleasanter. An "old man's love," he thought humorously, though at thirty-three, he did not yet feel completely ancient.

He smiled as she came striding to him, and she smiled, too, her eyes fiercely proud and shining. She'd come out to the field on a needless errand, and that pleased him. She wanted to be near him. He slipped an arm around her waist and walked her along the cut cane rows, staying clear of the oozing, sticky stubble. Fresh cut, the field smelled of sugar. They strolled along companionably, estimating the morning's tonnage together, talking, walking. His shirt was so wet with sweat the tail of it flapped in the trade winds, yet she didn't object to being near him.

During the first noisy half of the midday meal at Crawford Hall's table, Matthew Plum failed to notice anything different. Then, suddenly, he became aware. His eyebrows lifted. Something was different here.

He stopped chewing in midbite and glanced at Edwinna, then at Drake. Edwinna glowed. There was a radiance to her, and whenever Drake made the slightest comment conversing with the men, her eyes flew to him.

He looked at Drake. Something was different here, too. Drake had never looked more relaxed, more the master. He sat at the master's place with an easy grace, speaking no more than his share, but speaking sense whenever he opened his mouth. Drake's eyes went often to Edwinna, and he asked her opinion on every issue that came up.

Something lovely was happening here. Plum didn't want to spoil it. He finished chewing his mouthful of food, rose, and directed his overseers to get back to their work. They looked up in surprise, but promptly got up and went out. Plum courteously thanked Edwinna and Drake for the meal, then left himself, telling Edwinna he did not wish to look at accounts this noon. He wanted a nap.

"How very odd," Edwinna said to Drake, when Matthew Plum had left. Striding away from the house whistling, he scarcely sounded like a man who needed a nap.

Drake smiled against his propped hands.

"It isn't odd at all. Plum's an astute man. He has eyes."

"What do you mean?" She felt breathless with Drake looking at her that way. Awareness heightened, like the smell of a fresh wind. What a beautiful feeling.

"How about you, Mrs. Steel? Do you ever nap?"

"No, never."

"I do. Would you care to join me?"

Gazing into the frank invitation in his eyes, she felt her heart thrash against her ribs. *I want this! I'm a woman. I want what other women have. I want to love and be loved.*

Upstairs, they bolted the door against Tutu and Priscilla and reached for each other. They kissed, mouths open, warm, moist, seeking. She trembled at the touch of Drake's mouth as he roamed everywhere—her breast, her neck, her waist, her armpit. He was shameless, avid. He took her hand and brought it to his stiff, hot erection, teaching her to move sensually on it.

When the time came to undress, she began to shake.

"Don't be afraid."

"I'm not." But she couldn't stop shaking, so he undressed her himself, his hands gentle, his eyes hot. He slowly stripped away her shirt, shift, breeches, stockings, shoes, and her sex-moist drawers, which he kissed. Then he undressed himself, keeping his eyes on hers, shrugging out of his clothes with an urgency that took her breath away, made her know she was needed. When she threw a terrified glance at the bed, he didn't take her there.

Planting his feet on the floor, strong legs spread, he put

his hands under her arms and raised her straight up the length of his strong body. His chest hair brushed her breasts soft as a kitten.

"Wrap your arms around my neck, Edwinna," he ordered. "Hold on tight." One at a time, he fitted her legs around his waist. "Lock your ankles at my waist. Don't be afraid."

"I'm not."

He gripped her buttocks and lowered her onto his shaft. She gasped at the shock of it, the initial probing, then the sudden burgeoning fullness inside her. She panted. Sweat broke on his forehead, his chest. Gripping her tightly, he began to sway from side to side, gently swinging her. She clawed his hot shoulders.

"Oh, dear God . . ."

"Edwinna."

The swinging grew wilder. He pumped, panted, sweated. It was wild and sweet. When her spasms started she cried out, "Drake," and he plunged a hand to her throbbing spot.

"Come for me, Edwinna, come." She did. So wildly that when it was over she melted against him. With a pleased moan, he thrust and took his moment, gripping her close, his body stiff as wood. When he finished, he shook, as she had. His knees buckled a little, but he caught himself and held her until his erection went down and he could safely set her on her feet. Then he helped her to bed.

They lay breathing deeply, Drake on his back, one knee raised, his organ limp, wet, glistening. Edwinna lay on her stomach and inched closer, her forehead touching his shoulder. He wearily patted her buttocks. The pat spoke of affection. Blissful, content, she fell asleep to the monotonous drone of the grinder.

They awoke, startled, when the two o'clock work bell clanged. Jolted awake, they lifted their heads and looked at each other in surprise, happiness.

"That, Mrs. Steel," Drake murmured, "is what I call a *nap*."

Mrs. Steel. The name filled her with pride. She gazed at him, aware that her eyes must be shining much too proudly. Obedient to the bell by long habit, she got out of bed and began to dress. He lay watching her. When she stooped to retrieve her clothes, a wet, lustrous globule ran down her inner thigh. She took the shirt, which needed changing, and patted it away. Drake watched, his eyes growing dark, sexual.

"Do you mind?" he asked softly. "My seed in you?"

Drake felt himself grow tense, waiting for her answer. Anne had minded. He'd loved her so much. Wanted her so much. Wanted her to want him, all of him, himself, his seed.

Edwinna looked at him, her eyes uncertain, honest.

"No. Not if it's of you."

"Come here," he said, his voice husky.

She did. He drew her onto the bed, took her into his arms, laid her under him, and kissed her passionately. They didn't return to the harvest fields until four.

CHAPTER
* 16 *

The months of spring passed in a golden idyll. Years later when Drake recalled this time of his life, he would remember blue skies, green cane fields, and contentment. He saw the island with new eyes now and appreciated its savage beauty. He took satisfaction in small things—in a day's work well done, in a slave running to him and calling him Papa. Except for missing his children and his wine business, he was happy.

He was fond of Edwinna. She proved to be as staunch and loyal a mate as he could want. She wasn't Anne. He didn't love her, couldn't. Anne still owned that part of him. But his fondness for Edwinna deepened every day. In bed she was all that a man could want—passionate, teachable, willing.

Whenever he thought about returning to England, he felt a pang. He would miss her. He thought about taking her with him, but that would be a cruelty, a gross self-indulgence on his part. London wasn't Barbados. She would be unhappy there. London was a smoky, crowded, close-packed city where in winter the sun seldom shone and where you could walk blocks without seeing a single blade of green grass. Drake loved it; he'd been born there. But Edwinna wouldn't. She would pine for her cane fields, for her Barbados sun, for blue skies and trade winds.

His contentment troubled him. The ease with which he was slipping into his role as master of Crawford Plantation drove a spike through his conscience. What was he, a hypocrite? He loathed slavery, yet spent his days contentedly being "Papa."

His keen interest in sugar also troubled him. On the day the first batch of cured sugar pots had been brought to the knocking house, he'd waited as excitedly as Edwinna to see if the sugar would be top-quality muscovado or if it would have to be sold at a lesser price. He found sugar as interesting as wine, and it bothered him.

He didn't want to get attached to anything or anyone on this island, but his relationship with others grew daily: to Plum; to David, with his compassionate doctoring; to Kena, with her gentle ways; to Tutu, whom he carried about in his arms the way he'd carried Katherine. He'd even grown fond of Dinny and her Jumbo and that sexual scamp Macaw, who needed three wives in order to boil good sugar.

He smiled walking up from the cane fields in the blowing wind, recalling Macaw's latest outrageous demand.

"Macaw still wants a new wife," Edwinna had said as they had sat at supper the night before. He'd grown used to dining in semidarkness, candles always being in short supply. He'd even grown used to sugar on everything, although Honor had tempered her use of it after he'd barked at her a few hundred times.

Drake had put his spoon down. "He wants *what*?"

"He gave Juba and the twins to Kinto. He wants another wife to replace her."

"Edwinna, are we running a plantation or a brothel?"

She'd smiled broadly. "A plantation." He'd smiled, too.

They'd discovered companionship, an easiness with each other, enjoyment in each other's company. It wasn't what he'd had with Anne, but it was . . . special.

"Macaw already has two wives," he'd complained. "How many wives does a man need in his bed?"

"It's not a matter of bed," she'd assured him, dipping into her food and beginning to eat. "It's pride. Macaw is head boiling house slave, and head boiling house slave always gets three wives. It's a matter of pride."

He'd had to grin. "Is that what the liar told you? That it's a matter of pride?"

"Yes."

"Let me educate you, Edwinna. With a man, it is *always* a matter of bed. Tell him no. Or give him the wife of the Ashanti who died."

"I tried to. He doesn't want a used wife."

He'd returned to his eating, thoroughly amused. "Picky, isn't he?"

"If he does not get a third wife, he will sulk. When he sulks he boils sugar poorly."

"Well, he has that down pat, hasn't he? If I thought sulking would get me everything I wanted, I would sulk my head off, too."

As she'd rushed on in her explanation, his eyes had rested on her hair, shining long and lovely in the candlelight. She wore it that way for him, brushed out, soft and thick to touch, fragrant to smell.

"I told him you would buy a wife for him the next time you go to Bridgetown."

He'd stared, incredulous. "Edwinna. I am *not* going to shop for a woman to give to Macaw. Good God! I'm a wine merchant, not a brothel keeper."

"Don't be ridiculous. It is a small matter to choose one. You are a wine merchant; if you can select good wine, you can certainly select a slave's wife."

He'd gone on eating, amusement growing.

"Very well," he'd conceded. "I'll do it. While I'm at it, I'll buy one for myself. Every planter on the island has one."

Her head had come up, her eyes narrowing. He'd seen a flash of jealousy, possessiveness. He'd smiled.

"I'm teasing."

She drew a breath. "Well, never mind about buying Macaw's wife. I will do it myself!"

He had smiled then, but now, walking into the wind, he frowned. All of this made him content? He ought to be ashamed.

He was glad Arthur's letters came with frequency, full of detail, business, home. The letters preserved his sanity and kept him focused on London.

During that idyllic spring Edwinna was happy, too—so happy it scared her. She knew from experience that happiness was a transitory thing—here one day, gone the next. She loved Drake—loved him too much. Every day, every night she fell more deeply in love. What would she do when he left? How could she bear up?

He *would* leave. She knew it. Each time he received a letter from his brother-in-law, he became pensive, distant, as if he'd already gone. He shared the letters with her, particularly the sweet anecdotes about William or Katherine. They chuckled together, but underneath the companionship, she knew what he was thinking. *I want to be home. With my children.*

If she truly loved him, she would send him home, but she wanted to keep him a little longer. She couldn't send him home. Not yet. But soon, she vowed silently. *I swear to you, Drake, I will send you home to your children soon. Just stay with me a little longer—just a little longer.*

Drake and Edwinna received a jolt in March when a letter came from the governor informing them that George and Clive Crawford's legal heir, a second cousin in England, had preceded them in death, and the ecclesiastical court of London had awarded George Crawford's plantation to his nearest kin—Edwinna, Harry, and Thomas Crawford.

Edwinna was elated, and Drake was elated for her. They rode over to the plantation at once, taking Plum with them. Alerted to expect their visit, George Crawford's overseer came riding out to meet them. He was a sullen man with the stink of kill-devil clinging to him. He saw the handwriting on the wall—dismissal.

They rode into the cane fields first and recoiled at the neglect: unweeded fields, cut cane that had been piled in the paths and allowed to rot. Edwinna's cane fields grew lush and green, so thick a man couldn't walk into a ripe field without getting slashed to ribbons by the stiff, healthy foliage, but George Crawford's fields grew sparsely, like cornfields. Fourth-year rattoon cane had been allowed to spring up in half of the fields, a sign of a neglectful overseer. When they finally came to decent acreage and a field of cane that stood fully ripe, Edwinna's outrage spilled over.

"This field is overripe. Why haven't you cut it?" she demanded of the overseer.

"Ain't got to it yet." A cheeky answer.

Drake kneed his horse forward. "Get to it! Today. I'll be back tomorrow to check it's done. This is Mrs. Steel's plantation now. You'll answer to her, and so help me God, if I come back tomorrow and smell you stinking of rum, you're dismissed on the spot, without your year's pay. Do you understand?"

The fellow shot him a sullen look. "Yes sir."

They rode on. The more they saw, the angrier they became. Edwinna grew flushed, upset. Plum's eyebrows knitted into a harsh line across his brow. The slaves' condition was appalling. They were sick with malnutrition. Out in the fields, they chopped listlessly at the ground, lacking the energy to lift the hoe.

"What do you feed them?" Edwinna demanded.

"Lob lollie."

"What else? Surely plantain. It's their native food."

"Nay."

"Surely dried fish, beans, vegetables from the provisions fields?"

"Mr. Crawford, he didn't b'lieve in overfeeding 'em."

"Overfeeding them?" Drake felt as if he would explode. "God in heaven, Edwinna!"

"Yes." Her eyes blazed with anger. She turned to Plum. "I want two cartfuls of my plantain cut and brought here at once, then two cartfuls every Saturday afternoon. Also, two barrels of dried fish and three barrels of dried beans."

"And tomorrow," Drake said quietly to Plum, "let's bring James McCarran here. He can tear out a few acres of that worthless rattoon cane and put in provisions fields and plantain groves."

Plum nodded approvingly. "Soil's poor. Worn out by the cane and not enough dunging. But we'll dung it, bring it back proper within two, three years."

They found the mill in working condition, the grinder grinding, the boilers boiling. But the output was meager and of low quality. When they lighted a candle and went into the curing house to knock on sugar pots, even Drake could tell that molasses permeated the sugar from top to bottom.

"What about Alvis Nansellock?" Edwinna said to Plum when they emerged from the curing house and blew out the candle.

"My very choice. He will make an excellent head overseer."

"Drake, what do you think?"

"Absolutely, Nansellock."

They rode next to the slave village, and as expected, they found the slaves underfed and many of them sick. Edwinna picked up a baby of about twelve months and felt his forehead.

"This baby is sick," she snapped at the overseer. "Where is your plantation doctor?"

"Ain't got one. Mr. Crawford, he said 'twas a waste o'

money to hire a plantation doctor. Them niggers 'n bond slaves what's going to die, they'll die anyways.''

Drake riffled a hand through his hair. He wished George Crawford were alive so he could strangle him.

"I'm taking this baby to my plantation. And his mother. Where is she?"

"Weeding in the fields, I s'ppose."

"Find her," Drake ordered, "and find the father, too. The poor devil will despair if he comes in from the fields and finds his family gone. He'll think they've been sold."

Drake found another sick child in one of the slave huts, a little girl. "Don't be afraid, sweetheart," he said tenderly as he picked her up. "We're going to find your mother and then take you to a doctor." She was a little thing, no bigger than Katherine.

When the overseer produced the key to George Crawford's house, they saw the ultimate obscenity. While his slaves had lived in squalor, Crawford himself had lived like royalty, surrounding himself with every amenity. Silk upholstered furniture stood in the parlor. Oriental carpets graced the floors. Silver chandeliers hung from the ceilings.

They made a quick tour. In George Crawford's plantation office, Drake packed up business ledgers and financial papers and arranged for them to be brought to Crawford Plantation. They belonged to Edwinna now, and he intended to study them for her.

A week later, working by candlelight across from her in her plantation office, Drake closed the last of the ledgers.

"Congratulations. You are a wealthy woman." He glanced at his work sheet. "Less seven thousand pounds in creditors' bills that must be paid, the total value of your uncle's property—including land, slaves, bond slaves, millworks, house, furnishings—amounts to forty thousand pounds. That's a conservative estimate because I'm a conservative businessman. It may be more."

She gazed at him, stunned. "So much?"

"Yes. So much. What will you do with it?"

She propped her elbows on the table and held her head in her hands for a moment, taking it all in. "What will I do with it? Plant the land and sell the furnishings to improve the mill. Why are you smiling?"

"I'm smiling because you love land the way most women love pretty gowns and jewels." He leaned back in his chair and folded his arms. "I'm also smiling because I'm thinking that my entire London property—warehouse, wine shop, and house—amounts to only one-third of an acre. With your two plantations, you oversee eight hundred acres."

"But London property is valuable. And someday you will reclaim Highgate Hall, and that's a grand estate."

His smile broadened. "It's grand because it's my home and I love it, not because it's worth a lot of money. It isn't. The house is a handsome old Tudor that needs repair. The grounds consist of an orchard, a produce field, a small shooting woods where the Steels have hunted deer and pheasant for a hundred and fifty years. It is only twenty acres."

"Still," she said loyally, "it sounds beautiful. I–I would like to see it someday. And see your Thames Street house and wine shop and warehouse, too."

"I would like you to see it someday," he said.

Her heart pounded. Did he mean it? Pushing the candle aside, he leaned across the table, his lips parting. She leaned toward him and gave him her mouth. He was so sexually eager it thrilled her. He made her feel like . . . a woman. He reached out and pinched the candle flame, snuffing it out.

"Let's go to bed, Mrs. Steel."

At supper a few nights later, David Alleyne joyfully announced that Kena was pregnant. It was a blow for Edwinna. Drake congratulated David and sent to the kitchen for wine to toast the event. Edwinna congratulated both of them, hugged them, kissed them. She even took a sip of wine to honor the announcement, a thing she did not normally do. But behind her happy smile, she felt bruised, injured. She felt as if life were passing her by.

Drake noticed her distress and broached the subject in bed that night. They had just finished making love, and they lay in drowsy contentment, slightly dazed by the wonders they'd shared. Aroused by David's news, Drake had been in an erotic mood, tender and passionate. It had been wonderful for both of them, and when they finished, he'd gathered her into his arms and kissed her, whispering words of fondness, praise, gratitude. It still thrilled her to think of it. Now he brushed his lips across her temple, found the pulse point, and kissed it.

"Are you unhappy about the baby?"

"A little," she admitted. "I'm happy for them, but sad for myself." She turned her head on the pillow to look at him. The linen rasped under her thick, curly hair. At night she wore it the way he liked it—unbraided, loose for love.

"I have always wanted to be a mother, Drake."

He kissed her forehead in sympathy. She knew he felt sorry for her, but she also knew he had reservations. He was not the sort of man who would sire a child in the Caribbean and be willing to leave it behind. He was too possessive a father.

"What is the cause? Do you know?"

He gave his hand to her to hold while she told him. She gripped it tightly. "I am not a normal woman."

"Yes, you are. Our marriage bed is testimony to that. You are normal in every way."

"I do not get my monthly courses, Drake. I have not had them since I was fifteen or sixteen."

He lifted up on one elbow and looked at her in the moonlight. He smoothed a lock of her hair from her forehead. "Have you consulted anyone?"

"Yes. Midwives. Also, a doctor in Bridgetown a few years ago. They all say the same. I will never have a child."

"Maybe they are wrong. You're very slender, and I've heard that women who are too slender sometimes do not get their courses. When they gain weight, their bodies adjust."

Unwilling to be morose for him, she gave him a humorous smile. "Then I hope I get fat as a cow."

Because she gazed at him with such love and humor, he smiled and said, "I hope so, too." But she knew he did not. He didn't want to leave a child in the Caribbean.

With two plantations to oversee, and one of them in wretched condition, life became so busy Edwinna scarcely had time to think. She worked. Drake worked beside her. Each night they slept in each other's arms, and she found it harder and harder to think of parting with him. But she had promised he could leave at the close of his first year, and that year was fast slipping away.

Truly a planter, she couldn't stay away from George Crawford's plantation, which she'd renamed the Thomas and Harry Crawford Plantation. The slaves were her prime concern, and then the poor condition of the soil. Drake was always grinning at her, teasing her because she was ecstatic about every cartful of cattle dung that was brought from Crawford Plantation to fertilize the new fields.

Physicians in the Caribbean proved to be as scarce as icebergs. She failed to get one. She had to write London. In the meantime, David Alleyne nobly covered both plantations. Overworked, he remained cheerful, exuberant. His love for Kena filled him with zest. On the day Kena began to show and exchanged her gowns for loose smocks, he was jubilant. Edwinna was not. She felt devastated. Drake sensed it, and that night he made tender, gentle love to her. When it was over he held her in his arms and whispered consolations in her ear. She had lots of children, children who loved her. She had her slave children.

But it wasn't the same. She knew it. Drake knew it.

* * *

Drake and Plum accompanied the season's first load of sugar down to Speightstown, where they watched with pride as the top-quality muscovado was emptied out of the barrels into enormous, two-thousand-pound hogsheads and then loaded aboard ship for transport to England. Drake was surprised at the immense satisfaction he felt. Sugar was a long, arduous undertaking, but a man could take pride in seeing it done right, from the first cut in the cane field to this final step, seeing it off to England. He felt as if he were sending a child off. No wonder Edwinna was passionate about planting.

He and Plum stayed the night with Simon Tarcher, partaking of Tarcher's hospitality, dining companionably on fish, lingering long at table, drinking wine, talking.

"So, Mr. Steel. Now that you've been through a harvest with us, what are your plans?" Tarcher asked, using the table candle to light his pipe. Aside from the single candle, the cottage lay dark. Plum took up a pipe, too, and gestured to Drake, who declined. He disliked Barbados tobacco.

"The same. I haven't changed. I am who I am—a London wine merchant. My business is wine. My home is London."

"Meaning you will leave Barbados at your twelfth month."

"Yes."

"Will you come back?" Plum asked bluntly.

Drake first looked Tarcher in the eye, then Plum. "No." He liked and respected Tarcher and Plum, and he had no intention of lying to either of these men. "By now you know I'm not a pirate. Edwinna knows it, too. I've worked hard during harvest. I deserve my freedom. I have my family and my wine business to tend."

Tarcher sucked on his pipe, bushy white eyebrows meeting in a frown. "What about Edwinna?"

Plum seconded the question, smoking on his pipe. "Yes. What about Edwinna?" The scent of Barbados tobacco curled into the air, rank, raw.

"She is my legal wife. She will remain so. I will do nothing to change that—nothing to jeopardize her legal status or her right to rule her plantations. I would never hurt her in that way."

"We mean her feelings," Tarcher said plainly.

Drake felt his hackles rise. He disliked people probing into his private matters. But Tarcher and Plum were not being inquisitive. They were concerned. They loved Edwinna. Between the two of them, they'd been far more of a father to her than had that bastard, Peter Crawford. Drake owed them answers.

He swirled the wine in his cup and gazed at it. "I'd thought of taking her with me, but that would be a cruelty. London is not Barbados. She would be unhappy there, shut in a city. She would pine for her cane fields, her sugar making."

Plum sucked on his pipe. "Ay, she'd be a fish out of water."

Tarcher took the wine pitcher and refilled their cups, one by one: Drake's, Plum's, his own. "Tell us, Mr. Steel. What can we say or do to persuade you to stay?"

Drake shook his head. "Nothing. I have children, Mr. Tarcher. I have a wine business that has been in the Steel family six generations. I have a commitment to it. I owe it my loyalty."

They drank and smoked in silence. Tarcher looked at him from beneath white, bushy eyebrows—an acute, alert look.

"You must know, of course, that Harry and Thomas are dead. They must be. They have not been heard from in three years. If they were alive, they would have sent word, written."

Drake drew a slow, deep breath. "I have hoped, for Edwinna's sake, that they're alive. That at worst they are prisoners aboard some pirate ship, as I was, and will one day be freed."

"Your fate was an exceptionally lucky one, Mr. Steel." Plum spat a shred of tobacco leaf into his palm and discarded it. "Few men are fortunate enough to survive captivity on a pirate ship. 'Dead men tell no tales.' That is the pirate's credo."

"I hope Edwinna doesn't begin to realize they're dead. It will destroy her."

"It is up to the three of us to see she does not."

"Yes." Drake agreed. "Yes, it is."

They drank and smoked in silence, their hearts heavy with the thought of two vital, vigorous young men, probably dead, their bones possibly at the bottom of the sea.

"Mr. Steel," Tarcher said, breaking the silence, "if the day should ever come that Thomas and Harry are proved dead, Edwinna will need you. She will need you more than she has ever needed any human being on this earth."

Plum's nod, his worried eyes, seconded it.

Drake brooded on the words, took them to bed with him, lay in the darkness in his hammock and turned them over and over in his head, then slept with them and awoke in the morning still thinking about them.

The thing Edwinna had dreaded with all her heart happened so suddenly, so unexpectedly, she hadn't even a moment to shield her heart for the blow.

It was the Sabbath. Finished with bond slave prayers and slave petitions, she and Drake were alone eating midday meal, talking together, enjoying the Sunday respite, when a packet of letters arrived, sent up from Bridgetown. She quickly riffled through them with a momentary lowering of spirits. Again, there was nothing from Thomas and Harry. But a letter had come for Drake from Verity. She passed it to him and he received it with both a smile and a look of uneasiness. She understood. Letters could bring bad news as well as good.

He broke the seal instantly and had read for only a moment when he looked up with enormous excitement. "Edwinna, it's happened. The Protectorate government is gone, abolished. Parliament voted to restore the monarchy, and King

Charles has returned from exile. He set foot on English soil May the twenty-fifth!''

Edwinna smiled happily. She didn't care who ruled England, monarchy or Protectorate, so long as they didn't meddle in Barbados sugar, but she knew Drake cared passionately, and his father had cared to the point of sacrificing his life for the king.

"Drake, it's wonderful."

"Yes, yes, it is." Blue eyes bright with excitement, he read his letter swiftly, silently, raking his hand through his black hair. He glanced up often to share bits and pieces aloud. Not all of it was pleasant to hear. The Restoration had meant another bloodbath. Eager for revenge, the persecuted cavaliers and Royalists were now doing to Cromwell's followers what Cromwell had done to them. They were hunting them down, throwing them in the Tower of London, hanging them, drawing and quartering them, and displaying their decapitated heads publicly.

Edwinna shuddered. When King Charles and his procession had ridden into London by way of London Bridge, they'd been able to look up and see impaled on spikes the heads of the very men who'd beheaded King Charles's father, a dozen years earlier. Radical Royalists did even more. Burning for revenge, they had disinterred Oliver Cromwell's body, which was two years buried, cut off the head, climbed with it to the tallest spire of Westminister Abbey, and impaled it there for all of London to see.

King Charles, Drake read, had stopped the bloodshed. Determined to heal the wounds of the civil war and to knit the divided country together, he'd granted amnesty to all of Cromwell's supporters except the actual regicides.

Drake grew silent, reading on by himself, lost in the text. She watched his excitement grow. He drew a deep breath and raked a hand through his hair, then looked up with a smile.

"How does this sound: *Sir Drake Steel*."

For a moment she didn't comprehend. Then she gasped. "Drake! You're to be knighted?"

He nodded happily. "Listen to this, Edwinna." Too excited to sit, he leapt up and paced the dining chamber as he read the rest of Verity's letter to her. As reward for the Steel family's loyalty to the crown, the Steel family home, Highgate Hall, was to be restored to the family immediately. The present owners were to be turned out and ordered to pay restitution for the years they'd occupied it. Further, for his service to the king and to the secret organization known as the Sealed Knot during the years of exile, Drake was to be granted a knighthood. The grant of arms would be a hereditary title, remaining in the Steel family with the right to be passed down from generation to generation.

Drake looked at her, eyes alive with excitement. "When I am long gone from this earth, William will be Sir William, and when William is gone, *his* son. . . ."

"Drake, it's wonderful," she said softly.

"It is, isn't it, Edwinna?" He gave her a dazzling smile, then paced and finished reading the letter to her. The king's coronation would take place in Westminster Abbey in April of next year. Drake's knighting would be one month after the coronation in the assembly of others to be knighted. Further, having been petitioned by Verity, the king had ordered all charges of piracy to be stricken from Drake's name and ordered Drake to present himself at Whitehall Palace in London as soon as possible.

Drake read on, providing details from Verity's letter, but Edwinna heard nothing more. She sat shattered, stunned. The king had ordered . . . Drake was leaving!

He finished the letter and looked at her with an excited, happy smile, wanting her to be proud. She forced herself to say what she had to, but her lips were wooden.

"You must go, of course."

"Yes! As soon as possible." He headed out of the room. "Excuse me, Edwinna. I'm too excited to eat. I want to draft my letters and send them to Bridgetown at once—one to His Majesty and one to Verity. I'll use the privacy of the office.'' His footfalls faded down the corridor.

Edwinna couldn't breathe she hurt so badly. With effort, she pushed herself to her feet and left the house, dazed.

At the stable, she saddled her mare and rode east into the trade winds to the privacy of the desolate Atlantic shore. The trade winds blew hard, drying the tears on her cheeks as they spilled. Without consciously searching for it, she reached the spot where Drake had kept her company the day of the Bridgetown executions, comforted her, talked with her. She tethered her horse and sat alone where they'd sat together, her arms wrapped around her knees. The tears wouldn't stop.

She wiped them away. It was so foolish to cry. Before Drake had come into her life, she'd never cried. She hadn't cried when her mother left. She hadn't cried when her father died. She hadn't cried when Thomas and Harry had run off to sea.

But here she was, weeping for a London wine merchant she'd known less than a year—a man she could surely live without if she would but try. She wished Drake had never come to Barbados. She wished she'd never gone to Speightstown on pirate execution day.

No. That wasn't true. She could never wish that. She wanted Drake alive, even if she would never see him again.

She rested her forehead on her knees and let the tears flow. Deep in her heart, she knew she was not crying for Drake alone. She was crying tears that were years overdue. She was crying because she'd loved her mother, because she'd loved her father, despite what he'd done to her. She was crying because she missed Thomas and Harry. She was crying for Marigold and Jeremy. And—stupid!—she was crying for Jocko. She sensed the tears were Drake's gift to her. He had taught her how to cry, how to be alive, how to feel.

When the tears were done, she lifted her face and let the

wind dry her cheeks. She felt cleansed, reborn. She stayed past sunset and waited for moonrise so she would be able to ride home by its light. She'd just stood to go when she saw Drake riding toward her.

She could see from the set of his shoulders that he was angry. He leapt down from his horse, strode toward her, grabbed her by one shoulder, and wrenched her chin up so he could see her face plainly in the moonlight. It was the first roughness she'd ever had from him, and it would have scared her, except that his eyes shone with worry, not meanness.

"What's the meaning of this?" he demanded. "Where in hell have you been?"

"Here."

"All day? Why?"

"I had to be alone."

"Why?" he demanded again. "This was my happy day. My triumph. You belonged at my side, sharing it. You owed me that much. Now I want to know *why*. Why did you go off alone?"

"To—to get used to living without you."

He was taken aback. His anger slackened, and so did his grip. His eyes searched hers. "Good lord, Edwinna. Did you think I would go to London without you? Take my honor and be knighted with no regard for you? Have you been sitting here all afternoon, alone, thinking that?"

"Yes."

"You damned idiot." He crushed her close. "Edwinna, you are my *wife*. I want you at my side. When the king knights me, I want you standing there, taking pride in me. Of what use is an honor if a man's wife is not there to share it?"

For a moment she thought her heart might burst.

"You want me with you? Me?"

He smiled. "You." He pressed a soft kiss on her lips. "You."

"But, my plantations—I can't live in London."

"I know that. But you can visit. Stay a year. Then I'll bring you safely back to Barbados. I swear it. I've already talked to Plum and Nansellock while I searched for you this afternoon. They agreed. They can manage both plantations for a year."

"Drake, I love you!"

He cupped her face and leaned his forehead against hers. "Edwinna. I once told you that what I liked best about you is your good clean soul. That's true. Because it is, I want to be honest with you. I want to speak to you about my feelings for Anne, if you can bear it."

"I can."

He smoothed her cheeks with his thumbs, a husband's affectionate gesture. She wanted him to go on doing it forever. She placed her hands fiercely over his.

"I loved her more than it's possible for a man to love a woman—more than it's sensible to love. Beyond all reason, all logic, all sanity. I cannot explain it. I do not understand it myself. It simply was. It was like . . . lightning between us. Can you understand that?"

"Yes."

"Anne still owns my love. Even in death."

"I know that."

"But what I feel for you is a fondness so deep and so satisfying it leaves me entirely at peace. Edwinna, you give me the one thing Anne never was able to give me . . . peace. I'm not a fool. I cherish that. And you. If you can make do with me, if you can make do with fondness, with a husband who will not always be with you, who may be gone for years on end . . . if you can make do with a husband who hates slavery and will fight you tooth and nail on the issue until the end of our days . . ."

She gazed at him with shining eyes.

"I can," she said fiercely. "I can make do, Drake."

"So can I."

* * *

The weeks flew by at an exhilarating pace. Leaving a plantation for an entire year was no small matter. There was much to do—preparations to make, problems to foresee and prevent.

Working together, she and Drake tended to the details. They stocked up on supplies: tools, clothing, food staples, medicines. They ordered extra parts for the grinders, agreeing that it was better to be prepared than to take a chance Matthew Plum and Alvis Nansellock might reach midharvest and find themselves with a broken grinder. They applied to the governor for tickets to leave the colony, and notified the other planters. Determined to avoid pirates, Drake booked passage for them on a safe, well-armed ship.

As the time to leave drew near, Edwinna's anxiety grew. She was leaving her home, her plantation, everyone she loved. She began carrying Tutu everywhere, hugging and kissing him. She wouldn't see him for a whole year.

"Mixed feelings?" Drake said as they lay in bed too excited to sleep the night before they were to sail.

"Yes. I will miss being here for Kena's baby."

"David will write us."

"I know. But it's not the same. And I worry that Thomas and Harry will come home while I'm gone."

Drake lifted up on one elbow and gazed at her. "That would be all to the good, would it not? Then they'll be here when you return."

"That's true. But . . . I will miss them all—Tutu, Kena, Matthew Plum, David, Macaw, the boiling house, the grinder, everything." Then, lest he think she didn't want to go with him, she gave him a fierce look. "But it will be thrilling to be in London. I can watch my sugar come in by ship."

He looked at her with amusement. "I'll take you down to the docks every day and let you knock on sugar hogsheads to your heart's content." She smiled. She liked it when he teased her. She felt loved, even though the extent of that love was limited.

"Do you have regrets, Edwinna?" Drake asked.

She shook her head. "No. Do you?"

He covered her mouth with his and kissed her with passion. "None. Not one."

They sailed out of Bridgetown on the afternoon tide, standing in the stern of the ship, watching the island slip past them. Sailing past Speightstown, they looked up the terraced hillsides to the plateau and saw the tip of their own windmill above the cane fields. Edwinna swallowed with emotion. Drake squeezed her waist.

"You'll come back."

"I know." But she could not help wondering. Would *he*?

CHAPTER
* 17 *

Years later, when Edwinna looked back on it, she remembered the voyage as the happiest time of her life—a honeymoon spent in the arms of the man she'd sworn to love, honor, and obey.

The trip was glorious. She was seasick the first two days when the ship left the calm Caribbean and plowed into the rough Atlantic Ocean, but she soon got better and took to sailing with zest. When she'd recovered, she found Drake eager—his arms waiting for her, his mouth curved with passion, and his ways in bed wildly exciting.

If she never got to heaven, this would do, this bit of paradise with Drake—lying in his arms every night, being his companion every day. With the vast, unending sea surrounding them, the ship became their little world and they the only people in it.

At leisure for the first time in their hardworking lives, they spent all of their time together, and with immense pleasure. They made love, they talked for hours on end. Drake shared himself with her, told her private things: his goals, his aspirations, his disappointments, his philosophy of life, his intense love for his children. He didn't speak of Anne. He kept that private, sacrosanct, shut away from her. More than if he'd spoken of her, it told Edwinna how much he'd loved Anne.

Yet Edwinna knew he was pleased with her. She saw the fondness in his eyes. She tried to please him in small ways. Because he liked it that way, she wore her hair unbraided, loose, wind-tossed, full of sea air and sunshine. Occasionally, she put on a gown because he smiled so whenever she did. She would wear gowns in London, of course. She wouldn't embarrass Drake. But aboard ship, breeches and shirt were more practical. Sometimes, sunning themselves in the privacy of the rear deck, Drake's muscular chest bare, he would gently remove her shirt, too, giving her sun; and he would lie there with his spiky black lashes partly closed, watching her. Now and then he would lean over and take her swollen nipple into his warm, wet mouth and suckle. She trembled with anticipation whenever that private, intimate gleam came into his eyes. She wondered if all the things they did in bed were normal. Then she decided she didn't care. If she and Drake were happy doing them, that was all that mattered.

Drake encouraged her to talk on that long, leisurely voyage. With her love for him growing every day and her trust deepening, she unlocked her heart and told him things she'd never revealed to anyone. Painful things. Childhood things. How she'd felt when her mother had left. Her father's beatings. How she'd loved her father despite the beatings. His terrifying bouts of drunkenness. And the worst—his ultimate violation. Drake held her in his arms in the darkness of their small cabin, rocking her back and forth.

"The wounds need to heal, Edwinna. They won't heal unless you speak of these things. You need to say them with your own lips. You need to hear yourself saying them. And you need to grieve a little. I'm here for you. Lean on me. I'm here."

So she experienced a deep cleansing on that voyage. She gained a sweet peace. Not a complete peace; she would never have that. She knew she would never be completely healed. So did Drake. But at least the bitterness was passing. In its wake came an aching wish: She wished her father had loved her.

The ship anchored in Lisbon, Portugal, for two weeks, and here Edwinna saw a new side of Drake—the businessman. He shopped wine, buying for his business.

Taking an interpreter along, they visited a different winery every day. She watched and listened with admiration. Wine was his element. He knew it as well as she knew sugar. He knew everything about it—what it should taste like in each stage of its fermentation, what it should smell like, look like. He knew which sediments should be in it and which should not. He also knew the price he wanted to pay and drove a hard bargain. He bought sixty barrels of assorted Portuguese wine, and they paid for it with sugar that they'd shipped with them.

When he gave her an odd look one day and said, "I'm truly surprised to find you interested in my wine business," she suddenly guessed Anne had not been.

"Of course, I'm interested," she assured him. She wondered if it had hurt him, Anne not being interested. He would never say. That was private. But she knew the answer. Of course it had.

As the ship sailed north, Edwinna experienced her first cold weather. Though Drake insisted the weather was merely cool, she shivered, bundled in the wool cloak he'd had made for her in Bridgetown. She huddled in it for the rest of the journey. The ship made one more stop—a cold one in the Channel Islands—where she piled on clothing by the layers while Drake strode about, comfortable in his shirtsleeves, relieved to be out of the Barbados climate.

"Will we see ice soon?" she asked, her teeth chattering.

He laughed and took her into his arms. He kissed her nose. "No, Mrs. Steel. This is only October. It's not cold enough for ice."

She shivered. "That is news to me. I've never been so cold in my life."

"There's only one tried and true way to get you warm, Mrs. Steel." He whispered in her ear, and she smiled. He held her close. She rested her cheek against his warm shoulder and thought about what he'd whispered, about what they would do later. She loved him so much it scared her. She wasn't used to this much happiness. In her experience, happiness didn't last. She shivered in foreboding.

"Still cold?"

"No. Just—an unpleasant thought."

"Then, we'll have to give you a more pleasant thought."

They sailed into London by way of the upper Thames River, heading for St. Katherine's Docks. Drake grew more tense with every passing minute. She knew his signs. He grew private, quiet. She didn't intrude. She left him to his thoughts, which were surely of the children he hadn't seen in almost two years.

When they debarked at St. Katherine's Docks, Drake moved swiftly. He presented their Barbados permits to the customs officer, filled out the necessary paperwork, received their tickets to enter England, then made brisk arrangements for their cargo and trunks. Impatient to be gone, he hired a hackney coach.

They clattered through the streets of London, Drake tense, she uneasy. She'd dressed carefully, wanting to make Drake proud. Under her cloak was a gown of teal blue wool with a low collar of lace, and she wore a matching hat. She suspected she wasn't fashionable, but when Drake told her she looked lovely, she smiled proudly. If he was satisfied, so was she. He was all that mattered.

Drake had dressed carefully, too. He looked incredibly handsome with his deep Caribbean tan, his intense blue eyes, his black hair clubbed neatly to the nape of his neck and tied there with a black ribbon. His broad shoulders were comfortable for once under the coat of the black wool suit made especially for him. Gazing at him with fierce pride, she thought him the handsomest man in the world.

While Drake sat tensely in the coach, enjoying the city as they rattled by, she watched it with dismay. She disliked London on sight. The sooty air and the close-packed houses made her feel breathless, trapped, as if she might suffocate. The London sun was a pale thing, not the fiery white ball of light it was in the Caribbean. For a moment she missed Barbados unbearably, but when Drake smiled at her, she smiled, too, and said nothing about disliking London. She loved him. If London was where he wanted to be, then so did she.

"We're almost there," he said tensely, taking her hand and kissing it. "My house on Thames Street is closest. We'll stop there first, to make sure it and my shop and warehouse are still standing. Then we'll go to Verity's at Cornhill. The children will be there."

Drake's house on Thames Street was as small and old as he'd described it. The whole of it could fit into Crawford Plantation's great hall with room to spare. It was locked tight. Drake couldn't get in. Since it was the Sabbath, his wine shop and warehouse were locked tight, also.

They climbed into the coach and rumbled on to Cornhill, where Drake leaped out of the coach and banged on Verity's door. Verity's house was also small and shabby. The Steel family had indeed suffered for the king's cause, Edwinna thought with sympathy.

As Edwinna watched from the coach, Verity's servant came to the door. Recognizing Drake, the elderly man exploded with joy. The two embraced, talked briefly, then Drake came striding back, gave instructions to the coachman, and leaped in. With a lurch, the coach clattered off smartly.

"They're at Highgate Hall—the whole family. My children are well and healthy. Verity and Arthur have a son, born four months ago."

"That's wonderful!"

"Yes, it is." Then he frowned. "Old Peel said some confusing things. Never mind. Young or old, he never had but half his wits about him. Verity keeps him on out of compassion, because no one else would be likely to hire him."

Drake smiled, took her hand and kissed it, then held it tensely all the way out of London, through the city gate, and out into the countryside. They went about a mile and then turned down a lane, with the coach rumbling along under trees that wore autumn color—burnished brown and saffron yellow.

"Drake, it's a beautiful old house!" Edwinna exclaimed when he'd helped her dismount at Highgate Hall and sent his hired coach to the stable.

He smiled broadly, pleased with her praise. She stood in the lane, charmed. The old Tudor mansion had a multitude of gables and steep, irregular, peaked roofs. Each generation of Steels had put its stamp on the house, adding its own contribution—a small wing here, a new gable there. The surrounding hickory nut trees bathed the old house in a blaze of golden glory. It was breathtaking.

In the side yard, two children frolicked in fallen leaves and chased each other and shrieked, throwing leaves. Arrested by the sound of the coach, they stopped and turned to look, alert, bright as new pennies. Drake drew a ragged breath and gripped her arm. One child was a little boy of about seven who had glistening black hair and wore a Sabbath suit of black wool. The other was a little girl half his age. She had blond curls and wore a long gown of green wool, a matching cape, and a little white cap that tied sweetly under her chin.

"Oh, Drake," Edwinna breathed reverently.

"I feared I would never see them again." His voice was hoarse.

With the natural curiosity of children, they came running. William was the faster. He stopped six feet away from them and stared. Katherine followed and stopped beside him.

Drake went down on one knee and held out his arms.

"William."

William's intelligent eyes blazed. "Papa!" he whooped and hurled himself into Drake's arms so hard he nearly knocked Drake over. Drake laughed and hugged him, kissed him. "William. How you've grown. You're so tall."

"Papa, Papa, I can ride a pony. Do you want to see me ride? And I caught a fish *this* long."

Precocious, a chatterbox, William talked nonstop while Drake lovingly held him and extended a hand to Katherine. "Katherine? Sweetheart, it's your papa." Shy, she stayed where she was and stared, thumb in her mouth. She'd been a baby when he'd left England. She didn't remember him. Meanwhile, William jumped all over Drake, pulling at him, trying to ride his back. Drake hugged him and kissed him but kept his gaze on Katherine. The eyes he lifted to Edwinna shone with tearful joy.

"Drake, they're wonderful," she said with feeling.

He smiled with enormous pride, then gave his attention to Katherine. "Katherine," he coaxed, trying to contain William, who wanted Drake's entire attention and nothing less. "Do you see this lady? This is the lady who owns Priscilla."

The little girl's eyes grew big. Edwinna dropped to her knees, crisp yellow leaves rustling under her as she brought herself to the child's level.

"Katherine?" Edwinna said gently. "Priscilla sent a hug for you. Do you want the hug?"

Katherine nodded solemnly, and Drake and Edwinna looked at each other with their hearts in their throats as Katherine came into Edwinna's arms with a child's accepting trust. "Oh, you're so sweet." Edwinna hugged her, eyes closed to savor the sweetness. It was like having Tutu in her arms again. "Priscilla also told your papa to give you a hug. Will you let your papa give you Priscilla's hug?" Katherine nodded and trustingly went into Drake's arms, or, rather, into his arm, there being only one free, with William tugging on the other. "Katherine," he said emotionally. He squeezed her, kissed her, then kissed William.

Edwinna watched with eyes brimming. She'd been wrong not to send Drake home the instant she'd rescued him from Speightstown's cove. He loved his children so. He belonged with them.

The four of them sat happily on the warm, sunny ground in the autumn leaves, the children chattering incessantly, she and Drake answering them as best they could. William wanted to drag Drake off and show him everything at once: the roof he'd leaped off when he'd knocked out a baby tooth, a mashed squirrel carcass he'd found, his fishing pole, a dozen other things.

"But where is Priscilla?" Katherine chirped sweetly.

"I had to leave her in Barbados, Katherine," Edwinna said.

"Can't you go get her? Right now?"

Edwinna and Drake shared a smile, Drake's full of paternal pride. "I'm so sorry, darling. I can't bring Priscilla to England. She has to stay on my plantation. England is too cold for her. She would get sick."

Drake seized Edwinna's hand and kissed it. "Perhaps, Katherine, we'll all four of us make a trip to see Priscilla one day. Would you like that?" Though he spoke to Katherine, he looked into Edwinna's eyes. She gazed at him, stunned, love welling up.

"Oh, Drake."

"I mean it, Edwinna. We'll do it."

Her heart swelled. They played with the children, Drake tussling and roughhousing with William, who shrieked in delight while Katherine shunned this wild stuff and sat contentedly in Edwinna's lap, the two of them talking about Priscilla. Then Drake took each child by the hand, and they all four walked to the house. He suffered an emotional moment standing in front of the old arched front door, his voice going hoarse.

"It's been twenty years since I've been inside this house."

William wrenched the door open and went bounding in, shouting for his Aunt Verity. When they stepped into the entry hall, Drake looked about somberly, choked with emotion. Edwinna looked, too. She saw dark paneling everywhere. It was an old, staunch house. A dark, wide, handsomely carved wooden staircase dominated the entry hall, leading up to a landing and on up to the second floor.

"Aunt Verity!" William shouted, bounding down an echoing corridor. "Aunt Verity, Papa's home!" Katherine went bounding after him, taking up the chant. Edwinna smiled. Evidently, Katherine worshiped the ground William walked on.

"Edwinna," Drake said with emotion and hugged her close. She could feel the joy in him. He trembled with it.

"Drake, they're marvelous. They're darlings."

William and Katherine went bounding out a door at the end of the corridor, into the yard and the fallen leaves, shrieking. Drake grinned. "So much for 'Papa.' "

A door clicked open in the opposite corridor and a woman came clipping toward them. Edwinna stepped back, leaving Drake free. This had to be Verity. She was much as Edwinna had pictured her—sensible looking, of medium build, with Drake's black hair, which she wore plainly, parted in the middle. Her gown was brown wool, conservatively high-necked.

"Drake."

"Verity." They hugged and kissed. A fair-haired man who looked slightly older than Drake came following Verity, a broad smile on his delighted face. Arthur, Edwinna thought.

"You great fool," Verity scolded, giving Drake's ears a

tug. "That will teach you to book passage on ships ill-equipped to fight pirates."

Drake kissed her forehead. "I'll try to remember the lesson. You were safely delivered?"

"Absolutely. The midwife tells me I am built like an ox and will likely have a dozen more now that Arthur and I at last have made a proper start."

Drake laughed. "Then I look forward to meeting the first of my dozen nephews." He released Verity, and reached for his brother-in-law. "Arthur."

"Drake, it's good to have you home." The two men embraced fondly and shook each other by the shoulder.

"It's good to *be* home. Especially here." His sweeping nod took in the house, eyes joyful. "I will tell you all about my so-called pirate adventures, but first . . ."

Drake reached for Edwinna's hand and drew her forward. She smiled uneasily. She wanted Verity to like her. Verity gave her a steady, straightforward look, her expression puzzled but open.

"Verity? Arthur? This is Edwinna Crawford Steel," he said with unmistakable pride. "My wife."

Verity's expressive face went blank for a moment. She looked from Drake to her to Drake. Arthur's mouth went slack.

"Your wife?" Verity drew two sharp breaths. "Drake, didn't you get my letter? The instant we received the news, three months ago, Arthur and I scraped together the ransom money—"

Edwinna gripped Drake's hand. She didn't understand, but she felt frightened. "What are you talking about, Verity?" Drake asked calmly.

Silk rustled on the staircase landing. All eyes swung there—Edwinna's, too. A woman—no, a fairy goddess—stood poised on the landing, the light from the small window silhouetting the graceful curve of shoulder, breast, hip. Edwinna clutched Drake's hand. Instantly, she knew. That exquisite face, that sheaf of fair hair, silvery as an angel's wing. Katherine's hair. Edwinna lifted her eyes to Drake.

His face was white, all the blood gone, his expression stricken. He stood motionless, like marble, like some magnificent statue that someone had dressed in clothes.

"Anne." He whispered the word, then said it again, louder. "Anne!" The word tore out of his viscera, raw, ragged, like the bloody stump of a wound. There was so much agony in it Edwinna didn't wait to hear more. She pulled free. He didn't even notice. She threw herself at the front door and let herself out.

Stunned, her mind raw with shock, she stood there unable to think, her chest banging. What had happened? Anne was supposed to be dead. Playing in the side yard, the children shrieked at each other, threw leaves, chased a barking puppy. Edwinna went in the opposite direction, running through the sunny woodland, awkward in her skirts, running . . . to where? She couldn't think, couldn't breathe. When she'd left the house far behind, she stopped running and rested her palms on the smooth trunk of a hickory tree, pressing her forehead to the backs of her hands.

No. No! She drew shattered breaths, trying to absorb the shock of it, but it went too deep.

Inside the entry hall, Verity threw Anne a look of fury as Anne cast her usual magical spell over Drake, sweeping down the stairs in a silken rustle and into her brother's stunned, worshipping arms. He was totally overwhelmed.

"Anne—you're dead."

"No, darling, I'm alive! Drake, hold me, touch me, love me. I'm alive, darling, alive."

Verity watched as he crushed her to him, his powerful shoulders and arms clamping her like a vise. "Anne, Anne, Anne, Anne—you're not real. I'm afraid to blink, afraid to close my eyes. I'm scared you'll vanish."

"No, darling, no. I'm real. I didn't die at sea. The ship was captured and sunk by pirates. They took us to Northern Africa and held us hostage."

"Anne, beloved!" Drake crushed her so close he might have been trying to press his body into hers. He worshiped her with his mouth, kissing her eyes, her nose, her ears, her cheeks, her throat, her mouth. "Anne. Is it you? Is it?"

"Oh, yes, my darling!"

Verity glared at Anne's silken back. *Why did you have to show up like a bad penny? You're no good for him, you never were. That woman out there who is probably crying her eyes out is worth ten of you. Yet he will kneel at your feet and worship you.*

"Anne—Anne!" Drake's hands were groping in stunned disbelief, squeezing her shoulders, touching her. Then he swung around. "My God, Verity, Edwinna—"

"I'll take care of her," Verity said crisply.

"Anne, tell me everything, everything!"

Verity seized a shawl that was draped over the staircase rail, whipped it on, and went out. She banged the door closed on the love talk. *Drake, you great fool.* The afternoon sun was waning and a chill stole into the crisp autumn air. Folding the ends of the shawl across her breast, she went briskly about finding Edwinna. It wasn't difficult. Her skirts had swept a trail through the fallen leaves. Verity strode on for ten minutes and found her standing in a hickory grove, huddled in her cloak, her face pale. She wasn't crying. Verity liked that. A sensible woman, Edwinna Crawford. Verity had assumed she was from the very start, from the first of Drake's letters. She marched to her through the rustling leaves.

"Shall you be all right, Edwinna?"

"Yes. Thank you. It's just the . . . shock."

"Of course, it is. Arthur and I were shocked when we received the letter, demanding ransom for Anne's release."

"I don't understand!"

"Nor does anyone. Anne's story is most unlikely. But

Drake will believe her. According to Anne, she was captured by pirates and held hostage for two years in Northern Africa.''

"As . . . as happened to Drake?''

"Well . . . yes." Verity prided herself on being a fair-minded woman. If it had happened to Drake, it *could* have happened to Anne. She mustn't let her dislike of Anne color everything. England had been besieged with pirates since the civil war. "Edwinna, let's walk. And talk. If you're not feeling too cold.''

"I'm not. I'm feeling nothing but the shock of it.''

"Of course you are. The pain will come later." Verity scrutinized her. "But you look staunch enough to bear it.'' The woman *was* dazed. Verity had to take her elbow to get her to move. They walked through the rustling leaves, into the setting sun. Verity firmly believed in physical movement, and she kept a hand on Edwinna Crawford's elbow, even though the woman did not look the weak sort who would faint. Anne would faint—gracefully, and with great drama, Verity thought tartly. But Edwinna would not.

Verity walked her a half mile before she spoke again.

"He is a great fool, of course. You love him.''

"She is his wife.'' Edwinna stopped and pressed the heels of her hands to her forehead. "I don't know what that means! *I* am his wife. I know I am. We are wed. But she is his wife, too. She is the one he wants.''

"More's the pity,'' Verity said tartly. "I have never liked her and never shall. Drake knows it. Anne knows it, also. I see no need to pretend otherwise.''

Edwinna glanced at her, still numb, but startled by Verity's bluntness. She was surprised by it, but not greatly. Verity's letters had been blunt, straightforward, plain-spoken. They walked on through crisp leaves, their gowns sweeping a path. Verity was a comfort to be with, and oh, dear God, she needed comforting.

"I have grown to like you through Drake's letters, Edwinna. You are a sensible woman.''

The pain was starting. Oh, the pain. She felt as if her cutters were slashing her heart with a bill-cane knife. *I want to go home! I want my work, my plantation.* "I would've thought his earliest letters would carry complaints about me."

"They did," Verity agreed. "That is what made me like you. The very things Drake complained of were the things I valued. *A sturdy, hardworking woman,* I thought. *I like her.* I truly knew I liked you when I saw your drawings. For what I saw in them was love. You love my brother. I value that, for I love him myself." Verity scrutinized her. "Shall I tell you something? There is a bond between brother and sister that is like nothing else. Drake and I are born of the same father, the same mother. The same blood runs in our veins. Because of that I love him intensely, even more than I love my own Arthur, possibly even as much as I love my own son. Can you understand a love that strong?"

"I have two brothers. If need be, I would give up my life for them."

Verity took a tighter hold of Edwinna's elbow and walked her on.

"Then we think the same."

"Verity, I cannot go back to that house."

"And you shan't. Not for an instant. When we finish our walk, we will go directly to Drake's hired coach. I shall fetch Arthur and my babe and we'll start for London at once. You will stay with Arthur and me for as long as you like. Anne can take care of her own children. *If* she knows how, that is. She wasn't any good at it before. It's wishing for the moon to hope the past two years have improved her."

"I'm very grateful." Edwinna couldn't bear to see Drake. Not at this time.

"Horse feathers. You *love* my brother, and I would do anything for the woman who truly loves him."

Overwhelmed, touched by Verity's kindness, she put her arms around Drake's sister, and they hugged, cheek to cheek.

The warmth, the comfort of Verity! Then, arm in arm, they headed for the coach.

"I want to leave for Barbados as soon as possible."

"Arthur and I will help you."

Inside the house, Drake was beside himself with joy. "Anne. Anne." He couldn't stop kissing her eyes—eyes he'd given up all hope of ever looking into again. He couldn't stop kissing her mouth—the mouth he'd thought he would never again taste. "Anne, Anne."

She held him in her arms and stroked his cheek as if he were a wild animal in need of calming. "Drake." She gentled him with word and touch until with one final, ferocious shudder the shock reached its peak and began, raggedly, to subside. Then they held each other, rocking and kissing softly. Still, he couldn't let go of her. Every few moments a tremor rippled through him.

"Anne. Tell me everything. They didn't hurt you, rape you?"

"No. I'm fine. Drake, don't tremble so, darling. I wasn't hurt. A Dutch privateer took our ship, not Barbary Coast pirates."

He gripped her shoulders, still drawing shattered breaths. A door banged and the children came galloping in, squabbling.

"*Anne.*" He crushed her in his arms for one last embrace. "I want to hear everything that befell you. But right now—" He glanced out the window. "I must find Edwinna. She's probably feeling very hurt."

"Did you really *marry* that tall, plain woman, Drake?"

He drew back, surprised. He'd thought that of Edwinna when he'd first met her, but he didn't now. Now he thought her lovely. How could anyone look at Edwinna and think anything else?

"She isn't plain, she's lovely, and I had to marry her, Anne," he said soberly. "She saved my life."

"Poor Drake."

"Anne, she's a fine, decent woman. If you knew her, you would like her."

Anne laughed prettily. "That I doubt. I caught a glimpse of her gown under her cloak. How unfashionable. Never mind, darling. You have me now. Oh, Drake, isn't it exciting, your knighthood? You will be Sir Drake Steel and I will be Lady Anne Steel!"

Her comments jarred him. How could she think of fashion and knighthoods at a time like this? His own heart was so full of her that everything else was inconsequential. His heart was so full of family—Anne, William, Katherine, himself, a family reunited.

"Anne, I want to see to Edwinna."

"Do that, darling. Poor, plain woman."

As he went out the door the children threw themselves at Anne with happy, demanding shouts, and he heard Anne deal with them crossly. "What do you want?" Her tone stabbed him, but he credited her irritability to the stress of the day. This emotional reunion had been hard on Anne, too.

Outside the door he collided with Verity, who was heading in. They stood in the autumn leaves to talk.

"Where is she, Verity?"

"I'm taking her to London to stay with Arthur and me."

"Verity, I need to talk to her. We lived together as man and wife. In the complete sense."

"Don't you *dare* go near her," Verity said vehemently. "She is in enormous pain. What can you say to her right now that will ease her pain? Nothing. And she at her lowest ebb—humiliated, shorn of poise and pride. No! Give her three days to recover, and then you may come and visit her. Not a moment before. Go back to Anne, Drake. Go back to the wife you so blindly adore. She is all you have ever wanted, is she not?"

His anger flared. "Verity, you are a bitch. You've always been against Anne, from the very start."

"Yes! I *am* against Anne and I *am* a bitch—a bitch who loves you. As for you? You are a great fool who doesn't know a good woman from a bad one when they are right under your nose."

They glared at each other. Then, because in his heart he knew she was right about one thing—what could he say to Edwinna at this moment that wouldn't cause her more pain?—he went into the house and slammed the door. Fifteen minutes later the coach rumbled off to London.

That night, after he'd bedded the children and explored the old house for the small wonders he remembered from boyhood, Drake made a cozy fire in the parlor, pulled the old threadbare chaise up to the hearth, and got a goose-down quilt and a goose-down pillow. He and Anne settled into each other's arms as they used to do evenings in their small house on Thames Street, cozy and content, drinking wine, talking, watching the firelight.

He felt immensely happy, except for his sorrow and worry about Edwinna. He'd managed to steal an hour from the children to take Anne to bed and make love to her. It had been magic, breathless and thrilling as ever, he and Anne kneeling naked on the bed, seizing each other and kissing so deeply they became one. For the first time he could remember, she hadn't insisted that he withdraw at the final moment to spare her a pregnancy. He came, exploding in her gloriously. He hoped their wild, unfettered lovemaking meant she was willing to have another child.

"Now, tell me what happened, sweetheart. All of it." They settled down to talk and drink wine, Anne's head on his shoulder, her hair soft, a mass of fair silk that he kissed constantly.

"You were off in Holland on wine business, darling. You'll remember I was angry that you were going. I had wanted you to take me to France to see my sister."

"I couldn't, Anne. Now I can reveal why. I had to go to

Holland. It was vital. I was delivering letters and money to King Charles from the Sealed Knot.''

''The Sealed Knot?'' She lifted her head in surprise. ''Why didn't you tell me you were in league with the Sealed Knot?''

''The knowledge would've put you in danger.'' He kissed her forehead and took a sip of wine—the first good wine he'd had since he'd landed in Barbados. He ached. What was Edwinna feeling tonight? Thank God for Verity.

''Is that why King Charles is granting you a knighthood?'' He kissed her cheek. ''Yes.''

She settled against him with a smile and purred, a pretty sound, low in her throat. ''I'm glad. I shall like being Lady Anne Steel. They say the royal court is very merry, with its bachelor king. There is dancing and music every day. Will we be allowed to come and go at court?''

''Yes. As a matter of fact, I should present myself to King Charles next week—a courtesy visit.''

She reared up in excitement. He sheltered his wine cup to keep her from spilling it. ''May I go with you?''

''Of course. I shall enjoy showing you off.''

''I'll need a new gown!''

''Of course.'' But he stirred uneasily. ''Don't spend too much on it. I'm not sure yet of our financial situation, and I want to repay Verity and Arthur for the ransom they sent for your release.''

''They can wait. Pink silk, I think! Would that please you, Drake? It would please me.''

He kissed her mouth. ''Everything about you pleases me. Now tell me what happened. The voyage, the pirates.''

She seemed reluctant to talk about the capture and spoke in vague terms. He credited that to the terror of the experience. Essentially, she'd taken the children to Verity's, then booked passage on a ship leaving that day for France—a ship called the *Fair Wind*. But the wind had not been fair. A storm had come up. Mastless and foundering, the ship had been set upon by Dutch pirates who took the passengers and the cargo.

They'd left the crew to sink with the ship. Committing acts of piracy all the way, they had sailed to North Africa, where they'd imprisoned the passengers in a villa. Considering the captors, the passengers had been treated well. Drake held Anne close, trembling for what might have befallen her, thanking God it had not.

Anne lifted her head. "If you don't believe me, you can get in touch with a wool draper in Leeds—a Mr. Christopher Stiles. He and his wife, Mercy, were held also."

His lips parted with surprise. He gazed at her. "Why would I not believe you, sweetheart?"

"Verity doesn't. She is extremely mean to me, Drake."

His anger stirred. "Verity is Verity. We won't pay any attention to what she thinks or says."

"Good. Now tell me what happened to you, Drake." They sipped wine, lounged in each other's arms, and watched the firelight for two whole hours while Drake told her every detail. The only ones he omitted were those of his intimate life with Edwinna. That was private, between himself and Edwinna, no one else.

When he'd finished, Anne said, "Is she very rich, Drake?"

The question struck him as odd. "Well . . . I suppose she is. Not in coin, but in land, plantations, slaves, bond slaves, sugar."

"It isn't fair, her being rich while we are poor."

He looked at her in surprise. "We're not *poor*, Anne."

"If we can't even afford a decent gown for court . . ."

"Buy what you like," he said decisively. "I'll manage. As for unfairness, it is on our side. Edwinna has only her wealth, while we have each other. We have our love and our children. It is Edwinna who has little. We have so much, Anne. In fact, tonight I feel like the richest man in the world."

Just then, Katherine cried out upstairs. Tipsy with wine, Anne started to get up and collapsed in a giggle. Drake kissed her and settled her into the goose-down quilt. "Don't bother. I'll go, darling."

"She's a pest," Anne murmured. "She still wets the bed."

The comment pierced Drake. He frowned. "Isn't that to be expected? She's been through a lot in the past two years. She lost her mother, her father, and now she suddenly has them with her again. It's no wonder she wets."

"Hurry back. I want to kiss." He smiled and kissed her wine-sweet mouth.

"So do I."

Upstairs in the moonlit nursery he found William sound asleep on his cot, and Katherine wide awake, sitting up on hers. He squatted beside her cot. He loved her hair. It was as silken and silvery blonde as Anne's.

"Papa? Where is the lady with Priscilla?"

The question cut, caught him in the heart. "She . . . couldn't stay with us, sweetheart. She's in London with Aunt Verity and Uncle Arthur. She'll stay there."

"She's a nice lady, Papa."

"Yes, she's a very nice lady."

"When are we going to see Priscilla?"

He hedged. He couldn't say never. "I'm not sure, sweetheart."

"Tomorrow?"

"No, not tomorrow," he said gently.

"Papa? I didn't kiss Priscilla good night. I want to kiss her good night." He glanced to where she was looking. There was enough moonlight in the room for him to see, tacked to the wall, the letters he'd written her. He saw his own script and Edwinna's drawings of Priscilla.

"Well, why don't you run and kiss her?"

She twisted her blanket. "Because there's bad things under the bed and they'll get me."

"Now, who told you that?"

"William. William says the bad things will grab my feet if I get out of bed in the dark."

He made a mental note to have a father and son talk with

William—a stern one. Meanwhile, he made a show of looking under her cot. "Goodness. So there are. I'd best squash them, stomp them, and get rid of them. He made a silent pantomime of eliminating demons, bogeymen, animals, whatever it was she feared in her little girl's mind. She giggled. "There. All done. They're all dead. Now you can get out of bed and kiss Priscilla."

She hesitated, then gingerly got out of bed, flew across the room, kissed the drawing of Priscilla, flew back, and flung herself into bed. He covered her up and tucked her rag animal into the crook of her arm. It looked suspiciously like a monkey. He smiled. Verity's handiwork, no doubt, based upon Edwinna's drawings. Verity might be a bitch about Anne, but she loved his children.

Drake broached a delicate subject. "Katherine, sweetheart, there's a chamber pot under your cot. Do you ever use it in the night?"

She shook her head. "The bad things might grab me."

"But they're gone. Papa stomped them." She looked dubious. He squatted beside her cot. "Let's make a bargain. If you need to use the chamber pot in the night, call out to Papa. Call very loud and Papa will hear you and come. Will you do that?"

"Yes, Papa." She nodded enthusiastically.

"Now, go to sleep, sweetheart." She nodded, her eyelids heavy. He kissed her, and because she begged him to wait until she fell asleep, he did so. When her breathing leveled off, he stood.

Leaving the nursery, he paused and touched the letters and drawings on the wall. His script, Edwinna's drawings. He patted Priscilla and smiled. She had grubby kiss marks all over her. He ran a finger along the drawing of himself, of the cane fields, the mill, the slaves at work, Macaw at his boiling kettle.

Gazing at the sketches, he could almost smell the fragrant

trade winds. He could almost see the flocks of golden plovers soaring in the blue Caribbean sky. He felt as if he'd been gone from that lovely tropical island for a hundred years. He wondered if Edwinna felt the same way. Edwinna . . . He cringed in remorse. His strong, brave, lovely Edwinna. He ached with the need to comfort her.

CHAPTER

* 18 *

Drake didn't wait three days. He came on the second day, Verity be damned. He was worried about Edwinna. And why not! She'd been a wife to him, in the best sense of the word. She'd given him loyalty, fidelity, companionship. He was fond of her. Dammit, he was not so morally deficient as to feel fondness one day and nothing the next. Of course he cared.

Prepared for a quarrel with Verity, he knocked on her front door. To his surprise, Verity gave him none. She answered the door herself and let him come in, her bunting-wrapped infant in her arms.

A gust of chill November wind blew in with him. He shucked his cloak, dropping it onto a stool that stood beside the door. Verity's entry hall was so tiny it scarcely qualified as one. Verity and Arthur lived frugally. They were not ones to spend money they did not have. He felt a stab of worry about his own finances. The pink silk and the Flemish lace

Anne had bought for her court gown had come to more than he could afford.

"How is she?"

"Bearing up."

"I want to see her privately."

"Meaning you wish me to pay a visit to a neighbor."

"Preferably a long visit." Verity's house was so small that privacy was impossible. She eyed him with the look he knew so well: sisterly contempt leavened with tolerance.

"You can use the parlor. First you must say hello to your nephew. You haven't even looked at him properly."

Drake smiled and took the baby out of Verity's arms, careful not to touch him with wind-chilled hands. He settled the babe in the crook of his arm. "He's a fine boy, Verity." Four months old, he had Arthur's brown eyes, but his feisty spirit, as he seized Drake's finger and drove one pearly tooth into it, was pure Verity. "What's his name?"

"John Drake."

Drake smiled. "So I'm to be godfather?"

"Who else?" Verity said crisply. "I put off the christening until your return."

"And if I had not returned? If God had granted I die a 'pirate' in the Caribbean?"

"*My* God," she said emphatically, "would not have dared!"

Drake grinned. "Thank the Lord for sisters," he said, returning John Drake to his mother. The baby wanted to keep Drake's thumb. Smile fading, becoming somber, Drake changed the subject. "Verity, I want you to stop baiting Anne."

Plumping John Drake to one shoulder, Verity gave him a caustic look.

"Is that what she is accusing me of?"

"*Verity.*"

She glanced away in vexation. "Very well. I shall stop baiting Anne, if that's what she says I am doing." Lifting her skirts with her free hand, she went briskly up the narrow staircase that led to the sleeping floor, muttering, "You are a great fool, Drake."

He waited for Edwinna in the parlor, a room so small that its four well-worn, upholstered chairs crowded it. The baby's parlor cradle stood near the hearth. A fire burned cozily. Drake added a log, then stood gazing into the flames.

His mind drifted to Anne. He'd made the mistake of telling her about today's visit. He hadn't thought he needed to hide his intention to visit Edwinna. He'd assumed Anne would feel compassion for her, under the circumstances, and would agree that he was morally obligated to offer Edwinna all the help he could. He'd been wrong. She'd flown into a jealous tizzy. They'd quarreled, and it had upset him. A quarrel with Anne always upset him. He loved her so much.

Edwinna didn't keep him waiting. She came down at once, into the parlor, and softly shut the door. They looked at each other, feeling a welter of emotions, each of them all too aware that everything had changed between them. She wore a gown of soft mauve wool and a shawl to match. The color suited her, lent a glow to her skin and eyes. Her hair hung long and curly. His lips parted under the force of his emotions. How could Anne think her plain? How could anyone?

Edwinna ached. How wonderful he looked. He'd dressed handsomely to come to see her. He wore his best black serge suit and a white silk shirt with a lavish collar. His dressing up told her he cared. She felt grateful, for she herself cared so much it hurt. They gazed at each other, the fire crackling.

"Edwinna, I don't know what to say . . ."

"There is nothing you need say, Drake. It isn't your fault. It was nothing you could have foreseen."

"I never meant for you to be hurt."

"I know that."

They talked softly, gently, tenderly with each other.

"If I had known about Anne, I would not have . . ."

Wed her? Is that what he meant to say? He left it unsaid, and she was grateful. Said aloud, the words would have been cruel, and he was not a cruel man. He was the gentlest, kindest . . . most exciting man she'd ever known.

"No, don't think that." She gazed into the fire, watching it crackle and flare. "I lay awake one whole night thinking it out. I decided I will always be glad we wed. If we hadn't, you would be dead, executed as a pirate." She looked at him. "I couldn't bear that, Drake. I want you alive. I want you with your children. I think . . . I think perhaps I may have wanted that from the very first moment I looked down into Speightstown's cove and saw you shackled to the rocks, suffering. I remember thinking: He is a man with children. So, no. Don't say that, don't think it. I'm glad we wed. I will always be glad we wed. I will always be glad you're alive."

She watched him draw a slow, ragged breath. Verity's parlor had a high, small, glass double window. Drake rested his elbow up on the sill. He gazed at Edwinna so intensely she knew he wanted to take her into his arms and hold her. She was glad he didn't. That would have made a mockery out of what they'd shared together. She couldn't have borne it—his holding her, kissing her—knowing he'd shared a bed with Anne last night.

Because he didn't touch her, she felt filled with love for him—pride and love. She looked at him, standing tall and handsome, his eyes shining with the worry he felt on her behalf, eyes as clear and blue as the waters of Carlisle Bay.

"Edwinna, our Barbados marriage is void."

"I understand that."

"But there's no need to reveal that fact in Barbados. It's nobody's business. If you wish to keep my name, do so. It will spare you humiliation, and it will ease my heart when I think of you. I won't have you gossiped about, made the butt of cruel jokes."

Her throat tightened. "That's very kind of you, Drake.

I'm not sure what I will tell anyone. I haven't thought it out, yet."

"Do as you wish, of course. But I suggest you tell the whole story only to Matthew Plum and Simon Tarcher. David and Kena, if you wish. No one else need know. If others ask of my whereabouts, simply tell them the truth. I am in London tending to my wine business."

"I'm not sure what I will say."

"Do as you wish in the matter, Edwinna. But be kind to yourself." He swallowed. "I would be proud to know you call yourself Edwinna Steel."

"Thank you, Drake."

They had not sat, nor had it occurred to either of them to do so—a mark of the emotion gripping them. Rain spattered the window, thrown by a gust of wind. The panes rattled. Edwinna's glance followed the sound. Suddenly, she ached for her warm, fragrant trade winds. Even Drake looked toward the window as if remembering gentler, sweeter winds.

"I . . . plan to leave for Barbados as soon as possible. There is no point in staying."

"No," he said reluctantly. "I suppose there isn't. But if you plan to go, I want to be the one to make the arrangements for you, if you will let me. I want you on a safe ship, nothing less."

"Thank you, Drake. That would be very kind." The fondness in his deep, rich voice made her own voice tremble. She loved him so much.

"Also, I want to do one more thing for you. I want to be your sugar factor here in London."

She looked up with surprise, feeling the glow start deep within her and spread through her body, rise to her eyes. He wanted to stay in communication with her.

"That would be wonderful, Drake."

"I will do my level best for you, Edwinna. Too many sugar planters are cheated here in London. I mean to see that you are not one of them."

"I will want to pay you more than the usual five percent."

"No," he said flatly. "Three."

"That's not enough."

"It's more than enough."

"It will scarcely cover the work. No sugar factor works for that little."

He smiled. "Three percent. Take it or leave it."

She smiled, too. "I'll take it." She wanted to give him more. She knew of his financial straits. Verity had made no secret of it. The two thousand pounds raised for Anne's ransom had taken all of Verity and Arthur's slender savings, plus a loan against Drake's wine shop and warehouse. He was deeply in debt.

The afternoon passed too quickly as they settled in chairs by the fire and talked business: the delicate problem of dismissing her present, inept sugar factor, inventorying his books, his warehouse. Drake knew how to do these things. They discussed setting up a new banking account for Drake as sugar factor, dealing with the sugar now at the dock and the customs tax. She wanted the afternoon to go on forever.

Gazing into his blue eyes, she thought, *Oh, dear God, how will I ever bear it? How will I ever again sit at my worktable in my office at Crawford Plantation without Drake across from me?* It was all she could do to maintain her dignity and composure.

Their talk ended too soon. When it was time for him to go, she went with him to the door and even managed to return his smile, but when the door closed behind that decent, handsome London wine merchant, she leaned against it and wept.

Anne was a huge success at Whitehall Palace. The Steels went by hired coach to the palace on a midweek morning, Anne gorgeous in a shell pink gown of silk that had a low neckline lavished with lace and silk sleeves crisscrossed with yards of delicate gold ribbon. Drake was immensely proud of her and felt small-minded, stingy, at having quibbled over the cost of the gown. It was worth every shilling. In it she looked like an angel.

Rumbling along in the hackney coach, his "angel" radiated breathless excitement. Drake was more amused than excited. Speaking with the king was nothing new to him. He'd met privately with His Majesty on numerous occasions during the king's exile in Holland and France, but for Anne, this was the event of a lifetime.

Even the shabby condition of Whitehall Palace failed to dampen her enthusiasm. Whitehall's acres of buildings, some of wood, some of brick, had lain deserted and unoccupied during the Cromwell years. Neglect had taken a toll. Some of the structures looked as if they should be torn down and rebuilt. Only a few of the buildings were used for royal apartments. Most were government offices.

Awaiting their time to speak with the king, Anne and Drake strolled in the king's garden, which was fashioned in the French manner, with clipped hedges and graveled walks. They walked along the stone gallery that ran beside the garden and looked at the rows of apartments that housed the ladies and gentlemen of the court.

"Wouldn't it be wonderful to live here!" Anne enthused.

Drake laughed. "I think it would be awful living on a public road running right through Whitehall Palace. Sightseers like us would be going by all day, standing on your doorstep, gawking."

"I don't mind being looked at."

He kissed her cheek. "That's because you're pretty. I'm not."

"Drake." Her smile dazzled. So did her silvery blond hair. Her gown was the perfect complement, an angelic shade of pink, like the interior of a seashell. He felt so proud of her he wanted to burst. All eyes were on her—both men's and women's. She knew it and flushed in the happy excitement of it all.

A gracious man, the king himself came out to escort them

into his royal apartment, striding with his long-legged gait, the ever-present pack of spaniels yapping at his heels. Anne was awestruck. The king was easily the tallest man in England, standing several inches taller than six feet. He was a vital man with ruddy skin, devil black hair, and a smile that could charm a fence post into falling at his feet in adoration.

The king behaved charmingly to Anne, engaging her in conversation, saying pretty things to her. He was taken with her, Drake noted with a stab of worry. Jealous idiot that he was, he felt relieved when King Charles escorted Anne to a group of court ladies and gentlemen in his outer apartment who were playing parlor games and left her there in their company.

The king honored him, taking him not only to his inner chamber, but into his bedchamber, where they conversed in privacy for twenty minutes. Drake emerged from the interview pleased but uneasy at the king's "request" that he and Anne stay the day, dine with his court, partake of the afternoon's entertainments, and remain to sup in the evening.

Drake had better things to do. Work, for one. He needed to give his attention to his wine shop, to Edwinna's sugar, to the matter of Thomas and Harry Crawford. He and Arthur were attempting to get the Department of the Admiralty to trace the Crawford twins' whereabouts. Edwinna knew that and held high hopes. Drake wanted with all his heart to be able to send her good news, but his sixth sense told him Plum and Tarcher might be right. Thomas and Harry were probably dead. Dear God, he hoped not.

Anne, however, was thrilled with the king's request that they stay the day. Attracted by her beauty and wit, several of the ladies had attached themselves to her, and Anne was fast making friends. The men were attracted, too, Drake noticed with a jealous eye.

He was acquainted with most of the men. If he hadn't known them to be loyal supporters of the king who'd accompanied him into exile, sharing His Majesty's poverty there, starving when food was short, going threadbare and ragged and living in unheated quarters in the dead of winter when there was no money even to buy wood for the king's fireplace, he would have dismissed them as a bunch of wastrels, lounging about lazy as lizards, drinking wine, flirting with women, playing parlor games.

When the women withdrew to the garderobe room to primp and pee, Drake went out and strode across the grounds to the Office of the Admiralty, intent on Thomas and Harry. He mounted the stairs to the third-floor Office of Records, went in, and felt the same sense of frustration he'd had on his first visit. It was a slipshod place manned by indifferent, slow-moving clerks who sat at their worktables doing as little as possible. Wooden boxes heaped with unattended correspondence stood everywhere.

Realizing he would get nowhere without a bribe, he slipped the chief clerk five pounds sterling and promised him another five when information on Thomas and Harry Crawford was produced. He could ill afford to spend ten pounds, but Edwinna's peace of mind was worth it. It was the least he could do for her. The clerk's greedy eyes lighted up like lanterns, and he promised to expedite the records search.

Going down the narrow stairway, Drake nearly collided with a man coming out of another government office. They both stepped back, second-glanced at each other, and burst into pleased laughter.

"Charles!"

"Drake!"

"Good lord, Charles, you're back. I'd feared you dead. It's been so long since anyone heard from you."

"Dead? Not me. Where'd you get such a flea-brain idea?"

They embraced heartily and shook each other by the shoulders. Drake's smile spread ear to ear. Charles looked the same—a big, handsome blond man with a rakehell smile—but his manner seemed skittish.

"Where in hell have you been for the past year and a half?"

"Italy."

"Italy? And you just got back today?"

"A mite earlier than that."

"What ship?"

"The *Bountiful Queen*."

Drake was taken aback. "She's been in port two weeks. You mean you've been back two weeks and you couldn't take a minute to let your best friend know it? Lord Almighty, you're William's godfather."

Charles hedged. "I'd heard you were in Barbados."

"You could have come to the wine shop and checked."

Charles shifted uncomfortably, then smiled in his rakehell way. "Ah, Drake! You know how it is. I've a woman—a hot-blooded Italian petticoat. She doesn't like to let me out of her sight. She's a real terror. If I don't keep her sheets warm, she'll look for someone else."

Drake smiled a little. That could explain it. Charles could be a perfect idiot over a petticoat. They talked a while longer. Drake gave Charles a quick, sketchy account of all that had happened to him and Anne, and then, needing to get back to court, he and Charles parted company on the promise they would dine together soon. Charles seemed glad to go. It bothered Drake. It bothered him even more that Charles had been in the city two whole weeks. Preoccupied, he rejoined the court.

As the day wore on, the ladies switched to music for amusement, and here Anne shone. She was an extraordinarily accomplished singer. Invited to take her turn, she eagerly did so, and Drake glowed with pride. She had a faultless voice —a trained, silvery soprano. She adored singing and had studied music during her youth. Accompanied on the virginal by Lord Kersey, Anne's voice soared like a lark's, her control perfect. It was a thrilling performance. She put all the other singers to shame.

When she finished, she received a standing ovation, which she acknowledged with charming modesty, a flush of pink excitement on her cheeks. Drake was extremely proud of her. She was asked to sing again, and this time, drawn out of his chamber and away from his business by the purity of Anne's voice, even the king strolled out to listen.

"You had quite a triumphant day," Drake murmured, kissing her flushed cheek and holding her in his arms as the hackney coach clattered through the dark streets, carrying them home, swinging them to and fro.

"It was thrilling. It was marvelous. It was splendid!"

"I'm glad you had a good time."

"A good time? Drake, it was the best day of my life. The ladies begged me to come back on Thursday and sing with them. May I?"

He would have thought the best day of her life was the day they'd wed. That was his best day. Drake hesitated. The king's court had a sordid reputation. It was a bachelor court. Affairs ran rampant. But Anne was in a glow—so happy, so thrilled with her triumph, he hadn't the heart to say no. One more visit couldn't bring harm.

"If you like."

"Oh, thank you, Drake!" She threw her arms around his neck and kissed him—a bumpy kiss in the hackney coach. They both laughed a little when their teeth clicked. Their breath smelled of wine and happiness.

"Tell me about your interview with the king. When will you be knighted? When will I be *Lady* Anne Steel?"

"June first, *Lady* Anne. In the royal banqueting house."

"Oh, Drake, how exciting. What else?"

"Well . . . I now have the patent to supply all the wine sold to Whitehall Palace. I am now the king's royal vintner."

"Drake, that's splendid!"

He smiled ruefully. "We'll see. I'm not sure it's splendid. It may be dreadful. It may cost me a fortune. The king hasn't any money. He's poor as a street beggar and can't pay his bills. At least, he can't until he refills England's treasury, which is completely empty. To do that, he will have to start a war with the Dutch, they say, to get back the rich colonial trade routes the Dutch stole from us during our civil war. In the meantime, Lady Anne Steel—" he kissed her cheek "—I am likely to become impoverished if I'm obligated to supply free wine to the king's household. Either that or drive myself and Arthur crazy, pounding on the king's steward's door every week to collect what is owed."

"*I* think it's splendid. It is a great honor."

He laughed. "An honor likely to drive us right into the almshouse." Still Drake smiled. He *was* proud—proud for the Steel family name, for his father's sake, for Verity, and most of all, for Anne. She loved honors. She would delight in being married to the king's royal vintner.

In the midst of his contented reverie, he felt a pang. Edwinna would be pleased, too. Above all, she was loyal. She would be proud of everything he accomplished. He wished he could share it with her right now and watch her eyes glow on his behalf.

"What was it like, being in the king's bedchamber? Was it rich and beautiful?"

He smiled in amusement. "It stank to high heaven. The king's favorite spaniel bitch had whelped there three weeks earlier. There were puppies, dog shit, and pee everywhere." Anne giggled. They held each other, content, bumping along, basking in the afterglow of a glorious day.

Only one incident had marred the day, Drake thought sadly, and that incident should have filled him with joy—Charles Dare.

"Guess who I saw when I ducked out to the privy and went over to the Admiralty office for a moment? Charles Dare. I nearly dropped in my tracks. I'd thought him dead."

Anne stiffened and sat upright. "What did he say?"

He gazed at her, perplexed by her reaction. "What should he say? He told me he'd been in Italy, that he'd returned two weeks earlier. He hadn't realized people thought him dead. He said he'd written to me during his time in Italy, but likely the letters hadn't reached the wine shop. And of course he hadn't known about my pirate experience or Barbados. But I admit I felt a stab, Anne, knowing he'd been in the city two whole weeks and hadn't tried to see me. I'd thought we were best friends."

"Oh. Well, I meant only that Charles Dare can be a great liar. I wouldn't put credence in anything he says."

"That's true." Drake smiled. "He was always a rake, but he's never lied to *me*, so far as I know. I invited him to dine with us tomorrow, but he can't. I invited him for the next day, and he made vague excuses. I admit it hurts. It puzzles me. I'd thought us best friends."

She threw her arms around his neck. "Never mind, darling! We don't need Charles Dare. We'll have our new friends at court."

She gave him her mouth to kiss, and he kissed it. She smelled so sweet. "They're not friends, Anne," he warned. "They're acquaintances. And questionable ones. I don't want you becoming overinvolved with them. They live fast lives. They tread too near the borderline."

She laughed, her breath wine-sweet on his lips. "Just because they flirt? Drake. Don't be foolish."

"Foolish." The word bothered him. She'd called him that once before. Doubtless she'd forgotten. He hadn't. She'd called him that at William's Breeching Day party when he'd caught Charles kissing her in the garden. He gently leaned his forehead against hers.

"Anne, answer me truly. Do you love me?" It was silly the way his heart pounded as he waited for her answer. He loved her so much.

"You idiot! I love you terribly." To prove it, she seized

him by the hair, nearly wrenching it out by the roots, and thrust her sweet, quick tongue into his mouth. Low in his throat he growled with pleasure. She aroused and satisfied him as no other woman could.

"Anne, let's have another child. To crown our love." He kissed her flushed temple. In bed she'd reverted to her old disappointing habit of insisting he withdraw before climaxing to protect her from quickening.

She smoothed his warm, moist brow with two pretty fingers, trailing the ridge, then stroking each eyebrow, petting the black, bushy hair into obedience.

"Let's talk about it next year, darling. Not this year. I'm having such a splendid time. I don't want to go to court, to your *knighting*, in an ugly, great-bellied condition."

"There is nothing ugly in it. A woman's crested beauty is lovely to behold. Especially to her husband. It thrills me to see you carrying my child, Anne."

"Let's talk about it next year, Drake. Please?"

She was a beautiful woman. She deserved her moment in the sun—deserved to be looked at, admired. Still, he felt disappointed. He could not help but think of Edwinna, Edwinna, who had wanted with all her heart to have his child, but couldn't.

* * *

My dearest brother,
   Come at once. Edwinna has just received a visit from a representative of the Office of the Admiralty. Thomas and Harry Crawford are dead. Fever. Last year. Tangier, North Africa.

Your loving sister,
Verity

Drake looked up from the message, incensed. It had been two nights since the note had been delivered, and he'd received it just now from Anne as they supped by candlelight.

"Why didn't you give this letter to me the instant it arrived? You read it; you can see the seriousness of this."

Wearing a frock of red wool with a white linen cape collar, angel blond hair tumbling, Anne drew herself up defensively.

"For all I knew it was some trick of Verity's to spirit you away from me to that Barbados woman. Verity hates me."

"Trick! Verity has nothing to do with this." His chair scraped. He angrily threw down his napkin and strode to the dark entry hall. Anne followed, voice high-pitched, wobbly.

"Where are you going?"

"Where do you think? To Verity's, of course."

"Drake, you can't go in the dark. You'll never get a coach."

"Is that why you waited until *now* to give me the letter?"

"Drake! I don't like to be alone at night."

He grabbed his short sword and buckler from where it hung on a wall peg and buckled it on. He might need it, walking three miles through pitch-dark London. He swung into his cloak and grabbed his hat.

"You're not alone, Anne. You have two servants and two children. That is hardly being alone." He was furious with her. How could she have done this? Edwinna, suffering this blow without him . . .

Anne's lower lip trembled in a pout.

"You can at least eat supper with me first."

"*You* eat it. You seem to have the stomach for eating, despite such news. *I* haven't."

He wrenched open the door, trotted down the brick steps into the moonless darkness. His swift, angry stride crunched fallen leaves.

"Drake, I hate you!" Anne shouted, infuriated at his leaving.

He turned. She stood in the doorway, silhouetted in the glow of the candlelight that spilled from the dining chamber.

"You know? Sometimes I think you *do*."

He strode off, boiling. Her pretty pleas sprinkled the night.

"Drake? Come back. I love you. I do. I love you!"

He made it to Verity's door without incident, despite the footpads who roamed thick as rats in London's streets every night. They doubtless recognized fury when they saw it and feared the thrust of his sword in their belly.

Verity answered the door the instant he banged on it. "Why didn't you come at once—the moment you got my note?" Verity scolded.

Drake ignored it. No point in driving the wedge between Anne and Verity any deeper than it was. He shucked his outer clothes, sword and buckler. "How is she?"

Verity shook her head. "She should cry—she needs to— but she can't. It's all been too much, Drake. First you. Now this."

"I know," he said softly. "Is Arthur with her?"

"Yes. In the parlor."

Drake let himself into the parlor, and Arthur, his kind face compassionate in the firelight, rose at once, nodded to him, and left. Edwinna got up, too. Tightly. Her face was ravaged with shock. She wore the mauve wool gown and shawl she'd worn on his first visit, and it struck him, irrelevantly, that she was not like Anne—she didn't require a new gown for every day of the month. He went to her and took her into his arms. She leaned against him, her head drifting to his shoulder. He rocked her back and forth as they stood before the crackling fire.

"Edwinna, I'm so sorry—so damned sorry."

"Drake, I can't think. The blow. I can't believe it."

"That goddamned savage sea."

Verity was right. She needed to cry. It was all too much. His strong, brave Edwinna was at her lowest. He pressed her head to his shoulder, holding it there, cradling her soft hair, her warm head, in his hand. He wished he could repair her life, make it come right again, but he couldn't. He wasn't God. Sometimes he wasn't even much of a man.

"Drake, they were on a naval ship—the *Abundant*. While

it was in port in Tangier, a fever swept through the ship. Half the crew died, including the captain and the officers. In the confusion, the death lists were mislaid and didn't arrive at the Office of the Admiralty until now.''

"Edwinna, Edwinna.'' He rocked her, wishing she would cry.

"Drake, they were only nineteen.''

"I know, Edwinna. Cry, weep, rant, rave, be angry. Do anything you wish. I'll stay with you as long as you need me.''

He heard, felt, the catch in her breast.

"Drake, thank you for coming.''

"I *want* to be here. I want to be with you. There's nowhere else I want to be at a time like this. Don't be afraid that I'm going to walk out that door. I'm not. I'm going to stay with you, sit with you, all night.''

"Drake, thank you.'' It broke his heart, her thanking him like this. For what? He'd brought nothing into her life but misery. He held her, rocked her.

"The worst part is, they've been dead a whole year, and I didn't know it. I didn't know they were sick, suffering, dying, perhaps delirious with fever, calling for me.''

"Edwinna, Edwinna.''

"All that time I was planting, making sugar, being happy, being with you, and they were dying.''

"I know, I know,'' he soothed. "That's what hurts most.''

She began to weep then—weak, defenseless crying, her entire weight upon him. She cried in his arms for a long time as he rocked her. The log in the fire slowly burned through, and a sliver of moon rose hazily in the smoky London sky. When she wept herself dry, she wiped her eyes with one finger in that dignified, spinsterish manner he knew and loved.

"Let's sit by the fire, Edwinna.''

She nodded wearily. He settled her into a chair before the fire, pulled another one close beside her, took her hand, and kept it securely in his. They sat for hours like this, gazing into the flames, talking when she felt like it, being silent, companionable.

Exhausted, she was unfit for sleep. So he went to Verity's kitchen, found the Brazilian coffee beans, grinder, and tin pot Edwinna had brought with her from Barbados. He prepared the coffee and boiled it in the fireplace in the parlor. The rich fragrance steamed into the air, and they sat together drinking it.

The rest of the household had gone to bed hours earlier, but Drake kept vigil with her throughout the night. She never closed her eyes. Then, an hour before dawn, she let her head loll back and drifted to sleep in her chair. Drake slipped a footstool under her feet. Verity thoughtfully had put a goose-down quilt in the parlor, and Drake covered Edwinna with it and sat watching over her until dawn streaked the sky and he heard the sounds of the household rousing. He looked out at the cold winter sunrise, startled to realize he hadn't given Anne a thought all night. He felt remiss, guilty, but he was still angry with her. It had been a jealous, childish thing to do, keeping Verity's note from him, even though she'd read it and knew its seriousness.

When he heard Verity's step on the stair, he reluctantly dropped a soft kiss on Edwinna's hair and went out to leave her in Verity's capable hands. He and Verity conferred quietly in the entry hall as he drew on cloak and hat and gathered sword and buckler.

"How is she, Drake?"

"As well as can be expected under the circumstances." Weary as he was, Drake felt anger surging. "Damnation, Verity. I wanted good things for her, not this. I wanted her to have a good life. Instead? This! God damn it."

Verity smiled gently. "You're fond of her, aren't you?"

"Yes!"

"You should lie down and rest, Drake."

"I will. I'll nap at my Thames Street house. Tell Arthur to open the wine shop at the usual hour. I'll join him when

I've rested. Tell Edwinna . . . tell her I'll come see her again tomorrow.''

Verity scrutinized him, older sister fashion. "I take back what I said. You are not a great fool, Drake. You are rather nice.''

He opened the door. A gust of November wind blew in.

"Is that official? Or just a momentary opinion?''

"Momentary, I'm sure.'' She kissed him good-bye—a peck on the cheek.

When Drake returned home that night, he found Anne contrite and sweet and apologetic. Her attitude diffused his anger instantly. When she came running into his arms, he felt a surge of love that seemed greater than anything he'd ever felt for her. What they had that night was a honeymoon, sensual and erotic, with wine sipping in bed and endless sex play. When he came to climax—to that glorious moment men called *sudden vehemence*—she didn't ask him to withdraw. He came in her ferociously, spasm after spasm. It was glory.

Worried about Edwinna, Drake stole an hour from his business every day and walked up to Cornhill from his wine shop. He made no secret of the visits, and they irritated Anne. But then, her visits to court irritated *him*. Without asking his permission, she'd begun to go to court regularly. He hated it. The thought of lazy, lounging lords ogling his beautiful wife—particularly, promiscuous lizards like the duke of Buckingham and Lord Jermyn, who it was said slept with men as willingly as they slept with women, revolted him.

But he couldn't forbid Anne. It would be a cruelty. She'd never been so happy. Her heart was set on court. Even the king had sent him a very pretty letter requesting "Lady Anne" be allowed to sing at court as often as possible. So Drake granted her two days a week at court. He thought himself generous, but Anne did not. On the five days of each week she could *not* go, she smoldered with resentment. It was a sore point between them, sparking many a quarrel. So it was a relief to Drake to sit with Edwinna for a few minutes every day, talking companionably in Verity's parlor. This sensible woman, he knew, wouldn't give two pins to go to court.

On a sunny Sabbath when Anne turned up her nose at his suggestion of giving the children a day's outing at the Tower of London, to let them see the lions and the elephant that were kept in cages there on public display, he went with the children to Verity's house and took Edwinna with them. The children liked her and she liked them. She was as patient with them as she'd been in Barbados with Tutu and her slave children. Katherine, especially, took to Edwinna at once and put her little hand into Edwinna's as they strolled among the sightseers in the Tower. Edwinna told her a story of Priscilla's adventures in the boiling house and the cane fields, and Katherine clamored for more. Drake and Edwinna shared a smile over the top of Katherine's silvery blond head.

The autumn wind blew briskly. The Tower of London was a cold place. Drake wouldn't come here but for the children's pleasure. His father had caught his final fatal illness here, imprisoned in the dungeon. Drake hated the place.

"What do I call you?" Katherine piped, looking up at Edwinna.

"Well, my black children on my plantation call me *Mama*. You could call me Mama Edwinna." She shot Drake an uncertain look. "If that's all right?"

He smiled. "It's perfect. I like the ring of it." She smiled then, relieved, and they gazed at each other, their eyes filling with remembrance. They'd shared a lot: cane fields, middle-of-the-night treks, the bond slave revolt, Marigold and Jeremy, happier things . . . bed. Their eyes met intimately. She quickly looked away.

"Mama Edwinna, when are we going to Priscilla's house?"

"Well, I'm not sure, Katherine. But I will be leaving soon

for Barbados, and when I get there I will have Priscilla write you a letter. Will you like that?''

"Yes! With lots of drawings."

"Lots of them," Edwinna promised.

"I want a letter, too," William demanded. "I want mine to be written by a slave. He should be very tall—even taller than Mama says the king is. And he should be very black and very fierce. And he should draw pictures."

Drake and Edwinna shared a smile.

"I have the very slave, William," Edwinna told him. "His name is Macaw. He is my boiling house slave. He is tall, black, and very fierce. He once tried to hang his own wife. Your papa stopped him."

"You *did*, Papa?" William screwed up his face and looked up at him with admiration.

"If Mama Edwinna says so, I guess I did." Macaw. Incredible how a name could bring back such vivid sensations: the trade winds blowing sweetly, the sugary smell of a fresh cut cane field, blue herons flying into the sunset, pink coral dawns. With surprise, he realized he missed it all a little.

"Papa, that's brave."

"Thank you! I consider that my finest compliment."

The day passed too soon. Edwinna was easy to be with. She made no demands on him emotionally. She didn't drain him, as Anne often did, keeping him in a state of jealous agitation. But then, there was reason. He loved Anne, so of course she drained him. Now and then when his eyes met Edwinna's, intimacy sparked between them, but she always quickly looked away.

When he delivered Edwinna back to Cornhill, Katherine didn't want to let her go. She hugged the children, then got out of the hackney coach. He walked her to the door.

A pale winter sun was about to set. Cold wind gusted. London winter was about as different from a Barbados winter as the moon from the sun.

At the door, she smiled. "Thank you, Drake, for today. Thank you for letting me get to know your children."

"I wanted you to know them."

"And I wanted to know them."

They looked at each other uncertainly. She pressed her lips together—that wide, pretty mouth that he'd kissed so often and with such pleasure such a long time ago.

"Drake? The ship that you arranged for me to take passage on arrives tomorrow. It will leave two days later for Barbados."

He drew a breath. "So soon?"

She nodded. "I would like to say good-bye right now."

"No. I want to bring you a farewell gift."

"You already did. You gave me today, the children."

"No. I will come tomorrow. I want to bring you something."

"You needn't."

"I want to."

The next afternoon he brought a gift he could ill afford— an opal ring set in gold, which he gave to her in the privacy of Verity's parlor and which made her cry, and which, a month later, served as the occasion of a heated quarrel between himself and Anne when she found the bill for it.

"Drake, it's beautiful," Edwinna said, slipping it on her finger.

"I wanted you to have something beautiful to remember me by."

The November wind howled. The fire crackled and sent forth its warmth. She wiped her eyes with one finger. His strong, brave Edwinna, who had saved him from the sea. Edwinna, who'd shot a bond slave dead to save his life. His tall, plain, spinster bride. Lord, had he ever truly thought her that? She seemed so lovely to him now.

She laughed a little, a teary laugh.

"Did you really think I would need a ring to remember you?"

He smiled. "I'm vain enough to think not, but I wanted you to have it anyway. I wanted to give you something beautiful."

"I'll wear it always."

"But *not* when you knock on sugar pots."

She smiled, her voice choked. "But *not* when I knock on sugar pots." She looked up, eyes shining. "I have a gift for you, too, Drake. Not really for you, but for Katherine and William." He frowned in curiosity as she went to a side table and brought him a thick sheaf of folded parchment paper.

"Please read it. I suppose . . . because of Thomas and Harry, death is on my mind."

It was her will. Frowning, he took it to the window light to scan it. She'd made bequests of money to Plum, Tarcher, and smaller ones to Verity and her overseers. She'd named slaves whom she wanted manumitted. To Kena, Tutu, and David she'd willed George Crawford's plantation. Drake read on, then looked up in astonishment. She'd left her largest, most valuable possession—Crawford Plantation—to his children!

"Edwinna, you cannot do this. You are not thinking clearly."

"I'm thinking very clearly, Drake. I want them to have it."

"No! You'll marry again someday. Who knows, you may have children of your own. At least, you will want your plantation to belong to your husband."

She shook her head, her thick hair sweeping her shoulder. "No. I won't marry again. As for children . . ." She left the rest unsaid.

"Nevertheless, I will *not* keep this." He put it back on the table with a firm hand. "Rethink it, Edwinna. It's too much. It's great wealth."

"I wish you would keep this copy of my will."

"No. I want you to reconsider."

"If you wish. But I won't change my mind. I intend to leave a copy with Verity and Arthur."

They looked at each other. He drew a deep breath. It was time to go. He didn't want to, and she didn't want him to. They gazed into each other's eyes. He refused to cheapen the moment by taking her in his arms and kissing her. He didn't have that right. She was no longer his wife. It would insult her. So, simply, humbly, he said his farewell in words.

"Good-bye, then, Edwinna."

"Good-bye, Drake."

He looked at her a moment longer, picked up his cloak, and strode out of the parlor, pausing in the doorway to say it again.

"Good-bye."

"Good-bye."

Edwinna stood at the window and numbly watched him go. With the wind whipping his cloak and the broad brim of his hat, he stood at the street and took one last look back at her. He lifted his hand. She lifted hers. Then he walked down Cornhill and out of her life.

CHAPTER

* 19 *

Drake worked to exhaustion that winter. He wanted to—
for William and Katherine and Anne, for Verity and Arthur.

He had a new sign made for the shop, identifying himself
as the king's royal vintner. Suddenly, London found it fashionable to buy wine from him. Business increased a hun-
dredfold, which meant hasty trips across the Channel to the
wine cellars of France and freezing cold vigils on the wintry
docks of London whenever a ship came in bearing a cargo
of wine that he might wish to purchase. He sold nothing that
was not fine quality. The Steel Wine Shop on Thames Street
had represented quality and honesty for two centuries. He
intended to uphold that tradition.

Yet, finances tormented him. He was deeply in debt. Much
of the indebtedness stemmed from the Cromwell years when
his father, and later he, had been taxed, dunned, persecuted,
harassed. Striving to repay these debts, the money Verity and
Arthur had advanced, and the ransom loan levied against the
shop, he sometimes sat in his wine shop well past midnight,

his head in his hands. The mounting bills for Anne's pretty court clothes seemed the last straw.

He would glance up from his ledgers and long to see Edwinna sitting across the worktable from him, working on her own ledgers—his sensible Edwinna, with her silly hair braid and her zeal for work. Thoughts of Edwinna calmed his heart.

Anne made him uneasy in his heart. She was so . . . restless. His refusal to allow her more than two court days a week smoldered between them like an underground peat pit fire, difficult to detect with the naked eye, but smoking and apt to blaze into a conflagration quarrel at any moment.

Yet he remained adamant. He was *not* a liberal husband. He was not about to send Anne, like an unprotected chick, into that den of foxes. She was under the king's protection, Anne argued. Ha! In Drake's opinion, the king was the least trustworthy of all when it came to pretty women.

He wished she would show more interest in the children, but she seemed content to leave their upbringing in the hands of tutor and housemaid. She loved them; Drake felt certain of it. Sometimes she romped and played with them as merrily as a child herself. Sometimes he would come home to find Anne seated at the virginal, Katherine in her lap, teaching Katherine to play and sing. Those moments warmed his heart, but they came rarely. In the main she treated the children like playthings, to be enjoyed one day, ignored the next. He didn't know what to make of her.

Still, in bed she was the center of his universe. There she was passionate, her nature as inventively erotic as his own. They thrilled each other. In bed no other woman existed for him. Only Anne. Anne!

On a night like tonight, however, sitting alone in his drafty wine shop at midnight, with only the winter wind and a candle and a scuttling mouse for company, and with financial worries weighing him down, he longed for Edwinna. Edwinna, who could understand a man's money problems; Edwinna, who wouldn't care what she wore to court or if she even went; Edwinna, who cheered his soul, who gave him . . . peace.

Edwinna welcomed the long, arduous voyage—the solitary nature of it, the loneliness. She badly needed to be alone. She needed privacy to grieve for Thomas and Harry. She hadn't been able to do so properly in Verity's small, crowded house.

As the ship plowed south she allowed the days and weeks and nautical miles to wash over her until time and distance blended into a blur and she scarcely noticed or cared when one week ended and the next began.

A month into the voyage she awoke to a startling event. She was bleeding. She was stunned to discover she'd gotten her monthly courses. She tended herself, then curled into the goose-down quilt in her bunk and savored the unfamiliar feminine cramping and the wonder of it. Her courses. She was a woman!

She lay there filled with joy, and at the same time, infinitely sad. Had it happened two months earlier, she might have been carrying Drake's child. She might have had something of Drake to keep and carry back to Barbados with her.

Her lips parted with surprise. This was Drake's doing—Drake, who had helped her become a real woman; Drake, who'd given her his companionship by day and his passion by night; Drake, who'd given her fondness. Drake had re-awakened her womanhood. She contemplated it with wonder.

He'd thought his parting gift had been an opal ring, but he'd given her much more. He'd given her back her femininity.

Drake's heart leapt with pleasure when he received his first letter from Barbados, from Edwinna. She'd written cordially—a letter dealing mainly with sugar and needed supplies. She told him all the news. Her voyage had been safe and uneventful. In her absence Kena had been safely delivered of a pretty baby girl whom David had named Mary Rose Edwinna. Tutu was a little jealous but loved the baby. Harvest was going well, although an out-of-season hurricane had struck Barbados, flattening three cane fields, which she'd had to dig up and replant. Last, she hoped it might amuse him to hear that Macaw was bedeviling her, requesting a fourth wife.

Drake smiled reading this last dab of news, but his smile was bittersweet. He missed Edwinna. He was surprised at how much. He missed her sensible ways and her lovely eyes and, bastard that he was, he missed her in his bed.

The letter so gladdened his heart that he kept it in his pocket, which gave rise to a quarrel when Anne found it there while brushing his jacket. They fought hotly. Anne accused him of being in love with Edwinna. Drake denied it. They fought until bedtime. When the quarrel spilled over into bed, Drake lost patience and ravished her.

The quarrel melted away in the heat of passion, and later, when they lay lovingly entwined, both sated, both content, watching moonlit clouds sail past the window, Drake scarcely remembered what the quarrel had been about.

He pressed a kiss to her temple. "It's *you* I love. *You*."

"I do love you, Drake." Her confession thrilled him, for of late he had wondered. Sometimes she seemed to hate him for not letting her spend more time at court. Now they lay content in each other's arms and talked drowsily. This, he loved—this intimacy of spirit, this closeness.

"I'm only sorry we're poor."

"We're not poor, Anne. If business continues as well as it has, I will have my head above water in five years."

"That long?"

He smiled. "That's not long—not for indebtedness."

"Why don't you ignore your debts? The gentlemen of the court pay theirs not the least attention."

"Perhaps that's why I'm not a courtier," he said caustically.

She peered at him in the darkness, not much liking that. "At least they don't take their debts so seriously and boringly as you do. They all jest about how much they owe their tailors. Drake, you would have laughed at the funny story Lord Kersey told about climbing out the window of his lodgings to avoid his tailor when the poor, befuddled man came collecting."

"I'm a tradesman. I like to be paid for my wine so I doubt I would have been amused."

She trailed a soft hand down his chest and his belly, to his groin. "Don't be foolish." Foolish. It was a word that bothered him. He drew her hand away. "Drake, they all are ordering grand new suits of clothes for the coronation. Petticoat breeches with Flemish lace. Capes of cloth of gold. Lord Kersey is having seed pearls sewn on his waistcoat."

"He would." Drake yawned.

She turned a vexed expression on him. "What will you wear, Drake? I doubt you even care."

"Unlike Lord Kersey, I'll wear something I can afford and will have paid for." Then, because he sounded like a penny-pinching grouch even to his own ears, he kissed her cheek. "I want you to have a beautiful coronation gown—the loveliest in the city."

"It *is* beautiful. I had a fitting last week." She sighed. "I would *die* for a strand of pearls to wear with it."

He smiled in the darkness. "Truly *die*?"

"Perish."

"You needn't do that. I'll provide them."

"Oh, Drake." She lunged up, threw her arms around him, and strangled his neck. "Drake, you're so good to me."

"That's because I love you."

"And I love you."

Elated about the pearls, she snuggled in his arms and happily went to sleep. Drake lay awake, worrying. He ran his finances through his head. A good strand of pearls would cost all of thirty pounds.

In his attempt to make Anne happy, Drake stole time from the wine shop, which he could ill afford to do, and took her to the afternoon theatrical performances as often as possible. Theater enchanted her. Closed during the strict Puritan Cromwell years, the theaters of London had reopened with a flourish.

Female actors appeared on stage for the first time in the history of England. While London professed to be shocked, all the city flocked to see the spectacle. Drake refused to pretend he was shocked when he was genuinely delighted. He enjoyed looking at a beautiful woman as much as any man, especially when the actresses played in costume farces, prancing about the stage in tights, their shapely legs on display for all of London to see.

It was at a Drury Lane playhouse on a blustery February day that he spotted Charles Dare in the stalls. Despite Charles's promise to visit Drake, he hadn't come. The omission hurt. They'd once been best friends. What in hell had happened?

Determined to get to the bottom of it, he kept an eye on Charles, and when Charles rose in midperformance to go out to the privy, Drake went, too. They pissed side by side, their two trails of steam rising in the cold air.

"What's wrong, Charles? What's happened between us?"

"What d'you mean?"

"You know damn well what I mean. We used to be best friends."

"We still are," Charles protested.

"The hell we are. You haven't come to the wine shop, or to dine with us. You haven't invited me to dine with you."

"Been busy." Charles gave him a broad wink. "Got me

a new mistress. An actress. That girl in the blue tights? Mine.''

Drake looked at him in the waning winter sunlight. That could explain it, of course. Whenever Charles fell in love, which he did as regularly as other men pared their toenails, he became consumed with his *paramour*. Drake smiled.

''Well, you're not busy now. Come with Anne and me to the George and Vulture after the performance. We'll sup on lobster. My treat.''

Charles seemed uncomfortable with the invitation. He took his hat off and nervously rippled a gloved hand through his fair hair. Charles was as good-looking as ever—broad of brow and jowl. He had a face women took to. With a reluctant nod and a broad smile, Charles accepted. *There's something wrong here*, Drake thought.

He thought it even more as the three of them walked the short distance through the blustery wind to Cornhill, Anne giving Charles the cold shoulder, scarcely even willing to speak to him. When they'd seated themselves in a tall wooden booth near the fire in the noisy taproom and sat thawing out, Anne remained stiff, a flush of anger tinting her cheeks. She plainly didn't want Charles with them. Drake could not understand why. She'd always liked Charles.

Charles was not himself, either. He talked too loudly, laughed too hard. As they drank wine, shucked and ate oysters, and enjoyed sweet, buttery lobster, Charles talked nonstop about his two years in Italy. Drake gazed at him, puzzled. He hadn't invited Charles for a travel recitation. He'd hoped to reestablish intimacy and friendship. At one point Anne, who'd been entirely silent, burst out at Charles.

''Oh, do shut up!''

Startled, Charles fell silent, then recovered and babbled faster and louder than ever. Drake put down his lobster-cracking utensil and looked at Anne. ''Do shut up'' was such an intimate thing to say. Drake's heart beat oddly, and he looked piercingly at Charles, who was raving now about his visit to Rome, almost frantically piling detail upon detail of it. Drake's uneasiness grew. There was an undercurrent here, something out of reach. He felt a searing sensation in his brain. The undercurrent rippled away in the mundane ordinariness of talk and drink and food, but the memory of it lingered, deeply disturbing him.

Edwinna cherished every letter that came from Drake. He wrote with faithful regularity and accepted his responsibility as sugar factor seriously. She read each letter a hundred times, even though the contents dealt mainly with business: tonnage received, sugar prices, supplies ordered, dates sent. Drake was not one to put his personal life on paper, but she sensed that all was not well and she worried about him.

As for herself, she thought of Drake constantly and saw him everywhere. She saw his broad-shouldered figure in the cane fields, his black hair glistening in the bright sunshine. She saw him at noon table, sitting relaxed and easy in the place now empty, talking harvest with the overseers. She heard his voice, his step on the stair. Sometimes she imagined she smelled his scent, the sugary smell of fresh-cut cane. Whenever her need for him overwhelmed her, she spent the night sleeping in his bed, her arms tightly wrapped around his pillow.

As if she were important to him, Drake took time to write her a long, detailed letter describing the king's coronation, which took place in April. Reading the letter nightly in bed by candlelight, she would cease to hear the rumble of the grinder and would hear, instead, Drake's magnificent voice telling her about the event.

Drake counted himself lucky to witness it. The coronation of His Majesty, King Charles II, was the celebration of the century. In splendor and richness and pomp, its like had never before been seen in England and never would be again.

Drake set business aside during Coronation Week and witnessed all that he could, every bit of it, beginning with the majestic ceremony of the Knights of the Bath in the painted chamber in Westminster. Drake watched, dazzled by the rich robes and the glittering coronets of the knights. He was touched to the very soul by the religious rite, as the king put off his own robes to humble himself and take the ritual bath that signified his cleansing in preparation to rule England.

Similar pageantry went on each day of Coronation Week, each event richer and more dazzling than the last. But the most exciting was the coronation parade.

The participants gathered at the Tower of London the night before. Slated to take a minor part in it, Drake went to the Tower, too, and watched the thousands of participants arrive throughout the night: Swiss guards in white ruffs and uniforms of Stuart scarlet; the London militia in new tunics of blue and white linen; General Monck's army, wearing capes of gold cloth; splendidly garbed generals, bishops, dukes, earls, barons, viscounts. The richness of their attire hurt the eye. The Tower glittered with gold and jewels and diamonds.

As Drake wrote Edwinna later, he was glad he'd let Anne badger him into buying a new suit of black brocade silk. He didn't "glitter," but he felt appropriately dressed. He also wore two Steel family heirlooms—his great-great-grandfather's gold gorget at his throat, and his grandfather's gold-and-diamond ring on his finger.

But the lords' horses were attired even better than he. They wore gold-tooled saddles, blankets of gold cloth, and their grooms spent the entire night working by torchlight, braiding gold ribbons into their manes and tails. A few of the horses wore diamonds as large as hens' eggs on their forelocks.

With a great deal of pomp and ceremony, the mile-long procession started out from the Tower at nine in the morning, led by the king, bands playing, thousands of scarlet silk flags flying. In the bright sunshine, the procession was a glittering sea of diamonds and gold. London screamed with joy. Church bells rang ceaselessly. Wine flowed freely in the public fountains. People grew merry and drunk. The flower-strewn streets had been graveled for the event, and families throughout London had decorated their houses, hanging out flags and tapestries.

When Drake reached Cornhill, he eagerly looked up at Verity's windows and waved to his family, who cheered and tossed flowers to him. Lord, how beautiful Anne looked. He threw her a kiss, and she excitedly threw kisses to him. With her silvery blond hair dressed with pink flowers and her slender figure clad in low-necked pink silk, she was easily the most beautiful woman in London—a sight to capture any man, king or beggar. He had a moment of uneasiness, picturing the king passing this spot, looking up and seeing Anne so beautiful and desirable.

Marching on with the other men who would soon be knighted, Drake suddenly felt a lowering of spirits that was incongruous with the joyful day. He'd had such uncomfortable thoughts lately. When Anne came home from court these days she seemed overexcited, wound up like a child's toy top, a flush on her cheeks, her eyes bright and distant, shutting him out. He fought against his burgeoning suspicions; he didn't want to discover the reasons behind her altered behaviors. Yet, two week earlier he'd discovered a rent in her moral fabric, and, for that matter, a damned big hole in his own. He'd touched Anne with violence—a thing he'd never done before. Just thinking about the incident left him shaken.

The quarrel had begun without warning. He'd worked late, wrestling with his financial problems, and had come home to a midnight supper with Anne. As they sat at the table in candlelight, he'd made the simple request that she not commit him to any more creditors this year. The request had escalated into another argument about money.

"If that homely Barbados woman had not begged you to take only three percent as sugar factor we would have plenty of money," Anne had declared.

He'd looked up with a flash of anger. He didn't like Edwinna being called homely. She was lovely.

"She did not beg me. I insisted. She offered ten."

"And you didn't take it? Drake, how ridiculous. You should write her and change your fee."

"No."

"Then I will."

"You will not!"

"Why? It isn't as if you owe her anything."

He'd looked up sharply. "I owe her my life. Or would you rather have money than me?" It was a thought that had been occurring to him lately. He'd gone on eating his soup.

"Darling. I am only saying that she has pots of money and we have none. It isn't fair. What would it hurt if you kept back some of the sugar money, overcharged her for supplies? She would never know."

He'd looked up, utterly astonished. "Anne! Good lord, where do you get such thoughts? I would never cheat Edwinna. Never."

She'd tossed her head, silvery hair shinning in the candlelight. "Oh, don't be so righteous. 'Tis a common enough practice among sugar factors."

"Not," he said, growing harsh, "in the Steel family. Anne, sometimes I think I don't know you anymore."

"Oh. Now it is *my* fault we have no money, is it?"

"If you want the truth, *yes.*"

The quarrel had grown hotter from that point on. They'd both said harsh things they would not have said had the hour not been so late and had Drake not been so damned tired. Her dressmaker bills, her preoccupation with court, and the undercurrent he felt lately frightened him.

"Then, do you know what I hope?" Anne said curtly. "I hope she dies. Then William and Katherine will inherit her plantation and we will finally have enough money to live decently!"

Drake was out of his chair instantly. He grabbed her, yanked her to her feet, and gave her a vicious shake.

"Don't you dare say that! Don't you dare wish her dead." He shook her until her teeth rattled, until she cried out in fear. Not until he heard her pathetic weeping did he come to himself and realize what he was doing. He looked down at his beautiful Anne, aghast. Her eyes were wide with terror, and she stared at him as if he were a monster.

"Oh, my God." He crushed her close. "Darling, I'm sorry. Anne, I'm so sorry." She clung to him, sobbing against his chest. "I'm sorry, Anne, I'm sorry." He petted and comforted her and buried his mouth in her hair. "Anne, Anne, what's become of us? What's happening to us?"

She sobbed into his shirt, contrite. "Drake. If you want, I won't go to court anymore—I'll stay home."

"No, no, sweetheart," he whispered into her angel-soft hair. "I'm no tyrant. I'm just a stupid, jealous husband. Go to court. All I ask is your loyalty. Without it, I am unmanned—useless to myself, to you, to the children, to everyone. I need your loyalty, Anne."

She wept in his arms like a heartbroken child.

The coronation of King Charles II took place the day after the parade. Again and even more loudly, church bells pealed all over London. More wine flowed in the public fountains. Londoners shouted and cheered and danced in the streets.

To get a seat on the scaffolding erected for the proceedings inside Westminster Abbey, Drake and Arthur came at four in the morning, making their way through the dark city. By six in the morning all of the seats were taken. They then sat and waited until eleven for the ceremony to begin. Outside the abbey the crowd roared like thunder and massed so thickly the militia had to hold them back. People occupied every inch of space and perched on rooftops and in trees. The Thames River was a solid carpet of boats. People walked across the Thames from one shore to the other by stepping from boat to boat, full of high spirits, merry with wine.

The ceremony was worth the long wait. Drake and Arthur heard little of the actual rites with the crowd roaring so loudly outside, but the pageant itself proved splendid and rich, so religious that it swelled his heart, and when the time came to shout, "God Save King Charles the Second," he and Arthur shouted as zealously as peasants and with tears in their eyes. The civil war and the wretched Cromwell years were indeed at an end. The monarchy was restored. Drake wished that his father had lived to see it.

Two weeks after the coronation, Drake's world began to unravel. It began with one slip of the tongue—Anne's tongue.

Drake and Anne were at the royal theater on Drury Lane when Charles Dare walked in on the opposite side of the playhouse. Drake glanced in his direction. So did Anne. She said tartly, "I see Charles Dare is growing his mustache again. He looks ridiculous. Some men look well in a mustache, the king being one, but Charles Dare does not. Someone should tell him how foolish he looks."

Drake felt the chill all through his body. He stared at her, unsure he'd heard right, hoping he hadn't.

"Growing his mustache again? Anne, Charles has never grown a mustache. Not in all the years I've known him, and I've known him all my life."

Her eyebrows lifted. Her breath caught. She flushed.

"Well, then, I disremember. Likely it is someone else I am thinking of."

"Surely."

The play began. Anne leaned forward with zest. Drake stared at the stage, but saw nothing. For three hours as the play went on, he sat neither seeing nor hearing. *I see Charles Dare is growing his mustache again. Oh, do shut up! What do you do at court, Anne? Do you ever see the king? Oh, no! Very rarely. I spend all my time with Lady Elizabeth and Lady Edith. I am teaching them to sing. I see Charles Dare is growing his mustache again. Oh, do shut up! What do you do at court, Anne? Do you ever see the king?*

He spent a sleepless night. He watched Anne as she slept beside him and he agonized. He arose haggard in the morning and sent word to Arthur that he would not be in. Without waiting to break his fast, he dressed and went directly to St. Katherine's Docks, to the shipping office that had owned the *Fair Wind*, the ship on which Anne had set sail for France.

"I want to see the passenger records for the *Fair Wind*," he told the clerk on duty.

"She's sunk. Pirates. Two years ago." The clerk was a thin young man with a whiny voice and smallpox scars on his face.

"I know. I want to see the records for her last sailing."

"'Tis a passel o' work, diggin' em out."

Drake stacked five shillings on the countertop. With a furtive glance, the clerk whipped his head to the right and to the left, making sure his superiors were not watching. Then he swept the coins off the counter and into his pocket and scuttled off.

Drake waited a half hour.

"'Twas a passel o' work," the clerk said again, hinting for more money.

"You've been paid." Drake jerked the manifest out of the man's hands. For a moment, he couldn't look at it. Tension made his head throb, blackened his vision. He drew a deep breath to clear his head, then forced himself to look. He traced a finger down the passenger list. *Mrs. Anne Steel.* Expected. He continued to draw his finger down the list and found it. *Mr. Charles Dare.*

For a moment his head spun. He braced his hands on the counter and drew a ragged breath.

"You sick, sir?"

"No."

"Will that be all?" the clerk inquired.

"Yes."

Drake shoved the manifest at the clerk and strode out. He passed blindly through the city, trudging for hours, uncaring in what direction he traveled or where he was going, unaware of pedestrians except when someone barked, "Look where ye be going. Ye near knocked me down. Are ye drunk?" He walked and walked, pushing his way through crowds, now cursing, now shedding tears, vaguely aware that he must look demented or drunk or both, for people gave him a wide berth, crossing to the other side of the street. Anne and Charles!

When he finally looked up, he found himself on the south side of the Thames, near the bear-baiting pit in Southwark, without the foggiest memory of crossing London Bridge or hiring a water coach. How had he arrived here? Exhausted from the roar and tumult of his emotions, he went into an obscure inn, bought bread and beer, and ate and drank, lifting the tankard to his lips with a hand that shook. Then he sat for an eternity, his head against the smoke-blackened wall, eyes closed, mind empty, heart emptier. The innkeeper glanced his way frequently, warily.

It was late afternoon by the time he had thought through his plans and reshaped his life. He felt ten years older, a hundred years wiser. He traveled back into the city by water coach and had the oarsman let him off at Whitehall Palace. There were additional things he had to find out, pleasant or not. He didn't go into the royal apartments. Anne was there. This was her court day. He mustn't see her yet; he might kill her. Instead, he scanned the posted listing to see which of the nobles and ladies were in residence and which were gone from the city. Then he recrossed the Thames by water coach and went to the residence of the bishop of London. The bishop received him. Then he went home to his children.

Darkness had fallen by the time he heard Anne's hackney coach rattle down Highgate Hall's dirt lane. Her court days had grown longer. Now he knew why. He sat at the old oak table in the dining chamber and waited for her to come in. The candles in the wrought-iron chandelier cast a fluttering light in the May breeze. He could smell the first of the spring lilacs blooming in the yard. How incongruous to smell the sweetness of lilacs on such a day. He knew intuitively that from this moment on, for the rest of his life, he would always connect the scent of lilacs with Anne.

He heard the heavy front door open and close, then her light footsteps. Drawn by the candles, she came into the dining chamber. She stopped, startled to find him sitting there at the empty table, then offered a bright, tense smile—her court day smile.

"Darling, you're home from the wine shop early."

"Sit down, Anne."

"Why? What are you doing sitting here looking so odd?" The chair scraped as she took her seat opposite him. He sat with his elbows on the table, arms propped up, chin resting on folded hands. He gazed at her and saw things he'd never noticed before. The strong, selfish set of her pretty mouth. The evasiveness of her eyes. They never quite met his, or if they did, the meeting lasted only a second, no longer.

She looked about, uneasy in the silence.

"Where are the servants? The children?"

Drake observed the order of her questions and what they revealed. She cared little for the children. He'd failed to notice that before, fool that he was. He'd assumed a woman who bore children loved them. Untrue. Another of his delusions shattered. He thought of Edwinna, of her love for children —Edwinna, who was unable to have them.

"Are you going to answer me?" she asked, laughing nervously.

"I sent the servants on holiday, the children to Verity's."

"Why? You know I cannot do without servant help."

He drew a painful breath. She couldn't do without the

servants, but she could do without the children. The truth had been before his eyes all along. He'd been blind—an idiot in love.

"I sent them away because I don't want the servants or the children to hear what I have to say to you. I want the servants to continue to think you are a lady. I want your children to continue to respect their mother."

She grew wary. Her fingers moved tensely to the edge of the table. He looked at her pretty hands—hands that did no work. Edwinna's hands were not so carefully tended; sometimes they bore a torn nail. They were always working, or holding a child.

"What do you mean?"

"Where have you been today, Anne?" he said. He was astonished at how calm he felt—how little he felt, in fact. Was it possible for love to die in the short space of one day? No. It would take longer, probably forever. Perhaps a part of him would always love her, but he no longer liked her. That made the difference.

"In court. You know that."

"With whom?"

"The usual. Lady Elizabeth, Lady Edith. I'm teaching them to sing. They're progressing very well."

"Lady Elizabeth and Lady Edith left for Bath two days ago, with several other ladies of the court. They will not return until next week. I checked."

She drew a breath, nostrils flaring. Caught in her lie, she sharply swung her head away, looking anywhere but at him.

"You have been in bed with the king, Anne."

"No! That is—" Taking courage, she treated him to a scathing look, her eyes fiery. How little love was in the look. He'd never before noticed: Fool that he was, he'd thought she loved him. "'Tis an honor!"

He laughed. "An 'honor' you share with ten thousand other Englishwomen. Prostitutes are brought up and down the king's privy staircase every night, conveyed to Whitehall by water coach. They pass each other coming and going, their little sacks of coins in their hands."

She flared. "I am *not* a prostitute. If you must know, Drake, King Charles has asked me to become one of his mistresses. You—you should feel honored that the *king* of England has selected your wife."

Again, he chuckled, sat back in his chair. "Should I, by God?" His voice rasped. This wasn't easy. "I didn't know that. I didn't know a man should feel 'honored' to be made a cuckold by his king and his wife."

Confident in her position at court, she taunted him, spitefully. "For your information, Drake, I am already with child by the king. His Majesty says you will own it. You have to."

This was too much. He reared up from the chair, went to the window, and gripped the sill with both hands—gripped it so hard the old wood creaked. He must grip the sill to keep from killing her. He didn't speak until he had control of himself.

"You're wrong, Anne. And His Majesty is wrong. I will not cover his bastard with my name. You and His Majesty can dispose of the matter as you wish."

"You have to own the child," she spat at him. "We are married. It is the law. You have to own any child I bear, whether 'tis yours or not."

"True. If we were married when you gave birth to your royal bastard, I would have to own it. But you see, we will not be married. This afternoon I paid a call on the bishop of London. I have applied to the ecclesiastical court for a divorce from bed and board on the grounds of adultery."

Her face went white. "You—cannot do that."

"But I *can*. And I have."

Her fingers scratched at the table, as if she were in shock, as if she were trying to find something to grip. He was almost sorry for her. He knew what she was thinking. Divorced, she could not appear in court—at least, not openly. She would be reduced to using the privy staircase like a common prostitute.

"You cannot! Your knighthood, Drake. The king cannot grant a knighthood to a divorced subject."

"Ah. Now we are at the truth. You long to be Lady Anne Steel, don't you? Is that why you came back to me?"

She looked up at him, white-faced.

"What do you mean?"

"I know about Charles Dare." Her face went even whiter; her eyes became huge. "I know you sailed together on the *Fair Wind*." When she opened her mouth to protest, he shook his head. "Oh, I know you intended to go to your sick sister in France. I don't doubt it. But you also intended a dalliance with Charles. Your plans went awry when the Dutch pirates captured the ship. It must have been very disconcerting to both of you."

"He—Charles merely escorted me. *You* were gone, Drake, on one of your constant wine-buying trips. I—I needed someone to escort me."

He grimaced. "Anne, credit me with a little intelligence. If Charles had merely escorted you, you and he would not have kept the fact a secret."

"But it's true!"

Drake laughed.

"You cannot divorce me. You cannot mean to forfeit your knighthood. What—what about William? He will inherit your knighthood. You can't take the knighthood away from William!"

He gazed at her with intense dislike. *Now she brings up the children.* He shook his head. *Oh, my God. What a fool you've been, Drake Steel. A fool in love.*

"If you think, Anne, that I intend to raise my son with so few moral values that he would welcome inheriting a knighthood that has as part of its foundation his mother's prostitution with the king—well, you are quite wrong. I intend to raise

William to value what I value: honesty, decency. I mean to have my divorce from bed and board, my poor, foolish darling. I've already made my first payment to the ecclesiastical court.''

With a wounded cry—"Drake, please!"—she leapt up and came flying to him, the high heels of her pretty go-to-court shoes clattering on the ancient floorboards. She threw her arms around his neck and pressed her breasts to his chest. "Drake, don't do this. I love you, I do. I'll be good, I will, I promise. I'll be good.''

He peeled her hands from his neck as he would peel away an unwelcome snake. "Anne, you don't love me. You have never loved anyone but yourself. As for being good, you don't know the meaning of the word.''

"But you love me, you do." Sobbing now, she crumpled to her knees, wrapping her arms around his legs, clutching him, burying her face against the rough serge of his breeches.

"I probably do," he admitted. "And that's the hell of it." He touched her shaking shoulders. "But love doesn't live forever, Anne—not without being nurtured and fed. And today my love for you received poison. It will take a while for it to die, and the death will be an agony, but it assuredly will die.''

"Drake," she begged, her eyes wet, beautiful, beseeching, "don't do this, don't.''

"Now, my darling, go upstairs and gather your belongings.''

"Why?" she asked, a shot of fear piercing her tearful voice.

"Because tomorrow, Arthur will come and take you to find new lodgings. He will help you.''

"Lodgings?"

"I don't want you in this house, Anne. This is the Steel family home, and it has stood for honor and decency for six generations. You don't belong in it. You don't belong here.''

"Drake, please!" she begged.

"No." It was the hardest word he'd ever uttered. For indeed, he still loved her.

"But what will become of me?" she said in panic. The tears coursed down her cheeks.

He touched her lovely hair gently. "I will see to it that you have a roof over your head, food to eat, clothes to wear, a servant to serve you. You will have an allowance of one hundred pounds a year."

"I can't live on that little," she sobbed.

He stroked her hair. "Anne, Anne. You and I and William and Katherine lived on half that amount, and happily. At least, I was happy, though perhaps you were not."

"But what about the children?"

Again they were her last concern. He gazed down at her with pity and dislike. He wondered if she would ever realize what she'd lost? Probably not. She was resilient, like a cat, and with as little real affection.

"I'm taking them with me."

She looked up, face tear-streaked, roughened from the serge.

"Take—taking? What do you mean?"

"I'm taking them with me to Barbados."

"You're going to that woman? That tall, homely woman?"

He had to smile, pityingly, in sympathy for Anne's values.

"I thought that once. I thought her tall and plain. But later, Anne, I was privileged to know her. Right now she seems to me the most beautiful woman in the world—the only woman I want to be with."

"You can't marry her," Anne cried out vindictively. "You can't marry anyone. A divorce from bed and board doesn't allow remarriage."

He smiled sympathetically. "But you see, Anne, that won't matter to Edwinna. She will want me with or without marriage. She loves me."

"But you love *me*, Drake, you do!" Pathetically, she began to lavish kisses on his groin, trying to arouse him. He gently took her face and pushed it away.

"Gather your things, Anne. Get ready for the morning."

He strode out of the dining room, into the entry hall, and picked up hat, cloak, and sword. She jumped up and came flying after him, heels racketing, hair disheveled.

"Where are you going!" She cried out in alarm.

"To Verity's. To the children."

"You can't leave me alone," she said, panicky.

Alone? How ironic. He'd been alone all of his marriage and he'd been too stupid to know it. Ignoring her, he opened the door and descended the steps into the lovely spring evening. The hickory trees arched overhead, bare of leaves but budding. Spring, summer, autumn, winter—a lovely succession. Each of the seasons held its special joys and its small sorrows. He wouldn't have missed one of them. He was glad he had been married to Anne. Without her, he wouldn't have had William and Katherine.

"Drake," she cried out, panic growing. "I don't like to be alone!"

He turned for a moment before striding on. Silhouetted in the doorway, in candle glow, she had never looked more beautiful to him or less appealing.

"Nor do I, Anne," he returned. "But you see, if I stayed with you tonight, I would be exactly that. *Alone*."

He strode off into the lilac-scented evening, his step eager. He longed to be with his children.

CHAPTER

* 20 *

Drake caught the fragrance of the Caribbean when the ship was still two days out from shore. The huge continent of South America, with its vast landmass of steaming jungles, exerted that much influence. He inhaled deeply, breathing in the balmy air, the familiar scent, and gripped the rail with excitement. Edwinna . . .

The voyage had been easy and uneventful. They'd sailed directly south, with stops to take on fresh food and water in Portugal and along the northwest coast of Africa. When they'd reached the latitude of Barbados, they'd changed course and sailed due west, catching the trade winds. The ship galloped over the sea like a mare.

For his children's sake, Drake had chosen a stout, sea-worthy ship that had formidable deck cannons and a well-seasoned captain in command. A contingent of soldiers bound for Bridgetown rounded out the passenger list, eliminating the fear of pirates.

He glanced at the deck where William and his tutor sat

with a slate, studying the basic elements of celestial navigation, then at Katherine, who romped with a puppy born on the voyage to the captain's bitch. He smiled. The children were healthy and as brown as nuts. They'd taken to sailing. They liked their tutor, a cheerful young man who'd agreed to tutor them for two years in exchange for Drake's paying his passage to the Caribbean.

Drake leaned on the rail, content, happy, the trade winds ruffling his hair. He couldn't wait to see Edwinna. She would be so surprised. He'd taken a month to put his affairs in order before sailing. Some of the business had been unpleasant. He'd courteously written the king, declining the knighthood, thereby saving His Majesty the embarrassment of having to withdraw the honor. The king had written back with equal courtesy acknowledging Drake's refusal. Neither had mentioned Anne, but the crux of the matter had stood plain between them. King Charles had requested that Drake keep the patent of royal vintner, with the understanding the patent would remain in the Steel family permanently, to be handed down from generation to generation. Drake had accepted gladly. He was not so great a fool as to cut off his nose to spite his face. The patent would make his fortune, and William's, and William's sons'.

Drake smiled. "Not so great a fool." Those had been Verity's parting words, along with a ferocious hug and a demand he show his "handsome face" in London two years hence. He'd promised her and he'd promised Arthur. He couldn't overburden Arthur with the responsibility of the wine business and duties as sugar factor, as well. It was too much.

He intended to return in two years with Edwinna and the children, stay two years in London, and then go back to Barbados. He intended to be fair with Edwinna, dividing their time between London and Barbados, but he would *not*, by God, live without her. Not a year, not a month, not a day. He wanted her at his side, with him.

Edwinna. His heart beat oddly. He, respected and admired her, wanted her in his bed, but the feeling in his breast was something more, something larger than fondness, and it surprised him.

The ship plunged into a tall wave, the timbers creaking and the deck rolling gently. He glanced at the children. They'd become such sailors they'd hardly noticed. They'd leaned naturally in the opposite direction, expertly keeping their balance.

Another piece of nasty business had been Charles Dare. Drake was not a man to sweep dirt under the rug and forget it. He'd gone to Charles and confronted him. They'd had hot words. Only God's providence, and Drake's realization that Anne wasn't worth it, had kept the words from escalating into blows. When Drake had walked out from that meeting, the friendship was severed, dead—*if* a friendship had ever existed in the first place.

He'd asked Arthur to deal with Anne, to see to her needs. Drake couldn't and well knew why. He still loved her. He didn't want to love her. He prayed God to take it out of his heart, to liberate him. Standing there at the ship's rail, watching the waves slide by, mesmerized by the rhythmic rolling sea, he slowly became host to a new thought. Maybe it hadn't been love at all! Maybe he'd been the victim of a habit, the habit of loving Anne. His chest lightened. Habits could be broken.

Gazing at the hypnotic sea, examining the new thought, he suddenly jerked to attention, noticing the jetsam and flotsam on the waves. Whole cane plants drifted in the waves —small plants, large ones, unripe ones, fully ripe ones. It alarmed him. He was just turning to go find the captain when the man strolled up to rail and frowned down into the sea. He took a long draw on his clay pipe.

"Ay, 'tis cane, Mr. Steel."

"What does it mean, uprooted cane out here?"

"Means they've had themselves a bad time in Barbados. Likely a hurricane. Happens sometimes. Flattens and uproots all the cane fields on the island."

"A storm could carry the cane way out here? Against the trade winds?"

"Ay. If it's a bad storm, a powerful hurricane."

"Good God." His chest tightened. Was Edwinna all right? Not only Edwinna, but others he cared for: Matthew Plum, David Alleyne, Kena, Tutu, Simon Tarcher. "Perhaps the storm hit the cane fields of Brazil, not Barbados. Maybe this is Brazilian cane."

The captain sucked on his pipe and said with grim humor, "If it's Brazilian cane carried this far out, we won't even bother to look for Barbados. If the storm was *that* bad, she's sunk, gone to the bottom of the sea, like the lost continent Atlantis."

Drake worried all day, into the night. He was out at the rail by dawn the next morning, keeping watch. The seaman in the crow's nest shouted land-ho about nine in the morning, and ten minutes later Drake saw the outline of Barbados appear on the horizon. He watched, his nerves strung tight. Impatiently he waited for the ship to get closer.

The Atlantic coast looked the same, hurricane or not, for it was uninhabited and rugged and always looked storm-ravaged, but when the captain brought his ship around the southern end of the island, entering the calmer Caribbean sea, heading along the coast for Carlisle Bay and Bridgetown, Drake winced at the destruction, the devastation, he saw. Terraced cane fields lay flattened. Stone windmills had collapsed into heaps of rubble. Millworks lay in shambles. He saw the house of a planter he knew, its roof gone, its upper story shredded to sticks. God in heaven. The island looked as if some demon had taken an ax to it.

He grew panicky. Crawford Plantation would have been hit even harder, for it was on the spine of the island, the plateau, a thousand feet above sea level, in the direct path of the wind.

A seasoned sailor, the captain did not try to enter Bridgetown harbor, but scouted it first, staying outside the reef, tacking into the wind, making several passes at Carlisle Bay. Drake stood with him at the rail, looking at the horrors as they presented themselves. The harbor looked like a bucket of toy ships dumped out by a willful child. Oceangoing vessels floated keel up. Other ships that had managed to stay upright had lost masts, rigging. Two ships had been picked up by the wind and cast onto the beach. Bridgetown itself lay decimated, every tenth building in shambles. He could see people scrambling in the wreckage, salvaging things. Drake scanned the waterfront for Edwinna's warehouse. It was gone.

Unable to put in at Bridgetown harbor because of the floating wreckage, they sailed on to Speightstown. Drake gripped the rail tensely. The Caribbean coast lay devastated. They sailed past mile after mile of ruined cane fields, collapsed windmills. Whole trees bobbing in the water bumped the hull of the ship: banana trees, papaya trees, mahogany trees, queen palms. Approaching Speightstown, Drake borrowed the captain's spyglass and searched three miles inland, hoping to see Edwinna's stone windmill high on the plateau. He couldn't find it. His gut twisted.

Speightstown had sustained less damage than Bridgetown. The sturdy storehouses still stood, though minus roofs. The more flimsy buildings were gone, blown away. He drew a relieved breath when he spotted Simon Tarcher's limestone coral cottage. It was intact, only a few roof tiles missing.

The captain anchored in the cove and sent the passengers ashore in rowing boats, a hazardous enough undertaking with trees and wreckage bobbing in the surf. Filled with worry about Edwinna, Drake cradled Katherine on his lap. When they landed, Simon Tarcher came running to meet him, his white, feathery hair blowing in the trade winds. He'd spotted them through his spyglass. Amazed to see Drake, Tarcher nevertheless was sensible enough to speak at once of the important things.

"The storm hit thirty-six hours ago, Mr. Steel."

"What of Edwinna?"

"I haven't been able to send anyone up. Nor has she sent anyone down. The ravines are flooded with rushing water. A man could get swept away and drowned."

"Can you get me a rope, a knapsack, a bottle of drinking water, and a bill-cane knife?"

Tarcher nodded approvingly. "That I can, Mr. Steel."

Drake quickly presented his children and their tutor. It was agreed that they would stay with Tarcher while Drake made his way up to Crawford Plantation. While Tarcher hurried to get his supplies, Drake squatted to talk to his children.

"Katherine, sweetheart, I have to go to . . . to find Priscilla. To make sure Priscilla is all right. I want you to be a big girl for Papa and stay here with William and your tutor. Tonight you will sleep in Mr. Tarcher's nice house, and Papa will come back for you in the morning. Will you be a good girl and do that for me, sweetheart?"

She nodded staunchly, her little face brown from her stint at sea and her fair hair, Anne's hair, sun-bleached and more silvery than ever. "Will you bring Priscilla back here so I can play with her?"

"Well . . . Priscilla likes to stay at Mama Edwinna's house. But I'll take you to Mama Edwinna's house as soon as I can."

"Papa, I'm going with you," William declared. "I can find Priscilla—I can."

Drake tousled his hair. "I know you can, but you're needed here, William. I need you to be a man and take care of Katherine for me until I come back in the morning."

William sulked a moment, then changed his mind and said

importantly, "Katherine, I'm going to take care of you. You have to mind me and do every single thing I say."

"I do not!"

"You do, too!" Drake nodded at the young tutor, who adroitly took over. The young man had an excellent way with children, neither lenient nor harsh, but always managing to make William cooperate. At the tutor's suggestion, the three of them ran off to search the beach for "treasures" the storm might have washed in.

Lord, the destruction. Heading up into cane country, Drake grew more worried with every half mile he walked. He slogged his way through mud, slashed through vines that hung like green snakes, and occasionally sank into mire up to his knees. The storm had uprooted everything, from towering mahogany trees to terraced cane fields.

The affingoes' trail was gone, washed away. He couldn't even find it. The cane had begun to rot in the blazing sun, and the dense, musky stink permeated everything. The ravines were the worst. He had to cross two of them. Long before he came to them, he heard the thundering sound of rushing storm water. Routed out of their holes in the ravines, brown snakes slithered everywhere and rats ran as blatantly in the sunlight as if it were night. Descending into the first ravine, he lost his footing, slid in mud, and rolled fifty feet, flinging out his arms to break his fall. He grabbed at a brown vine to catch himself. It was a snake. The damned thing bit him. It was a glancing bite, but it hurt like hell. He sucked the wound, thanking his lucky stars that Barbados had no poisonous vipers.

He had to swim the ravine in roaring water that thundered in his ears, shutting out every other sound. The force of the rushing water swept him two hundred feet down the ravine, bashing him with uprooted trees that stabbed him with their hairy roots. When he finally found his footing and climbed out, exhausted, panting, he'd lost his rope, but he still had the knapsack with the leather water bottle and bill-cane knife in it. He drank thirstily.

He climbed to the top of the ravine, stood panting for a moment, and slogged on. When he came to the second ravine, he shuddered and descended into it with its snakes and rats and roaring water. This time, he found a mahogany tree that the storm had plucked up somewhere on the island and had cast into the ravine. It had come down in such a way as to make a precarious bridge over the rushing water. He inched across it on his knees, and then, reaching the other side, climbed way to the top of the ravine, his breath roaring in his lungs as loudly as the gully water.

High in cane country again, he looked about and tried to get his bearings. All of the familiar landmarks were gone. He had to navigate by keeping an eye on the terraced hills and the sea behind him, on the Speightstown coast, and on the shape of the cove. He plodded on in water-soaked boots.

In one of the flattened cane fields, he found a body, a black, and it brought tears to his eyes. Not for this particular black, whom he didn't know, but for all on the island who might have died in the horrendous storm. He dragged the body out of the mud, but he had nowhere to shelter it. He cursed in frustration, knowing wild pigs would come for it, feed on it.

When he came to another flattened cane field, he found red roof tiles scattered like grapeshot. He shucked his knapsack and ran slogging through the mud. Lord. Crawford Hall's roof was red tile.

He tore across a flattened cane field, jumping stubble and roots and whole plants. At last he saw the familiar lane with its mahogany trees, most of them down, flung every which way, as if a giant fist had bashed them. Red tiles littered the field. He spotted something grotesque sticking up in the field—one of the wrought-iron front gates curled, twisted like rope. God in heaven! Crawford Hall reared into view, its walls still standing, but the roof gone, bare beams shining in the sun. He sprinted through the garden, past the demolished coral drip. The front door swung in the wind, hanging by one latch. He ran inside, heart pounding.

"Edwinna?" he bellowed. "David, Kena?"

No one answered. The house stank of rainwater and mud. He ran down the debris-strewn path, leaping tree limbs, dodging masses of roots. He ran to where the millworks had stood. They were demolished. His chest tightened. He'd never told Edwinna he loved her. And he did! If she'd died without knowing he loved her, he would never forgive himself. God damn it, it wasn't fondness, it was love. *Love!* You proud jackass. His own words thundered in his ears. *I'm fond of you, Edwinna*. Jackass. She had wanted to hear *I love you*, not *I'm fond of you*. God damn you, if you get another chance—if you're that lucky—tell her. Tell her, God damn you. It's not Anne you love, it's her—her!

There had been three deaths and twenty-five injuries.

Edwinna had been working without sleep for thirty hours. So had David and Kena and Matthew Plum and the others. She was exhausted, numb.

When she stepped out of the makeshift hospital and heard a ferocious shout—"Edwinna!"—she nearly burst into tears of frustration, for it seemed so cruel that she should imagine Drake's magnificent voice ringing out in all this devastation and suffering. Yet, a crueler thing could happen, for she heard it again.

"Edwinna!" his voice bellowed.

She whirled and rubbed her tired eyes. She swiped a muddy sleeve across her face. "Edwinna!" The bellow was persistent. Kena poked her head out of the hospital tent to look, then David peered out, and Matthew Plum. Someone was running down the tree-strewn hill, his clothes wet and muddy, his shoulders broad, his black hair glistening in the bright sunshine. Edwinna stood stock still, stunned.

"Oh, dear God, oh, dear God," she murmured.

Matthew Plum smiled broadly and gave her a shove.

"Go, girl! If he's what you want, show him."

"Oh, dear God!" She drew a ragged breath, threw out her arms, and ran like a madwoman straight into warm, strong arms that caught her and crushed her close, hugged her so hard she was lifted right off her feet. She clutched him fiercely, buried her face in his hot neck, and closed her eyes.

"Oh, dear God."

For a moment she couldn't open her eyes, scared it was a dream born of fatigue, scared it wasn't he. A moment after that, she didn't *want* to open her eyes. She only wanted to be held and to listen forever.

For in his hoarse, magnificent voice he was saying, "I love you, I love you, I love you, I love you, I love you, I love you, Edwinna . . .

One year later, to the exact date and minute, Drake was still saying those words—saying them as he looked down at her, his handsome face tense, beaded with sweat.

"I love you, I love you . . ."

She couldn't answer. She could only pant, caught in the vise of pain so excruciating she wondered if she could bear it. Each contraction tore through her like the blow of a billcane knife through cane. Her bottom burned as the flesh began to tear there. She wanted to scream, but had no breath to do it. Pain gripped her lungs. She panted.

"David!"

"She's doing fine, Drake."

"Give her something for the pain!"

"I cannot. It might harm the babies."

Drake swung his head sharply. "Babies?"

David leaned down over her, his fair hair spilling forward. He smiled and braced an arm on either side of her pillow.

"Edwinna? There will be two. Do not be afraid. You're doing fine."

She tried to smile, but couldn't. The pain came bearing down so excruciatingly that a cry of agony tore out of her. She lost her breathing rhythm, the panting she seemed to need so as not to panic. She struggled, thrashed about to get air, found it, went on panting.

"It's time, Edwinna," David directed calmly. "When I tell you to push, you can push. Not before, not after. Drake, get on your knees behind her on the bed. Support her shoulders and give her your hand to grip."

Edwinna panted, panicking as a new pain began to build, greater than any she'd felt before. "Drake—" Drake knelt behind, his head above her. Sweat beaded his forehead.

"I love you," he whispered. "I love you."

The pain came bearing down. "Push," David ordered.

She screamed and pushed. Nothing happened. She lay back, panting. Drake mopped the sweat from her brow, then gave her his hand to hold again. She gripped it. The pains came faster now, fierce, savage, throwing her toward the bottom of the bed.

"Push."

"Push."

"Push."

She screamed in agony as her bottom tore open. Something wet slid between her legs. She lay back, panting. A newborn's soft, crowlike cawing filled the room. David smiled. Kena smiled. Above her, Drake smiled. Edwinna panted.

The pain came again, an ax blow. "Only two more pushes, Edwinna," David directed calmly. "I'm going to help this little fellow's brother along a bit, by reaching in. 'Twill be a bit painful. Here we go." She screamed in agony. The pains came bearing down in fast, wild succession. "Push. Push."

She bore down and something else wet and slippery slid out between her legs, followed by afterbirth in a strong, primitive surge. Now, two newborns cawed loudly. Exhausted as she was, she had to smile. "They sound like magpies.'' She fell back against Drake, light-headed, black spots swimming before her eyes. The moment passed. When she could see again, it was to look up into Drake's fierce, happy face.

''I love you . . . God in heaven, how I love you!''

''Is it—are they healthy?''

''They are magnificent.''

''Is it really—two of them?''

He smiled broadly and kissed her forehead. ''I love you.''

The room smelled of birth and blood and sweat, but she'd never smelled anything so wonderful in her life. David flopped her loud, complaining sons on her belly to work on them, and Drake lifted her shoulders so she could watch.

''Don't hurt them!'' she commanded.

David smiled at her and then shared a smile with Drake. ''Very well.'' Kena stood smiling, too, ready with cloths and sweet oil.

Holding her up, letting her lean against him, Drake put his cheek against hers and watched, too, whispering in her ear words she never tired of hearing. ''I love you . . . I love you . . .''

Later, after she'd drifted to sleep, she awoke to a shimmering coral sunset and to a scene she would never forget. Absorbed in his sons, having a private talk with them, Drake was holding the swaddled, sleeping babies, one in each of his strong arms, and kissing them. She could hear him whispering, telling them over and over, ''I love you, my little sons, I love you.''

Her heart filled to bursting. She lay quietly watching, listening, adoring him as the Caribbean sunset painted the room with light. She loved him so much, this handsome London wine merchant who had come into her life so unexpectedly, who had taken away her fears and made her a woman, a wife, a mother.

When he noticed she'd wakened, he ambled to the bed, smiling.

"Well, Mrs. Steel. Which of your sons would you like to hold first?

"Both of them."

"Greedy."

She smiled at him, so in love with him she glowed. She knew she glowed because she saw the reflection in his eyes.

She eased up in the bed and held out her arms. "What shall we name them? We didn't expect two."

"It's already been done. William and Katherine and I have already named them, while you slept. Even Priscilla put in her suggestion, or so Katherine insists."

Edwinna's smile faltered a little. She was disappointed. She had two special names she'd wanted to suggest.

"Make a cradle of your arms, Mrs. Steel, and I'll introduce you. This little fellow's name is—" He gently put the baby into her arms and she looked into the tiny face and melted. Oh, dear God, she was a mother! "—Harry Crawford Steel." Her head jerked up and she looked at Drake intensely. He smiled into her eyes. "And this little fellow—" He gently deposited the second baby into her arms. "—is Thomas Crawford Steel."

Her breath caught in her throat.

"Oh, Drake."

He carefully sat on the bed, cupped her face in his hands, and put a soft kiss on her lips, a lingering kiss. She closed her eyes to savor it, to savor him, to savor the feeling of babies in her arms, her babies, Drake's babies.

It was joy that sent a tear trickling down her cheek. Drake knew it, for he kissed the teardrop and the next and the next, then sat on the bed with her as they watched the brilliant coral sunset paint its glory all over Crawford Plantation—the plantation that would one day belong to the two young men for whom it was meant—Thomas and Harry.